Tom Wood is a full-time writer born in Burton-on-Trent who now lives in London. After a stint as freelance editor and film-maker, he completed his first novel, *The Hunter*, which was an instant bestseller and introduced readers to a genuine antihero, Victor, an assassin with a purely logical view on life and whose morals are deeply questionable. Like Victor, Tom is passionate about physical sport, being both a huge boxing fan and practising Krav Maga martial arts, which has seen him sustain a number of injuries. He has not, however, ever killed anyone. Tom also publishes standalone psychological thrillers, including *A Knock at the Door*.

TRAITOR

TOM WOOD

SPHERE

SPHERE

First published in Great Britain in 2022 by Sphere
This paperback edition published by Sphere in 2023

1 3 5 7 9 10 8 6 4 2

A CIP catalogue record for this book
is available from the British Library.

ISBN 978-0-7515-8485-1

Typeset in Sabon by M Rules
Printed and bound in Great Britain by
Clays Ltd, Elcograf S.p.A.

Papers used by Sphere are from well-managed forests
and other responsible sources.

Sphere
An imprint of
Little, Brown Book Group
Carmelite House
50 Victoria Embankment
London EC4Y 0DZ

An Hachette UK Company
www.hachette.co.uk

www.littlebrown.co.uk

For Kirk

PART ONE

PART ONE

ONE

Stairs were dangerous. They killed more people per year than Victor could in ten lifetimes. If a person died of an accident in the home then chances were it would be the stairs that killed them. Despite a long career, he had never once assassinated a target by pushing them down the stairs. So, for now at least, that particular methodology remained in waiting.

The stairs ahead of him were more dangerous than most. Not from any risk of falling. They formed a perfect chokepoint.

If his enemies were any good, at least one would be covering them.

The first flight rose only ten steps until it met a mezzanine-hallway that extended perpendicularly left and right deeper into the building. A longer flight of stairs rose parallel to the first before it reached a strip of bare landing from which more stairs led to the next floor. Victor leaned over the banister to glance up – a darting motion in case an ambusher

3

was on a higher storey and looking down with a gun aimed.

He saw no one.

Just stairs and banisters rising up and stretching towards a vanishing point beyond the uppermost ceiling.

These stairs were designed for large volumes of foot traffic. They had wide steps – almost two metres from wall to banister, which might have been wrought iron beneath the heavy layer of gloss green paint. He saw where the once sharp edge of each step had been smoothed away, an uneven distribution of wear that stretched from the banister to about the midpoint. This area of the step had been dulled by the soles of dozens or even hundreds of people every weekday.

This was where Victor ascended, close to the banister, where he knew the erosion of the stone meant a rougher texture that absorbed the energy of his footfalls more than the less worn areas would. An imperceptible reduction in noise to him. Yet a gunman on the floor above might misjudge Victor's location on sound alone, failing to hear his assault for a second longer than he might have otherwise.

Long experience had taught him a single second was exactly enough time to be a second too late.

He climbed the stairs one at a time, a slow deliberate pattern, knowing anyone lurking out of sight in the hallway ahead would hear each quiet tap of his sole on the stone steps and picture him coming closer and closer. The corridor extending to both the left and the right meant two potential ambush points, but not both at the same time. A gunman in each might kill one another if they both shot at an enemy appearing between them.

If there was an ambusher, he would be in the hallway to Victor's right.

That hallway because it provided a shooter a greater chance of catching an ascending target in the back as he headed for the next flight of stairs. A gunman in the left hallway was more likely to meet that same target face to face, and assassins weren't exactly known for playing fair.

They weren't known for poor tactical positioning, either. They wouldn't be standing in the middle of the hallway, as exposed and vulnerable as the day they were born. They would be close to a wall. Nine-in-ten odds a gunman would be right-handed, and that right-handed shooter would want his left shoulder near a wall so his weapon wasn't impeded by one. Those walls all had a two-tone paint job. The lower third had an almost clinical washed-out green whereas the upper two-thirds was a warm beige.

When Victor reached the eighth of the ten steps, he paused, interrupting the rhythmic pattern of his footfalls – just long enough to throw off the mental image of a potential ambusher – before he switched the gun into his left hand and sprang up the final two steps in a single bound, ducking low as he swivelled his head to peer down the right hallway, his left arm bent at the elbow and flat against his chest so the pistol extended past his lead shoulder.

The first enemy was hiding where Victor had anticipated.

Reaction was always slower than action, so Victor had a split-second advantage, which he needed to find his mark because the gunman had positioned himself halfway into an adjoining room. Most of his person was out of sight, only his head, arms and shoulder were through the doorway.

They shot at the same time, the gunman surprised by the sudden appearance of Victor and firing a panicked snapshot with his aim too high, expecting an upright man caught off guard from behind, not one doubled over and looking straight at him.

Victor's first round was a little off, catching his target on the side of his skull and glancing away as blood erupted in an atomised cloud from the superficial temporal artery. The second hit him in the upper chest as he jerked in response to the glancing headshot and staggered out of the doorway's cover.

The gunman stayed upright, alive but suffering the shock of sudden injury, so Victor took an extra beat before he squeezed the trigger a third time, putting the bullet between the man's eyes. He fell down to the floor.

A young guy. Twenty-two or -three.

He didn't look like a professional under Victor's definition. No doubt ex-military and maybe he had even executed his share of paid targets, yet this could have been the kid's first proper gunfight.

Blood drained from the hole in his forehead to form a glossy pool. Little pieces of brain were ferried along by the current, funnelled by gaps in the parquet flooring into stretching red fingers.

A messy end, yet quick. All over inside two seconds. Whatever the kid's expectations for how the ambush was going to play out, this hadn't been it.

Victor sympathised to an extent. He had understood nothing at that age too.

But he had been a quick learner.

He kept his pistol pointed down the corridor in case another enemy responding to the gunshots appeared through one of the many doors. They had had the same green colour as the lower third of the walls, although they seemed a little brighter and cleaner except where flakes of paint had chipped away. The morning sun brightened the space before the occasional open doorway, leaving shadowed sections between.

Several offices. Too many spaces to clear.

He didn't like the idea of leaving rooms uncleared behind him as he ascended, but he knew for certain that more enemies were higher up in the building. He couldn't imagine individuals already down here running to hide deeper into the building in one of those offices. And if they had, it meant they were scared and had no stomach for confronting him, which was fine for the time being.

Victor let off a bullet down the empty hallway, both in case anyone was so hiding and to encourage them to stay there, and also to signal to his enemies higher in the building that his focus was elsewhere. He hurried forward a couple of steps and shot the young guy's corpse, extending the audible tale he was telling to those on the floors above him. Different acoustics than the previous shot. Maybe interpreted as an extended shootout between him and the still-alive ambusher, or maybe as him stalking deeper into the building in pursuit of a fleeing enemy or to finish off a wounded one. Either way, if anyone above was inclined to exploit Victor's perceived distraction, now would be the time.

He gave them a few seconds to descend then darted back out into the stairwell.

Again, he took his enemy by surprise, only this gunman was on the stairs above and out in the open without the concealment and cover of a doorway to protect him.

As such, Victor needed no split-second to find his aim.

He double-tapped the man on the stairs, both bullets punching bloody holes through his T-shirt, before a third hit him in the forehead and painted the two-tone wall behind him in a single shade. He had already been on the move, descending the stairs, and that forward momentum tipped him over and he tumbled down the remaining steps, smearing them with blood and brain matter, before coming to a stop at the foot of the stairs, a confused expression on his dead face where eagerness and anticipation had been moments beforehand.

Muscle spasms had kept the pistol in his hand. Victor prised it free and tucked it into the rear of his waistband. While not the best pistol in the world, it was always good to have a backup with a full magazine.

He noticed an elevator in the hallway to the left of the stairwell. He did a quick check to make sure no one else was inching down the stairs, then used a knuckle to hit the call button. A slight delay, then the steel door retracted and he stepped inside the car. The walls were bare steel, scuffed and marked except where it had been polished smooth on the rear wall by the countless coats and jackets of weary workers leaning against it. Again using his knuckle, he tapped the buttons for every floor above in ascending order. They each lit up in a dim yellow glow, one after the other.

He stepped back out before the steel door could extend back to seal the car. A slow process. He heard the hum and whine of old machinery.

He was already creeping up the stairs when the elevator started to rise.

Not the most imaginative of mis-directions. Still, no competent kill team consisted of only two gunmen, so if the

8

elevator ascending and stopping on every floor caused even a single enemy a mere moment's distraction then it would give Victor a huge advantage.

He might need every advantage he could engineer because no competent kill team organised by his own long-term broker to assassinate her most experienced contractor would be counted in single figures.

He could flee, of course, although that would not solve the problem, only delay it. They would try again, maybe with greater numbers, and with a better understanding of their target after this warm-up. Maybe he wouldn't spot them coming next time and he already had them on the back foot now. They had been expecting to ambush him, not have him assault their position before they were ready to act themselves.

No way was Victor prepared to waste such an advantage.

Given the choice, he always attacked.

TWO

The elevator sounded a *ding* when it stopped on the first floor.

Victor, crouched halfway up the intervening staircase, waited. Shoulder blades pressed against the two-tone wall, restricting the width of the target he presented to any enemy above.

Should one or more be waiting for him, at the very least they would glance towards the elevator as the door opened. If they had been covering the stairs they couldn't afford for a threat to emerge behind them, and if they were covering the elevator itself – fooled into thinking Victor was suicidal enough to trap himself when he didn't need to – they were already facing the wrong way.

Either worked for him.

There were other possible scenarios, though Victor gave them no thought. After so many years in the world's most dangerous profession he considered himself pretty adept at reading likely eventualities.

He was still alive, after all.

He always imagined what he would do if the roles were reversed. That way, if that worst-case scenario proved true, he already had a head start in countering it. If he overestimated his enemy's proficiency then it hardly mattered that he gave incompetents too much credit.

In this instance, he gave about the right amount.

Someone had been covering the elevator, because a roar of automatic gunfire sounded an instant after the *ding* – before the doors had fully opened to reveal the car and who was inside, which meant he was twitchy.

He, because twitchy gunmen were always gun*men* in Victor's experience.

Testosterone's powerful effect on subcortical signalling, he expected. It encouraged impulsiveness in stressful situations.

Instincts could not be overruled, he knew, only circumvented. At best they could be delayed after endless practice.

A couple of seconds' panicked fire emptied the guy's gun. He hadn't practised.

Victor used that painful roar of sound – suppressed and yet still as loud as thunder echoing in the stairwell – to cover his dashing footsteps on the stone stairs.

He reached the floor to see the gunman near the elevator fumbling to reload his sub-machine gun. A second guy with an SMG – positioned to cover the stairs – wasn't looking at what he should be doing.

The thirty-two bullets unloaded in close proximity had drawn his attention away from the stairs for longer than any elevator's *ding*. No matter how composed, no one could ignore all that nearby noise.

He pivoted back towards the staircase when he received a

headshake from the other guy to say the elevator was empty and all those bullets were for nothing.

Nothing for them, not for Victor.

He shot the guy covering the stairs before he had finished pivoting so he collapsed down in a spiralling motion.

The corpse ended up in a neat folded pile that caused Victor no delay dashing by, his sudden appearance and the unexpected death of the gunman covering the stairs combining to startle the twitchy shooter so much that he dropped his replacement mag before it could be slammed into the receiver.

Two squeezes of the trigger and the shooter fell through the open door of the elevator, ending up facedown inside the car, legs left out in the hallway.

Before reloading himself, Victor put a second bullet in the guy folded into a neat pile when a hissing groan sounded. Maybe the man's last breath or the first breath of renewed consciousness but for certain the last breath now.

Victor still had a few rounds in the magazine, although nowhere near enough if there were another four guys elsewhere in the building – which he expected, and more besides. His pistol was a Five-seveN made by Fabrique Nationale of Belgium: his preferred weapon in most professional situations at close range. He had managed to obtain a couple of the twenty-round magazines usually only available to military or law-enforcement personnel. He was neither, of course. A German fixer named Georg could often do what most others could not. She kept stressing arms dealing was not her true business and this transaction would be the final time she did him a favour.

There had been many such final favours over the years.

He had only the single spare magazine, however. She was not a miracle worker, as she told him often. Still, that was why he had the collected pistol in his waistband. He ignored the SMG dropped by the shooter half inside the elevator. A nine-millimetre Ingram. Incredible rate of fire, as the twitchy shooter had demonstrated, yet Victor would take accuracy and control over raw firepower in almost every circumstance.

All of their weapons were suppressed, as was his own. Combined with subsonic ammunition, the generated decibels were greatly reduced. Nowhere near silent, however. More than loud enough to hide approaching footsteps and carry to the city outside.

A quiet Sunday morning in Nice's Old Town. Less busy than on a weekday, although the café across the street had three patrons enjoying breakfast or a coffee. Victor had been one himself only moments beforehand as he sipped one of the best espressos he had ever tasted outside of Italy. Cops might already have been called, which was why he wasted no time continuing his attack.

He had maybe four minutes to kill the rest of Phoenix's team and obtain some answers before he had to flee. He wanted to do both but would settle for achieving only the former. Answers alone could shoot no one.

Behind him, the elevator door tried to close. The door stopped on contact with the dead legs, retracted, and then tried again.

The pattern would repeat long after Victor had gone, he was sure, only stopping when some official examining the scene grew annoyed and frustrated with the noise and ordered a subordinate to shut it down.

The twitchy shooter's left foot twitched.

THREE

Only the triumphant yell of an over-eager gunman warned Victor of the impending danger another two floors up. The gunman ascended the stairs behind him, having elected to wait until he was sure Victor had passed by unlike the four dead guys had done.

A smart move, because now Victor had enemies above and below him.

He reacted by dashing along one of the hallways leading from the stairwell, and throwing himself into the cover of the closest open doorway, chased by bullets that the gunman unloaded from his MP5 in a brief burst that splintered the wood of the frame a split-second after he passed it.

The gunman called out again, this time with more control, as he raced up the remaining steps.

'*Hurry, hurry*,' he yelled, speaking English with a coarse British accent. 'I've got him.'

Not entirely accurate, but Victor didn't correct the man just yet. He would do so without words in a few moments.

Popping back out of cover, they exchanged fire down the hallway, maybe ten metres of open space between them made greater by the difference in elevation. The guy was using the stairs as cover, the angle hiding at least half of his silhouette. Victor was shooting down while the gunman aimed back up at him.

Automatic fire from the MP5 didn't need to be accurate to catch him, whereas Victor needed a truer aim to find his target. One of his bullets hit the floor mere centimetres in front of the gunman, encouraging him to duck out of sight after he had unleashed another burst Victor's way.

He heard eager footsteps pounding on the stone stairs and pictured another man – from below or above – rushing to aid the one already there, so Victor changed position.

Bullets hounded him as he dashed further down the hallway until he was out of their line of sight.

He took cover at the corner of an intersecting corridor, waited a couple of seconds to encourage them to leave the stairwell and pursue, then leaned out to catch them while they were vulnerable.

They had expected such a tactic, their SMGs putting so much volume of fire his way he had to withdraw before he could squeeze the trigger even once.

Bullets exploded plaster and sent clouds of dust into the air as the corner of the wall disintegrated.

Fragments of masonry peppered the floor at Victor's feet.

With a better picture of their positions, he tried again, although he dared not pop out of cover for longer than an instant to loose a couple of snapshots their way.

They rushed forward as they shot back, each one now close to a different wall and making it harder for him to exploit his better position. Rounds shot at one man slowed his advance yet let the other hurry closer. If Victor switched between both targets then his shooting was not accurate enough to delay either.

He saw he wasn't going to win this particular firefight. These guys were a step above the previous four. They had the initiative and he was the one reacting this time.

Leaving the cover of the corner, Victor backed deeper inside the building. He needed a more defensible location to stand his ground or, better still, an entirely different battlefield that neutered their superior numbers and firepower.

He hurried down the corridor, trying door handles as he went. Every door was locked. No time to kick one open in case the first kick was not enough. When the two guys with SMGs made it around the corner he could not be out in the open. They would shred him before a second kick did its job. He had to gamble one of the doors would be unlocked.

One handle emitted the telltale click of a bolt retracting and he shoved it open, throwing himself through it as he saw in his peripheral vision the two guys appearing.

Bullets zipped his way. Some struck the doorframe, others the walls around it.

His error was immediately apparent.

The reason the door had been unlocked was because this office was unoccupied. Either no one was leasing it or there was no current use for the space. Not entirely empty – there were some desks and chairs – but he saw nothing he could use to his advantage and nowhere to make an effective stand.

He had trapped himself.

Rushing to the closest window, he peered through the dusty glass to see no convenient fire escape or terrace. He would have taken a drainpipe had there been one, whatever its rigidity. Nowhere to leap to, either. It had to be ten metres to the other side of the street. He had ascended too many floors even to think about dropping from the window. He would risk a turned ankle; he wasn't so keen on breaking his neck.

The two guys with MP5s didn't rush. They might not understand the full extent of Victor's lack of options, yet their instincts told them he was going nowhere. They remained cautious. They had the numerical advantage and a considerable edge in firepower so neither wanted to rush needlessly into the inevitable path of his bullets. He pictured them whispering and gesturing, maybe each urging the other to be the first one through the doorway. In his rush to escape the hallway, he'd had no time to close the door again without staying within their line of fire. For this reason, they were staying back. He figured they were waiting maybe a metre or two from the doorway, working on the assumption Victor had his gun aimed at the open space.

Which would be correct of them, because as he tested out potential positions he kept the muzzle of the pistol pointed at the doorway at all times. It would have been ideal if they had pursued him with more recklessness and dashed into the empty office moments after him. He would have dropped the first, and there would have been a small chance he could have hit the second in a vital area before the SMG swung his way.

Maybe one-in-ten odds of living through it.

Nowhere near good enough to be a course of action worth gambling on.

He needed an edge.

He just couldn't think of one.

FOUR

Victor's only advantage was they couldn't know where in the office he would be positioned, while he knew for sure they had to come through the doorway. Had their roles been reversed, he would be tapping the internal wall between them to test if it was part of the original structure and composed of brick, or a newer construction and only aluminium-framed plasterboard painted to blend in with the original features. The building was old and had been refurbished and remodelled many times over the years.

Which was the conclusion they came to themselves a few moments later.

Only they did not understand how to test the wall by sound alone and so used bullets instead.

Plaster dust sprayed from the wall in dense, violent clouds. The MP5s were no Ingrams. They could unleash around eight hundred rounds per minute to the Ingram's twelve hundred. The former was still an incredible rate of fire from Victor's perspective when on the receiving end of it. Dozens of bullet holes appeared in crazed lines on his side of the wall.

He dropped prone to the thin carpet and waited. There was not much else he could do besides waste rounds he could not spare shooting back at them. He could not deduce their exact positions based on the pattern of random bullet holes. He guessed they were not standing still as they squeezed their triggers, instead stepping back and forth along the wall to cover the largest possible area inside the office.

They aimed at too steep an angle, however, not realising the extent of the space available for Victor to be within. After passing through the partition wall, most of the bullets buried themselves in the floor in the middle of the room. Victor, near the external wall, was well clear, although a ricochet caused plaster and brick dust to shower him from above.

The shooting only lasted a few seconds, the two gunmen firing in controlled bursts, each unleashing three or four bullets at a time. Though he tried to count their rounds, the high cyclic rate and their overlapping bursts made it impossible. He wanted to time it so he was leaping to his feet at the exact moment they were empty so he could dash out of the doorway and kill them both while they were mid-reload.

Perhaps they understood this possibility themselves because they staggered their reloads. When the shooting did stop he caught the sound of a fresh magazine being slammed home.

They were smart, so Victor abandoned that plan.

Instead, he played a hunch and rolled laterally across the floor of the office while the second gunman reloaded. That guy was competent, although no expert, and it took him a few seconds longer than necessary to discard the empty mag and push in another. Victor had plenty of time to cross the floor and come to a stop parallel to the partition wall. The carpet was thin, as was the wall, but he made far less noise going shoulder to shoulder than he would have with even his lightest footstep. No doubt while the guy was reloading, the other gunman was straining to hear any movement in an attempt to gauge Victor's position.

More than anyone, Victor knew reaction was slower than action. If they rushed inside the office – even if they didn't notice him straightaway – he would be playing catch-up by default. He had no reason to think they had any abnormal sluggishness, and ready for violence and expecting resistance, stress hormones were elevating their speed and response times. Lying on the floor by the wall might put him in their blind spot, although for no longer than a moment. If he didn't react to their presence and kill them both fast enough, he would be the easiest target in the world to a spray of automatic fire.

Victor didn't like these odds, either.

With no better option, he took the looted gun from his waistband into his left hand. Maybe two pistols' worth of gunfire could make up the shortfall in his plan.

Once the second guy had finished reloading, there was silence. In that silence, Victor knew they were preparing to enter. Whether that would be in two seconds or nine, he couldn't know for sure. Even though he could predict a lot, there was always a limit.

Reaction slower than action.

Playing catch-up by default.

He blinked sweat from his eyes.

'Are you as ready for this as I am?' he heard one whisper on the other side of the wall.

The over-eager gunman, of course.

The return whisper answered, 'Let's do this.'

Victor appreciated the heads-up.

'On three,' the first whispered.

Victor almost smiled. It wasn't often those trying to kill him were considerate enough to warn him in advance, let alone volunteer their exact schedule.

'Three, two . . .'

Right on cue, they charged in.

The open doorway provided them with a view into the room so they had already seen the door was in the corner with a wall running perpendicular to it. Which meant they knew Victor could only be to their right as they entered and so that was the direction in which they charged. They had their weapons up before their faces, gazes fixed along the iron sights for fast target acquisition but at the cost of peripheral vision.

To make room for the second guy, the first had to dash in a few more steps, taking him past Victor's position without the man noticing, so Victor shot him in the back of the head with the Five-seveN.

He used the pistol in his offhand to kill the second with a headshot too, only to the side of the skull as that guy didn't rush in as far, partly to give the lead gunman room to manoeuvre and partly because the first guy's head disintegrated right in front of him. He had just enough time to see Victor out of the corner of his eye before the wall above and to the left of where he stood was plastered with a glistening smear.

The resulting muscle spasms caused the dead guy's index finger to compress the MP5's trigger and the gun unloaded as the corpse tumbled to the floor, bullets blowing holes in the ceiling and wall.

The gun clicked dry as the body hit the thin carpet and Victor found himself peering at the black void of the smoking muzzle pointing his way.

He took a breath and hopped to his feet.

It seemed pointless to thank two corpses and yet he really was grateful for all of their assistance.

And their guns, too, one of which had a fresh magazine, fully loaded.

Excellent weapons. Much better than the Ingram downstairs. Each was an MP5K. The compact version of the Heckler & Koch sub-machine gun had been around for decades yet was still the first choice when it came to close-quarters battle for many militaries, police forces and intelligence agencies the world over. He wasn't a huge fan of nine-millimetre ammunition in general, preferring something better able to penetrate body armour or makeshift cover – hence the Five-seveN – but the MP5K's rate of fire, accuracy and target acquisition were beyond reproach. They had forgone any straps, however, so Victor only took one of the two weapons.

The one with the fresh mag because he saw they had no spares, which was unfortunate. He supposed taking three each had seemed enough when they had sourced them. One-hundred-and-eighty rounds between them to kill one man would seem enough on paper, especially when they had other teammates with guns of their own. But most things seemed adequate until they did not on the battlefield.

He discarded the looted pistol and replaced it with his Five-seveN, even though it was almost empty, tucking it into the back of his waistband. It could never be traced back to him, although there was a chance it could be linked to Georg and he did not want to put her at needless risk of repercussions. And he might need another one of her final favours before too long.

He couldn't be certain how many more were in the team or if backup was on the way. The six might be all those inside the building with more nearby. Maybe on standby in vehicles ready to make a getaway after the finished assassination, or on surveillance or guarding the perimeter. Or the rest of the team could still be ahead of him, which he expected to find because they hadn't been ready for him.

Regardless of the remaining opposition's locations he wanted to manage his ammunition better than these two guys had, especially with no spare mags, so he thumbed the selector on the MP5 to single shot.

If he had been correct in his prediction regarding the composition of Phoenix's kill team then there were still at least four enemies who now had had plenty of time to organise a proper resistance. However, with six dead and an SMG in hand Victor still felt good about the odds.

The only trouble was he had perhaps as little as three minutes left before the cops arrived on the scene.

After his recent interactions with US law enforcement, Victor didn't relish another brush with the police any time soon.

Protocol dictated that he should withdraw from an uncontrollable situation as soon as an opportunity presented itself. However, protocol also stated that threats in close proximity should never be disregarded.

Victor took the stairs to the next floor.

FIVE

He found the window with the open shutters that looked out over the street. From this height, the café opposite seemed benign, almost tranquil, and not the site of a trap organised by his broker.

Such a simple ambush, and yet he had almost walked straight into it.

Victor felt naïve.

Of all flaws, this one seemed the most egregious to a man who strived for professional perfection. She had betrayed him, yes, and yet he could not have made it any easier for her.

The window was in one of the large offices on the sixth floor. This office had an expansive open-plan area filled with desks and cubicles, surrounded on three sides by conference rooms and individual offices. Nothing Victor could see indicated what kind of work took place here. What little wall art broke up the greys and beige tones was abstract and revealed nothing. Could be an insurance firm. Could be for professional phishing scams.

The kill team had chosen a decent enough observation point. Victor would have gone a floor lower, to improve the angle on the café and provide a clearer view of the strike point. Perhaps they had favoured seeing more of the street itself because in the Old Town the streets were narrow and the buildings tall. They could have preferred to give themselves a better chance of seeing their target coming, instead of seeing him more clearly when he arrived. Regardless, Victor would never have chosen to wait in an unoccupied building like this one. Any activity where there should be none was always easier to spot than that which was hidden inside the crowd of regularity.

Still, no strike point was ever perfect. There were always compromises. Victor was sure they, like himself, planned every single facet of their work to the nth degree. No matter the validity of a plan, some things always came down to improvisation.

They had done their best with what they had.

It just hadn't been good enough.

He saw waxed-card coffee cups as he stalked through the open-plan area and checked the adjoining rooms. Eight coffee cups in total. No doubt from the café across the street, which seemed unnecessarily crass given they intended to fill it full of lead soon afterwards. The cup he tested was room temperature against the back of his hand so they had been here a while. Did the number of cups mean there were eight of them in the kill team or just that not all of them had wanted caffeine? All he knew for sure was that eight of them had been gathered in this office at some point in the last few hours.

He expected they had been planning to wait a few more

minutes before attacking. The café might as well have been a shooting gallery: small, with only one way in and out because the staff door to the rear of the establishment had a push-button lock and the customer lavatory needed a key from behind the counter. Given some had SMGs, they could have stood in the street and emptied their weapons through the plate-glass front of the café and killed him and everyone else inside within seconds.

If so, they had waited far too long. They had allowed him more than enough time in which to give themselves away. Or maybe they had been waiting for him to leave again, to follow him and kill him elsewhere with a little more subtlety. It didn't matter, although he was curious as to whether they had all been here finishing their preparations when he had crossed the street or if they had already been spread out in the building. The kill team as a whole might have been comprised of several smaller elements who kept to themselves when they didn't need to be together.

Assassins weren't famous for their social skills, after all.

Spread out or not, they should have organised their defence better. Numbers always beat proficiency if those numbers were utilised. On the back foot, they had not been able to coordinate. Victor had given them no time in which to exploit their numerical advantage.

He figured those remaining had caught up by now, however. The firefights on the floors below had lasted maybe two minutes, including ascending up the stairs. If the remainder of the kill team could not get themselves together within two minutes they would never have been granted the contract to murder him in the first place. They had to have proved their competency in advance. Phoenix knew exactly what

Victor would do if they failed. They must have convinced her somehow.

He had no more time to speculate. Cops were on their way and there were still more gunmen nearby—

One of which, in baggy joggers and matching sweatshirt, appeared from a blind spot in the next office.

Victor was first to react, his snapshot missing by millimetres and tearing a chunk from a doorframe. The second missed too because the gunman retreated, almost falling over in panic as the bullets came his way. Victor chased after him, letting go of the MP5's foregrip with his left hand so he could extend his right arm at full length and pivot it through the doorway ahead of the rest of him, the muzzle already pointed in the direction of the panicked gunman before Victor caught up.

He shot the man in the back as he tried to scramble away, already losing his balance in his desperation to flee and using the wall for support to stop himself falling. The bullet hit high on his left side, entering through his shoulder blade and into his chest cavity. He cried out and twisted, rebounding away from the wall and tumbling over a desk, knocking over a letter tray and scattering paperwork before he hit the floor behind it.

Victor hurried forward, rounding the desk to see the gunman lying on his back with his palms out before him. He was shaking his head, a terrified expression on his face. A tiny .22 pocket gun lay nearby – close enough to reach and use, and yet the guy had no interest in going for it. No blood stained the front of the sweatshirt so the bullet had not exited from his chest. Victor pictured it buried in a rib.

With the side of his foot, he kicked the .22 away and it slid beneath a desk. The guy on the floor seemed to have no other weapons and the pocket gun was no good for the primary weapon of a hired killer going after a fellow professional. It was for protection not attack. This guy wasn't expecting to have to use a gun at all.

'You're in charge,' Victor said.

The guy said nothing in response, only gasping as he struggled to breathe.

'Tell me your name.'

'Walker,' a weak voice said.

Another British accent, so no thrown-together assortment of Phoenix's contractors; this was a tried-and-tested unit. The offshoot of a single private security enterprise, Victor figured, or a loyal cohort of soldiers turned mercenaries, then assassins.

Irrelevant, because all Victor needed to know right now was—

'How many?'

Walker shook his head as if he did not understand, only pushing his raised hands higher.

Victor checked his flanks, then shot Walker in the guts.

The bullet in the back was already affecting his breathing, so Walker's cries emitted as keening exhales. He clutched a hand to the hole in his belly. It made no real difference to the rate of blood loss because the wound was no immediate threat. Victor had aimed to miss the abdominal aorta and vital organs. He didn't want Walker bleeding out or succumbing to shock, only to suffer.

He managed to control his pain enough to make a whispered grunt that could be an attempt to talk or a pretence of muteness. His eyes begged for patience, for mercy.

Victor, no stranger to such pleas, was unmoved.

Which was clear to Walker. He swallowed and opened his mouth to answer ... and then didn't. Instead, he broke eye contact, glancing to somewhere behind Victor.

Who was throwing himself to the floor before bullets came his way.

Automatic fire. More MP5s. Two for sure.

Three if it really wasn't his day.

SIX

Victor scrambled behind a desk – then darted to another – nine-millimetre subsonics chasing him, plugging holes through wood and fibreboard; burying themselves in the floor or wall.

He returned fire, shooting blind in the direction of the gunfire, switching to automatic himself to increase the chances that one of his bullets would find a target he hadn't even yet seen.

Prone on the carpet, he peered beneath the desk shielding him, viewing a skewed slice of the office: carpet, chair casters, table legs ... legs.

A quick squeeze of the trigger and he shredded the shins of one of his attackers.

That man fell straight down, falling into Victor's skewed line of sight, so he put a second burst into the guy's contorted face.

'*Coward*,' another gunman yelled in response, loosing off a burst of his own.

He must have forgotten they weren't playing to any rules, Victor thought, using the sound of the guy's shout to better picture his position before popping up to shoot in that direction.

A single gunman stalking closer.

Victor's abrupt appearance gave him a split second in which to shoot. He hadn't pictured the guy's exact location so he had to adjust his aim before letting off a burst.

One of the bullets hit the guy in the shoulder and he flinched and stumbled, throwing off the aim of his returning fire, providing Victor with the perfect opportunity to finish him.

Except the MP5 was empty.

Victor dropped it, snapped a hand to the back of his waistband – to draw the Five-seveN while the guy was still vulnerable – but his fingers found only the leather of his belt.

The pistol must have fallen free when he had thrown himself to the floor.

Not good.

With no gun, and far too much distance between them to have any chance of getting to him, Victor dashed for the closest door.

He charged into an adjoining office room and flung the door shut behind him. A small square box of a room that might as well have been a coffin. A desk and chair, a filing cabinet. Little else. On the desk sat a large monitor, keyboard, mouse, in- and out-trays, a tidy of pens and a chunk of volcanic rock used as a paperweight. Nothing that would make a good improvised weapon against a guy with an SMG.

No way out except a single window.

31

'*Coward*,' the guy yelled again.

Victor was in no position to disagree.

He passed the desk to hurry to the window, which over-looked a narrow side street and had no shutters like the ones at the front of the building. Just as before there was nowhere to go: no drainpipe, no terrace, nowhere he could hope to reach with a jump.

The gunman's footsteps sounded on the floor beyond the room and Victor was already rolling over the desk – knocking away everything but the monitor in the process – on to the carpet before bullets punched through the door.

They blew neat holes through the computer monitor, the wall beyond, the desk and the floor as the gunman adjusted his aim.

Victor scrambled to his feet before the shooting ceased, keeping outside of the cone of fire coming through the door. When the silence came, he was stood along the wall with his shoulder against the doorframe.

For a moment, it seemed to Victor that the wounded man would empty the MP5, and yet there was no sudden click. He must have reloaded before chasing Victor here.

The door would shield him when it opened inward. He might remain unseen just long enough to catch the guy by surprise. Unless he anticipated that this was Victor's only real option and simply shot him through the door once it was open.

Either way, the gunman didn't charge into the room. He must have deduced the confined space on the other side and wasn't prepared to give away his advantage in firepower by allowing Victor any opportunity to get close. Victor didn't blame him.

The guy wasn't coming in and there was no way Victor was stepping out into the line of fire.

A temporary standoff.

Except Victor could do nothing in the small office to improve his odds, whereas the gunman outside could be calling for backup, preparing to set the building on fire, or simply waiting him out.

Within the next minute or so, the cops were going to arrive and Victor could not let that happen.

He scooped up the chunk of volcanic rock from the floor where it had fallen and tossed it at the window. He threw it in a fast, snapping motion.

The pane shattered as the rock smashed straight through it and sailed out into the air beyond.

In response, the door flew open, kicked in by—

The wounded gunman, who rushed into the room and headed to the window to pursue a fleeing coward.

A big guy, quick and agile on his feet, the MP5K held tight to his chest to minimise the risk of being disarmed. A competent professional. A significant threat eager to complete his job, who realised his error as he reached the broken pane and noticed the jagged shards around the frame that would have been cleared before someone climbed through.

The realisation came fast, yet not fast enough to stop Victor rushing up from behind, dropping to a squat that he exploded out of as he planted two open palms against the man's shoulder blades to shove him straight through the broken window.

With both hands clutching the SMG, the guy could do nothing to prevent it.

33

Victor would have liked to have taken the weapon to use himself, but it had been far too good an opportunity to waste.

The guy's screech of surprise and terror was also somewhat satisfying.

Turned out he wasn't so brave himself when it came to it.

SEVEN

After locating his Five-seveN, Victor found Walker was now breathing in a fast, erratic pattern. He was still on the floor where Victor had left him, still on his back, still clutching his wounded abdomen. The way he breathed told Victor the pressure of his chest cavity had been compromised by the bullet through the shoulder blade, making it increasingly difficult for his lungs to inflate and deflate. It helped that he lay on his back. He might already be dead otherwise. The floor was doing a passable job at closing the hole in his shoulder blade so not all of the internal pressure could escape. If he rolled on to his side, it would hiss out of him in seconds and he would not be able to breathe at all.

Victor used a foot to roll Walker on to his side.

The man's lungs deflated and he gasped in a vain, desperate effort to suck in air.

'I take no pleasure from this,' Victor assured. 'I assume you, like me, are one of Phoenix's contractors. Which means we're almost colleagues. In a different line of work we might both have been on the company bowling team.'

He waited until Walker's face had turned as blue as his sweatshirt before rolling him on to his back. He made a sharp wheezing sound as the hole in his shoulder blade closed enough for the internal pressure to increase sufficiently for his lungs to reinflate.

'Where's Phoenix?'

Walker's face reddened in seconds and he took in massive, gasping gulps of air.

'This must be because of what took place in the US,' Victor began. 'The Russian contracts, naturally. But was killing me part of the terms, or is this just Phoenix's personalised way of saying my services are no longer required?'

Walker let out coughing exhales that spattered frothy blood over his chin and chest.

'Whatever she told you, you need to tell me. Any scrap of information you overheard, anything you might have figured out on your own, even educated guesses ... You understand, I'm sure, that you need to tell me something if you value oxygen at all.'

Victor wasn't certain Walker heard him or, if he had heard, that he understood. All his efforts were on each desperate and agonising breath, none of which were anything close to enough to take away the feeling of suffocation.

'You're a smoker, aren't you?' Victor said with a sigh. 'Which is unfortunate. Because it means your cardiovascular health was a mess and your lung capacity a joke back when they could inflate unimpeded. I used to be a smoker too, so I do sympathise.' He paused, pad of index finger rubbing against thumb. 'Of course, I say "used to", only that's not entirely accurate, is it? No one is ever a former smoker, are they? I'm just a smoker not currently smoking.'

Walker gasped.

'Trouble is,' Victor continued, 'that's where my sympathies end. I look human, granted, but I may as well be an entirely different species. I am capable of empathy now and again, much to my chagrin, though you really have to catch me in the right kind of mood.'

Walker gasped again.

'Be a sport and at least try to say something,' Victor said. 'Because if you're admitting this impasse can only be broken with you on an operating table surrounded by talented surgeons then we can skip to the end. Likewise, if this happens to be a bluff then now would be the right moment to let me in on the performance as neither of us has time on our side. I'm in a rush, true, yet your life happens to be tethered to my good nature.' He shrugged a little. 'By now you may have guessed that today I'm not in one of those rare merciful moods we talked about.'

Walker *really* tried to speak, Victor could see, though only a strange, guttural sound escaped his lips. Croaking, almost.

Victor took this as a definite answer. He used the same foot to roll the man back on to his side and then tipped him over on to his front.

'This is not cruelty,' Victor assured him, backing away. 'I'm simply low on ammunition, and your choice of pistol is as bad as your sense of fashion.'

Walker was too weak to roll himself back, as Victor knew would be the case, but he tried anyway, managing little more than to wriggle and shudder for a few seconds before he just lay there trembling until even that was too much.

Since Walker seemed to be the last of them, that made nine gunmen organised by Phoenix. Given Victor would never have expected her to send a kill team numbering single figures, he was a little insulted.

Did she genuinely have such a low opinion of him?

Just before he killed her, he intended to ask Phoenix exactly that.

Sirens growing louder by the second urged Victor to leave without delay, so he hurried down the stairwell, leaping the last four or five steps of every flight. Though he knew he had spent too long with Walker, it had been the best and only chance of finding the answers he needed to track down Phoenix. Still, if Victor was fast, he could be out of the building before the first responders had reached it.

He was not fast enough.

When he was passing the bloody corpses of the first two gunmen, with only one flight of steps left before him, the building entrance was already swinging open to reveal the bright blue uniform of a man rushing into the building.

The police had arrived.

PART TWO

One week earlier

EIGHT

The first cop looked young from a few metres away. His narrow jaw and clean shave gave his face an immature appearance. The blue eyes and light eyebrows only exaggerated the air of youthfulness. As he approached, he seemed to age at an exponential rate. The blue eyes became washed out and the shadows beneath them darker. Up close, the lines at the corners became apparent, as did the creases either side of his mouth. He was thin, too. Beneath the weak chin, his Adam's apple jutted out, sharp and prominent. It might as well have been a flashing target to Victor, who assessed everyone he encountered on the level of threat they posed, and then on the most efficient ways to maim and kill them.

He was sitting in the booth furthest from the door. The sports bar was the basic small-town kind, yet had a certain charm Victor had come to appreciate on top of its uncommon cleanliness. He never liked keeping to a routine – even in character – yet his options were limited in a town of only a few thousand inhabitants. Still, he hadn't yet eaten here enough times to be recognised by the serving staff. The big screens helped him out in that department. He could appear distracted by the game, never needing to make small talk, although those screens were now showing sports news during the lunchtime slot.

Which meant the bar was busy with diners eating burgers and wings. The waitress running his section never stopped moving and yet never seemed rushed. She was a stone-cold pro. No one ever had to wait more than a moment for service. No order was served incorrectly. No pick-up grew cold on the counter. No customer reached the end of their first coffee without it refreshed. Victor was pretty sure he hadn't needed to tell her how he wanted his omelettes; she had simply read his mind instead.

He put down his knife and fork. Useful implements for all sorts of attacks, but he preferred open hands until he knew for sure he needed weapons.

Especially given the fact his dexterity was currently impeded.

The cop was safe for now. He had his service handgun on his hip, as well as a baton and mace, all of which made for effective weapons, although the cop wasn't planning on using any of them. The holster was clasped. Mittens protected his hands from the Minnesota cold outside. Should it come to it, Victor could take the cop's gun into his own hand quicker than the cop could.

A safe town. Low crime rate. The kind of place where police officers didn't feel the need to have their weapons ready. The kind of cops who only shot those weapons at the range and only when there was an evaluation.

Victor liked it here. No one cursed. No one blasphemed

either. They said *oh, shoot*, and *ah, heck*, and some even followed up such exclamations with apologies for their bad language.

It was chilly, too. The kind of temperature that reminded him of Iceland and Saint-Maurice in the winter. Victor was no fan of the sun. He preferred it when everyone wore long coats and hats, when covering up was the norm, when he could disappear into any crowd without even trying.

He estimated the first cop was in his mid-thirties. Maybe seventy kilograms in weight if he stepped on the scales right now in uniform, winter coat, and with all his gear. Six feet tall in his shoes.

The second cop was a little taller and a lot heavier – a hundred kilos, give or take. Most of it around the waist. He had a thick moustache and a haze of stubble despite the middling hour. His eyes seemed small, shaded under bushy brows and half hidden by rounded cheeks reddened by the cold and high blood pressure. He looked tired. He looked like he hadn't slept in days.

His size made him a minor threat. A hundred kilos was a lot of inertia. He took off his mittens as he neared, stuffing them into a pocket of his department-issue coat. He had thick fingers that would take some effort to break. The kind of hands that wouldn't give up a weapon with ease. If it came to it, Victor would attack him first. He would go for the legs – knees or ankles – using those hundred kilos against the cop. He would be writhing on the floor before the thin cop could react. Victor wasn't sure if he would go for the gun next or put the thin cop on the ground first. A half-decent strike would be all it took. Victor didn't need to overcomplicate the details.

He wouldn't kill them, whatever happened. He knew that for sure.

The thin cop might come out of it with nothing worse than a concussion. The big cop was looking at a cast and crutches. Maybe a wheelchair. But only after the surgery to set bones and reattach tendons. Or multiple surgeries could be needed. Either way it would be weeks of convalescing. Potentially months of physical therapy to help him walk again. Then more to address the muscle wastage and imbalances. A good chance he would never fully recover. Joints were complicated, after all. He might need further surgeries a year or more down the line. A limp and consigned to a desk for the rest of his career was as likely as not.

A steep price to pay for removing his mittens.

They were here for him, of course. Which was a novelty. Victor had killed no one. Recently, at least. He had committed more crimes than both officers had investigated between them in their careers, he was sure. They wouldn't believe him if he told them the extent of his criminal activities. They would laugh. They would think he was joking.

He was in their town for business. That went without saying, although he had no intention of telling them about the intricacies of his current contract.

'Got a minute?' the big cop asked.

Victor nodded. 'Sure.'

The cop slid into the booth, opposite him. The shiny vinyl seat covering squeaked. The thin cop took a seat at the table perpendicular to Victor. Which was either a smart, tactical move or an accident of chance. Either way, Victor was boxed in – not a feeling he liked even when there was no threat. He made a subtle adjustment to how he sat so he could see both cops without needing to first turn his head.

'That's quite the lunch,' the big cop noted.

It was supper for Victor, who spent the night awake. He preferred to sleep in the morning or afternoon when he could, although that did not suit his plans for later today. He had two omelettes on his plate and had already eaten the third. He wanted lots of slow-digesting fats and protein in his system because he didn't know when he would get another meal.

'What can I do for you?' Victor asked.

The big cop said, 'Are you William Pendleton?'

'I am,' Victor said. 'What's this about?'

The thin cop answered. 'Where were you last night? Around three.'

Victor had been sat in an armchair, studying his next target while he kept watch for enemies, so he said, 'I was sleeping.'

'Anyone to corroborate that?' the thin cop asked.

'No.'

The two cops exchanged glances.

The big cop fished out a black notebook, opened it. 'Do you happen to drive an olive-green pickup?' He recited a licence.

Victor said, 'I do,' and the two police officers exchanged glances again. 'It's outside, if that matters.'

'Where was your truck while you were at home?'

'Parked on the driveway, where else?'

The big cop said, 'Then you need to come with us.'

'Why?'

'Because that truck is connected to a crime committed last

night. While you were supposedly at home asleep and it was parked on your drive. Can you explain that?'

'No.'

The big cop said again, 'Then you need to come with us.'

'What kind of crime are we talking about?' Victor asked.

The thin cop said, 'A murder.'

The big cop said, 'So either you come with us willingly to the station to have a little chat,' still polite, 'or I'm afraid we'll have to put you under arrest.'

Victor gestured for the cheque.

NINE

He paid up and left a good tip. In any other circumstances he would have left just enough to avoid the displeasure of the serving staff. Normally, he didn't want to leave any impression at all. He wanted whoever served him to like him and then forget him within moments of him leaving. That wasn't possible here. Everyone nearby was looking his way or pretending they were not. All were wondering why two local cops were escorting him out. The waitress would remember him regardless, so he paid well over the odds. If she wasn't going to forget him anyway, he may as well make her day in the process.

'Do you want the rest of your coffee to go?' she asked him.

'I'm fine.'

She gave him a smile, but it was forced. She didn't know what was happening or how to react to it. He was still her customer, however, and her service had been stellar.

The thin cop and the big cop were patient. They didn't try to hurry him. Either they wanted to keep things civil or this was just their manner. Polite Midwesterners even when they didn't need to be cordial. They could make a scene. They could use raised voices and shove him along or take his arm. There were lots of ways other cops would be less polite. If it came to it, he decided, he would go for the big cop's ankle instead of the knee. Easier for a surgeon to repair than a damaged knee joint. A few weeks less in a cast. A few months less physical therapy. Victor's way of repaying their politeness in kind.

As with the perpendicular seating arrangement, the cops had him walk in front. Could be tactical or could be for no particular reason. They didn't seem afraid of him so the latter seemed more likely. The thin cop still had not taken off his mittens.

They didn't know the truth about him. They thought he was Bill Pendleton. Had they known the truth, the entire department would be here to take him down, and only after SWAT teams had surrounded the building and snipers were stationed on each overlooking rooftop and every road was barricaded.

There would be nothing polite about it.

He kept his gaze forward as he headed for the exit. Most of the diners were interested and curious in what was going on, though four seemed especially enraptured. A lone man, a lone woman and a young couple. The lone man had a tanned, leathery face and a bald head that pooled the fluorescent lights above. The woman had curly grey hair and a book of sudoku open on her table. The young couple both had black hair, T-shirts emblazoned with the names of old bands. The waitress was a little older than the couple, though not by much. If they were twenty, she was twenty-two. They almost certainly went to the same high school and maybe all three knew one another. The owner looked as if he was related to the waitress. They had the same kind of nose, a little upturned with prominent nostrils. They could be siblings, or cousins.

Maybe Victor escorted out of the local sports bar was the most exciting thing to have happened all year.

He pushed open the door and cold air rushed over him. He wore cargo trousers and a polo-neck sweater under a puffer jacket. All dark and muted colours. The jacket had more bulk to it than he would typically wear – he always wanted freedom of movement – but he needed protection from the weather and it was hard to grab hold of the slippery, synthetic material. A reasonable trade. He had no scarf – he tried to avoid offering attackers convenient ways to strangle him – so he needed the polo collar to block the icy wind.

The sidewalk had been gritted, leaving only a strip of ice where the pavement met the building. He saw where the cops had parked a little further down the street. He waited on the pavement for them in case they just wanted to talk outside.

They didn't.

'Let's put some pace on it,' the big cop said. 'Far too cold to stand around.'

His eyes had an irritated red look to them. Victor imagined he was tired and kept rubbing at them. The big cop had probably been at the scene in the middle of the night and should have been in bed hours ago.

Once he was in the cruiser, Victor's options would reduce dramatically. And yet he did as he was told. Each step towards the vehicle felt difficult, as if his feet had taken on sudden additional mass. It was an effort of will not to attack the cops by default.

Don't let them take you, he had been told long ago when his worst crime had been stealing cars. *Never let yourself get captured*, he had been warned by wily veterans before setting off on his first patrol.

Now, he had his own rules. He had his own warnings.

The thin cop gestured for Victor to stop when they reached the cruiser. In the glare of daylight, the thin cop seemed thinner. His nose was sharper, a bump on the ridge more prominent. His weak chin was sharp, too. A small triangle. His cheekbones looked as though they might cut through the skin at any moment.

He would be a bleeder, Victor knew.

The thin cop unlocked the vehicle and held open the near-side rear door for Victor, who glanced at him for a moment and then looked at the big cop nearby. The same tactics could work here on the pavement as they would have inside the diner. But this was Victor's last chance. Once he was inside the cruiser, everything would change.

'If you please,' the thin cop said, motioning.

The big cop said, 'We'll run you straight back once we're done.'

Victor knew a fallacy when he heard one.

TEN

A pine air-freshener scented the car's interior. There was no scent of coffee or cigarettes or body odour. The footwells were clean. The backseat was clean. The windows were clean. The big cop climbed behind the steering wheel and the thin cop spent a moment outside. Victor couldn't see what he was doing and heard no muted voice. Whatever the reason, the thin cop then settled into the passenger seat.

They exchanged looks, the big cop making some gesture Victor didn't understand. The thin cop shrugged in response.

Twelve minutes along the highway and they pulled up in front of the police station, which was a single-storey building with a pale brown exterior. A couple of cruisers were parked next to it along with some civilian vehicles.

For the twelve-minute drive, Victor had been silent. The cops were silent too. Exchanging small talk might have been useful. He could have gleaned a little information about what to expect, yet he preferred to use the time to think. He ran through his actions over the preceding night, picturing where he had been and what he had done, who he had seen and who had seen him in return. He thought about what could be construed as suspicious and what he might need to hide. More importantly, he thought about what truths he could share without compromising himself or his contract. The more truth, the better. Even though he had murdered no one, he needed to be careful if this was not to devolve into something beyond his control. He wanted to risk as few lies as possible because on paper he would look suspicious. His legend had no parking tickets. No criminal background, either. But a good cop might see a man from out of town, with no family, no friends. A man with almost no history. That good cop might suspect that finding so little meant there was something to keep hidden.

The thin cop opened the back door and motioned for Victor to climb out, which made no sense to Victor. He wasn't going to stay in the car for the fun of it.

He acted like it was a little effort to climb out, as though he had a bad back or generally poor health. It was a subtle signal to his enemies that he was weaker than the reality, to encourage them to underestimate him. He considered this because he had deemed the cops were no threat. Over the years it had become a reflex whether he needed it or not.

Once again, they were vulnerable to the same tactics: big cop first – kick to the ankle – then the thin cop. The strategy, however, was terrible. If he attacked them here in front of their own station the only option was to then flee in their cruiser. With the other cruisers speeding after him moments later while backup was called to intercept him along the highway. That was no kind of plan.

A few broad steps led up to the entrance, where the big

cop pushed open the plate-glass door and led Victor into the foyer. He felt a blast of warm air from overhead. The foyer had rows of plastic chairs fixed to the floor. Framed photographs hung from the walls, showing smiling men and women in crisp uniforms. A stand by the entrance displayed flyers of many kinds, all warning of the dangers of drugs or gangs, or offering advice and support to the victims of crime.

The big cop went over to the front desk, where a uniformed woman was busy at a computer terminal. She raised a palm to the big cop to both acknowledge him and request he wait a moment until she finished up what she was doing. An incredibly efficient gesture, Victor thought: so much said without saying anything at all. The big cop waited so Victor waited. The thin cop hummed a tune Victor didn't recognise.

The palm from the woman behind the desk rose again, although this time she closed her thumb and two fingers to leave two protruding to make the shape of a gun.

'Shoot,' she said to the big cop.

He went to say something and didn't because she saw Victor then, and she nodded.

'Take him through.'

The two cops escorted him through doors that the woman behind the desk buzzed open. Then they took him a short distance along a hallway and into an interview room. An uninteresting space. Bare walls. A functional table and three chairs. Nothing on the tabletop.

The big cop waited outside and the thin cop followed Victor inside a step. 'You want a coffee?'

'I'm good.'

'You sure?' he asked. 'You could be here a while.'

'Why would I be here a while?'

The thin cop didn't answer. He backed out of the room and pulled the door shut.

Victor reminded himself that he had murdered no one. He was in control. He sat down although he wanted to stand. He preferred to be on his feet in unfamiliar areas, but he knew they would perceive that as nervousness. They couldn't know that he was never nervous.

The chair was hard plastic, deliberately uncomfortable. It was too warm as well. The fluorescent lights were too bright. He wondered if all the interview rooms were like this or was this particular room unique.

The door opened and a heavyset woman entered. She had a file under one arm and a cup she slurped from in the other hand.

'Detective Spector,' she announced.

'Bill Pendleton,' Victor said.

She nodded because she knew. She let the door swing shut behind her and set her cup down. A bag of herbal tea floated inside, staining the water yellow. He could smell ginger.

She sat down opposite him and said, 'Do you know why you're here?'

'Something to do with my truck.'

'Something to do with your truck being sighted at the scene of a murder.'

Victor said, 'This must be a mistake.'

She opened up the file and slid it over to Victor. The file contained photographs of a corpse. A man. 'Keep going.'

Victor did as instructed, turning over the loose photographs, all showing the same man, both crime-scene pictures and ones showing him alive.

'Do you recognise that man?' Spector asked.

Victor said, 'No,' because the dead guy was the target he was in town to kill.

ELEVEN

Spector looked about forty. Her hair was short and neat. He imagined it would be huge and untameable if the curls were allowed to have their own way. She was a little overweight and her eyes had a little puffiness beneath. She fidgeted with her pen a lot. She kept it in her hand even when she wasn't writing. It never stopped moving. He put her as a fellow smoker who no longer smoked.

Spector watched his reaction with a careful, considered gaze. She just looked at him, waiting for him to say more. Victor remained silent.

Spector adjusted the way she sat, pulling the chair a little closer to the table. She was done waiting.

'His name is Grigori Orlov,' she said. 'Born in Russia and a citizen of the US for the past fifteen years. Someone shot him last night.' She tapped her head three times. 'Bang, bang, bang.'

Victor did not react. His target had been christened by a different name long ago. He hadn't just become a citizen.

He reinvented himself in America. On the surface, a regular citizen.

'A businessman,' Spector continued. 'He owns a fleet of delivery trucks, an aggregate yard, and even has the franchise on a big-box store out of town.'

Victor waited for more. He acted as he expected a normal person would act in such a situation. He appeared expectant and confused.

She said, 'Rumour has it that Grigori, despite the legitimate businesses, was part of the Russian mafia. Do you know what these guys call themselves?'

He shook his head.

'Bratva,' she said. 'Means the Brotherhood. I'm no expert on them but I know a little. They are serious characters. To call them mafia is like calling a great white a big fish.'

'They sound scary,' he said.

'Obviously, they're way above my paygrade. The Feds are the ones going after them, naturally. But Grigori died on my turf so here we are for now before it gets passed up the tree.'

'I thought you said he was a businessman.'

'Sure did. But organised crime doesn't happen in its own bubble, does it? Like any other mafia group, the Bratva have legit businesses like restaurants or construction firms so they can launder money. Did you know it's estimated that something like eighty per cent of building permits in Moscow go to Bratva-owned companies?'

Victor shook his head. 'How would I know?'

'The FBI think Grigori answers to a guy called Kirill Lebedev, who runs the show for the Bratva here in the Midwest. Ran, I should say. He's currently awaiting trial for, well, all sorts of things.' Spector sipped her ginger and lemon tea, then said, 'Where were you at three a.m. last night?'

'I already told the two officers.'

'Then you can tell me too.'

Victor said, 'I was asleep.'

'Anyone with you at the time?'

'I was alone.'

'And this would be at your residence, yes? On Fairview Drive?'

'That's it.'

Spector checked her notes. 'You moved in – what was it? – six weeks ago. Is that right?'

'That's right.'

'Why did you move here?' she asked.

'I wanted a change of scenery.'

She furrowed her brow and gestured that she didn't understand or expected elaboration. Which was what Victor wanted. When lying, people almost always give too much information in an effort to appear veracious. When telling the truth it's commonplace to reveal too little. If Spector wanted more then it meant Victor was being convincing.

'I came for a job offer,' he explained. 'It didn't work out.'

'I'm sorry to hear that,' she said. 'That must make it hard to pay the rent.'

'It's a short-term lease and I have savings.'

She tried to build some rapport with a self-deprecating smile. 'Must be nice to have money in the bank. Mine slips away so fast you'd think it was deposited smeared with grease.'

He smiled a little in response. 'You have a family then, I take it.'

She nodded. 'And an ex-husband and two dogs and a cat.'

'I like dogs,' he admitted.

'You don't like cats?'

'I don't dislike any organism.'

Her head moved back. 'That's a curious turn of phrase.'

He said nothing.

The rapport was over because she said, 'Why would someone have seen your truck in the vicinity of a crime scene?'

'I don't know why,' he said, shaking his head and shrugging as he expected an innocent and confused man would do.

She said, 'Would you consent to a GSR test?'

Victor knew what the abbreviation stood for but gave her a questioning look.

'Gunshot residue,' she explained. 'Someone wipes your hands. It's quick. Doesn't hurt. Doesn't even smell bad.'

The innocent and confused man Victor was playing might be suspicious of such a test, so Victor said, 'Do I have to do it?'

'Nuh, uh,' Spector answered. 'That's why I asked if you would consent to it. You understand what consent means, don't you?'

'I do.'

'Then you know it's entirely up to you. Of course, if you don't want to take the test then I'm going to want to know why you don't want to take the test. And off the top of my head I can't think of many good reasons why you wouldn't want to consent.' She raised a sudden finger into the air. 'I'm sorry, I can't actually think of any good reasons why you wouldn't want to take the test.' She lowered the finger in a slow, deliberate way. 'I can only think of a bad reason why.'

'Then I guess I'll take the test.'

'Great,' she said with a small smile. She pushed herself and the chair away from the table, and stood. 'Come with me, please.'

TWELVE

The situation was still novel for Victor, although he garnered no enjoyment from it. Simply being a suspect inside a police station had been unthinkable once. Every instinct he had said he should have done everything possible to avoid this situation at all costs. Whatever the fallout, this should never happen.

Now, Victor had to play it through regardless. He would have to jump through whatever hoops they presented to him. They were investigating a murder. They suspected him of killing the target he had planned to kill. They couldn't prove he had murdered Grigori Orlov because he hadn't shot the man.

GSR test or not.

He stood waiting with his palms out in front of him as he had been instructed.

Though Spector wasn't doing the test herself, she was watching it.

The thin cop snapped on some blue nitrile gloves and

wiped Victor's palms with two cotton swabs. One for the left and one for the right. Each swab went into a separate test tube. The thin cop pulled off the gloves and filled out a form.

'Is that it?' Victor said.

Spector nodded. 'All done. Told you it wouldn't take long.'

'Can I go now?'

'Sure,' she said, then added, 'Once the test comes back clean, I mean.'

'How long will that take?'

She exchanged looks with the thin cop, who said, 'Fifteen minutes, maybe.'

She looked back at Victor. 'That okay?'

'I guess.'

'I knew you would consent.'

Victor remained silent.

Spector said, 'You can wait in the interview room. Coffee?'

'Sure.'

Before they went back, the big cop appeared and gave Spector a pointed look.

Spector asked him, 'They're here already?'

The big cop said, 'Yeah.'

Spector looked at Victor. 'Coffee's going to have to wait, I'm afraid.'

Victor asked, 'What's going on?'

'Time for your line-up.'

It was done in a bright room. Which made sense. The fluorescent ceiling lights were as intense as daylight, exaggerated by the white paint on exposed wall and the mirrored window. He stood with four other men. No one really looked like anyone else beyond broad features. One guy was taller than Victor. The other three were shorter. Two had lost most of their hair. Only one was about the same age. Two were much younger. One was older. Three of the four were wider around the waist. Victor had a short beard, as did two of the others. The youngest guy had no trace of stubble.

He was third in the line. The two in front entered before him and took their places. The big cop had given a few seconds of instructions before opening the door. Not much more than *go in, stand on your number.* Not complicated.

Victor stood over the number three that had been spray painted on to the floor. Behind him was a chart for height. He looked forward at the mirrored wall and his reflection looked back at him.

He pictured Spector on the other side of the glass. The thin cop and the big cop might be there too. And the witness, of course.

Only no one had seen Victor commit the crime. They couldn't have seen him near the crime scene, either.

No one said anything. He wasn't sure how long it was supposed to take. He imagined it would be a quick process if the witness immediately made an identification. Which had to be a good sign. They hadn't picked him out of the line-up because he wasn't the man they had seen. Maybe they were explaining that to Spector behind the mirrored glass. Spector could be reminding them to take their time and have a really good look. Or perhaps there was some briefing they had to go through first.

He didn't feel so much observed as evaluated.

His posture and demeanour were non-threatening enough

without needing to change them now. He carried himself as if he were no danger to anyone. He realised that this might be part of the problem. Since he tried so hard to blend in he also wouldn't stand out and be obvious it wasn't him the witness had seen. His forgettable demeanour could be a good enough proxy for lots of generic individuals, especially if a witness hadn't had a good look. In the dark or at distance or for a brief moment.

A speaker squealed and the big cop said, 'Number Three step forward.'

Victor did as he was told.

He stood a step in front of the other men, a step closer to the glass. He wasn't sure how much difference that could realistically make.

'Turn to your left,' the voice told him.

He did.

'Now turn to your right.'

Again, he did so. Then there was silence for a moment. There were no distinguishing features on either side of his face, so he expected the witness had seen a man from their profile only. Or was this just part of the routine?

'Step back into line.'

He noticed the guy next to him, the youngest, glance his way, as if now identifying Victor as the suspect the others had been brought in to stand with, but Victor saw it was for some other reason. Like the young guy wanted to tell him something.

The door then opened and the big cop gestured for Victor and the four men to leave.

'That's it,' the cop said. 'All done. Thank you, everyone, for your assistance.'

The other guys began filing away.

Victor said, 'Why do I get the impression that didn't go to plan?'

The big cop had an unreadable face. 'I don't know why you would have that impression.'

Spector joined them. 'I have some more questions for you.'

'I think I'm going to go now,' Victor said. 'I'm not under arrest, am I?'

'Not yet,' Spector said.

'So that means I'm here by consent, yes?'

She made a slow nod.

'Then I'm going. We can talk again another time.'

She said, 'Why not just talk now? We can get this all over with in one go. It's not like you have a job to get back to, is it?'

He said, 'The witness couldn't say for sure they saw me because they didn't see me. I didn't kill that guy, so this is a waste of all our time.'

'You think a murder investigation is a waste of time? That's not an especially community-driven response, Mr Pendleton. Even if you had nothing to do with last night's homicide, it's important we eliminate you from our inquiries as quickly as possible. I'm sure you understand that.'

She was speaking in a reasonable voice, as if they were all reasonable people discussing a mundane problem. Only nothing about this situation was reasonable to Victor, who said:

'I'm going now. We can talk more tomorrow.'

'I'm sorry you feel that way,' Spector said, then to the big cop, 'Officer, if you would.'

The big cop reached for his belt, for the handcuffs.

'The GSR results came back positive,' Spector said to

Victor. 'So if you're not going to stay here voluntarily I have no choice but to arrest you on suspicion of murder. You have the right to remain silent. Anything you say can and will be used against you in a court of law ...'

THIRTEEN

Victor let it happen. He wasn't going to maim or kill cops inside their own police station under any circumstances. He would be a wanted man far beyond the county or state borders. He would be a fugitive on a national scale. Even if he fought his way out of the station past the other cops – and he didn't know how many more there were – he might not make it out of the country. Not with his face passed to every agency and flagged on every database.

The big cop put him in handcuffs, ratcheting them tight around his wrists, yet not too tight. Polite to a fault. Spector finished reading him his rights.

'Who processed the test?' Victor asked.

The big cop said, 'Why does that matter?'

Spector said, 'The test doesn't lie. It's a chemical reaction. No false positives.'

'Who processed the test?' Victor asked again. 'This has to be a mistake.'

The thin cop, close by, said, 'I did it right, don't worry.'

'I want a lawyer,' he said.

'Course you do,' Spector said. 'I'm amazed it's taken you this long to ask for one.'

'I didn't need one before.'

'Thought you were going to get away with it?'

Victor said, 'What's my motive?'

The big cop answered, 'Probably money related.'

'Maybe he's the one who promised you that job,' Spector said. 'At the aggregate yard, maybe. Then he pulled it away once you'd already moved and it left you high and dry. You've been sat watching your savings evaporate, knowing he did you wrong, and that anger and resentment built and built and then you just snapped.'

'Makes sense,' the big cop said.

'I snapped,' Victor said. 'And in my rage I then went to the local bar for distinctly average omelettes and left my green truck parked outside for all to see?'

The big cop just shrugged in response. Spector gave Victor a look like he'd made a good point, and yet she didn't comment. She was doing her job with the evidence she had.

'I'll be gone in twenty-four hours,' Victor said. 'All you have is a witness who described a truck like mine, but who couldn't pull me out of a line-up, and a GSR test that at most says I shot a gun recently. You don't have enough to charge me.'

Spector said, 'Let us worry about that, okay?'

'There's nothing to connect me to the murder.'

'A lot can change in twenty-four hours,' she said, then to the big cop, 'Take him to the holding cell.'

'You don't want to ask me any more questions?'

'Sure I do,' Spector answered. 'But after we've searched

that truck of yours, and your house. Who knows what we're going to find there?'

Victor remained silent.

The big cop took him by the upper arm and led him away to a room containing a single holding cell. Bars extended floor to ceiling, and wall to wall across the middle of the room. Enough benches in the cell to hold a dozen men. No occupants so far today.

The big cop had him turn around inside the cell and uncuffed him through the safety of the bars.

Perceived safety only, because there was a moment's opportunity when Victor's first hand was free, a moment for him to yank the big cop closer, into the bars, stunning him long enough for Victor to spin around. Then, with one of the big cop's arms between the bars, there was all sorts of horrors Victor could inflict.

'Dial zero for room service,' the big cop said with a smirk as he put away the handcuffs.

He looked very pleased with himself.

Victor said, 'Do you use that line with every detainee?'

A frown replaced the smirk.

The big cop stared at him, the bars between them, and Victor understood what it must be like to be a wild animal in a zoo.

'We don't get a lot of murderers here.'

'I can imagine,' Victor said. 'Everyone's too polite to kill each other.'

'Exactly. Whenever we do have a homicide it's always someone from out of town. Usually out of state.'

'Is it you?'

The big cop said, 'What?'

'One in three,' Victor said.

The big cop said, 'What?' again.

'Spector, the thin cop . . . you.'

The big cop shrugged with his hands. 'You can count to three. Amazing. I hadn't realised we'd arrested a certified genius.'

'I'm assuming not all of you are in this together,' Victor began. 'That seems too much of a stretch, doesn't it? Three bad cops working together. I imagine there's maybe only three bad cops in this entire state. What are the odds they all work in the same county? What are the odds they all work in the same building? On the same shift?'

'What are you talking about?'

'Someone tampered with the GSR test or the results. I don't suppose it really matters what they did exactly. But it wasn't all of you. It wasn't every bad cop in the whole state working together. Like I said: it's a one-in-three chance it's you.'

The big cop was silent.

'Is it you?' Victor asked.

The big cop looked at him as though he had misheard or as though Victor was talking nonsense. He took a backwards step. Could be instinctual defensiveness or because he had had enough.

Victor said, 'Because I'll find out.'

'What are you talking about?'

'I'm talking about your best interests.'

'Are you threatening me? That's not a very good idea.'

Victor shook his head. 'I'm going to be out of here soon and then I'm going to find out why I was here in the first place.'

'Sure you are,' the big cop said. 'Sure you will. This is all some big coincidence. A conspiracy, yeah?'

'So,' Victor continued, 'if you are part of the reason why I'm here, you need to tell me. If you tell me, I'll take that into consideration. But it's a one-time deal. The second you're out of the door it's off the table.'

The big cop listened and then was quiet, as if he was replaying the words over in his mind, thinking he had misunderstood the first time. When he realised he hadn't, he took another involuntary step backwards away from the bars, away from Victor. Who said nothing more, just stared into the big cop's eyes with a careful measure of the danger he posed.

The big cop looked back at him as though Victor were a lion in a zoo, looking casually back at visitors who would be lunch if not for the bars.

'Save your energy, chief,' the big cop said, forcing a chuckle to mask his unease. 'Use this time for quiet reflection on the error of your ways.'

FOURTEEN

Victor was going nowhere fast. He took a seat on one of the benches inside the cage. He didn't want anyone watching via CCTV to think he was standing because he was concerned. Whatever Spector had said, he wouldn't be here for twenty-four hours. And they wouldn't actually charge him for the murder he hadn't committed. He just had to wait.

He did as the big cop had told him. Victor used the time in the holding cell for quiet reflection on the error of his ways. He thought a lot about potential errors he had made and whether they might come back to haunt him.

He was a perfectionist by trade because an imperfect professional assassin would not remain alive for long. He made mistakes, of course, although rarely. He ran through the weeks of preparations he had done for the Orlov contract. Everything he had planned. He thought about what might have been done in error and what he should have done instead. He thought about what the big cop had said: homicides were always perpetrated by outsiders. He was technically an outsider. Although they couldn't possibly know who he was or why he had come to this town in the first place.

The big cop had joked that this must be some coincidence. Victor didn't believe in coincidences as a rule. If he saw the same face twice in a crowd then that person was shadowing him. If nothing came of it, there was no loss in him behaving as though he were being shadowed. Coincidences were never coincidences until proved otherwise. Possible threats whether he was working or not.

As well as the Orlov contract, he had a second job to complete worth even more. Both contracts had come his way, as all of his contracts did these days, from his only broker, a woman named Phoenix. He thought about her now; he found himself thinking about her a lot these days.

He had been in the holding cell for almost an hour before the door to the room opened and the big cop entered.

He was not alone this time.

He pushed forward a young man with a sheen to his skin. His hair was long and greasy. He had sunken cheeks and thin lips. His pupils were so dilated Victor couldn't tell the colour of his irises.

'Thought you might like some company,' the big cop said to Victor.

The young guy with greasy hair said, 'I didn't do nothing.'

'No one ever does,' the big cop said.

'I've been set up,' he protested. 'It's not my fault. It's a mistake.'

The big cop glanced at Victor. 'Lot of those going about these days.'

He ushered him closer to the cage, then motioned

for Victor to move away from the cage door. He did as he was told.

The big cop opened up the cage and shoved the young guy inside, who then backed up to the bars once the cop had closed the door again. Victor heard the handcuffs open and saw the young guy's arms fall loose at his sides. He had thin wrists and long, pale fingers.

The big cop smiled and opened his mouth to say something to the young guy, but then looked Victor's way and thought better of it.

'Busy day,' Victor said to him.

There was no reply. The big cop left the room. This time he didn't look back.

This time Victor didn't sit down.

The young guy did. He dropped his weight on to a bench and his hair fell forward over his face. He swiped it back and some grease-reinforced clumps stood up. He cast a glance at Victor.

'What's your name?'

'Bill,' Victor said.

The young guy nodded.

'And you are?' Victor asked.

'Finlay.'

He picked at his cuticles as one knee bounced up and down. Finlay cast another glance at Victor, then looked away again.

Victor checked where the CCTV camera was positioned, judging where he and Finlay sat in its perspective and what it could detect at this distance.

Finlay continued picking at his cuticles. His nails were short and dirty.

Victor said, 'Are you sure?'

'What?'

'It's not chance you're here right now, is it?'

Finlay tore off a little chunk of dry cuticle and flicked it away.

'I know what you're thinking,' Victor said, adjusting where he stood. 'You're wondering if you can do what you've agreed.'

The huge pupils stared Victor's way.

'You wouldn't be here now if you couldn't, so shall we quit wasting time and get it done?'

The knee kept bouncing up and down. He pulled at the same cuticle, tearing away another chunk but this time some live skin came with it. The pain made him hiss and grimace. Several teeth were missing or rotten.

A tiny dot of blood welled on Finlay's finger. He looked at it, then at Victor.

Finlay stood fast, springing to his feet and turning to face Victor. Reaching into his sleeve, he drew out a knife.

Victor nodded. 'I knew you had it in you.'

FIFTEEN

Finlay was no physical threat. He was skinny and weak. The drugs ballooning his pupils would play havoc with his coordination and timing. They might make him more resilient, however. So Victor made a mental note not to pull his punches too much.

The knife was pocket sized. A short, single-edged blade. Maybe sharp. Maybe not. Finlay held it low, near his waist level, so he intended to stab instead of cut. Sharp or not, it still had a point that would pierce flesh without too much effort. They had taken his coat so Victor only had his sweater for protection, which was no protection from pointed steel, however dulled.

No knife-fighter, that was clear. Finlay had already burned precious seconds by rocking from side to side, adjusting his footing, and trying out different positions for his arms. The first seconds of any combat were the most important. Surprise won more fights than skill. Unskilled people managed to stab and kill one another all the time.

Victor waited, using the seconds the young guy was wasting to mentally rehearse different strikes and takedowns. He wasn't looking to disarm the knife because he didn't want to touch it. If the opportunity arose, he would make Finlay release it by shocking the arm or causing so much pain elsewhere he would let go of it of his own accord.

He could not avoid causing pain, but he didn't want to maim Finlay too much. He didn't want the cops to think he was capable of true violence unless he had no other choice. The longer those cops thought Victor was a regular citizen, the better.

No advanced techniques, then. Nothing that would look impressive on camera or leave significant injuries.

A regular citizen might be able to throw a half-decent punch but was unlikely to hit vital areas by design. No kicks or elbows, either. Victor was a lot bigger than Finlay so it was conceivable a regular citizen could use that size to then overpower the stunned younger man, to wrestle him to the ground and pin him there with mass alone. Perhaps one of that citizen's knees would happen to fall on to the young guy's solar plexus as they struck the floor. The paralysing of the diaphragm and subsequent agonising breathlessness could be interpreted as fortunate happenstance.

Finlay might still be holding the knife in such a scenario, but he wouldn't be able to make use of it.

Moments later, cops would be spilling into the room in response to the commotion, finding Finlay foetal and gasping, and Victor stepping away, wide-eyed in pretend shock at what had just occurred.

A lot of pain, though no lasting injuries. A clear case of self-defence and no reason to detain him longer than necessary. And a cop scolded for not searching the new arrival properly. Would that be the big cop who had brought Finlay in here, or had the thin cop been the one to conduct the search? Too polite for their own good.

No way to disguise the deftness of footwork that Victor would employ to make Finlay miss with his initial attack. But maybe the camera wouldn't pick it up or the cops wouldn't pay attention to the details.

Finlay had finished psyching himself up. He said, 'Are you ready?'

'Absolutely.'

The young guy sprang forward with speed, which Victor had expected based on how fast Finlay had been on his feet from the bench.

He jerked out his right arm in a slight, upwards arc, aiming at Victor's midsection, which—

Wasn't where Finlay expected it to be and he stumbled off-balance with Victor now outside of the attacking arm, the small blade behind him and harmless.

Victor was at the perfect distance to land a devastating elbow strike to his opponent's nose or temple, the latter being a blow from which the young guy might never recover.

Instead, he fought the instinct to inflict maximum damage and swung a clumsy left hook, making sure to flare his elbow too wide, increasing the distance his fist had to travel, looping into the side of Finlay's neck.

He connected just under the ear, as if aiming for the jaw and missing, sparing his knuckles any damage as they impacted muscle and skin instead of bone.

The young guy took it well – the drugs numbing his brain to shock – and he staggered only a little before twisting around to send a backhand slash of the blade at Victor's ribs.

This time Victor stepped closer so Finlay's inner forearm struck the intended target and the knife went past Victor again.

He trapped that arm to his side and threw his weight at Finlay, who was too small and too weak and too unstable to offer any resistance.

He stumbled backwards and Victor barrelled him into the cage wall. Pinned against the bars, the young guy was in a perfect position to receive a headbutt, but again Victor resisted the compulsion. He didn't send any knees upwards to the groin or abdomen either. He didn't snake his arm around his opponent's trapped limb. He didn't break it at the elbow.

He simply hurled him to the floor, landing on top of him with the knee to the base of the young guy's sternum.

No recreational drugs could numb this pain. Finlay's face turned an intense red. He gasped, airless, unable to inflate his lungs. His eyes streamed with tears. He writhed on the floor while screaming in silence.

Victor stood.

The big cop and the thin cop were opening the door an instant later, and hearing this, the young guy, still holding the knife, turned it around in his palm, from a regular hold to an ice-pick grip.

The cops didn't see.

They didn't see as Finlay locked eyes with Victor and then stabbed himself in the abdomen.

The big cop and thin cop were yelling for Victor to get back as they came closer.

They rushed up to the holding cell to see Finlay on the

floor, clutching his belly with bloody hands, the knife released and on the floor between him and Victor.

Despite the wound and his breathlessness, Finlay looked relieved.

I'm sorry, he mouthed to Victor.

SIXTEEN

There were no polite Midwestern manners this time. Victor made no effort to resist as the big cop charged into the cell to slap handcuffs on him while the thin cop hurried to where Finlay lay. Spector was next into the room, rushing closer with wide eyes.

'What the heck is this?'

The big cop said, 'What does it look like?'

'Where did that knife come from? How the heck did you miss it?'

She looked between Victor and the big cop for answers.

Victor said, 'I didn't do that. He stabbed himself.'

'He tried to kill me,' Finlay wheezed.

Spector stared at Victor. 'Wh–why?'

'Check the grip for fingerprints,' he told her. 'You won't find mine.'

The big cop huffed at that. 'Whatever you say, chief.'

Victor ignored him and said to Spector, 'Do you want to find out what's really going on?'

She didn't answer. She had a look of utter disbelief, glancing between the wounded young guy and Victor. It didn't make any sense to her because it didn't make any rational kind of sense.

'Be there when the knife is dusted for prints,' he said to her. 'Be there when they're checked against mine.'

'Why don't you just shut up for a minute?' the big cop told him. 'We're getting awful tired of your mouth.'

Spector was looking at Victor. The disbelief was still on her face, although now she was curious too. She didn't know quite what to make of what Victor had said, and yet she wasn't going to dismiss it till she heard more.

A groan from Finlay broke the spell.

'How is he?' she asked the thin cop, busy dressing the wound.

The thin cop said, 'He needs the hospital.'

The big cop asked her, 'What do we do about him?'

He meant Victor, who he had by one arm.

She exhaled, unsure. A lot to process.

'You know this doesn't feel right,' Victor said to her.

She listened.

'I'm sure your instincts have been good before,' he continued. 'Heed them now.'

She hesitated.

'Let me guess,' Victor began. 'Finlay has a rap sheet inches thick. Drug offences, mostly. But with addiction comes poverty and from poverty we get burglaries, handling stolen goods, shoplifting. Maybe some violence, too. At home or on the street. Nothing serious, though. He would be no good like that. Definitely nothing with a knife. That needs to be out of character. If he had even been in possession of one in the past then he wouldn't have been hired.'

'Wait, what? *Hired?*'

It was an incredulous tone. Nothing he had said could make any difference because Finlay had a hole in his abdomen and Victor was already suspected of murder. The simplest explanation was usually the correct one in a detective's experience and Spector had it all laid out before her.

'But why?' she asked, just as incredulous.

'To keep me here,' Victor answered.

'Who wants to keep you here?'

'I don't know.'

The thin cop said, 'I can't stop the bleeding. We need to get him to the ER right away.'

'Do it,' she said.

The big cop pointed a thumb in Victor's direction. 'What about our resident psychopath? We can't bring anyone else in while he's here waiting to pounce.'

Spector was holding Victor's gaze when she said, 'Send Mr Pendleton here to county lockup. He can be their problem for a while.'

SEVENTEEN

The seats of the county jail bus were textured vinyl worn down to shiny slickness. They reminded him of the chicken buses of Guatemala, and of a bus in Bulgaria. He tried not to think of waking up in the latter and the night that followed. There were many such nights he did everything in his power to forget.

It had been a long wait for the bus to arrive at the police station. He had been left on his own in the holding cell the entire time once Finlay had been taken away to the hospital. The jail bus had ferried almost a dozen men from various police stations across the county. Victor had been one of the last to be picked up, so it was well into the afternoon when he was taken outside into the cold. Snow fell and dusted the ground. He felt it in his hair and on the back of his neck and then it melted fast once he was on the bus.

An old man sat next to him. 'You ever been to jail before?'

Victor shook his head.

'That's what I figured. You don't look like the rest of these bozos.'

He had a deep tan. Deep lines bisected his forehead. Deep recesses lay behind his eyes. He had a grey beard and what hair he had left was grey on top and at the temples and blacker the further around the skull it reached. Bushy white eyebrows shadowed his eyes. His nose was broad and long. His chin jutted out to a sharp point beneath the haze of grey beard.

Victor could tell the old man wanted to talk, and even though Victor was content with silence, he humoured him.

'Have you been before?'

He nodded with some vigour. 'Yeah, I'm a bozo too, you'd better believe it. Can't seem to keep my nose clean for more than five minutes. Some of us are just born bad, aren't we?'

Victor remained silent.

'You probably think jail will be a lot better than prison, but that isn't right. Prisons are nicely organised by security level. The serious criminals go to maximum security and the white-collar tax dodgers go to minimum. Everyone mixes in county. It's like a watering hole in the African savannah. You got lions and crocodiles and zebras and wildebeest all in close proximity. Only in county you can't tell who's a croc on sight alone.'

'Why are you telling me this?'

'Because they're going to eat you alive in there. You're not just a zebra but a lame zebra who stands out from the herd. The lions and the crocodiles will be fighting over who gets you for dinner.'

'You don't need to worry about me,' Victor said.

The old guy paid no attention. 'Don't ignore the skinny kids. Just because they're weak doesn't mean you don't have to watch out. They're full of hormones and self-doubt, so

85

they're on a hair trigger. Because they haven't finished grow-ing, they look puny and they know it. So they have to prove they're not, and because they're not, they'll have shanks. They won't bother with me as I won't make them feel small. You ... you're perfect. You're big enough to give them some status for bringing you down, but not so big they'll be scared to try.'

'I'll take that as a compliment.'

'It wasn't.'

'That's the good thing about compliments,' Victor said. 'We can take from them what we will.'

The bus rattled along at a steady speed. The highway was quiet. One of the passengers sang a song Victor didn't know. Some sad ballad about love and loss. The singer had a pretty good voice but someone yelled at him to shut up and then there were no more songs for the rest of the journey.

'It's not just the watering-hole effect that makes county bad news,' the old man told him, 'it's the disorganisation. I've been everywhere and you can go a month in a federal penitentiary where they have the nastiest pieces of work you'll find anywhere and not see a single violent incident. That's cuz the inmates have a pecking order. Alliances. Gangs. Peace through mutually assured destruction. In jail, we're all the same. No one is in long enough for order to form. Some inmates are in jail only until the system is ready to send them to a supermax, so they have nothing to lose and time to kill. People will act the fool in county. You act the fool in the real pen and someone will straighten you out real quick. A week in county is worse than a year in prison, trust me on that.'

'You don't seem down about the prospect of going back.'

'Why worry about it? Worrying doesn't help. It's not going to turn back time and stop me robbing, is it? What's done is done. This is what I've got so I'm not going to sit here feeling sorry for myself. If I've only got a can of beans to eat today I'm going to eat those beans like they're some fancy, gourmet delicacy and I should count my lucky stars I've even got them to eat at all.'

'I like beans,' Victor said. 'Lots of protein. Lots of micronutrients.'

'That's not my point.'

'I understand your point,' Victor assured. 'It's good to be optimistic.'

The snow drew a white veil around the bus. The flakes were now coming down in clumps that glued themselves to the window glass and collected in little drifts in the rounded corners. The driver had the heating cranked up to hold off the cold. The air became humid before too long. The dozen guys were not all clean and a few stank. In time, the air took on a rank smell that reached Victor. The old guy next to him grimaced.

'I've slept on the street more nights than I ever slept in a bed and I never let myself stink up the place. There's never an excuse to let yourself go when it comes to hygiene.'

'I'd scoop out water from a fountain,' Victor said. 'I'd use a plastic bottle or a coffee cup. Soak a coarse scrap of fabric and even without soap you can get pretty clean.'

'Exactly,' the old guy said, gesticulating as much as the chains let him. 'Hold on, wait. You were on the streets?' The old guy's eyes grew larger. '*You* were on the streets?'

'Is that so hard to believe?'

'You don't look like a bum.'

'It was a long time ago,' Victor said. 'I was a kid.'

'Broken home?'

Victor looked out into the snowstorm. 'I never had one to break.'

'Ah, institutionalised, then?' The old guy winked. 'You'll fit right in.'

EIGHTEEN

The bus stopped at the county jail in the middle of the afternoon. The snow had settled into a thick carpet of white across the ground. Clouds darkened the sky and blocked the sun so much there were almost no shadows. The old guy stuck out his tongue to catch snowflakes and gestured for Victor to do the same. He did not. The county jail looked as he had imagined. No walls, although lots of tall chain-link fences. Not a maximum-security prison facility. Secure enough, however.

The corrections officer who processed Victor had a neat, almost military haircut. Clipped on the sides with a little length on top. Black and grey hairs competing for limited space. He had a thick moustache over thick, shiny lips. His face was round with fat and bright pink in colour. He had wide shoulders and a massive back. He seemed too cumbersome to move. The size, no doubt, helped subdue inmates. Victor couldn't imagine him running for more than a few seconds before that pink face darkened to red and he gasped and wheezed.

'Open your mouth, please.'

Victor did so and a beam of light from a small torch was shone inside. The huge corrections officer gripped Victor's jaw with the other hand to keep it open and manipulate that opening.

When he was finished, he had Victor pull up his sweater.

The corrections officer did not react to the sight of Victor's many scars. The man was well used to violence.

'Further,' he said. 'Let me see your armpits.'

There was a curiosity in being restrained. Other times he had been held against his will were to facilitate questioning before inevitable demise. Not here. No one was going to interrogate him. Those who held him had no personal stake in his captivity. They wanted nothing from him except his acceptance. He was content enough to give them that until release.

Victor stood before a camera to have his photograph taken. First his face, and then either profile.

His thumb was scanned and then his whole hand. He watched it happen with a careful gaze, imagining the scan appearing on the nearby monitor. The corrections officer glanced once at the screen to make sure the print had gone through, then waved Victor away.

Although he did not like having his photograph taken, there was little potential fallout as he would not be charged with a crime, and the arrest would go on the record of William Pendleton, who only existed on paper. The fingerprints were of even less concern.

He continued on to the screening classification deputy, who interviewed Victor to determine where he should be housed in the facility.

'Are you going to be trouble?' she asked him, blunt and to the point.

'I'll be gone come tomorrow.'

'We'll see,' she said, checking her screen. 'Have you ever been arrested before?'

'No.'

'What other convictions have you had against you?'

'None.'

'Are you currently, or have you ever been, a member of a gang?'

For a moment, he thought about his time on the streets with his small crew. They had never thought of themselves as a gang. They hadn't thought of themselves as anything worthy of a label. Just kids up to no good. No ambitions.

Victor shook his head.

She said, 'There's a note on the file saying you stabbed a guy in your holding cell.'

'I didn't, but that's why I'm here.'

'Do you have any tattoos?'

'No.'

'Do you have any scars?'

'One or two.'

'Are they, or could they be construed as ritual scarring?'

'No.'

'Do you take drugs?'

'No.'

'Have you ever taken drugs?'

'Yes.'

She asked more questions – Do you hear voices? Have you ever tried to kill yourself? Are you currently thinking about hurting or killing yourself? Do you sometimes feel that people are out to get you? – before explaining: 'You're here because you're too dangerous to be held at a local facility. Even though you haven't been charged with a crime at the present time you'll have to stay here overnight. Tomorrow, either you'll be charged and have an arraignment where the judge will set your bond or you will be released. Do you understand everything I've explained to you?'

He was given the privacy of a booth in which to change. He removed his own clothes and dressed in the bright inmate trousers and shirt. Both were too big for him, or perhaps they were supposed to be so loose. Footwear was a pair of rubberised sandals. No good for running or fighting but he was surprised by just how comfortable they were to walk in.

He bagged away his clothes and handed them over. In return he was given a cot matt folded into a spiral and a clear plastic bag of basic toiletries.

Dozens of eyes looked his way as he walked into the pod. It was a bright, open space with many tables fixed to the floor and weak plastic chairs surrounding them, red in colour. A crescent-shaped counter was near the door, behind which stood a corrections officer, busy at her computer. Maybe a third of the corrections officers he had seen were female.

He saw some of the guys from the bus already at tables, so he guessed they had been here before and were already comfortable. Maybe the rest were in their cells, wary and nervous, or they had been sent to a different part of the facility.

There were several pods that made up the jail. Each pod housed maybe one hundred prisoners, which were organised by the severity of the charge or the security risk posed by the prisoner. Those charged with misdemeanours were held

in the same pod, whereas a felony charge meant incarceration with other felons. Women were kept separate from
men, and those with mental health problems had their own
pods. Given Victor was here for violence, he was sent to the
most secure pod that housed all those charged with a violent
crime, as well as theft, burglary, drug abuse violations, and
even some DUIs.

'You can't tell who's who,' the old guy from the bus had
told him. 'That's why you can't ever let your guard down.
Anyone could be a threat.'

Victor's guard was never down, jail or not. And he could
tell. Not the inmate's crime, but who was a threat. A sixty-
kilo murderer who had no idea how to fight was no threat to
Victor, whatever murderous intent that man might harbour.

'New guys need to watch their backs the most. Most of
the inmates are repeat offenders who have been here before.
They know what to expect and what to do. New guys don't.
They stick out from a mile away. The biggest threat in jail
is boredom. Not your own, but the other inmates' boredom.
Some of them will mess with you because they've got nothing else to do with their time. Some know they're going to
be shipped to a supermax and might never get the chance to
attack someone again. For some, it's now or never.' The old
man had stressed this last point. 'Make sure you ain't the
guy they pick for their last hurrah.'

Insults and taunts came his way as he approached the
counter. The woman behind it didn't look at him as she
read out his cell number. She didn't offer directions and he
didn't ask.

Most inmates ignored him and continued playing cards or
watching a TV positioned high on one wall. But the old guy

from the bus had been right: it was the younger men who called out to Victor in the kind of coarse language he would not usually be willing to tolerate.

He gave the impression of indifference.

One of the inmates was stood by a bank of phones. He was fighting back tears and failing. They glistened on his cheeks and mucus leaked from his nose.

In a corner of the open space, a group of men stood around a table. They were a range of ages, and all white. The two men sitting at the table were also white. They played cards, uninterested in the men around them or the rest of the inmates. Aside from those around the table, the other inmates kept their distance. A clear borderland lay between, wherein a half-circle of tables were empty. As Victor glanced over, one of the two men at the table looked his way. That man had white hair and a white beard, both short and neat. The skin between had a tanned glow. His exposed forearms were dark with tattoos, although the distance was too great for Victor to make out the designs. The man with white hair and a beard watched him for a moment before turning back to his cards. Victor noticed a bottle of prescribed pills on the table.

As Victor moved out of line of sight, he glimpsed one of the men around the table leaning in to say something to the man with the white hair and a white beard.

Victor hadn't had cause to speak Russian for some time, though he read the words on the man's lips as easily as he had ever done.

That's the one who killed Grigori.

NINETEEN

Bolts held the tables to the floor of the pod so the inmates could not utilise them – either for barricades during riots or as weapons with which to pummel each other. The chairs did not require such measures. They were lightweight plastic and prone to flexing. They survived a year or two at most. A company who made chairs for nurseries had the contract. They were the same chairs toddlers sat on, only scaled up for adults. Collapsing under the weight of a larger inmate was not uncommon. For fun, veterans of the jail would engineer it so that the oldest and weakest chairs were set in place ready for an ignorant new arrival. In time, you learned how to sit on them with care in case your buddy had set you up. So such a trick tended not to work unless the inmate in question was fresh off the bus. If he was on the heavy side then most of the pod would gather round to watch the show. Almost as good as going to the movies.

The tables in the pod all had a checkerboard pattern on the surface so the inmates only required pieces to play.

Checkers was the most popular game. In part, because it was simpler to pick up than chess and quicker to play. In part, because playing pieces went missing all the time. Which wasn't so bad with checkers and yet it was a different story while playing chess without knights.

One chess set, however, never ran out of pieces. It had a letter K written on the front of the box. K for Kirill, so the American inmates understood.

No one in the jail screwed with that collection of pieces.

'That's the one who killed Grigori.'

They referred to a new inmate. He glanced their way for a moment while he crossed the pod towards the cells. He had dark hair and a short, dark beard. Maybe thirty. Maybe forty. It was hard to tell. Tall and lean, and yet the short-sleeve jail shirt showed forearms ridged with powerful muscle. A natural light heavyweight, maybe, boiled down dry for fight night.

'You're sure?'

A nod. 'That's what they say. They picked him up earlier today.'

'Fleeing the scene?'

Shake of the head. 'Eating lunch.'

'Is that a joke?'

'No, Kirill. That's what they told me. Omelettes.'

Kirill considered for a moment. 'How did Grigori die?'

'Three shots to the head.'

'You're certain it was three?'

'I wouldn't say if I wasn't sure.'

Kirill asked, 'They found the gun on him?'

'No, but he failed that test they do.'

'What test?'

'I don't know how to describe it. They do it and it shows you shot a gun recently.'

'He failed the test?'

'He failed the test.'

'But he's not been charged?' Kirill asked.

'That's right.'

'Then why is he here?'

'Separate thing. A fight at the station. He stabbed someone.'

Kirill said, 'A cop?'

'No, no, no. A junkie.'

'Why?'

'How would I know? I can't read his mind.'

Kirill shook his head. 'It doesn't make sense to me. He shoots Grigori. He doesn't run. He gets picked up for it. They don't charge him, but then he stabs someone?'

'Maybe he's crazy. People like that ... they're never right in the head.'

Kirill was silent. Contemplating. Then he squeezed his eyes shut tight in sudden pain. He fumbled blind with one hand on the tabletop while the other massaged his temples with finger and thumb.

After a few seconds, he found the small plastic bottle of pills and shook out a couple, or maybe three. He did not see or care. He swallowed them, took a moment to calm himself, then opened his eyes to see his man staring at him with concern Kirill did not appreciate, and made clear with his return stare of contempt.

'What do you want to do about him ... the guy who killed Grigori?'

Kirill said, 'What else is there? We take care of it.'

TWENTY

Victor's cellmate was perched on the top bunk reading a Bible when he entered.

'I'm JT,' he said as he turned a page.

'Bill,' Victor said.

JT was twenty at most. Maybe as young as eighteen. He had a well-fed but scrawny frame. A slight paunch and stick-thin arms. Buzzed hair. Acne on his forehead.

'I hope you're more chill than the last guy,' JT said.

Victor said, 'I expect so.'

JT had a goatee beard, or perhaps it was an overgrown chinstrap. Victor wasn't sure. He had no understanding of fashion. He had a beard for disguise purposes. It hid a large part of his face, changing its structure in the process. He could shave it off and be unrecognisable. Same with his hair. He grew it out in between jobs. He cut it shorter for those jobs, and could buzz it off entirely if he needed to be someone else.

'You're not going to freak out, are you? It's hard enough

to sleep in here without crying and sobbing like a li'l bitch all night.'

'I assure you I won't freak out if you watch your language in return.'

'Are you serious?'

Victor nodded.

JT shrugged and put the Bible down next to him on the cot. 'I can do that. But are you sure? If this is your first time it might not have hit you yet. That's what happened to me. Only when the lights went out and I'm staring up at the ceiling does it finally catch up with me where I am. I freaked, man. Woke the whole place up and they put me in solitary for two weeks.'

'That must have been hard.'

'At first, sure. But I found my peace through God.'

'So you slept better when you came out of solitary?'

'Yeah, man,' he said with a smile. 'Only cuz some inmates beat me black and blue for keeping them awake that first night. Spent a week in the infirmary.'

He was laughing as he finished.

'I won't freak out,' Victor assured.

'Is that a promise?'

'It's absolutely not a promise. The last time I made a promise I made life very difficult for myself. But you can nonetheless trust me that you'll get a good night's sleep tonight.'

JT looked him up and down. 'I'm going to guess something to do with finance. Fraud or insider trading or whatever.'

Victor remained silent.

JT laughed. 'Nah, I got it now. You ran one of them pyramid schemes, yeah? You robbed little old ladies of their pensions.' He laughed harder. 'You didn't raid their piggy banks too, did ya?'

Victor began to lay out his mattress on the bottom cot. 'They claim I stabbed a guy in the holding cell.'

JT formed a clamshell around one ear with his palm. 'Say again?'

'And murdered another guy,' Victor added.

'Ah, I get it,' JT said, nodding his head in understanding. 'You may not be a fool but you're a joker.'

'That's me,' Victor said, deadpan. 'I'm a comedian.'

He put the toiletries by the washbasin in the corner. He didn't ask why JT was here because he didn't care.

'They said I beat up on some guy and I never did,' he told Victor when it became clear there was going to be no enquiry. 'I mean, I wanted to do all sorts of damage to him since he cheated me, and I never did. Look at me. What am I going to do to anyone, least of all a big pimp? Seriously, does it make any sense to you?'

'Nothing you're telling me makes any sense.'

JT missed the nuance. 'Exactly. But that pimp is in a coma and my prints are all over his crib, so what can you do? They want me here so I am here.'

He hopped off the bunk and stood before Victor to size him up. JT was a few inches shorter and a lot thinner and weaker. He didn't seem to like that fact when he realised.

He lowered himself to the floor and into a push-up position. He swivelled his head to look up at Victor. 'How many can you do?'

'I'm pretty out of shape right now.'

JT's face was already red from the exertion of holding up his body weight for a few seconds. He turned back so he faced the floor and began exercising. He started grunting when he had performed five. At ten he was unable to hold his back straight and his whole body shook. By the time he reached fifteen he was barely performing a full rep and hurriedly brought his legs forward and entered a kneeling position to avoid collapsing.

He gasped and drew a wrist across his forehead to wipe away the sweat.

It took a few seconds before he was able to speak.

'Could've gone to twenty but I'd just done five sets before you got here.'

'Impressive,' Victor said.

'Got to get my hands on some sauce,' JT said as he pulled up a sleeve and flexed his arm so that there was almost the shadow of a triceps. 'I wanna be a proper fiend by the time I leave here.'

'Inmates have access to steroids?'

JT nodded with vigour. 'Yeah, man. Some do. You can get anything you want if you know how.'

'Do you know how?'

JT pulled his sleeve back down. 'I'm going to get them from someone who knows. In here, it's all about knowing the right people.'

'Do you know the right people?'

JT grunted. 'Why you got to disrespect me like this?'

'Asking a pertinent question is being disrespectful?'

JT was confused, so he became insulted. 'Watch your tone. I may not be jacked but I could still whoop your pyramid-scheme ass around this cell.'

Victor raised an eyebrow. 'Of that I have no doubt.'

JT wasn't sure of Victor's tone, but there was no

aggressive or threatening change in posture or behaviour, so he let it go. Whatever his words, JT had no belief in his own capabilities and was relieved to avoid having to back up his words. It was all bravado and Victor was content to allow JT the win he obviously needed and spare him unnecessary embarrassment.

Victor found the resulting change in JT's behaviour to be a curious thing. JT was energised, with a spring in his step. He had better posture, his shoulders squared and his neck straight. His chin was elevated as he spoke, telling Victor about himself and his illicit exploits. All petty crime, and yet JT spoke about shoplifting and dealing marijuana as if they were the high-stakes enterprises of top-tier criminals. He hadn't been selling grass to middle-class high-school students but trafficking narcotics under the radar of well-policed neighbourhoods.

With his confidence high, he was able to be honest without fear of reproach. 'Got cocky, didn't I?'

'Overconfidence is a killer,' Victor agreed.

'Literally,' JT said metaphorically.

'Literally,' Victor said and meant it.

JT tried to vault up to the top bunk and failed. He had nowhere near the requisite athleticism and had to first use the bottom bunk as a step. He cast a quick backwards glance at Victor, who made sure he was looking somewhere else so JT thought he hadn't noticed. Victor wanted JT to stay confident and remain calm as a result. Victor, while patient beyond the means of almost anyone, knew there was only so much he could take of a JT that felt the constant need to prove himself.

The bravado faded from JT when an inmate appeared in

the open doorway. It was one of the guys from the corner of the pod. Now close, Victor could see the Cyrillic alphabet amid his tattoos. The man said nothing. He just stood in the doorway and looked into the cell. At both Victor and JT, though mostly at Victor.

JT couldn't handle the scrutiny. 'What is it, Nikkitin?' he asked in a meek voice. 'What do you want now?'

In a thick Russian accent, the man said, 'I just want to take a look at your new friend, JT.'

'He's not my friend,' JT was quick to say in return. 'He's a pyramid scheme fraudster.'

Victor said, 'Something I can help you with?'

Nikkitin shrugged. Then he nodded. Grinned. 'You've been a great help already.'

'My pleasure,' Victor said.

Nikkitin withdrew and the tension left JT. For a moment, he stared at the wall before scooping up his Bible.

'Who was that?' Victor asked him.

JT turned a page. 'One of Kirill's guys.'

'And who is Kirill?'

'Russian mafia,' he explained. 'Since he arrived, they've practically taken over this place.' He sighed as he turned to Victor. 'I don't know why they're interested in you, Pyramid, but whatever it is you better fix it fast.'

TWENTY-ONE

Victor had told Spector the truth when he said he liked dogs. He always had. As a boy, there were always dogs around. Not as pets, but to work. He had never owned a dog himself, although in an alternate dimension he might live with several. Not owned, since he would never assume authority over any sentient being. He could imagine such a cohabitation, however. A mutually beneficial association. He couldn't quite bring himself to think of such an arrangement of friendship since he had never known friendship, only facsimiles of such relationships. In a way that he now found ironic, dogs had taught him a lot about people. Men, in particular.

Male hierarchies had much in common with the canine pack. They shared more similarities than differences. Strength – power – equalled authority. Such power came in many forms, although in dogs it was literal. In both, that authority brought prosperity and peace. The weak did not seek war on the strong, and the strong had no need to persecute the weak if cooperation was more beneficial. A pack was greater than an individual. Even a pack of the weak could overcome a singular strength.

While power in civilised human society could manifest in many ways, in jail most of those ways did not apply. In here, the hierarchy was closest to that of the canine. In jail, raw power was the greatest strength.

Victor had been captive before. Many times, in fact. In a way, he had spent his entire childhood as a captive. Even when he had been liberated from one penitentiary, it had only been because another awaited him.

He didn't find jail any different in that regard. Walls were walls. Aside from set times for meals, the inmates were mostly left to their own devices. Some guys stayed in their cells. Others socialised in the open area of the pod.

JT said, 'Do you like books, Pyramid?'

'Very much so.'

'I'll show you the library,' his cellmate offered. Then he leered. 'I know all the books that have some filth in them.'

'I'll choose my own titles, thank you.'

They didn't get far out of the cell before Victor saw a problem coming. It was impossible not to see, in fact.

The inmate who stepped into his path was massive.

Victor, who was an expert at estimating a person's weight, put him at one hundred and eighty kilos, or almost four hundred pounds. He was both hugely fat and hugely muscled. He was overweight even on the undernourishment of a jail's diet, so either he obtained extra food by other means or he had been even bigger before he ended up here. Which was an image Victor struggled to visualise.

The inmate stood with his hands on his hips, further increasing his breadth. His jail jumpsuit, which had to be the largest size available, was too small for his frame. The sleeves were skin tight across his shoulders, increasing the depth of the groove between the deltoid and bicep. That sleeve had been cut to further expand it, otherwise the massive circumference of his arm would be too big to fit. Faded tattoos sleeved his arms. Victor could make out many interwoven designs, contradictory cultural symbols, lurid images and inconsistent philosophical statements, inked in over many years by many different hands of greatly varying skill.

The inmate said, 'I'm Two Times.'

His head was shaved at the sides and left a little longer on top, where it was thin and patchy. Bare scalp reflected the harsh lights above. He had a beard, fair in colour, short and neat. His eyes seemed small between his bloated cheeks and jutting eyebrows.

Victor said, 'Good for you.'

'Do you know why they call me Two Times?'

'I can't possibly know because I've never met you before, but I imagine it's an incredibly clever handle based on the fact that you never have to hit a guy two times.'

Two Times frowned.

Victor was aware of JT and the other inmates looking his way. They had a look of anticipation and expectation. Therefore this was not the first time a new guy had faced such a welcome from Two Times. There were no corrections officers looking his way, however, which meant nothing was going to happen now. If a fight broke out every time a new guy arrived and it was always Two Times involved they would pay more attention. So Two Times rarely got to make sure his name was still accurate. Which was no surprise. Victor could not imagine many new inmates keen to be the subject of that particular test. Therefore Two Times was after something else instead of a fight. He assumed he had won the fight just by standing in Victor's way.

'Whatever you want from me the answer is no.'

Two Times said, 'You don't say no to me.'

'You're huge,' Victor said.

Two Times grinned.

'You're so huge you can't even remember what you did when you last had to actually fight someone.'

Two Times's smile faded.

'You probably just rushed them,' Victor said, 'and fell on them. The weight alone won the fight even before you threw any punches. Three or four and you're gasping. Five and you're drowning in your own sweat. Six and you're passing out.'

'I only need to throw one,' Two Times said. 'That's why they call me Two Times.'

'Maybe,' Victor said. 'Assuming it hits, of course. And then what? What do you gain? You maintain your position. So you gain nothing. You're top dog anyway. You're top dog if you didn't get off your chair.' He paused. 'But what if you need more than one punch? What if you need two or three or six? Worse still, what if you lose? What if I actually fight you back like no one has ever really done? What then? If you knock me down, no one cares. If I knock you down no one will ever take you seriously again. Is it worth the risk?'

'There's no risk,' Two Times said after a pause.

'For argument's sake, let's say you're right,' Victor said. 'Doesn't change the most important point: when was the last time someone punched you back? You probably don't even remember what it feels like, do you? It hurts. You remember that much, at least. But can you cope with it after so long without? Because all those hours lifting weights have done nothing for your pain tolerance. That's all willpower. That's inner strength. And let's face it: you haven't spent thousands of hours working out to get that big if you were overflowing with self-belief in the first place. When I start hurting you like no one ever has before, we might as well be travelling back in time to the day before you began lifting weights, when you looked like a pencil and everyone made fun out of you, asking "What's the air like up there?" and "Is everything about you so skinny?" So I won't be hurting you, I'm going to be hurting him. The real question, therefore, isn't do you think you can beat me, but do you think *he* even stands a chance?'

No answer came.

Victor stepped past Two Times, who made no effort to stop him.

JT followed after a moment, hurrying to catch up. He stared at Victor with wide eyes.

'*How did you do that?*'

TWENTY-TWO

The jail had an impressive library that inmates could visit with as much frequency as they liked throughout the day, JT explained. He had never read before his incarceration and now couldn't get enough. With little else to do to pass the time, Victor was content to peruse the book selection on offer. Equal parts fiction to non-fiction. He saw many law books; an entire wall of the library was dedicated to them.

JT said, 'Huh.'

Victor looked up from his reading. He saw JT perched on the edge of the table, the dog-eared paperback in his hand now dangling down by his side, held in a loose pincer of index finger and thumb. JT was chewing his bottom lip.

'What is it?' Victor asked.

'Nothing,' he said. 'Just something funny.'

There was something in his tone. It told Victor that JT wasn't talking about humour. He was using 'funny' as a synonym for unusual. He had thought of, or noticed, something that didn't feel right. In Victor's experience if something didn't feel right that was for a reason. The brain processed so much information it was impossible to be consciously aware of everything. In the civilian world, people dismissed such feelings on a regular basis because more often than not nothing came of them. Maybe it was noticing that someone was behaving in an odd manner. Maybe it was a noise from downstairs in the middle of the night. Probably nothing, they told themselves. Don't make a fuss.

'Tell me,' Victor said.

They were not in the civilian world now. They were not in Victor's world, either. Here, he couldn't process the same information as he could under normal circumstances. His threat radar was slowed in jail.

'It's nothing,' JT insisted. 'Just you never know someone until you know them.'

Victor rotated his head, scanning the library. It had another six inmates inside. Four had been here from the start, and two others had replaced the two that had left while Victor and JT sat at the desk. The original two continued perusing the law texts. One sat cross-legged on the floor, three books opened out around him. He made notes.

The other two were looking for novels in the literary fiction section, which occupied less than half a bookcase of space.

JT had his gaze in their direction.

'Let me guess,' Victor said. 'You didn't figure them for readers.'

JT grinned. 'Oh, they read. Everyone in here reads eventually. What else are you going to do? But they're the kind who only read certain pages of certain books.' He grinned wider. 'And they only read them after they've ripped them out and taken them back to their cells.'

JT made an obscene hand gesture.

Victor considered the two men. Lean, inmate builds suggesting they'd been inside long enough for the poor nutritional content of the food to have a detrimental effect. One had tattoos on his neck and on his cheeks. He was older than the second, whose narrow babyface had no hint of stubble. Both had buzzed hair. Neither faced Victor or JT. They weren't close, either. In Victor's blind spot unless he swivelled his head, but they had no direct path of attack.

Victor considered. Potential threats.

'Violent records?'

JT shook his head. 'Maybe, I think.'

'Affiliations?'

JT frowned. 'What?'

'Gang?'

JT shrugged and said, 'They're white,' as if that explained everything. Then in a lower tone, asked, 'Is it on?'

'Fifty-fifty right now,' Victor told him. 'Whatever happens, stay out of it.'

'What? No way, Pyramid. I got your back.'

'Go to the other side of the room,' Victor said. 'Stand with the others. That way it won't look like we're together.'

JT said, 'We *are* in this together.'

'You've known me for a matter of hours.'

JT said, 'Changes nothing. You're my cellmate. That means we're a team. I'm not going to let you take a beating here. I know I can't fight for shit but I can fight better than a pyramid fraudster.'

'No,' Victor said. 'You'll get in my way.'

'Nuh uh. It's two against one otherwise. If it kicks off, you need me.'

The door to the library opened and another man came in. Taller and broader than the other two, who looked straight towards him in expectation. He ignored them, his focus directed only at Victor.

When the new arrival stepped towards Victor, the other two followed a step behind.

Together, the three men edged closer.

'You definitely need me now.'

JT had a look of nervous excitement. It was the midpoint in the fight or flight reflex, when two very different instincts were still competing within his subconscious. Stress hormones were elevating his heart rate. His eyes were wide to take in as much visual information as possible, though his focus was narrow. His entire being – all of his senses – was fixed on the three threats. But JT did not understand the signs as well as Victor. JT's existence up until this point had not been the same.

'This isn't a fight,' he explained. 'They want to kill me. If you're with me, if you try and help, they'll try to kill you too. I won't be able to protect you while I'm dealing with three of them.'

'Kill a pyramid fraudster? No way. Why would you even think that?'

The three inmates answered for him.

They all had shanks. Previously hidden in their clothes, they revealed them now.

JT paled.

'Like I told you,' Victor said as he stood from his chair. 'Stay out of my way.'

TWENTY-THREE

The lead guy had a toothbrush, only a razorblade had been inserted into the head of the brush where bristles should be to form a small but deadly sharp cutting implement. Technically a shiv since it was for slashing instead of stabbing, although Victor doubted the man understood the difference in terminology. Given its size, it would be almost impossible to disarm. Too small to bat away, and any attempt to grab it or the hand would almost certainly create a deep laceration to the fingers or palm. But if it was close enough to cut him then the wielder was close enough to receive broken bones. Maybe an acceptable trade-off to the inmate if Victor had a slashed carotid.

The one with the babyface had a hard plastic spoon that had been shaved and filed down to a spike. It could make no cuts, and yet the tip could be driven through flesh with only a little force. Maybe not through his skull or ribs, and it was unlikely to do much damage to his arms, so it would come from a low angle, aiming for his abdomen, or downward to his groin and thighs. Like the toothbrush razor, it had no real advantage in reach, and there would be far less risk to grabbing it. The inmate had it in his fist, protruding between his index finger and middle finger in imitation of a push dagger.

The inmate with the tattoos had a crude triangular blade made of dark metal that looked like wrought iron. Too thin, though. It took Victor a moment to understand that it had been constructed from a baking tray. So the metal was weak and that was why it had been fashioned into a triangle. That meant some extra strength and rigidity, and it could both cut and stab.

'Go,' Victor told JT.

Now JT understood.

He stood up from the plastic chair now he was no longer caught in the middle of opposing instincts. Flight won and he did as instructed, backing away to the far side of the library.

The three inmates with weapons let him go.

Victor saw they had crafted their weapons well. As important as the blade or spike were the grips. One wound would almost never be enough with these kinds of improvised weapons, so keeping hold of it was essential. If the shank became slick with blood or sweat, it could slip from the hand. Each of the three had a strip of towel, bed linen or clothing wrapped around to form a grip. Such grips naturally moulded under pressure so they ergonomically suited the wielder, ensuring a secure hold even in the most extreme of circumstances. Beyond blood or sweat increasing the risk of dropping the weapon or having it taken, a stabbing implement could get stuck in the victim. Flesh alone could suck and stick, and bone could make an even stronger hold.

A poor grip on the shank would only increase the likelihood that such an unfortunate incident occurred.

Victor assessed his immediate area. While the library had plenty of open space, it also had lots of obstacles. Tables and chairs for a start, and several bookcases subdividing the space. And inmates. He expected no involvement from the latter. They looked scared. They were here to read, not witness a murder

Victor wanted no assistance from anyone. He preferred to operate alone, to fight alone, to kill alone. Even the most competent of partners could also be a liability. Any successful partnership required synchronicity. An expert combatant at his side was of no benefit if they got in each other's way. Victor had learned long ago that too many cooks could spoil more than just the broth. In his early days as a professional he had sometimes worked in teams. Often, those teams were comprised of highly skilled individuals. Specialists. Experts in surveillance, counter-surveillance, marksmanship, tactics, but who he witnessed first-hand could not operate effectively as a single entity, their superb individual skills neutered by a lack of coordination, teamwork or mutually aligned instinct. At other times, Victor had singlehandedly defeated such teams, whose numerical advantage had been their ultimate undoing. He, as a single entity, had no one else to get in his way.

He needed a weapon, however, against two shanks and a shiv.

A chair could make for an effective counter to any small melee weapons. In most hand-to-hand fighting, reach was often the single most important factor. Spears had been used on the battlefield for thousands of years, after all. A chair held by the back gave a huge advantage in reach over a shank. However, the plastic jail chairs had no useful mass and no structural integrity. They would provide an advantage in reach, although were no weapon in themselves. The library chair would only be useful as a shield. Only in defence. It would only delay a shank reaching him. It would not enable him to disarm or defeat his enemies.

Instead, Victor slid the non-fiction title he had been reading from the tabletop.

He held it in his left hand, pinched closed between thumb and fingers, spine facing away from him and towards the three inmates moving into attacking positions. They were eager and yet also confused by what he was holding.

Victor said, 'Never bring a shank to a book fight.'

TWENTY-FOUR

Either the three inmates with weapons thought he was joking or they were not deterred by the sight of the academic tome in his hand. When the inmate with the babyface charged first, lunging with the sharpened plastic spoon, Victor blocked its path to his abdomen with the spine of the textbook.

The book was over five hundred pages in length, three inches thick, reinforced with a hardcover of dense cardboard that may as well have been armour plating to the sharpened plastic spike. It deflected away, ricocheting as a bullet would do from a tank's hull, sending the inmate's arm up and to his right.

Victor sent an elbow strike down the resulting gap at the exposed babyface.

He aimed for the nose, to crush it, but his accuracy was a little off and his elbow collided low, hitting the inmate in the teeth. Which were clenched shut. They gave way under the impact, the forward momentum of the inmate multiplying the force of Victor's accelerating elbow.

Enamel shattered, roots tore free from jawbone, scattering teeth and chunks of them across the thin library carpet and the table surface.

Blood spattered everywhere. On the table, on the carpet, on books, on Victor's clothing.

The inmate dropped straight down at Victor's feet.

Who retreated a step to create distance. He didn't want the guy on the floor to get in his way, either as a deliberate act of attack or as a simple obstacle.

The other two were cautious now. Their energetic assault faltered. Neither wanted their own set of county jail dentures like the guy on the floor. He was a horrid sight. Bright blood ringed his mouth, had spilled over his jumpsuit, and the jagged remains of broken teeth were plain to see because he was wailing. That awful sound was as much a deterrent as the blood and scattered teeth. It was an alarm bell. A siren almost. An unmistakable warning. The only downside was the teeth embedded in Victor's elbow. Which was why he had aimed for the nose, which would have crushed beneath the strike, taking the guy out of the fight either through unconsciousness or sheer pain and debilitation. Victor wasn't quite at his best, he knew, so he cut himself some slack.

He used the textbook to brush the incisors out from his elbow.

The two other inmates did the right thing: they spread out, making use of their numerical advantage, one stepping to Victor's left and the other to his right. While he could see them both in his peripheral vision at the same time, he could not focus on both their weapons simultaneously. They were no perfectly in-sync duet, however. They were no trained team. Spreading out was an obvious tactic. Surrounding an enemy was as basic a strategy as they came. Humans had never been solitary predators; pack tactics were ingrained in DNA. Flanking a dangerous adversary was as good as hardwired.

The library and the bookshelves prevented them from getting behind him. In ideal two-versus-one situations there would be an enemy in his blind spot while the other occupied him from the front. They couldn't achieve that here because Victor did not let them. He moved when they moved and used the obstacles of furniture and the bookcases to ensure they were both in front of him at all times. If it came to it, he would back off into a corner with two walls converging, protecting his flanks and his rear. He didn't expect it to come to that because these guys weren't going to wait that long. Victor had no idea about the jail schedules, the corrections officers and their rotations, their movements, from how far away they would hear an altercation or how long it would take to intervene. Even if some distraction had taken place elsewhere, and his attackers were smart enough to have set up such a distraction, they wouldn't have long. Someone would hear. Someone would come past or would notice something was amiss. Maybe the disruption in the homeostasis of the jail could be detected. The corrections officers might have such awareness and instinct that they would just *know* something was amiss, some subtle sign detected, a tremor in the air, almost. The two guys knew what they had to do, whether compelled or hired or instructed, it did not matter. They were on the clock. They knew it. And Victor knew it.

'Tick tock,' he said.

They found their courage as the pressure built to unbearable levels.

The two inmates attacked.

Both at the same time, yet without coordination. Which was why he'd taunted them into hasty actions. He didn't want one taking the time to get behind him while he had to fight off the other.

The taller guy on the right swung the razorblade shiv an instant after the tattooed guy on the left stabbed with the folded baking-tray shank.

Victor batted the shank away with the textbook but could not bring it back in time to defend against the razorblade.

The guy aimed for his face or maybe the side of his neck. A downward attack coming from a raised stance.

Victor jerked his head backwards and the razorblade cut his chest, slicing through the cotton jumpsuit and drawing a vertical line of blood that he did not feel, only saw as it stained the fabric.

Now they were close, he whipped an elbow against the guy's skull, striking just above the ear. A solid blow, which made the inmate's knees buckle, yet did not take him out of the fight.

Victor retreated before the tattooed guy with the shank recovered and attacked again. He overextended himself in an effort to make up for that increased distance, giving Victor plenty of opportunity to block the weapon with the textbook. Though a makeshift blade, the shank had been patiently and expertly sharpened. It pierced the tough cover of the book and a few pages before it could pierce no further.

For an instant, it was trapped, although easy enough to pull free by a strong or determined hand. But Victor had anticipated this moment, whereas the attacker was in unpredicted territory.

Immediately, Victor rotated the book, and with it, the shank, which in turn twisted the guy's arm so that the elbow was pointing directly up, locking the limb and controlling the rest of the person attached to it.

Victor would have slammed his right wrist down upon that exposed elbow joint and smashed it open, but the guy with the razorblade was attacking him. With no way to dodge, Victor had to use the back of his forearm to block the incoming shiv. This time he felt it cut him before he saw the blood bloom out of the wound.

They were both within his personal space now, and there was not enough room for all three of them together. He stumbled backwards and they stumbled forwards with him, six legs competing for purchase on the same stretch of carpet. Victor's back collided with a bookcase and books fell to the floor, creating more obstacles, providing more reasons to trip and slip. The collision with the bookcase, however, kept Victor from falling over, which would have been bad, with two guys landing on top of him.

Victor was quicker on his feet, his reactions faster, his experience far greater. He slipped and weaved out from the subsequent attempts to grapple him. He found space and sprang back a step to create enough distance to launch a stomp kick at the nearest guy, the inmate with the razorblade toothbrush. The kick landed on the guy's hip. Not Victor's best placed or strongest kick, although more than enough in the instant of time he had to propel the guy into the other inmate, knocking them both back, creating more distance.

And with it, a greater window of time in which Victor had to pick his next attacks for most devastating effect. He used the textbook as a shield held out in front of him and delivered a right cross over the top of it that landed square and hard on the inmate's tattooed cheekbone as his head swivelled in an attempt to keep Victor in his focus.

Victor's hand stung but the inmate had it much worse. The cheekbone was broken and he staggered backwards as his brain rattled around inside his skull before he slid down with his back against a bookcase until his behind was on the carpet and his legs splayed out. Not knocked out, yet so dazed his eyes were wide open and yet looking at nothing at all. He wouldn't be getting back up any time soon.

At that point things looked pretty good to Victor, who had only one inmate standing before him, but two things happened to complicate matters.

Victor only saw one of them.

TWENTY-FIVE

The first complication came from the inmate with the razor-blade toothbrush in his right hand, who supplemented that armament by picking up the sharpened spoon that had been dropped by his babyfaced friend who now required emergency dental work. That made things difficult, although two weapons did not mean a doubling of the threat posed. As both were short, only one could be implemented while maintaining an effective fighting stance. One weapon would always be further back than the other unless a square posture was used, in which case any advantage in offence was tempered by the disadvantage of presenting a larger and more vulnerable target.

Regardless, at extreme close distance, within Victor's reach, it would be impossible to defend against two deadly weapons.

Worse, though, was the second complication.

One of the previously passive inmates huddled against the far wall found some courage. Victor did not hear him approach – all his focus was on the threats before him – and the inmate with the new-found courage crept up behind him.

This inmate did so with slow careful steps, getting close to Victor before charging into him. No real plan of attack, just simple mass and intent.

'*Watch out*,' JT yelled, far too late to be useful.

The new attacker was way bigger than the others and barrelled Victor down to the floor, falling with him, although less controlled. Victor reacted faster and flipped over from his front to his back before the guy on top of him could capitalise on that advantage.

Victor grabbed both of the big guy's ears and pushed him away, creating distance and exposing the guy's face enough for Victor to launch a relentless series of rapid, well-placed headbutts. The forehead has the strongest curve of bone in the human body, and Victor's broke the guy's nose at the ridge, then crushed the cartilage flat, then cracked the orbital bone of his left eye socket. Blood streamed from the wounds.

He was still conscious so Victor wasn't finished with him. Because of the risk of getting the guy's blood splashing in his eyes with more headbutts, Victor instead pushed the curve of his forehead into the damage he had already down, grinding bone against broken bone while he pulled on the inmate's ears to both increase the pressure and prevent his escape.

The inmate screeched louder than the guy who had lost half of his teeth.

Victor released the two ears, allowing the big guy to throw himself backwards to escape the merciless attack, and a quick lateral roll meant Victor avoided the stomping heel of the foot that was crashing down towards his exposed face.

He grabbed the leg before it could be withdrawn, and bit into the back of the calf muscle of the inmate holding both the razorblade toothbrush and the sharpened plastic spoon, biting with just his incisors to focus the force in the smallest possible area of flesh to maximise the pain caused.

That guy wailed, high pitched and shrill.

There was so much overlapping screaming by this point that one of the inmates keeping out of things pressed both palms over his ears.

Victor rolled away to avoid the responding downward swipes with the razorblade and the thrusts with the sharpened spoon.

Springing to his feet, it became messy then, with the three of them in close confines between bookcases. The big inmate with the busted face was behind Victor, and his injuries had not dissuaded him, although they impaired his effectiveness to only blocking Victor's line of retreat from the shiv and shank attacks.

He snatched another book to use as a shield, blocking and batting, stopping some attacks, not able to prevent others finding their mark, unable to dodge effectively with the guy behind him in the way.

Victor took superficial wounds to his arms and chest. The razorblade toothbrush cut him across the back of his right hand, nicking the artery protected by just thin skin. Blood coated his hand and dripped from his fingers. A significant wound but it would be hours before he would bleed to death.

His attacker saw this as a prelude to a violent, imminent victory.

The inmate, wounded and bleeding himself, said, 'Bet that hurts.'

Victor shrugged. 'It's not as bad as it looks. See . . .'

He motioned with his bloody hand, and his attacker instinctively glanced at it, creating the perfect opportunity for Victor to flick blood into his eyes.

At first, Victor did not know whether his blood found the guy's eyes. It didn't really matter because the flinch reaction did everything Victor needed.

The inmate blinked and jerked his head back at the same time, flinching to avoid the threat to his vision, changing his centre of gravity in the process so that he had to take a backwards step in order to stay balanced.

Victor never let an advantageous opportunity go to waste and he darted forward between the two weapons, inside the guy's reach.

The inmate's eyes only blinked open again long enough to see the blur of an accelerating elbow and then nothing more.

He collapsed to the floor, silent and unmoving.

Victor took a breath then turned to face the inmate who had joined in, the guy with the flattened nose and the cracked orbital bone. The big inmate hadn't needed to get involved, and who had only done so when Victor's back had been exposed.

With the rest of his attackers on the floor in varying states of unconsciousness and agony, and him now all alone, the inmate backed away and raised his hands in surrender.

'Ah,' Victor said. 'You want to call a timeout?'

The big guy said nothing, but nodded and thrust his hands higher as blood streamed from his broken nose.

'What do you say, JT?' Victor said without looking at his cellmate.

JT, who was open-mouthed and statue still at what he

had witnessed, had to clear his throat before he could find his voice.

'Well,' he said, swallowing. 'From where I'm standing the clock's still running.'

'Clock's still running,' Victor repeated with a nod, before beating the only inmate still standing to his knees, then holding him there to beat him a little longer.

TWENTY-SIX

When the corrections officers arrived there was a lot of shouting. They didn't seem to care about Victor's injuries, only restraining him. He didn't resist, though they used far more force than necessary. When they had things under control, they performed some basic first aid on him and the wounded inmates before taking them all to the infirmary. The doctor in charge tutted and rolled her eyes as Victor and the four others were brought inside.

'I hope it was worth it,' she said.

A nurse cleaned and dressed Victor's injuries. None of the cuts inflicted by the razorblade toothbrush required stitches. Bandages and tape were enough to close them. He had two puncture wounds from the sharpened spoon that required a little more attention. One to his right biceps, the other to his chest.

The cut to the back of his hand hurt more than any other of the small wounds. When he clenched his fist, a hot sting of discomfort radiated from the cut.

The nurse took extra time cleaning the wound and applying tape to keep the skin closed.

'You should take better care of these hands,' she told him afterwards. 'They're incredibly youthful.'

'Reassuring,' he said. 'They cost a pretty penny.'

She smiled as though he were joking.

'What have we here?' she asked, examining his right elbow and the indented and broken skin.

Her eyes widened when she found a shard of tooth embedded that the swipe with the book had not cleared. At first, she gasped, thinking it was a piece of bone from his radius, poking out.

'Incisors are sharp,' Victor explained. 'That's why I always aim for the nose or the jaw.'

Her eyes widened further. '*Always?*'

'Sometimes I miss,' he admitted.

When she had finished cleaning and dressing his wounds, she told him, 'You're very lucky to be in one piece.'

'I don't believe in luck.'

'That doesn't matter,' the nurse said. 'Luck believes in you.'

'That's an interesting way to look at it,' Victor replied.

'Oh, I'm interesting whichever way you look.'

He had no idea what she meant, and had no time to ask because she left him then with his pain. Not debilitating and yet uncomfortable. In his experience, superficial injuries always hurt more than serious ones.

After the nurse had gone, the huge corrections officer wanted to speak with him.

'Don't say anything,' he began, holding up a palm like a shield to block lies. 'They started it.'

Victor said, 'They did.'

'Four guys, of which three are due to be released soon, decided, with no prior provocation, to attack the new guy. And not just attack, no, that is not enough. A beating – a few bruises – just can't satiate this sudden, unquenchable, bloodlust. So they decided to arm themselves with a wide array of deadly weapons. They raided their armoury, the entire secret stash of shanks and shivs. All for the new guy.'

Victor nodded. 'That's what happened.'

He sighed and stared at Victor. 'So,' he said, 'please enlighten me. Tell me ... why? Did you happen to sleep with all their mothers before you came here? Were you their school bully? Or is it simply that they find your face so questionable, so irritating, that they can't share the same world with it?'

Victor remained silent.

The corrections officer continued. 'Because, and trust me on this, you're not actually *that* ugly.'

Victor said, 'You think that I started a fight with four other inmates on my first and only day here?'

The guy shrugged. 'Why not? We get all kinds of crazy in this joint.'

'I'm out of here tomorrow, and yet I risk that imminent release by starting a fight. Sounds reasonable.'

'I'm just saying how it looks. You have a couple of paper cuts while none of those four will be out of the infirmary for a week.'

'When you check the tapes later you'll see I was in the library before the third guy even entered. And you'll see them converge. Check the tapes of what was going on before then and you'll see them converse or at least acknowledge one another, because this wasn't random. That's why they all had weapons, and you know it.'

'Maybe I know it but I just don't believe it. Do you know how often an inmate survives a four-on-one ambush like that?'

'It wasn't a four-on-one ambush,' Victor said. 'It was three versus one. The fourth guy didn't join in until the end.'

The huge corrections officer huffed. 'My point still stands. No one walks away from something like that.'

'All records are set only to be broken.'

'You're a funny guy.'

'Are we done?'

'Yeah, we're done.'

Victor headed back in the pod in time for dinner, and he joined the line of inmates waiting to be served. He ignored all the glances and stares.

Word travelled fast in jail.

Aided by JT, who was miming elbow strikes and headbutts to the other inmates sitting at his table. When JT saw Victor with a tray of food, he beckoned him over to join them.

With a shake of his head, Victor took his dinner to an unoccupied bench to eat by himself. The food was bland and nutritionally dead, but calories were calories. Victor had eaten a lot worse in his time without complaint, and he needed to refuel after the fight in the library.

The Russian who had stopped by the cell earlier, Nikkitin, sat down opposite Victor and said in a quiet voice, 'Don't go to sleep tonight.'

It wasn't a threat. It was an instruction.

Victor gave him a questioning look.

'Kirill wants to talk to you,' Nikkitin said. 'In private.'

Victor used a plastic fork to chase an overcooked piece of penne pasta around the tray. The fork wasn't sharp and the

131

pasta was too soft and springy to comply. Victor's impeded dexterity didn't help.

'What about?' he asked.

'Doesn't matter what it's about. Kirill wants to talk so you go to him and talk.'

'After lights-out?'

'Yes.'

'When the cells are locked?'

Nikkitin nodded. 'Sometimes they don't work. Very old electronics. Okay?'

'Cameras?'

'Sometimes they get turned off by mistake,' Nikkitin explained. 'No one sees anything that Kirill doesn't want them to see. You'll get a knock on your door and then you wait five minutes. The door will be unlocked and the cameras will be off.'

'Which cell is Kirill in?'

'You'll work it out, I'm sure.'

Victor shrugged. 'If I'm tired, I'll be asleep.'

Nikkitin grew frustrated. 'You stay awake all night long if that's what Kirill wants. Or it won't be four in the library next time. It'll be everyone in here.'

With that, Nikkitin stood and left Victor alone with his meal.

TWENTY-SEVEN

A little after midnight, the knock came. JT was asleep and snoring quietly on the top bunk, having said nothing further to Victor. He waited the five minutes Nikkitin had told him to wait – counting off each and every second – and opened the door to the cell. It had been locked at lights-out like all the others.

Victor stepped out into the quiet corridor that had another twenty cells like his own. Nikkitin had not told him which cell was Kirill's, yet it was easy to tell. All the other cells had their doors closed except one. A faint light emerged from the doorway.

With quiet footfalls, Victor approached.

Kirill had a cell all to himself. He stood at its far end, washing his hands at the basin, when Victor entered. Kirill glanced his way and said nothing, giving Victor a moment to take in his surroundings. Before housing Kirill, the cell had been used by four inmates. The four bunks remained, although they had been adjusted. Only one top bunk remained used for its intended purpose. The bunk below it had become a sofa of sorts. The bunk opposite was now a desk. One of the chairs from the open area of the pod had been brought in for use with the desk. There was a disparity in height – the bunk was lower than the seat of the chair – and so plastic storage boxes had been placed on the bunk. Those boxes were filled with something heavy to stop them sliding around. They had lids so Victor could not see inside. The other top bunk was used for storage. Books, mostly. Kirill was a voracious reader.

Given the dimensions of the cell, Victor had no place to stand where he could watch the doorway and Kirill at the same time. Victor was no fan of having an open door in his blind spot, so he took a few steps further into the cell to increase the distance between the entrance and his back.

Kirill dried his hands on a towel. He took his time, drying each finger in turn. He said nothing until he had finished.

'You,' he said, and put the towel down.

'Me,' Victor said.

'My name is Kirill Lebedev.' He paused. 'And you're William Pendleton.'

Kirill was stripped to the waist. From a distance, he had seemed old with his white hair and beard. Up close, Victor saw he looked closer to forty than his actual fifty years. The blue eyes were intense, made brighter by the contrast to the darker shade of his skin. At that initial distance, Victor might have guessed Kirill had not been in jail for long, and had brought his tan with him. Now, Victor figured Kirill had been allowed to spend more time in the yard than other inmates during the summer months, and the effect on his skin endured.

Kirill's torso was covered in tattoos. On the right side of his chest were several words written in Cyrillic script: *brat*, *soldat* and *zakonnyy vor*. Brother, soldier and lawful thief. *Brat* and *soldat* each had a line through them, denoting his rise in ranks within the Bratva. Kirill was now a lawful thief. He had a cross on the right side of his chest. Even for Victor, who cared nothing for such body art, it was a beautiful image. Kirill saw Victor looking.

'We all have this,' Kirill said, touching the cross. 'It means much to us in Russia. Christ himself died upon it and yet when the godless communists took over they wanted to rid us of our faith. This is so we don't forget. And it reminds us never to kneel to any authority except that of God himself.'

Victor asked, 'Why am I in your cell in the middle of the night?'

'Because I need to see your face and look you in the eye.'

'You could have done that any time,' Victor said. 'You didn't need to wait until now.'

'Some things need to be done in private.'

Victor waited.

'That was quite a thing you did in the library,' Kirill began. 'You've only been in jail a day and now you're the scariest man in here.'

'I'm surprised to learn you're giving up your crown quite so easily.'

Kirill seemed confused. 'You find me scary?'

'That's not what I said.'

'Everyone in here is frightened of me,' Kirill admitted. 'That is true. Although it's because of what I can have done in here or outside, not because of what I can do personally. If four inmates come at me then they'll kill me. I'm no warrior.'

'Only they would never dare.'

Kirill nodded. 'What do you know of me?'

'My cellmate said you are Russian mafia,' Victor answered. 'Bratva.'

'The Brotherhood,' Kirill said. 'We are all *bratskaya*, little brothers.'

'Why am I here?'

'You killed Grigori Orlov. He was one of my little brothers.'

Victor said, 'It wasn't me who shot him.'

'Yet it was you who was arrested.'

'I haven't been charged.'

'Your truck was seen leaving the crime.'

'Hearsay,' Victor said. 'It's not been confirmed. Just an anonymous tip at this stage.'

'You failed a gunshot residue test.'

'You're well informed,' Victor said. 'So you also know I wasn't picked out of the line-up.'

Kirill smiled. 'Yes, yes, yes. Very impressive. You've done well. I've been thinking this through since you arrived, how you managed to pull it off.'

'Why do you care so much?'

'Because I am awaiting trial,' the Russian explained.

'What are the charges?'

'Drug trafficking, racketeering, bribery, murder ...' Kirill laughed. 'The usual. I was not as careful as I should have been.'

'Are you guilty?'

'Obviously I'm guilty. Of that and a lot more besides. I have a team of lawyers working around the clock to keep me here in relative luxury and not sent somewhere decidedly less pleasant. That won't work for ever. And when I stand trial, I'll lose. And then I'll be sent to prison for the rest of my life.'

'Tough break,' Victor said.

'So,' Kirill began, 'how did you end up in here?'

'Long story, but there was an altercation in the holding cell. An addict attacked me unprovoked. He got hurt. I got sent here.'

'I thought you'd be more careful than that.'

Victor waited for more.

'Did you know that Grigori was one of us, the Bratva?'

'Is that why you sent the guys to attack me in the library?'

Kirill laughed. 'They were nothing to do with me. The Bratva is not a single animal but many beasts of the same herd. Those men in the library were friends of Grigori's people, not mine. They merely wanted revenge for his murder. Although, had they known the truth about him, they wouldn't have been so eager for vengeance.'

'Why's that?'

'Because Grigori was a rat working for the FBI all along. He was going to be one of the District Attorney's star witnesses against me. Because he's dead, her case is suddenly a lot weaker.' He paused. 'Thank you for that.'

'Why are you thanking me when it wasn't me who shot him?'

'I think it's time you dropped the act,' Kirill said. 'I know you killed Grigori because it was me who hired you to do it.'

TWENTY-EIGHT

Victor said, 'It wasn't me who killed Grigori. I won't be charged. There's no evidence.'

Kirill shrugged. 'Evidence is for the courts. Exhibit this and exhibit that. All those plastic bags. Those labels. Weeks and months of back and forth and arguing. And for what exactly? Evidence doesn't prove guilt any more than it demonstrates innocence. Evidence is merely there to tell a story. The most believable story isn't necessarily the truth. It's a story, after all. I wanted to bring you here so I can look into your eyes.'

Victor stepped forward. 'Be my guest.'

Kirill did. He stared up without blinking for a long time. Victor let him.

When Kirill looked away, he seemed neither pleased nor disappointed.

'I can't wait to hear what you saw,' Victor said without enthusiasm.

'You think I was looking for the truth, do you? You think I could discern guilt and innocence from your eyes? If I gave you that impression, then I did not convey my intent properly. I only looked to see what kind of man you are, because eyes always tell.'

'They must have whispered,' Victor said, 'because I didn't hear anything.'

'You're funny,' he said. 'I like that about you. You killed Grigori, which I also like. You got yourself caught, which is something I don't like so much.'

His mouth stayed open as if he were to continue speaking, only he closed his eyes and groaned. Kirill bunched both hands into fists and massaged the sides of his skull with his knuckles. The thick skin of the scalp stretched and creased while he pushed and pulled, up and down, and in circular motions. He let out a quiet sigh of relief.

'I get headaches,' he said. 'In this place, I get no peace. The stress and boredom bubbles up inside me and I have no release from the pain in my skull. Sometimes I fear I would chop off my own head to find relief if only I had access to a large enough blade.'

'Aspirin might be a safer option.'

Kirill took a bottle of prescription pills and shook out a couple into his palm. 'I have access to a lot better than aspirin.'

'You're allowed to self-medicate in here?'

He swallowed. 'I'm allowed to do a lot of things.'

Victor watched him set the bottle back down. The label read TRAMADOL, a powerful opioid.

'I don't know your name,' the Russian said, 'but I know the name of your broker. Her handle, at least. I paid Phoenix a lot of money to have you kill Grigori so that I had no connection to it that the FBI could ever prove.'

'I didn't shoot him,' Victor said.

'Don't try to deny it again. It insults us both. My instructions were three shots in the head, just like it happened.'

'It's the truth,' Victor said. 'I wasn't the one who squeezed the trigger.'

Kirill's eyes narrowed, thinking. Then they widened. 'You had someone else do it for you?'

'Outsourcing might be a better term.'

Kirill chuckled. 'I knew it. I always know a killer when I see one.'

Victor remained silent.

'But what I can't understand is how you screwed it up and found yourself in here. Why outsource the job only to get yourself caught? I thought you were better than that. I was assured by your broker you didn't make avoidable mistakes.'

'I made no mistake,' Victor said.

'Now is not the time for ego. The walls around you send a clear enough message that you are not as good as your reputation suggested.' There was annoyance in his tone. 'I paid a small fortune for the best. At least, I thought you were the best. Whether you are charged or not, the police still picked you up for the murder you were hired to commit.' Kirill edged forward, one meaningful step at a time bringing him ever closer. From the far side of the cell to a couple of metres, then to arm's length. Then inside arm's length. Close enough for Victor to smell the man's body odour and sandalwood in his beard oil. 'If that's not a mistake, then what is it?'

'Careful design,' Victor explained.

Kirill was confused.

At least until Victor put him in a rear naked chokehold.

He thrust out both hands at the same time, his left grabbing Kirill's right shoulder and wrenching him closer while his right hand shoved the Russian's left shoulder, spinning the man around one hundred and eighty degrees.

As Kirill had admitted himself, he was no warrior. His reactions were slow. He didn't know how to resist as Victor spun him around and snapped on the chokehold.

'I expect your boss higher up in the Bratva is worried about you,' Victor said as he applied pressure to Kirill's carotid arteries. 'They probably think you'll be offered a deal and you'll take it to taste free air again. Assuming you haven't taken one already.'

Kirill struggled fruitlessly as the oxygen supply to his brain was impeded. He didn't know what to do to save himself. He had longer than most because Victor was careful with how much pressure he applied. He didn't want to leave marks on Kirill's neck.

'You really should have kept these midnight meetings a better secret,' Victor said as he felt Kirill's resistance begin to wane. 'Same goes for your headaches. Turns out, former inmates are very loose-lipped once you've bought them a few whiskies. Who could have guessed?'

After a few more seconds, the Russian went limp.

Still alive and not yet unconscious. Victor maintained the chokehold until Kirill was as close to passing out as he could take him without going over the edge. Victor paid attention to the strength of the man's pulse, to how much he struggled. Then he released Kirill, who would have fallen had Victor not supported his weight. The Russian was faint, his brain so oxygen deprived he could not coordinate his limbs or even his lips.

He could not resist as Victor laid him down on the bottom bunk that was used as a sofa.

He could not resist as Victor fed him the rest of the tramadol pills and held a palm over his mouth and nose until he had swallowed them all.

Tramadol helped Kirill's headaches by suppressing his central nervous system to dull the signals to his brain. A tramadol overdose led to respiratory depression, and an overdose could happen with as little as double the regular dose. Victor didn't need to count the remaining pills in the bottle to know he had given Kirill many times his regular dose.

Within a few minutes, Kirill had shaken off the effects of the chokehold. The tramadol had begun to work by then and his breathing became shallow with long pauses between breaths.

Victor watched him. Not because he needed to see Kirill die – he knew the opioid would do its job in minutes – but because he wanted to check no marks appeared on the Russian's neck.

Pleased to find none, Victor wiped down the bottle of pills, placed it in Kirill's dying hand, and left the cell.

Maybe at some point a thorough investigation into the overdose would take place and someone might find it odd that the cameras had been shut off at the same time Kirill died. And maybe Nikkitin would claim Bill Pendleton had been let out of his cell at the same time too.

There was even a chance someone would take Nikkitin's claim seriously.

Regardless, Victor would be long gone by then.

TWENTY-NINE

The pod was buzzing with activity in the morning. Victor acted as ignorant as the other inmates while corrections officers rushed around with anxious or stressed expressions, refusing to explain themselves. The only portion of the jail population who weren't confused were the Russians. They had solemn or angry faces. Victor assumed Nikkitin or one of the others had found Kirill soon after the cells were unlocked.

Maybe the corpse was still in the pod or maybe it had already been removed before the other inmates were aware of it.

At breakfast, JT was pensive. He sat opposite Victor to eat his cereal.

'I think someone's died,' he said, slurping from his spoon.

Victor remained silent.

Food still un-swallowed, JT said, 'Will you teach me how to fight?'

'Why?'

JT almost dropped his spoon. 'What do you mean, why? Because you absolutely monstered those guys yesterday, Pyramid. Those *four* guys. Three with *shanks*.'

'I did have the book,' Victor admitted.

'Will you?'

'I'll be gone this afternoon. There's nowhere near enough time.'

'Just a few techniques,' JT urged. 'I know we don't have time for a whole training montage. Show me how to do a couple of those moves you did.'

'What good will that do?'

He made a mocking expression. 'So I can defend myself, that's what. Duh. If a fraudster like you can learn karate then why can't I?'

'I don't know karate,' Victor said. 'And if you want to defend yourself then you've already lost the fight.'

'Excuse me?'

Victor said, 'You fight any fight with the intention of defending yourself, you'll lose.'

JT was lost.

Victor continued. 'You fight to kill.'

JT was even more lost.

'But you don't have to kill,' Victor explained. 'You can hurt them, or maim them, or take them to the absolute brink of death ... But it has to be your choice. That's how you win. Not because you're the biggest or the strongest. It's because of intent. *Will*. You try and kill that opponent when he's just trying to hurt you, you'll win. You try and kill the guy trying to be break you, you'll win. If he's trying to kill you too then it's the toss of a coin. But you only get that coin-toss if you go in with that mentality. Anything less and you might as well let him kill you. The longer it takes, the worse it is. You don't want to die, but you really don't want to die slowly. Believe me.'

JT seemed to understand. 'You're telling me I don't fight them, I try and kill them?'

Victor nodded. 'That's it. That's exactly it. Only you need to understand that it will only work if you mean it. You can't pretend to try to kill someone. Death is the fairest of all judges. Death plays no favourites.'

JT nodded several times. 'Yeah, yeah. I get it. I see what you're saying. Try and kill them ... but stop. Makes sense. I can do that. Sure. Easy.'

'No, it's not so easy,' Victor said, looking at JT and yet seeing someone else from a long time ago. 'Remember: when you're trying to kill someone, you're not simply killing a static, singular person. It's not only who they are that you are trying to kill. You are killing them. You are killing who they were. And – worst of all, depending on your perspective – you are killing all they will ever be. Every kindness they might enact. Every soul they could engage. You're not just killing them. You're killing futures not even written. Hopes, dreams, and more. And not only them, it's everyone they could touch throughout the rest of their lives. Is that what you're prepared to do?'

'Whoa, man. What the actual ...? No way. I'm not nuts.' He shook his head, threw his hands up in the air. 'I'm not killing anyone's hopes and dreams. Are you even serious right now, Pyramid?'

'That's why you've lost the fight,' Victor told him with honesty JT could never appreciate. 'So, forget the push-ups. Do something more productive with your time.'

'And you're cool with that? All that stuff you're telling me about hopes and dreams? You'd do that to dodge a beating?'

'Of course,' Victor said. 'And a lot worse besides.'

JT thought about what that could mean for a moment, then set his spoon in the bowl and pushed it away.

'No good?' Victor asked.

JT grimaced. 'I've lost my appetite.'

THIRTY

Spector was waiting for Victor when he left the county jail around one in the afternoon. She stood outside her car, wearing a sheepskin coat and beanie hat to ward off the cold.

'Figured you'd like a ride back to town,' she said as he approached. 'Beats waiting for the bus in this weather.'

'Very kind,' Victor said.

'And it's the least I can do,' she said with a sigh. 'I heard what happened in there. It's a miracle you weren't killed.'

He was silent.

She took a deep breath and said, 'I'm sorry.'

'Apology accepted. You weren't to know.'

'One per cent,' she said.

'Excuse me?'

'The chances of a GSR test coming up with a false positive,' she explained. 'Unless you fired a gun before you came to the station and didn't think to mention it.'

Victor remained silent.

'And your prints weren't on the knife either. Guy stabbed himself just like you said. Craziest thing I've ever come across. Finlay says he was paid to do it.'

'Paid?' Victor asked.

'In meth,' Spector answered. 'Claims he doesn't know who paid him.' She shook her head. 'He's spinning all sorts of stories about dead drops and instructions from some mysterious, unidentified backer. Who apparently gave him instructions on how to hide a knife so a pat-down wouldn't discover it.'

He said, 'I expect that will be hard to prove.'

'You're telling me.' She opened up her car. 'But something's going on,' Spector said with a sigh of incomprehension. 'If I were a betting woman I'd say it was the Bratva cleaning house. First Grigori Orlov, now Kirill Lebedev. Took too many painkillers last night, if appearances are to be believed.'

'There was a commotion this morning. No one knew what was happening.'

'Kind of odd, isn't it?' she asked without waiting for an answer. 'You're arrested for Grigori's murder and then Kirill dies on the very same night you're in the very same jail.'

She had a hunch something wasn't right, he could see, although the pieces of her thought process were too disparate to bring together into a whole. He imagined she had spent much of the day before now on the phone with corrections officers and the medical staff, trying hard to organise those pieces and failing. This was her last attempt to make them fit. Her instincts were good, of course, but she could not envision the whole she was trying to form.

Spector was still trying to fathom how Grigori Orlov and

Kirill Lebedev of the Russian mafia were connected to an ordinary nobody named Bill Pendleton.

Victor just stood there until, after only a few seconds, she realised there could be no possible connection.

She shrugged and waved a hand in a dismissive gesture. 'Ah heck, I'm not sure we're ever going to know exactly what's happening.' She smiled. 'Which is why I get to sleep at night, am I right?' The smile became a chuckle. 'But if I were of a wagering kind – and I'm not – I'd bet that you and Finlay have been unlucky enough to stumble on to someone's chess board.'

'There are too many rules in chess,' he said.

'FBI's problem, whatever the rules.' She gestured. 'Come on, hop in and let's go get some lunch. I'm guessing the food in that place is not what we'd call finest home cooking.'

Thinking of the soggy pasta, Victor said, 'You can say that again.'

'I'm buying,' she told him as they climbed inside the vehicle. 'My way of saying sorry.'

'You already did.'

'We take our good manners seriously in this part of the world,' she said with a self-deprecating smile. 'And over a burger I'll tell you how this business with Finlay gets even worse.'

'Worse?' he asked as she started the engine.

She cast him a sideways glance. 'Or better, depending on your perspective. For you, at least. Because not only were your prints absent from Finlay's knife but his prints were all over the gun used to kill Grigori. Which we found last night when we searched his place. Again, he's saying he was hired to do it but doesn't know who hired him. The same mystery backer who paid him in drugs to stab himself.' She smirked and shook her head. 'Can you believe that?'

Victor raised an eyebrow. 'It does sound pretty far-fetched.'

PART THREE

PART THREE

THIRTY-ONE

Maxim Borisyuk did not enjoy these engagements, and yet here he was wearing his tuxedo surrounded by celebrities, politicians and oligarchs, as well as the associated partners, executive assistants and essential hangers-on. There were more publicists in the room than billionaires, he was sure. The setting was lovely. The grand ballroom of Moscow's Pashkov House could not be more beautiful. The imperial mansion appealed to Maxim's love of history and art and was bursting at the seams with priceless oil paintings and artefacts, and yet banners and posters hid much of the decor, with punchy slogans and provocative calls to action bearing the organiser's logo. A string quartet provided an ethereal ambience that sadly could not quite mask the noise of so many monstrous egos competing to be heard. From the windows, the views of the Kremlin were impressive and gave Maxim an excuse for ignoring as many attendees as possible. But the food – *the food* – Maxim had eaten few better meals in his life.

That was charities for you, he thought; they spared no expense to get your money.

On the surface, everyone seemed to be having a good time. Everywhere he looked he saw smiles that could not dissuade him from the truth that no one liked one another. The chitchat, jokes, compliments and flirting could not disguise the fact that all these rich people would sooner be anywhere else, spending time with *anyone* else. Surely the point of wealth was to forgo anything one did not like to do? However, Maxim knew that wealth was a trap. Once you were used to money it ceased to provide any joy. Then, the closest thing to pleasure possible was to flaunt that wealth because there was always someone who had less of it. If you failed to extract any joy from your money you could always take pleasure in the envy of others.

Maxim no longer played such games. He was here for his daughter's benefit and not his own. It was her event. One of many she organised. Oksana had always had a caring soul, was always out to help the less fortunate. He had cherished this angelic trait in his daughter, nurtured it. He had told her many white lies to shield her from the grim reality of business in post-Soviet Russia so that she might remain that same caring soul for ever. Now she sat on the board of directors for several charities and never seemed to have a minute of time to herself.

'I'll take a day off when there are no more wars.'

She had no need to work even a single day and yet did not wish to live off her father's wealth. With some frequency he reminded her that it would all be hers one day, so why wait? She had numerous arguments as to why and he loved her all the more for it.

Of course, while Oksana refused any kind of allowance, she was happy to benefit from her father's influence every now and again. She was no longer a naïve child and knew exactly the reasons she had grown up in such luxury. She also knew that when the daughter of Maxim Borisyuk invited someone to a fundraiser, they went. It might be one thousand dollars a plate; they went. The funds might be on behalf of more sustainable energy and they were an oligarch of the coal and gas industry; they went. They cancelled every other plan and went. They went and smiled and made a separate donation. A generous one.

And they all wanted his ear as a result. Maxim's bodyguard did a good job of keeping all but the most important of guests away. It was hardly necessary to have one – Maxim was perfectly happy to outright ignore anyone he did not want to speak with – but his daughter would worry about him if he were unaccompanied. Not that she was concerned about his safety. Oksana worried about him being lonely. She often tried to set him up on dates with eligible divorcees and widows, even though he had been honest when he said he would not marry again. Three wives had been plenty. Maxim had a sneaking suspicion she also worried he would take another fall and not be able to get himself up again. Which was ridiculous. It had only happened the one time before the hip replacement. Now he joked about his bionic power to quell her concerns. Maybe she wanted him to find someone purely to be there to help out should he fall again. He had servants for that, naturally.

'You need someone in your life that isn't paid to be there,' Oksana would tell him.

When his bodyguard interrupted a discussion on plastic

waste in the oceans, the temper Maxim had spent decades learning to dampen rose in a sudden, fiery heat. His daughter was making an eloquent and compelling speech that almost seemed to be making some of Russia's worst polluters reconsider their positions.

'*What?*' Maxim snapped, turning sharply to the bodyguard who had so rudely interrupted his daughter.

The bodyguard had a head and more over him. He might have weighed quadruple Maxim. He could snap his spine as easily as a twig. And yet the man mountain took a quick step back in fear. He stammered an apology and gestured to where a woman waited on the outskirts of the ballroom.

Maxim swallowed his rage and reset his expression to something more appropriate for the occasion, apologised to his daughter and her company, and walked with the bodyguard to where Luda Zakharova waited.

She was a tall woman, much taller than Maxim. Young, too. At least, he thought of her as young despite her greying hair, because she had been very young back when Maxim had first known her. He could still picture that fresh-faced and overworked politician's aide. The politician had been in Maxim's pocket, naturally, though he could no longer remember the man's name. A pudgy fool who had wasted Zakharova's many talents. She had been a first-class student, earning scholarships abroad. A degree from Oxford. A master's from Stanford. It had taken much careful seduction to lure her into his business empire.

'I understand you're here for your daughter,' she began, straight to the point without need of small talk or even greetings, 'so I'll try to be brief.'

Maxim nodded to show his appreciation.

She told him, 'The Kremlin would like a sit-down at your earliest convenience.'

He huffed. 'I know what that means. They want another favour.'

'Of course,' she agreed, well used to the endless acts of goodwill Maxim had to perform to keep the government as friends instead of enemies. 'On a separate note, the lobbyists in London need additional funds transferred with haste to cover the excesses of our new friend in the Houses of Parliament.'

'There are none greedier than those born into wealth,' he said, shaking his head. 'Do it, though I want leverage in return.'

'They've compiled many emails at this point.'

'Too dry to make a scandal stick. Get photographs, or better yet, video.'

'I shall make sure our lobbyists understand what's required,' she said with a small nod. 'And don't forget I'm going to be in Belarus tomorrow to see the president. Would you like me to take him a gift?'

Borisyuk shook his head. 'Not after he gave me that hideous watch. Why would I want to know my resting heart rate or how many steps I've taken?'

'I believe his intentions were good.'

'He can wear it if he's so worried about health,' Maxim said. 'In fact, have it beautifully wrapped, and give it back to him. Make sure he knows it was my idea. Let him lose sleep trying to unravel what it means.' He smiled to himself at the thought. 'Make sure you have breakfast with him the following morning so you can tell me how tired he looked.'

Always the voice of measured restraint, Zakharova said,

'I will think of an appropriate show of our continued friendship to give to him.'

When her phone rang, she excused herself and turned away to answer. She could hide her emotions as well as anyone he had known and yet he saw creases of worry and concern in her face when she turned back to him after a brief exchange with the caller.

'Maxim,' she began, soft of tone, and holding the phone against her chest to muffle the microphone, 'you need to take this call.'

He was not convinced. 'The only person I truly care about is in this room.' He looked to where his daughter held court like a princess of old. 'So whatever this is about can wait.' Zakharova went to speak but Maxim was not finished. 'If I've lost a hundred million on the FTSE, so what? It'll still be lost in two hours' time when this function is over.'

Zakharova had not moved. She hadn't told the caller he was busy. She still had the phone against her chest.

'Please,' she said.

'What is this?'

She glanced at his daughter, then said, 'It's about your son-in-law. I'm so sorry, Maxim. Kirill's dead.'

His gaze fell towards Oksana, who caught his eye and gave a little wave of acknowledgement and a warm smile. Borisyuk kept his expression even so she would not deduce anything was wrong. Inside, however, he was already grieving for his daughter and her pain. He had never forgotten the sound of her cries when he had lowered himself down to look into her innocent little eyes to tell her that Mother would not be coming home from the hospital. Thirty years later his daughter was a strong, capable woman, a mother herself now, and Maxim knew he had to break her heart a second time.

His daughter went back to her conversation and he turned his attention to Zakharova, still waiting with the phone against her chest. He gestured and she handed it to him.

He said to the caller, 'Tell me everything.'

THIRTY-TWO

The beach lay somewhere below. Unseen, yet loud with laughter, raucous and carefree. Children playing, and adults too. Maybe kicking a ball or building sandcastles. Victor pictured parasols so white they almost glowed. He could imagine people without a single concern lounging beneath them, sipping cocktails and reading. Some were dozing, no doubt. Closing their eyes and willingly slipping into slumber in a public place, utterly exposed and as vulnerable as they might ever be and yet not even considering themselves in the remotest danger.

They could not even comprehend his envy.

If he leaned over the balustrade a little then he could peer down to see the beach. He did not. He stood back and kept his spine straight so as not to expose himself to an enemy lurking below who might be waiting for such a lapse in judgement. The odds of a competent professional risking such a visible attack were minimal. Still, an amateur might take a reckless approach, unbothered by the inevitable witnesses sunbathing and swimming, and amateurs were still capable of shooting straight now and again. He had no intention of making their job any easier.

Victor watched a pair of jet skis zipping along parallel to the shore, far enough away that he only heard a faint whizz from their engines. A couple, he assumed. They turned into the gentle surf, gaining air, splashing back down, before racing off into the distance, competitive and yet cooperative in their mutual joy.

Gulls glided overhead, in no hurry, content to bide their time until the hotel's private beach was less crowded and presented better opportunities for scavenging. He wished them good fortune in their endeavours. He thought of feral dogs in Central America.

The hotel sat on a small spur of land that jutted out into the Mediterranean. On that spur lay no other buildings. A small village of sorts was behind it, further inland, comprised of maybe a dozen expensive villas set back from the long coastal road that spanned almost the entire length of the Riviera. The hotel was the largest building in this particular area and overlooked the village from a steep elevation. On the far side of the houses, the land rose to form an unpopulated hillside covered in dense scrub. The hilltop lay some two hundred metres away, and could conceivably prove a good spot for a patient marksman. Victor had surveyed it already – had done so before even approaching the hotel – and had noted that the palm trees outside the hotel's entrance disrupted any useful line of sight. Knowing this, Victor could then take a moment to thank the doorman and engage in rare small talk.

The suite lay on the far side of the hotel, facing the sea.

Any sniper on the hillside hoping to catch Victor at a window would be sorely disappointed.

He had a fondness for a sea view that went far beyond the breathtaking beauty of the glossy turquoise water speckled with brilliant white sailboats. The paving stones of the terrace were rough beneath his feet. To prevent a guest slipping, he assumed. He breathed in the air and felt the warm sun on his skin. A gentle breeze ruffled his hair and cooled his face. He remained unmoving and staring out at the Mediterranean for several minutes. That was the reason he was so fond of the view. He could remain in one place without the need to evaluate the risk in doing so because the location took care of that for him.

Looking out at the sea, he was as safe as he had ever been. Looking to his left or right, to the east and the west he saw the Mediterranean, the concave coastline out of sight behind him, and then faraway land in the shape of two similar spurs. The spur to the west was about a kilometre away, while the one to the east was closer and yet still close to five hundred metres from his position. No one was making that shot with inconsistent and unpredictable prevailing winds coming from the sea. Not even with a .50-calibre round as big as a finger. And the best marksmen in the world would struggle to place a bullet anywhere near him when shooting from a sailboat moving to the will of the waves.

He wasn't sure if she had chosen the hotel to accommodate his particular idiosyncratic requirements, but if so, she could not have picked a more suitable place to stay.

The private beach below him was narrow and short, filling a shallow cleft in the cliff face. Fine golden sand and gently lapping surf. Given the protection of the cliffs at both flanks, the sea in front of him, and the isolated hotel behind, he was almost – *almost* – tempted to make use of the beach. After the chill of Minnesota he wanted to feel the sun on more than just his shoulders. At this time of the year, after the season's end, the temperature was still in the early twenties. He wondered if the old man from the bus had put on some much-needed weight and if JT had got his hands on those steroids he wanted.

With access to the beach limited to hotel guests, it reduced the chances of an enemy taking advantage of it. Victor could have the Five-seveN Georg had supplied in a small bag within arm's reach at all times. He could wait until the lounger furthest away from the hotel was free. He could reposition it so that he would see anyone approaching from the hotel proper. No one could predict when he would make use of the beach because he didn't know when he would himself, so no one could be waiting on a sailboat, ready in full scuba gear to drop into the sea and emerge from the surf to take him by surprise when he was most vulnerable. Board shorts and a linen shirt would cover the majority of his scars and recent minor wounds. Maybe he could read a whole chapter of his book before ignoring protocol became unbearable and he had to move elsewhere to spare his sanity.

The problem, of course, was the many rooms overlooking the beach. A gunman could use any one of them to shoot down at him. The wide parasol would be no obstacle, even if it shielded him completely. It would be simple enough to deduce where he lay beneath it based on the dimensions of the lounger and the resulting shadows. If he were at one of those overlooking windows, the parasol would be no real hindrance.

He could deduce no solution to this vulnerability.

So, no reading his book on the beach. He felt a little foolish for even taking a moment to think it through. His professional instincts were finely tuned enough for him to decide within an instant what level of risk was posed by almost any action and the level of risk that was acceptable at any given time. Still, taking a moment to play with the idea was almost the same as the real thing. Better a facsimile of reading his book on the beach than nothing at all.

He only moved when he heard footsteps behind him: bare feet padding closer on lush carpet, then paving.

'You were like a statue,' she said.

He turned to face Phoenix.

'I thought you might have accidentally fused with the balustrade.'

He almost smiled.

She wore his shirt like it was the oversized centrepiece of a designer's haute couture show. Seeing his look, and perhaps reading his thoughts, she fixed him with an intense stare and strode forward with one hand on her hip and the other swinging free. Her expression was both frozen and yet over-flowing with verve.

She had modelled a long time ago, Phoenix had told him once while they sipped a freshly opened bottle of champagne from the cellar of her chateau.

'Pretty unsuccessfully,' she had explained. 'I had the height and the cheekbones but a healthy appetite, which simply wouldn't do. When a certain designer with a giant ego and a wonky hairpiece told me I needed to have less width at my hips, I told him he needed more follicles on his head so we were both shit out of luck. The shows became quite scarce after that.'

It was the first time he had told her not to use foul language in his presence. She hadn't stopped then, nor since.

She stood next to him and stared out at the sea as he had done. 'What are we looking at exactly?'

'Nothing,' Victor answered with uncommon honesty. 'Nothing at all.'

She folded her arms on the rough stone and rested her head upon them. 'That's my favourite kind of nothing.'

The overhead sun gleamed from her cheek. She closed her eyes to protect them from the glare. She had a dusting of freckles on her nose. The golden tresses of her hair were pushed back behind her ears except for a few strays the sea breeze teased into a wild dance. He watched minuscule beads of sweat form at her temples. Victor was sweating too, he realised. While the sun was not too hot for him at this time of year, his body temperature was still high from all the exertion.

Eyes still closed, she told him, 'There's something I need to tell you.'

Leading her by the hand, he said, 'It can wait until later.'

THIRTY-THREE

The foundations of the Bratva were laid way back in the seventies when Maxim and those like him were just a collective of ragtag street gangs united by their shared dislike of authority. Simpler times, never to be repeated. He was often nostalgic for those years before the Wall came down, when opportunities had been so few. They had been happy then, he thought. Before greed and ambition took over, becoming more important than happiness in the fire sale that was the fall of the Soviet Union. As the oligarch class sprung out of those ashes, so the wealth and influence of the Bratva rose in unison. He had lost many friends since, plenty by his own hand. Some who betrayed him. Others he betrayed first. And then, when the current power came to the Kremlin, the Bratva were not only allowed to grow unimpeded, they were encouraged. Just so long as those who helped them grow were appropriately rewarded.

Not even Maxim himself knew just how much money passed through Brotherhood fingers, though many speculated that he sat at the head of an organisation with more than one hundred billion USD in annual revenue in Russia alone. No one had any idea how high the global figure reached.

The modern Bratva encompassed many separate entities who operated independently the world over yet all bowed before Maxim. It had been several years since he had made anyone literally bow at his feet. He found, in his twilight years, that such ceremony was not only unnecessary, it made him a little uncomfortable. Besides, true loyalty had to be earned. Servitude through fear lasted only as long as he was terrifying. Now, neither a young man nor one who still revelled in violence, it was too much effort to be terrifying himself. Besides, he had thousands of loyal little brothers who were happy to be terrifying on his behalf. He would probably retire were it not for the fact that the next to sit at the head of all the tables of the Bratva would likely feel impotent with him still alive.

Often, the activities of the Brotherhood did not require his oversight or intervention. The day-to-day business took care of itself, the lawful thieves taking care of the soldiers and the soldiers taking care of each other. He had long since ceased the bloody reign of terror that had insured his throne. Headless bodies no longer showed up floating in the river unless under exceptional circumstances; Maxim was almost exclusively a legitimate businessman these days. He couldn't quite believe it himself that the most feared person in post-Soviet Russia – besides the big man himself – was now little more than a real estate mogul building more and more condominiums for Russia's ever-expanding middle classes. Abroad, however, things were different. The Bratva continued its legacy of criminal enterprise and Maxim was happy to let them. He could remain as the seemingly benign face of the Russian mafia and rub shoulders with politicians and philanthropists without making either uncomfortable. As long as no one dug up the foundations of all those condominiums, of course.

As such, it had been a long time since he had cause to speak to anyone in the organisation other than Zakharova.

'Tell me everything,' Maxim had said to the caller.

It was one of the most senior loyal thieves, a man in Marseille who went by the name Castellan these days. He even had a little bit of a French accent to his Russian. Maxim had never really liked Castellan. Which was not uncommon. Maxim disliked most of the people who comprised the Brotherhood. They were criminals, after all.

Castellan said, 'I know very few of the details at this stage, so I'm afraid I cannot tell you very much, but I wanted you to hear it from me without any delay.'

'How?' was Maxim's only response.

'An overdose of painkillers, they say. His headaches had been getting worse in jail, everyone knew. He had a large supply of opioids.'

'How many pills did he take?'

'I can't tell you that,' Castellan answered. 'Only that an empty bottle was found next to him when they discovered his body.'

'A note?'

'I don't think so.'

'Evidence of a struggle?'

'Not that I know of.'

Maxim looked over to where Oksana had her guests hanging from her every word. 'When I disconnect this call

I'm going to tell my daughter that her husband is never coming home again.' He took a breath. 'Given he was in the US on your behalf, the next time we speak you better have something more to tell me. Do you understand?'

'I do,' Castellan assured.

Maxim handed the phone back to Zakharova and she hung up.

He gestured for his bodyguard. 'Tell Oksana I need to speak with her right away. In private.'

'I'm so sorry about Kirill, Maxim.'

'He was a son-in-law not a son so you don't need to say sorry to me,' Maxim said, no longer presenting himself a real estate mogul but as the head of the largest organised crime network in the world. 'However, if I don't see you weeping like a child in front of my daughter I'll rip out your eyeballs and squeeze the tears from them myself.'

THIRTY-FOUR

The suite was huge. Sheer indulgence. No two people could require so much space on a trip, certainly not for the short amount of time Phoenix and he would remain here. But she, like Victor, was a person who spent much of her time alone for security considerations. He had found that the longer he spent alone in one space, the more space he required. All walls inevitably became constraints slowly tightening. Maybe Phoenix felt the same and that was why she had booked such an extravagant suite for their short dalliance. He would never know because he would never ask her, and she would never reveal the inner workings of herself in the same way he would never reveal his own.

He knew only a little about her. Regardless of the physical intimacy, there was still a reservedness between them. They had been enemies for a time, back when she had brokered a contract on his life worth a considerable amount of money. When Phoenix had finally revealed the dollar amount, he had joked the purse was so high he seriously considered murdering himself for it. He had killed several of her sub-contractors before eventually tracking her down, which had required calling in favours, the assistance of an intelligence agency, and a huge amount of time and effort. His intention had been to end the threat she posed on his life and yet they had decided to work together instead. With her as broker and him as contractor, the arrangement proved most profitable to both parties.

A broker was a middleman in the most basic sense. They were the conduit between a client and a contractor. They provided protection for both by ensuring the client had no connection to the assassination and the killer had no connection to the motive. An imperfect system, as all were, but it was generally better for all concerned. Victor had dealt with clients directly when he had no other choice. In his experience, a client was much more likely to view him as an expendable asset if they had a direct association with him. With a broker providing a buffer, clients were generally less so inclined. There were other advantages too. The contract on his own life that Phoenix had once been keen to cash in with one of her stable of killers had ultimately lapsed when that client believed Victor dead. Which meant when they presented other contracts Phoenix's way there had been nothing to stop Victor fulfilling them. They were always happy with his services.

After she had showered, Phoenix scooped up some caviar from the room-service trolley and scraped it on to a triangle of toasted sourdough. 'You should tuck in. You could use it given you're a little skinny right now.'

He turned from the window and saw her ferry the toast to her mouth, her other palm cupped beneath to catch crumbs or wayward fish eggs. She had piled the caviar into an unstable pyramid that threatened to collapse at any moment.

'Say nothing.' Her gaze was fixed on the wobbling pile. 'I have this under complete control.'

'If you have my contracts under a similar level of control then we need to talk.'

She shook her head as she chewed, then said, 'If you're not quick I'll finish the rest.'

'Be my guest,' he said. 'I'd prefer a burger and a milkshake.'

'Honestly, I'm surprised they even allowed you inside the hotel. You're practically a barbarian.'

'You don't seem to mind.'

'That's because either way you're not my type,' she assured.

He gave her a look of scepticism.

In return, she looked at him with astonishment. 'If I actually liked you then I would keep you very, very far away from me for both our sakes. The very fact that we have these occasional trysts is precisely because I *don't* like you. I prefer a more intellectual companion, truth be told.'

He gave her another look.

'And all these lumps and bumps of yours.' She wrinkled her nose. 'Not for me. It's all a little try-hard, don't you think?'

He did not answer.

She was enjoying herself the more he stayed silent, although she tried to keep that hidden. 'A man who spends too much time taking care of himself is not very appealing. It's a bit sad, no? Can't be smitten with someone who's literally frightened of a sticky toffee pudding.'

If he believed that she would let their personal interactions cloud her professional judgement, he would have no choice but to expedite that inevitable conclusion. His broker was his most valuable connection, which meant a broker was his greatest vulnerability. He had to know at all times that her actions and decisions were driven from a purely business perspective. The moment he doubted that would be the moment he would sever that connection.

He took his suit jacket from the back of the armchair and slipped it on in front of the tall, brass-framed mirror.

'You should really try wearing one that fits you right,' she told him. 'Those lumps and bumps aren't so terrible they need such a masquerade.'

'One day,' he said without sincerity.

'I'm on very good terms with an exceptional tailor in Marseille,' she said with a click of fingers. 'Not that Marseille is another Paris, you understand.' She paused with a musing frown. 'But, in all honestly, I think you find a better quality of craftsmen outside of the obvious haunts. Let's face it, branding can so easily be mistaken for reputation and that can lead to laziness. Marseille doesn't have anything close to its own rue du Faubourg Saint-Honoré, but who actually cares?'

'There's a nice hotel just off that street,' Victor said. Then, thinking of Jackson Pollock, 'Lovely wallpaper.'

'*Fascinating*,' she said with unfiltered sarcasm. 'Anyway, you'll like Relou. He is quite the mystery man too.'

Something in her tone.

Victor said, 'Let me guess: he wasn't always a tailor.'

'Oh, he was always a tailor at heart. Merely took him a little while to answer the calling. All you need do is ask and I can make an appointment on your behalf.'

'I'll think about it.'

173

'Tremendous.' Phoenix smiled. 'I'll turn you into a gentleman yet.'

'Let's not get carried away.'

'Let's,' she said, then, 'Are you ever going to explain yourself?'

'I'm lost,' Victor admitted.

She gestured to him with aggressive waves of her hand. 'This,' she said, almost hissing the word. 'The aforementioned lumps and bumps. Over the top at the best of times and yet you look positively shrink-wrapped right now.' She perused him with a look of distaste. 'You're like a skewed-aspect ratio, all stretched and narrow.' She furrowed her brow to think. 'No, you're a balloon with all the inert gas forcibly sucked out.' She sucked in her cheeks for emphasis.

'Remind me again why I never killed you? I can't quite work it out.'

'Oh, that's an easy one,' she replied. 'You're absolutely smitten with me.' She made an L-shape with hands and used the L to frame her face while she fluttered her eyelashes. 'And who could blame you?'

He elected not to answer.

He had a story to explain his weight loss. He had composed and rehearsed an explanation for this very enquiry. It was not chance that he had avoided it before, but careful wordplay. He did not want to answer the query because he did not want to relive the circumstances that had compelled her questions in the first place. He realised now that he could not hide for ever.

He took a breath and said, 'I am still convalescing.'

She pursed her lips as she examined him. 'There was nothing in the ether to suggest any problems with the contract besides these scuffs and scrapes of yours.'

'Before that,' was his explanation. He touched his left thigh where he had a scar from a bullet wound. 'I'm sure you've noticed this particular addition.'

'I can't say I did. I lost track of what's new and what's always been there a good time ago.' She spread her fingers out before her to better examine them. 'Meanwhile, I have to say I would reconsider my life choices if I so much as cracked a nail.'

'Anyway,' Victor said as he approached the door, 'I have a plane to catch.'

Phoenix had never been one for goodbyes so he was expecting little more than a pithy *bon voyage*.

Instead, to his surprise, she said: 'After you've finished up with your procedure, come and see me again.'

THIRTY-FIVE

They called it a club. They were a part of the Bratva, the Brotherhood, and yet they had taken to referring to themselves as *the Club*. It had hundreds of members, with a board of eight seats. Those on the board had always been in the Club because they had set it up in the first place. A bit like the UN Security Council, they had realised at one point. The comparison was a good one, they agreed, because the members of the Club had won a war of sorts, using coordinated brutality and terror to displace the original bosses who had previously run the city. That was long ago, when few knew of the Bratva and none could yet guess what they would become. Now, the Club did everything in its considerable power to avoid fighting another war, at least between each other. Everyone else was fair game.

Marseille had 111 official districts divided into sixteen municipal arrondissements. The arrondissements were paired into eight sectors. Each member of the Club was a boss over one of those sectors whether the native criminals liked it or not. No single man could control an entire city, so each of the bosses ruled an entire operation with its own hierarchy, its own business interests, its own rules. No other member of the Club had a say in how another's operation was run. That would be impolite. But as interests overlapped, some-times by design and sometimes by accident, a certain level of consideration was necessary. Toes might get stepped on from time to time, they all understood that reality, so when it happened apologies were expected. Recompense was just good manners. Not a perfect system because one member's idea of compensation could be an insult to another. Hence the Club would arbitrate. The Security Council would agree a resolution.

Similarly, if there was a situation that affected multiple members then the Club would meet to work out a solution. Collectively, there wasn't much that couldn't be fixed. One do-gooder from the mayor's office bringing too much heat to a profitable section of the Sector Seven boss might have an illegitimate kid from an affair in a district controlled by the Sector Three boss. Maybe the mother decides to show up with the snot-nosed brat at the do-gooder's front door on the day of their summer garden party attended by the great and the good. Maybe a scandal is orchestrated and the do-gooder has to pull out of that promotion he wanted.

Everyone wins. Especially the mother, who has offshore accounts set up in her name so that she and the kid never want for anything again.

The Club preferred to work in such ways. Violence was always a last resort. They knew from their own wars that there was a domino effect to such things. *You kill one of my guys and I kill two of yours* ... And even if the victims did not belong to an operation, they still had loved ones. Everyone meant something to someone. Even those who had no one. Kill the wrong loser without a friend in the world and maybe a detective who doesn't give up is called to that scene. He's going through a divorce and not only is he losing the house but she's taking the dog too. That detective just happens to have nothing else to do except work the loser's case. His whole life is falling apart so he won't let the case fall apart. No way. Then there's a whole world of hurt coming for nothing.

Instead, they always tried to de-escalate a situation. If that loser was drawing attention to a member's operation because the loser was selling rock at the mouth of an alleyway that just so happens to contain a door leading to a whole lab, then they would ask him to sell elsewhere. If the sweet talk failed, they would give him a bag of cash. If the payoff didn't work, they would try words not so sweet. If the threats didn't work it would be where violence came in. At least, that's what most operations would do. The Club would try to circumvent the problem. They would have the loser followed and find out who supplied him with the rock he sold. The Club would try their sweet talk on the supplier to refuse to sell to the loser or to insist he sold elsewhere and they would try a payoff if that didn't work and threats would follow if neither had an effect. It would be rare if any problem went that far. Almost always there would be someone in the chain who responded to the sweet talk, or the money, or the threats.

If not, it got messy.

Members of the Club could not be seen to make idle threats. Certainly not twice.

The Club almost never dirtied their own hands. They had friends everywhere. Every member of the Club had any number of people they could call. If that loser selling rock was in the Sector Six boss's territory then the Sector Two boss would take care of it. He might put a few independent people together or he might call in a favour with a crew who owed him. They would go out to the countryside and make the loser selling rock suffer as well as his supplier who wouldn't comply.

Then, should that detective going through the divorce get called to the scene, it wouldn't matter. He could work that case for a hundred years and never deduce the loser and his supplier were killed by a crew who drove across the city to hack up two guys they had never met before on the behest of a boss doing a favour for another boss who simply wanted that loser to sell his rock from another alleyway.

A good system that Castellan was proud to have founded.

And should the matter require even greater subtlety, the Club brought in outside assistance. If there was no way of avoiding dirty hands, those hands would not be their own.

They met with some frequency, always at the port, because the best way to keep their interests aligned was to continually agree new resolutions. Unanimous agreement was unlikely, of course, given the Club was the United Nations Security Council, all with an equal vote. However, Castellan controlled the port, so he controlled the supply of heroin and anything else the Club imported or exported, so the votes tended to go his way. If Castellan needed something to happen then the Club needed it to happen. When Castellan made money, so did the Club. When he lost money, they all lost money.

Even if he would never say the words aloud, it wasn't just the Club, it was *his* Club.

Setting down the phone after his call with Maxim Borisyuk, Castellan took a deep breath and poured himself another shot of Finnish vodka. Fresh from the compact freezer he had in the meeting room, the bottle was frosted with ice and the vodka slipped down his throat with glacial smoothness. He gazed out of the window at the port where the largest gantry cranes in the world lifted containers off ships with efficient ease, before hybrid straddle carriers ferried them on land, stacking the containers in neat piles.

The port was a town unto itself, with over forty thousand employees. Beyond that, with crews, passengers and all the innumerable subsidiary duties, millions of people passed through it every year making it impossible to keep track of who should be there and who should not. Castellan had always liked that about the port beyond the smuggling operation he ran through it.

Castellan controlled the port because he controlled the inspections. He had enough customs agents on his payroll to ensure an uninterrupted smuggling operation. If the other members of the Club wanted to bring in, or move out, drugs or other contraband then they had to go through Castellan. His port. His Club.

'How did Maxim take the news?' the Sector Five boss asked him.

'He wants answers, naturally. As Kirill was in the US on my behalf, Maxim wants me to present those answers to him.'

Nothing they hadn't expected, so everyone maintained their cool, though they were all nervous. They may have thought of themselves as the UN Security Council, but

Marseille was the extent of their world and the world was much larger than Marseille.

That world belonged to Maxim Borisyuk.

The Sector Five boss said, 'Maxim is an old man who has lost his fire. He will accept whatever he's told because he doesn't have the stomach to ask questions for which he might not like the answers.'

'Others will ask on his behalf,' the Sector Two boss said.

While Castellan agreed to an extent, as far as he was concerned that was irrelevant. 'Our friend has assured me the link between us and Kirill's death will soon be severed.'

THIRTY-SIX

Victor stopped before the door and looked back at Phoenix. 'Twice in the same month? I don't think we should let the pursuit of pleasure lead us to taking avoidable risks.'

She gasped. 'You arrogant prick.'

'Don't sw—'

'Yeah, yeah,' she interrupted. 'Don't swear, don't blaspheme, don't call you a hitman ... I know all your little tics by now and I really don't give a flying *ph*easant.' She collected herself for a moment. 'As if you're such a good lover I would throw caution to the wind just for one more day in your bed. I just can't help myself. *Oh, please.*'

'Then I don't understand.'

'I have something to discuss,' she said. 'That's why I would like you to come back.'

'I'm here now,' Victor said. 'Why wait and increase the risk of being noticed or shadowed?'

'Because I have many plates currently spinning and I need

to wait and see which remain spinning and which fall from their poles and shatter on the floor.'

'Interesting imagery and it tells me absolutely nothing.'

'Will you return or not?'

He thought for a moment. It was already a considerable risk meeting his broker at all, let alone in the same region of the country in which she resided. And that country was one wherein his carefully constructed existence had first begun to irrecoverably unravel. Given there was no professional need to meet with Phoenix, the risk was entirely avoidable. A fact of which he was constantly aware. Any action that increased the level of risk should not be tolerated.

Almost always when he lowered his guard, problems arose. The bullet wound to his left thigh was an ugly reminder of that. Few of the protocols he had devised were not based on past experiences he had no wish to repeat.

She tutted. 'It's not an ambush, don't worry.'

'I don't worry.'

'We're long past all that silly business,' she said. 'And we're far too profitable as a team for either of us to go down that route again.'

He looked at his hands. 'Once I've had the procedure I'll want to lay low for a while. Go off the grid for a couple of weeks at least.'

'Waiting a few more days before you disappear won't make a difference.'

'It's already a risk going back to the US,' he said. 'It would be even riskier to return here.'

That he was even considering ignoring protocol for Phoenix meant he needed to end their arrangement without delay. He survived only because he identified and dealt with incoming threats before they could fully materialise.

It would be simple to murder her now, he found himself thinking.

She was fit, in excellent shape, but not a professional in the way he measured it. He could snap on a chokehold from behind and she would be unconscious in seconds as the blood supply to her brain slowed to a stop. He could maintain that choke until oxygen deprivation ensured brain death. He would feel the exact moment her pulse ceased. Only a little pain. He preferred to kill with a minimum of suffering, if possible. It would be discourteous to extend distress that could be avoided.

No real fallout, although he would never know how much intelligence she had compiled on him. She had to have a dossier with everything she knew, somewhere. Yet for her to stay safe, all such information had to be kept safe. Should she ever be apprehended by the authorities then all evidence of her many criminal activities would need to be inaccessible to anyone but her. He expected she changed computers and other electronic devices as often as regular people changed their underwear. Her home had to be clean. No paperwork or other physical items that could incriminate. As far as he was aware, she never conducted business from her residence. There were dozens of towns and villages within an hour along the coastline or inland from which she could access the internet and conduct her business.

She recognised the silence for what it was and sighed in disappointment. 'Given these extra-curricular activities of ours, I can't help but feel a little affronted that you still refuse to trust me.'

He wasn't sure whether she truly expected him to trust her or merely convinced herself he should. Regardless, she could never trust him, whatever their personal interactions. Once they parted ways, once business was resumed, she had to consider him a threat in the same way he thought of her. She was just as much a mercenary as Victor. Maybe she had forgotten, and yet he would play no part in any resulting charade.

'If I've given you the mistaken impression that I trust anyone on this Earth then I apologise.'

'Do you think I would even be here, putting my life on the line, if I didn't trust you?' she asked him, with a seriousness of tone he was not expecting. Not so much a question but a challenge. 'I don't even know your name.'

He knew her name. At least, he knew the name by which she booked their hotels. Her chateau was owned by a company registered in the Virgin Islands. That company paid all the utility bills. Nothing was in a private citizen's name. He imagined she had several identities. Maybe more than he did. However many forgers he had been connected with via Phoenix, he was sure she kept some purely for herself. It would be foolish of her to share all of her essential resources with him and despite the many things he did not know about her he knew for certain she was never foolish.

He knew every inch of her flesh and yet her mind was an unexplored expanse in which he was not allowed to wander unaccompanied. He respected that. Inevitably, they would become enemies again one day. Although neither of them expressed this, it was a given. At some point a contract would be placed on his head so large that she simply could not refuse. Or else her uniquely privileged knowledge of him would become too much of a liability to remain uncontested. Many other scenarios lay between these two most obvious culminations of their association. It served no purpose to raise them.

When the end result could only be one of their demises, why rush to rock the boat of an otherwise mutually beneficial association?

He was sure she felt the same.

But he saw he had hurt her in a way he had not intended. Phoenix was offended and he would never offend anyone if it could be avoided, least of all her.

'I'll come back,' he said. 'So I can hear all about those spinning plates of yours.'

She smiled and clapped her hands in overexcited glee.

'Let's play tourists when you return,' she said. 'I'll show you some hidden haunts and we can grab a coffee. I know a great little place in Nice's Old Town.'

Victor said, 'Then I'll see you there.'

THIRTY-SEVEN

Hyaluronic acid had become one of the most widely used dermal fillers the world over for good reason. Many different laboratories synthesised the chemical under a variety of brand names. Victor, who had frequent cosmetic procedures to continually alter his appearance, had learned much about the clear gel over the years. It was most commonly used to enhance lips, disguise dark circles and eye bags, and to smooth away wrinkles and lines. Victor maintained a low body-fat percentage year round and so had lean, defined facial features. Hyaluronic acid injections could change his face by rounding his cheekbones and jawline, widening his nose, even altering the shape of his eyes when injected into his eyelids. Victor had found that even small changes could have significant effects to his overall appearance, especially when out of direct lighting, when those subtle alterations made an exaggerated impact on the shadows cast by his face.

He was particularly partial to its use over other types of

filler because of the immediate yet temporary affects hyaluronic provided. Several vials' worth injected to re-contour his face in such a way as to make him unrecognisable at a distance would be broken down naturally over a number of months, creating a gradual reversion imperceptible to the naked eye. It had another benefit, too: those changes could be undone in seconds if he needed a sudden reversal. The enzyme hyaluronidase, when injected to the same site, would dissolve the hyaluronic acid on contact.

He preferred to forgo dermatologists and instead opted for high-street clinics and salons who offered cosmetic procedures. It was harder to get the best results that way, but he avoided the scrutinising questions and meticulous record-keeping of a doctor.

For his most recent injections, he had needed the sharp skills of an expert.

Dr Maddy Cho smiled when she saw him enter her office. She had gleaming teeth as white as her doctor's coat. Hair blacker than the night sky.

'Mr Pendleton,' she said, approaching him with an outstretched hand, 'how nice to see you again.'

'Call me Bill,' Victor said, taking the hand and shaking. 'Please.'

'Of course. Please, Bill, come in and take a seat.'

He did so in the chair provided and she sat down in her own and swivelled on the seat to face him.

'I have to say,' Cho began, 'I've been really quite curious to know how it went.' She held up her hand, showing crossed fingers. 'I've had them like this the entire time.'

'That must have made your job a little challenging.'

'You can say that again,' she said, playing along and

leaning forward. 'Just this morning I injected a woman with Botox to smooth out her crow's feet.' She grimaced. 'Only I kept missing.'

With her fingers still crossed she tried to pick up a pen from her desk, which she could just about manage, but it was impossible to control with any accuracy and she made erratic stabbing motions.

'Ouch,' Victor said.

Cho nodded and put the pen down. 'The poor woman is going to look like this for six months.'

She rested a fingertip under her eye and stretched down the lower eyelid to reveal the full eyeball and the wet, pinkish inner lining of the eyelid.

She noticed something and gasped.

'*What did you do to my babies?*' she cried in exaggerated horror.

Cho took his right hand in hers and leaned in closer for a look at the cut caused by the razorblade toothbrush. It was healing well, although it was less than a week since it happened.

'I suppose you wouldn't believe me if I told you I was reading a book at the time?'

'This is quite the papercut. Did the book also happen to be a deadly weapon?'

'More like a shield, actually.'

'I'm sorry, what?'

He said, 'Forget it. Let's just say I should have been more careful.'

'I'll say,' Cho agreed. 'At least it's been well taken care of. You're going to have a scar, though.' She said this as if it were an inconsolable tragedy. 'I can give you the details for some very good plastic surgeons. I'm afraid I don't have the lasers and such here.'

Victor, who had the details for many such specialists, said, 'Thank you, that would be useful.'

She fetched him some business cards and he placed them in a pocket. He knew from past experiences that many of the best specialists in the fields of cosmetic surgery were difficult to find without introductions and recommendations. Those who valued their services also valued discretion. Movie stars didn't want to be photographed entering such clinics or, worse, photographed leaving, bandaged and swollen.

This dermatology clinic had signage that might be for anything. Tall shrubs shielded the entrance and the parking lot. An A-list actor could pull up and get out without being observed by passers-by or even a patient paparazzo. The clinic had several doctors of differing specialities in both surgical and non-surgical procedures. The blinds were drawn at all times for the sake of privacy, which meant he could not see outside no matter where he sat. An entire team of assassins could park and he would only know about it when they came charging inside with their weapons up, angled in his direction. He would have no warning and no cover either. As good a chance to kill him as anyone could want. Thankfully, the clinic was run with incredible efficiency. Victor had barely sipped the complimentary cucumber-and-wheatgrass-infused water before he was told the doctor was ready to see him. He liked that. If waiting on his own terms, Victor's patience was limitless. In an environment he could not control, however, that patience could be tested.

When she had settled back into her seat, she said, 'So, did

you get the gig?' Cho grimaced more with each word, scared to ask and scared of the answer.

Victor sighed and looked away.

'*Oh, no*,' she cried. 'I can't believe it. That's ridiculous. I'm really quite furious on your behalf. Least of all because I know exactly how much the procedure cost you. It's unethical, as far as I'm concerned.'

With honesty, Victor said, 'I try not to worry too much about ethics in my line of work.'

'Fashion is ruthless.' She paused, thinking of something. 'Then I'm confused. I assumed you were here for a top-up before the campaign started ... or during. I'm afraid I have no idea how these hand modelling things work.'

'Neither do I,' Victor said, again with honesty. 'I'm not here for a top-up. I'd like a reversal.'

'Oh, is something wrong?'

He didn't tell her that he felt like he had lost a little dexterity, which he had expected, and that he didn't want to wait several months before a gun felt the same way as it used to in his grip. The hyaluronic acid had changed the dimensions of his hands, thickening the pads of his palm, changing the way the skin folded and the arrangement of creases. She had injected his fingers, too, again altering the skin folds and creases, but also changing the shape of them, the filler making them rounder and denser in appearance. Such differences didn't change the actual fingerprints themselves, which was why each fingertip had also been covered with an incredibly thin silicon membrane.

The rest of the time, a simple silicon solution was enough to keep him from leaving fingerprints behind.

He said, 'These hands are just not mine. If that makes sense.'

'Sure,' Cho replied. 'Sure. There was nothing wrong with them in the first place. A perfectly lovely set of hands. There was never any need to change them.'

'You're too kind,' he said.

She set about checking her notes to see the exact sites of the previous injections, then prepared the hyaluronidase.

'I can't remember,' she began, 'but I'm thinking you forwent the topical anaesthetic last time?'

He nodded. He hadn't wanted any numbness in his hands, however temporary, especially combined with the inevitable loss of dexterity his thicker fingers and denser palms gave him. And he didn't want that dexterity to return now only to then be dulled by local anaesthetic.

It was all over within five minutes. Aside from tiny injection marks, there was almost no visible change, though a reduction in volume of maybe ten per cent. They would shrink a little more over the coming days and creases would deepen.

They chatted more as she walked with him to the reception area. The clinic's decor had a palette of pastel yellow and cream tones complemented by lavender accents. Lavender fragranced the air, too. It was such a pleasant place and the doctor so talented that it was a real shame he would never be coming back.

'What's next then for you?' Cho asked. 'I assume you're retiring, or at least taking a break, from the hand modelling?'

'It's not my forte,' he admitted.

'Well, perhaps that's for the best,' she said. 'Maybe you should try doing something else that's a little less ... merciless?'

THIRTY-EIGHT

Because he had taken the train on the previous visit to meet with Phoenix, Victor flew directly to Nice this time. He preferred not to travel in a straight line, but he also never wanted to take the same route twice. The airport was always crowded and the city was always saturated with tourists, so while he increased his exposure by travelling direct he should be able to disappear into the crowds.

A sign at the airport proclaimed Nice as the GATEWAY TO THE CÔTE D'AZUR. It was always crowded, yet with the season not quite over it was his idea of hell and paradise at the same time. The airport seemed so busy it might burst open at any time. On the one hand that meant he was harder to spot in a crowd – almost impossible, in fact – yet on the other it meant he never had his personal space free of intrusion. In Victor's experience the already limited spatial awareness of the average human was massively diminished when they were on holiday. They became so singularly possessed by their own intent that the wider world almost ceased to exist. In a way, he supposed, it was a cousin of the survival instinct that focused all senses to the most immediate threat at the expense of all else.

Even for Victor, who could count the instances of losing his temper on one hand, his patience was pushed to breaking point more than once.

He took a taxi from the airport to the city centre, sitting in the back and directly behind the driver, who chatted the entire way. Victor was content to make small talk, pretending not to speak the language beyond a rudimentary understanding of words and phrases, so the exchange was stilted. The driver knew some English, although he was far from fluent, and his jovial nature ensured that any moments when he struggled to make himself understood soon developed into smiles and laughter.

Victor had the driver drop him off at a hotel a little way outside the centre of Nice. He paid the driver in cash and waved off a receipt. A doorman welcomed him through the hotel entrance and Victor found an armchair in a corner of the lobby in which to sit and wait and watch those who entered after him. He checked his watch on occasions and politely declined refreshments when they were offered to him.

He was only interested in those who entered the lobby and proceeded to look around. He had chosen a chair that put him as far away from the entrance as possible. The lobby had plenty of room for many chairs and tables. Nineteen guests drank coffee or sipped cocktails delivered by waiting staff in pristine uniforms from the nearby bar. Potted plants and pillars broke up lines of sight. Anyone who picked him out would have to really look for him first.

He gave it thirty minutes, ignored anyone too old or too

young to be a professional, and anyone with heavy suit-
cases, which left only six people who entered the hotel after
him. Of those, he dismissed anyone who made straight for
the reception desk or for the elevators, both of which were
immediately obvious even before setting foot in the lobby
thanks to the clear, plate-glass doors.

Which left two people.

A man and a woman who came in together. Both in smart
business attire. He wore a navy suit and she a black dress.
He was tall, with greying hair and a deep tan. Her hair
was black like her outfit and pulled back from her face. She
carried a black bag in her left hand. They entered the lobby
fifteen minutes after Victor sat down in the armchair.

He did not recognise them from the airport, although it
was entirely possible they had been there when he arrived.
Neither stood out enough to be notable among the hundreds
of other people at the airport. If they knew who they were
looking for then he would have been simple enough to spot
in comparison.

The tall man with grey hair was maybe forty and the
woman a little younger. Both were in decent shape, although
their clothing made it difficult to tell whether they were fit
and slim or simply thin and weak. Neither had any obvious
signs to mark them as threats. No gloves. No earpieces. The
guy's suit jacket did not show the bulge of a holstered pistol.
The woman's bag did not move in a way that suggested it
was weighed down by a heavy sub-machine gun.

Victor made sure to be facing elsewhere as they took a few
steps nearer. While he sat in a relaxed pose, gaze towards
the bar area that branched out from the lobby through an
arched opening, he kept the couple in his peripheral vision.

He wasn't sure about them just yet. They could be here for a business meeting or they could be professional assassins hunting him. Until he knew for certain he treated them as if they were the latter.

Which meant they were good. Following a taxi taking no preventative measures was simple enough, but they had had to have known he was coming to have been waiting for him at the airport. That meant they knew the legend he was travelling under was bogus or they were part of a larger operation that had been tracking him previously. Either way, they were too dangerous to leave alive.

So soon after his flight, he had no weapon. In any case, even if there had been a sidearm tucked into his waistband he wasn't going to start shooting inside a hotel unless he had no other choice. Such things tended to draw attention.

If they had seen him, he could not tell. If they were good, and he deemed they were, then they had to have seen him. That he failed to detect that meant they were better than good.

The man and the woman took seats in roughly the centre of the lobby. A poor choice in many ways, although they were facing the entrance. They would see him if he left, which might be their only intention right now. Waiting outside, he might see them. Here, in the lobby, they didn't look out of place. They could hide in plain sight. And with plenty of mirrors and other reflective surfaces throughout the lobby they could watch their flanks to a large degree.

Leaving dangerous enemies unattended to was against protocol, yet so was killing them in a public space full of witnesses. He thought for a moment, then stood.

He crossed the lobby, heading to the archway that led to

the bar area and, more importantly, a set of toilets identifiable by a discreet sign. If the man and the woman had seen him and were paying attention to their flanks through the mirrors, they would see him head in that direction. If they were here to kill him then the toilets offered them the perfect opportunity.

Passing under the archway, the bar opened up at the end of a short hallway. A corridor led off to Victor's right in which he could see four doors leading to separate toilets for men, women, disabled people, and a baby-changing room.

In the men's room, he was alone. He stepped inside the closest stall and waited.

Two minutes seemed about right: enough time for the man and the woman to consider the merits of the opportunity presented, and act. The man would come in first while the woman waited outside, both to serve as advance warning of anyone else incoming and to be close by if backup was needed. Any longer than two minutes and they risked Victor finishing up and leaving before they could strike.

He would attack the man in the blue suit three seconds after he was through the door. That was how long Victor deemed it would take the man to cross the short stretch of tiled floor to reach the first stall. Victor would charge out and take the assassin by surprise, disable him with elbow strikes to the face, aiming for the cheeks or jaw because he didn't want to open up a cut around the eye or inside the nose and bloody up his own suit in the process. Then, Victor would heave the man into the stall. If he remained standing, a choke hold. If he had fallen then a stamp to the back of the neck to break the spine.

Either way, ten seconds at most.

The woman outside would deter any random guest from walking in during those ten seconds, so that was one less problem to solve. She would be more difficult to handle. Maybe he would take the dead guy's gun and use it to usher her somewhere else. The baby-changing room made sense. Less chance of interruptions. If they had suppressed weapons then he could just shoot her, although he would press the muzzle against her flesh to further reduce the noise. No suppressors and he could club her to death with a gun instead. Two strikes to the temple or the brainstem would be plenty and he could still walk out the hotel with his suit free of bloodstains.

A momentary inconvenience and yet he would obtain a couple of disposable, almost certainly untraceable, weapons in the process, which was a reasonable trade for his troubles.

But the man in the blue suit didn't follow Victor inside within those two minutes. He waited another two in case they were slow to improvise, and still nothing.

He returned to the lobby to find both the man and the woman standing up and greeting another couple in business attire who had just arrived. Lots of smiles and hugs and air kisses. A meeting, although between fond acquaintances.

Victor complimented the woman in black's outfit before he left. '*Excusez-moi, je voulais juste vous dire à quel point votre tenue est joli.*'

'*Merci,*' she replied, flattered. '*C'est gentil de le dire.*'

As he left the hotel, he heard one of the new arrivals ask who Victor was and the woman replied that she had absolutely no idea.

THIRTY-NINE

'Excuse me,' a man said as he passed them, slowing in his stride to look at the woman in the black dress. 'I just wanted to say how fetching your outfit is.'

'Thank you,' she said in return, surprised and smiling. 'That's so kind of you to say.'

He seemed genuine and yet his manner seemed unconventional in a way she found hard to describe. He had dark hair, dark eyes, and wore a charcoal suit. He was both ordinary and paradoxically extraordinary. He passed their little group and headed to the exit with nothing further. He didn't look back.

'Who was that?'

The woman in the black dress said, 'I have absolutely no idea.'

The tall guy with the grey hair said, 'Well, whoever he is he's right, you know?' He asked this as if a sudden revelation had caught him off guard. 'That *really* is a wonderful outfit.' She smiled and waved a hand in a dismissive gesture.

Undeterred, he continued. 'Seriously, how did I not notice until now? You're a vision. So maybe I should get my eyes tested after this.'

'That's probably a good idea.' She glanced up at his grey hair. 'You are ageing at an exponential rate.'

She laughed and the others joined in.

He grinned in response, but feigned offence. '*That* is a very biting comment. *Ouch*. I'll have you know that I'm not ageing ... I'm improving instead.' He looked at the other two. 'You guys know it's true, right? Men get better with age.'

The man said, 'Hey, don't bring me into this lovers' tiff. I'm going to be on someone's bad side however I respond. I know when to stay neutral.'

The other woman said, 'Why can't it be both?'

The man with grey hair gestured for elaboration. 'Both of what?'

'Ageing and improving,' she answered. 'I see no reason why they have to be mutually exclusive. Ageing shouldn't be seen as an inherently negative part of life.'

He nodded. 'You know what? I like that. I'm improving *because* I'm ageing.'

The woman in the black dress said, 'Keep telling yourself that.'

'Oh, I shall. Don't you worry about that.'

The woman said, 'Do you even remember what it was like to be young? Youth isn't all that if we really think about it. So what if your skin is smoother and your hair has more colour? I wouldn't go back twenty years even if you paid me. Being young is a curse. You look the best you're ever going to look and yet you're so full of insecurities you can't begin to appreciate it. I'm happier with myself in my forties than I ever was at twenty-five. Aren't you?'

The guy with grey hair was nodding along, while the woman in the black dress shrugged in half-hearted agreement. Only the other man was not taking part in the discussion at that point because he was approaching the lobby's plate-glass entrance.

When he turned back towards the other three, he nodded.

The woman in the black dress released a sigh of relief.

The man with grey hair said, 'That was too close.'

She nodded. 'That was not just too close, it was *far* too close.'

When the other man returned to them, he said, 'What the hell just happened? I can feel sweat on my back right now.'

She said, 'He made us.'

'I know that. How did he make you?'

The man with grey hair said, 'Maybe drop the bass from your voice, okay? You didn't see him. You were outside.'

'And a good job we were outside, wasn't it? So we could rush in and save your asses.'

'Thank you,' the man with grey hair said in a sarcastic tone. 'Thank you so very much.'

'It's a team effort,' the woman in the black dress said. 'If our roles were reversed, he would have made you too.'

The other man said, 'I doubt that.'

She said, 'Let's just lose the blame game altogether because it gets us nowhere. What's done is done. When this is all over we can sit around a table and run through what might have happened in other circumstances, but that's for that glorious future day. This is now. We need to know what went wrong here and now so we can avoid it next time. Okay?'

The man with grey hair said, 'The only explanation I can give is that he just knew.'

'That doesn't make sense,' the other man said.

'He was sat in that far corner so he could watch the entrance. This is not his hotel, I guarantee you. He had the taxi stop outside and he came in and sat in that chair and watched for us to come in.'

A moment of quiet while they thought this through.

'So it was at the airport, then. That's when he made us,' the second woman said. 'Which means it could have been any of us he saw.'

The woman in black shook her head. 'I don't think that's the case at all. He didn't know we were going to walk through this door. He couldn't have known. We didn't, did we? We only decided to when we feared he wasn't coming out again. We did nothing wrong. He simply acted as though he was being followed. He picked a hotel that looked grand enough and large enough to have the right kind of lobby. Then he sat down and watched to see if anyone came in after him. And then we did.' She paused. 'He didn't know anyone was following him until the exact moment we showed ourselves. We did all the work for him.'

'Shit,' the man with grey hair said.

'No.' She shook her head. 'It's okay. He saw us, he suspected us, then he dismissed us. That's even better.'

'How could this possibly be better?'

'Because we passed his test. He doesn't know who we are.'

The other man said, 'Except if he sees any of us a second time then he will change his mind in a heartbeat. We passed this one test and that means we are guaranteed to fail any others.'

'Then we make sure he doesn't see us, don't we?' She didn't wait for a reply. 'The four of us are backup only from now on until the time is right. Tell the others to be *extremely* cautious with this one. He's even better than she warned.'

FORTY

Nice had been a tourist destination ever since the English aristocracy decided it was far better to spend the winter somewhere with a more agreeable climate than the British Isles. Victor had spent enough winters there to feel as though he knew exactly how those aristocrats had felt.

He was meeting Phoenix the next morning so had a whole day in which to perform counter-surveillance. It was always an extra risk seeing her, so that increased danger had to be offset with more thorough precautions.

The taxi he caught after leaving the hotel dropped him off near the railway station. He headed left from the station and joined the Avenue Jean Médecin, a pedestrianised thoroughfare lined with colourful storefronts and green with many trees. Sleek trams passed by every few minutes. As he walked south, the storefronts displayed increasingly expensive wares. A pair of American tourists, red faced and sweating in the heat, asked him for directions. He shrugged and pretended he did not speak English.

He found it not uncommon that strangers approached him. He looked and acted as though he were a respectable person, and though he tried not to appear too friendly, it was worse to stand out as belligerent. That balance was ever fluid and what worked one moment could fail the next.

Counter-surveillance was simple enough to perform in such a city bustling with tourists. Pleasurable, too. Victor could be a tourist himself while he kept a lookout for watchers and took steps to slip any shadows he failed to identify.

He let the crowds ferry him through the new town of Nice that lay west of the Paillon River, which had been built over to some degree. He strolled along the Promenade des Anglais, allowing the flow of the crowds to dictate his path and speed. The sea breeze coming across the waterfront was cool and pleasant, ruffling his shirt and swaying the palm trees that separated the two wide carriageways.

He saw many pickpockets as he walked. They were easy to spot because he had been one long ago. Pickpockets never looked ahead for long. Their gazes were always cast a little down: looking for pockets that bulged with a fat wallet or a sleek phone, a backpack or bag with an open zipper. They never walked in straight lines, either. They were always zig-zagging through crowds. They were on every street but most people would escape with their belongings. Pickpockets were opportunists. There was no need to attempt a risky theft when within the next minute more potential marks would wander along. All it took was one unobservant tourist with loose, comfortable clothes. Some of the pickpockets operated in small groups. Usually just two or three, although three was perfect. One spotter, usually tall to have the best view of a crowd. One distractor, often female so they were less threatening. And, of course, the pickpocket, who was probably short to better go unseen, and slim to more easily slip both in and out of tight spaces and tight pockets. For those reasons they tended to be young, and most often male. The simplest distraction was to ask for directions, drawing the eyes and ears of the mark deemed a good target by the spotter. Other times, the distractor would drop their guidebook or trip or otherwise create a sudden, attention-grabbing moment. The best distraction, but also the riskiest, was the bump. Stopping in front of the mark was the simplest way to do this, and the sudden physical contact created the perfect opportunity for the pickpocket to act. While best at chokepoints, it was workable anywhere.

Victor had always been the pickpocket in his crew; he had been the smallest and skinniest because he had been the youngest. When he had become too tall for an effective pickpocket, his crew had moved on to more profitable activities.

Later, in the wealthy neighbourhood of Cimiez, he admired the Franciscan monastery and the views of the city from its gardens, then explored the extensive Roman ruins. Georg's courier had hidden Victor's ordered Five-seveN behind a loose brick in one of the amphitheatre's remaining arches. While he was pleased to discover two twenty-round magazines, he made a mental note to tell Georg her couriers needed more respect for historical sites.

He overheard a woman ask her husband, 'Can you imagine what it must have been like to be a gladiator?' and Victor wondered what it was like to have someone with which to share such speculation. The husband only shrugged in answer and took a bite of his ice cream.

He spent a little longer than was optimal in the

amphitheatre itself, so he made sure to take only a brisk walk in the nearby park, sticking to the shade of olive trees and using them to block possible sniping lines. He saw many potential threats, as he always did, but none more than once and none that advanced from a potential threat to a definitive one.

He took a circuitous route back to the city centre by way of the university campus and the Parc de Valrose, in which he paused to watch a trio of young dancers perform energetic, almost acrobatic routines for an appreciative crowd, while he checked to see if anyone in the crowd was more interested in him than the dance act.

Certain he was free of shadows, he headed to the Old Town on the river's east side, spread around the foot of Le Château, a hill so named for the castle that once stood atop it. It was quieter here. Still busy, yet the streets were narrow and shielded from the sun and the noise by tall buildings, many five or more storeys high and painted in warm ochres, reds and oranges. At the harbour, he watched ferries taking passengers across to Corsica and bright sailing boats speckling the waves. Tourists rode by on rented bicycles.

He liked Nice as he liked visiting most of France. The city had a charming air to it, a combination of its French identity and Italian roots. It was a shame he could not come to France more often. When he had lived in Switzerland for a time he had made regular visits. That had all changed when a job in Paris had gone so wrong he had stayed away for several years afterwards. That incident had put him on the radar of too many powerful enemies. Most of whom now thought him to be dead. Still, better he did nothing to make them think otherwise.

And though his face now was different to how it had been then, and he used no legend from that time, he still had to limit how often he came here and for how long. If not for Phoenix, he might never have returned at all. He had a particular fondness for Normandy and Provence. He liked the history of those regions. He enjoyed exploring the medieval villages and castles in particular. In those excursions he could play a tourist with a fascination for history because he was that tourist.

The café where he was to meet her lay near to a *vélo bleu* docking station. It had capacity for twenty bicycles and yet only four were currently there. They were popular with tourists. He saw them on almost every street. The café itself was unremarkable. Small. The scent coming from within suggested the coffee would indeed be excellent.

Across the street an old building faced the café. Maybe built a century before. Maybe two centuries. Russet shingles. Pastel yellow façade. It occupied one corner of a small block. Six storeys. It had been modernised over the years, yet without losing the feel of the Old Town. It looked like maybe once it had belonged to a wealthy merchant and had been converted into offices in the middle of the last century. On Saturday it was empty.

Because it faced south, all the window shutters on this façade were closed to prevent the interior overheating.

He liked that it was unoccupied. He had no need to look out for snipers at windows. Not that he expected any, of course.

While their relationship could not last forever, he was certain it would be he who first decided when it was time to end it, not Phoenix.

FORTY-ONE

As usual, Victor woke in his hotel room way before his alarm buzzed. The alarm wasn't so much to wake him up but to tell him when he was losing his edge. Years of careful observation and training meant he knew how much rest he needed, how much fuel he had to consume, how long he would take to heal from wounds, how much exertion was required to maintain his fitness. The day the alarm roused him from sleep was the day he had failed to understand himself. That day was coming, he knew. The only thing he didn't know was if it would be age or a slip in discipline that brought it on.

He lay still for a moment, listening for any sounds out of place. He heard his own breathing, a motorcycle in the distance, and nothing else. No footsteps nearing. No clothes rustling. No door easing open.

Regardless, he reacted as though he had been woken. Until he knew otherwise, he was under attack. He snapped his hand to the pistol tucked in his waistband and bolted upright as he pulled the gun free and aimed it at each of the three points of the room where he deemed an enemy would wait.

A fast, practised movement, jerking the weapon from the right to the centre and then far left.

The door, the window, the armchair.

No one.

Only the shadows of murderers lurking at the edges of his unconsciousness.

He would have been by the door, which was why it was the first place he pointed the handgun. But he wouldn't have waited for a dangerous target to wake up. He would have killed them while they slept. Not every assassin was so efficient, he had learned.

Some professionals liked their prey to know what was coming. Others enjoyed saying a few words first, a power move or theatrics for the sake of theatrics.

It was rare they ever reached Victor's level. Not impossible, though. He had encountered such assassins before and had no doubt he would again.

He had moved the room's armchair so that it was in line with the doorway and hence in the line of sight of anyone who entered the room. Maybe its placement would shave off a split-second from an assassin's target acquisition as their attention was drawn to it. Some professionals slept in chairs, after all.

Which happened to be a terrible idea in Victor's opinion. Getting up faster was no consolation to the immobility of a stiff back and a sore neck. Let alone the cumulative effect of never sleeping well and hence the body and mind never fully recuperating. Or the slow debilitation of spending many hours every night in a position for which the human body had never been designed. Spending too much time sitting killed more people than Victor ever could in a hundred life-times, and he had killed more than he cared to count.

Professionals who slept in chairs were never at their best. They only ended up making it easier for their eventual executioners in every other way.

Climbing off the bed, Victor rubbed his hands together and flexed his fingers, glad to find they felt like his own once more. At a casual glance, they had seemed no different with the hyaluronic acid and yet they had seemed almost alien to Victor. He had become used to the tight feeling in his fingers after a couple of weeks. They had been uncomfortable, the hyaluronic acid swelling them and stretching the skin. Now, making a fist felt more natural. He could do it faster with the resulting fist tighter and stronger. With his dexterity reduced, he was glad he had only needed to contend with inmates with shanks, not assassins.

He applied his silicon solution and allowed it to dry before he touched anything in the room. It was a simple trick he had been using for a long time to create a barrier over his skin, preventing the oil from his fingers leaving prints behind. For the Kirill contract, of course, he had needed to forgo this protocol, and yet wasn't prepared to have his own fingerprints entered into the US criminal justice system.

The silicon membranes he had worn to fulfill the contract had each been indented with the fingerprint of a different person. Combined with the changes to the contours and creases of his hands and fingers from the hyaluronic acid filler, the prints the police officers had taken at the station, and those taken in jail, were nothing like his own. When heated, the silicon became soft and malleable. An actual finger would not be able to indent it with prints, but a 3D scan of a finger that was printed in hard resin could do the job with only a little pressure. The whole process was extremely delicate and time-consuming but the results were even better than Victor had needed.

Each tiny membrane was perforated at a level undetectable to the naked eye so that the skin beneath could breathe. That porous nature gave them a matte finish, and given its transparency, made it as good as invisible. The texture wasn't quite the same as skin. Victor could feel the difference, yet no one who had taken his prints had actually bothered to check his fingers first, let alone to touch them to see if they felt real. By sight alone, they were indistinguishable, and what the eyes saw the brain believed.

The membranes had been kept in place by medical-grade adhesive, the same kind used in the advanced modern hair systems used by many Hollywood actors. Which was another reason to have chosen a dermatologist in California. Neither oil nor water would break it down. Instead, it had to be scratched and peeled away and then isopropyl alcohol used to remove the residue. The only way to remove it was to scrape it clear. Which had taken Victor almost an hour to do once he had finished lunch with Spector.

Carrying the membranes across borders, however, was too much of a risk for frequent use. He kept the solution in a hand sanitiser bottle, which no one looked at twice.

Standing up, his left thigh ached. It seemed there was something about moving from horizontal to vertical that caused discomfort. Perhaps the change in blood pressure. He rubbed at his thigh until the discomfort eased. Phoenix had pretended not to notice the new scar, although it would be impossible to miss it.

He wasn't certain whether it did still cause him pain or if it was in his head. A bullet had nicked his femoral artery and sometimes he felt the need to make sure the wound – though repaired several months before by exceptional surgeons – had not reopened. He couldn't quite remember the agony of being shot, but he would never forget the sight of staccato crimson arcs originating from his leg. Victor was used to seeing such sights from his victims, not himself.

Convalescing had been hard. As Phoenix had noted, he was a little under his optimal weight. It had taken many weeks of recovery before he had been able to exercise, and even then it had been at a fraction of his usual intensity. Peak physical fitness was towards the top of Victor's qualifications and he was nowhere near his best. He was weaker and he tired quicker. In a strange way it was like being young again, back when he was a stringy kid who did everything possible not to exert himself. That kid was content stealing cars and jewellery and spending the proceeds on hedonistic pursuits. The kid who had wronged the wrong people and fled under the shade of an army recruitment stand to avoid a beating. The kid who had then lied about his age to a recruitment officer happy to turn a blind eye while faking signatures.

The memory made him pause because he had not thought about that time in years. He kept his focus on surviving the present, constantly taking in and analysing information, so memories were little more than distractions for him, and distractions could be fatal.

He pushed the unwanted memories away, bathed, dressed and set out to meet Phoenix.

FORTY-TWO

Early Sunday morning, the city seemed almost empty. He heard the wondrous sound of church bells as he made a circuitous route to the Old Town. By mid-morning Nice had come alive. He smelled coffee and cigarettes wherever he walked.

A woman in a wide-brimmed hat sat smoking and reading a magazine outside the café. From a distance he could tell she was not Phoenix. Something about her intrigued him nonetheless, although he had no idea why. The café had a narrow frontage. Beneath a bright blue awning was a handful of small round tables and low-backed chairs, all wood stained a dark hue. The furniture had been maintained to an immaculate degree considering they spent so much time outdoors. Victor could detect only a little wear on the legs and the odd patch of sun damage.

Inside, the café was quiet. One couple ate crêpes and drank orange juice in the far corner. A man with stubble up to his cheekbones worked the espresso machine after taking Victor's order.

He decided to sit outside. Maybe because of the woman in the wide-brimmed hat and maybe just to enjoy the fresh air while he sipped his coffee.

This part of the Old Town was already packed with visitors just one street over, yet this small corner had no real sights to see and little reason to linger. The office building with the closed shutters across the street was pleasant enough yet unremarkable. Only a few pedestrians passed by, going this way and that. He expected to have to wait for Phoenix given he arrived everywhere early.

She was right about the coffee. Delicious and strong, which made it a shame he would have to ignore the place after this for at least a couple of years. By the time he deemed it appropriate to return for another espresso the guy with the cheekbone-high stubble might have switched bean supplier. The coffee might never be this good again.

Then Victor saw he was never coming back to this café because one of the shutters had opened on the office building opposite. Yesterday, they had all been closed for the weekend.

We're long past all that silly business, she had said.

He finished his espresso, rocked his head from side to side to crack his neck, and crossed the street.

FORTY-THREE

They hadn't long finished their coffees when the killer stood up from his seat outside the café and crossed the street. At first, they figured there had to be something they missed. This had to be a mistake, surely. Maybe he was just stretching his legs while he waited for his broker.

No, they soon found out.

He was heading straight for them.

None of their plans had involved this particular course of action. For a few seconds, no one knew what to do about it. The leader, Walker, was slow to act. A fine tactician in his own right, his improvisational skills were lacking. The team was already somewhat spread out in the building while they waited. There had been no reason to all wait together and every reason not to get under each other's feet.

They had no sophisticated communications equipment because there had been no need. Now, Walker realised the depth of this oversight. He had to use a phone to hurriedly call some of the guys he knew were downstairs to tell them to expect company.

He had no advice to give them beyond a simple directive: don't miss.

They knew with whom they were dealing. This guy was bad news all day every day. She had told them.

Once the gunfire sounded, Walker got nervous. A couple of muted shots and he would have known his men downstairs had ended the intruder with swift efficiency. Instead, he heard multiple gunshots.

Phoenix's best contractor didn't die easily.

Walker ordered the others to intercept the uninvited guest. He had eight armed men at his command. However capable this guy was, he couldn't get through eight, could he?

Walker waited on the same floor from which they had kept the café under surveillance. He had a little .22 as his personal weapon and he was a good shot. He hadn't actually fired a gun in anger for a long time, however. He was a leader not a triggerman.

He paced back and forth through the offices, listening to the firefights below him.

Come on, he willed his men, *come on*.

Then there was silence and he wasn't sure what the result had been. He remained still for a while, wondering if one of his men would shout out that it was over – or not. When he could no longer bear not knowing he moved again, stepping back into the open-plan office area and seeing Phoenix's best contractor turning his way.

For Walker, things became painful after that.

PART FOUR

FORTY-FOUR

Leaving Walker to suffocate, Victor hurried back down through the office building, thoughts of Phoenix's betrayal at the forefront of his mind. He wasn't surprised because their business relationship had always had a limited shelf life, but he had been caught off guard nonetheless. He had not anticipated the end would come so soon. He corrected himself: he had not expected her to be the one who made the first move.

He felt foolish for having bought her carefree act when they were together.

Maybe it was more than just foolishness he felt.

He forced the introspection away, conscious of the ever-increasing volume of approaching sirens. Time seemed to have different rules during a firefight, so the four minutes it had taken him to clear the building of Walker's kill team might have been five or six. Which was far too long. He was glad Phoenix had chosen the café opposite as the location of the trap. The narrow, twisting streets of the Old Town would slow the police response. Had she elected to have him attacked elsewhere in the city, the building might already be surrounded.

When he reached the last set of stairs, the entrance was opening ahead of him and he saw the blue flash of a police uniform, so he stepped into the adjoining hallway where the young gunman lay in a pool of blood. His dead eyes seemed to watch Victor as he stood with his back to the wall, left shoulder close to the corner of the stairwell.

There were no cries of '*Arrêter, le policier*,' so the cop or cops hadn't seen him. Which meant he slipped the gun into his waistband.

He controlled his breathing to lower his heart rate, elevated after hurrying down the stairs.

He heard them coming. Three sets of feet. They were quiet, not silent. Careful footsteps on a hard floor. First responders. They didn't know what to expect, no doubt told the barest of details by a dispatcher who only knew enough to tell them nothing useful beyond witnesses reporting gunshots. They would have radioed in the dead guy on the street outside who had taken a dive from a six-storey window, so more units were on the way. Perhaps a tactical unit from RAID or GIGN.

Victor wanted to be long gone by then.

He urged the three first responders to approach faster than their careful pace. They were cautious in their ignorance of the facts and their understandable apprehension of walking into a potentially life-threatening situation.

They couldn't know Victor wasn't going to kill them unless they gave him no other choice.

He heard them on the stairs. A slow ascent. He pictured

two side-by-side and the third cop a few steps behind. Even odds whether the first two would initially look right to where he was hiding or left to where the second gunman lay at the foot of the next flight of stairs. Which Victor considered good enough. Either their attention would be grabbed by the corpse and Victor would attack them from behind or they would see him as they checked their flank and he would implement ferocity instead of stealth.

He preferred the first option but the end result would be the same.

They checked their flank.

Victor was exploding into motion before the two cops could react.

His left forearm pushed the first pistol to one side, creating room for a palm heel to strike the guy in the jaw. He took it well, dazed and standing instead of unconscious and falling.

It would have been better for Victor had the cop stumbled backwards into his partner, who was a couple of steps behind. Instead, he doubled over, blocking Victor's line of attack in the narrow hallway and simultaneously giving that partner a clear line of sight in which to fire.

Victor dropped low before the second cop had a chance to do just that, and sent another palm heel – an uppercut this time – into the first guy's face. That put him down, flipping him backwards and into the cop behind, who lost any opportunity to aim his weapon as he stumbled backwards in an effort to keep his balance.

Which gave Victor enough time to reach him.

He snatched the gun straight out from the cop's hand. Turned a fast ninety degrees to whip the weapon into the face of the third responder coming up behind the first two.

He fell straight down the stairs, nose streaming blood, and groaned at the foot of the staircase.

The second cop had recovered from his surprise by then and slipped Victor's attempt to do the exact same thing to him. An instinctual dodge, though. He flinched himself off balance.

Victor kicked his load-bearing leg, aiming for the side of the knee with the intention of folding the leg a way it was not built to go, but he struck a little too high.

No disabling trauma. Lots of pain, however. The cop became more unstable, falling to one side and only remaining standing because the hallway wall prevented him from tipping over. He managed to push himself away and turned into—

Victor's elbow strike.

Consciousness left the guy in an instant and he fell into the wall and slid down it, the skin of his cheek making a squeaking sound against the smooth paintwork.

Two unconscious and one disabled, so Victor held off following up with more strikes. The first two wouldn't be awake for several minutes, or even hours. When they did come to, concussion would keep them out of action for days. None had had the chance to get a good look at him, so there was no need to leave even more corpses in the building.

The cop lying at the bottom of the stairs was still conscious, however, so Victor leaned down to grab a fistful of the man's hair, then slammed his head against the floor to ensure he stayed there, before exiting the building in a slow, casual gait as if nothing had happened.

Should there be more police arriving or waiting, he wanted their first impression of him to be benign. He wanted them to think of him as a bystander, not the perpetrator. If only for a few seconds.

While he saw a single police vehicle and no more cops, he could hear them coming. Sirens wailed nearby. Perhaps a cruiser on a parallel street or at the end of this one.

Patrons from the café were looking in his direction, and pedestrians had begun to congregate. Only a small crowd because it was still early on Sunday morning, yet far too many witnesses for his liking. He presented the same benign persona so he wouldn't stick in their minds when asked about him later. Besides, there was something a whole more interesting to distract him.

The gunman Victor had shoved out of the window was a grisly sight in the road.

Blood surrounded the corpse and extended in a spatter almost two metres in length across the paving stones from where his head had cracked apart. Someone nearby, seeing the corpse for the first time, screamed.

Victor preferred to keep civilians out of such professional inevitabilities if it could be avoided. However, while he had caused someone temporary mental trauma he had also gifted them a story they would be telling at parties for decades to come. A reasonable trade to some, he supposed.

He noticed the bearded café owner, who had made him the excellent coffee, had stepped outside and was looking his way with a pensive gaze. The patrons were more interested in the mess, although Victor could not see the woman in the wide-brimmed hat. The bearded guy turned his head to track Victor as he walked away, which was a problem he could do nothing about without exponentially increasing the chances of being remembered.

The corpse lay in the road to Victor's left, so he headed right, away from the focal point for the gathering crowd.

Which expanded by the second as people hurried closer, rushing towards the sound of the scream and sirens, eager to discover their cause. Once they saw the dead guy, some would turn away. The majority wouldn't, Victor knew. They would stare at the corpse and the blood until the cops showed up and pushed them back. They would take pictures and record videos on their phones. Gruesome footage would be seen the world over by ghoulish voyeurs. The sight of death and trauma had never bothered Victor but he could not comprehend why anyone sought it out and revelled in it.

Plenty of rainbows were out there to look at instead.

There was a lot of blood. From the broken skull, naturally. Also from many instances of skin ruptured on impact. The voyeurs wouldn't know the guy had been pushed and the cops likely wouldn't either, but the paramedics might and the medical examiner would for sure. The explosion of blood said in no uncertain terms that the guy did not commit suicide. A suicide knows what's about to happen and the brain understands it too, so the body responds by pulling blood away from the skin and to vital organs. A survival mechanism that just so happens to mean less mess on the pavement.

The gunman hadn't known he was about to fall to his death, and less than a second's descent wasn't a lot of time to dwell on the situation. Just long enough for that short screech of terrified surprise.

Nowhere near long enough to complete repentance.

Victor knew if their roles were reversed he would need a very long fall to have any hope of repenting his many sins.

A cop car turned into the street ahead and screeched to a stop in front of the office building after passing him without so much as a glance. The benign-bystander guise was still working.

Victor resisted the temptation to break into a spring now he had some distance. That would only ensure they noticed, and focused on, him. He had to play the chance the arriving cops headed into the building, or at least began to manage the crowd and secure the integrity of the crime scene.

A glance over his shoulder told Victor to trust his instincts: he saw the cops as they climbed out of their vehicle and the bearded café owner rushing towards them and pointing Victor's way.

FORTY-FIVE

He darted around the first corner that opened up before him, sprinting along the narrow, cobbled street, glad of his resulting loud footfalls that acted as a horn so pedestrians had a warning to dart out of his path. He clipped stacks of flattened cardboard boxes left outside storefronts to be taken away, sending them scattering, before the side street opened up into a small square where market stalls sold sacks of rice, huge jars of olives, and many spices that flavoured the air. Women in burqas and men in tracksuits bought and bartered. Victor felt a few gazes on him but detected no hostility, just curiosity. He made his way through the square, slipping in and out of space as and when the crowd let him. He didn't rush. He had no wish to draw attention and while he had people all around him he was a harder target to hit if a pursuing police officer was reckless enough to shoot into the crowd.

He dashed down a sloping path, passing walls stained with grime and graffiti. The path took a sharp turn before the alleyway opened up to the adjoining street. An SUV blocked the exit to the alleyway, so Victor took a running leap up on to the bonnet and dropped off the other side. The owner, nearby, yelled abuse.

A park lay on the far side of the road, so Victor headed that way, not knowing if the police were running on foot behind him, but aware of blaring sirens no more than a street away.

In the park, he slowed to a jog, then a walk.

The most important thing to do when running away was to stop running, he had learned. A human being in motion was easy to see and easy to hear. Someone running stood out in almost every setting. A temporary increase in distance had no benefit if it could not be sustained. Better to move slower and make less noise and be less noticeable. People running tended to do so with their heads up and their eyes forward, looking into the distance. When moving at speed it was necessary to have plenty of warning as to what was coming up, because whatever it was, it was coming up fast. The downside of that was less attention could be paid to that which was closest.

Victor sat down on a bench at the far end to an elderly woman who was tossing breadcrumbs to nearby pigeons. They exchanged nods of polite greeting, and then he leaned back and stretched one arm across the top of the backrest as though he was enjoying the sunshine.

She muttered about how loud the sirens were and did they really need to make so much noise on a Sunday morning?

Victor nodded in agreement.

A few moments later, two cops ran straight past. Heads up. Eyes forward, looking into the distance for someone fleeing, not sitting in a relaxed pose out in the open.

The running cops had frightened the pigeons, who took off as a single flapping mass of wings.

The elderly woman tutted and raised the finger in the direction of the police officers.

Victor disliked cursing, even in gesture, though he found a certain amusement in the moment. He waited maybe half a minute until he could no longer hear the running footsteps, and stood again.

He shared a polite nod of farewell with the elderly woman, who sat alone, longing for the pigeons to return.

As useful as stopping could be when running away, hiding in plain sight could be even more beneficial, Victor often found. When he spotted an organised tour group taking in the sights of the Old Town, he changed direction to walk alongside them. He kept the same pace while he too angled up his head to take in the pretty architecture.

Two police cruisers with flashing lights and an ambulance had passed them by the time the group crossed the river into central Nice. Victor only peeled away when he saw an open barbershop and strolled inside for a haircut and shave.

With his cheeks and jaw as smooth as they had ever been, and his hair buzzed down to just a few millimetres, Victor bought a change of clothing from whichever stores he could find that opened on Sundays, throwing away his suit and replacing it with slacks, polo shirt and blazer. He swapped his good brogues for cheap hiking boots, leaving the former with a skinny homeless guy while he changed into the boots in the same alleyway.

'*Merci, merci*,' the man said, with wide, grateful eyes.

He had thin skin stretched over a face worn down by poor choices. Maybe twenty years old but he might as well have been seventy.

'I'll take good care of them,' the young man assured

him, saying, 'I promise, I promise ...' over and over again, clutching the shoes tight against his chest as though Victor might change his mind and take them back just for the cruel fun of it.

He reminded Victor of no single person, and yet of people he had known a long time ago, and in a moment of unforgiveable weakness, Victor handed over all the cash he had on him, politely declining the resulting offer to share the young man's precious bottle of cream liqueur.

As he left the alleyway, Victor couldn't be sure if it was laughter or sobbing he heard behind him but he made sure not to look back.

FORTY-SIX

Outside, the afternoon sea breeze was cooling. Inside, the air was thick and hot. Castellan could feel the humidity on his skin and the heat in his throat as he inhaled. Sweat glistened on his face. Thinning hair was plastered to his scalp in unruly wisps. Beads of sweat hung from the end of his nose and the point of his chin. His white undershirt had stains on it where he had wiped his hands, and was so soaked with sweat it had become almost transparent. He stank. He always stank.

From his office window, he watched a container ship pass through the harbour, heading out to sea. The ship was huge, loaded with well over twenty thousand containers. The port itself could easily accommodate more than one million containers at any one time. Every day, more than two dozen container ships ported in Marseille, coming from and going to hundreds of other ports across the globe. It was a mammoth operation back when Castellan had first arrived as a little brother accompanying a heroin shipment from the Black Sea. He had never left the city and had watched the port grow and grow over the years to its current gargantuan size with three million square metres of storage space.

Two separate harbours comprised the port. The eastern harbour, located in the city, handled cruise ships and handled goods coming and going to elsewhere in the Mediterranean. The western harbour at Fos – where Castellan was based – formed the commercial and industrial heart of the port. All day and all night ships arrived and cargo was loaded and unloaded; commercial trains arrived and departed; boats came and went along the Rhône.

This particular meeting of the Club was unplanned, naturally.

With so much at stake, the Security Council was having trouble agreeing on their resolutions. Castellan let their bickering voices fade into white noise. He watched his cranes load an enormous cargo ship packed with Black Sea heroin destined for Boston and the lucrative American market.

'Everything we have built is now at risk,' he heard one of the bosses say in a loud voice.

Another said, 'It's too late to have second thoughts. Kirill is dead. We can't bring him back because things have become a little messy.'

'We have an asset in the wind,' the Sector Five boss pointed out. 'Every second that remains the case is a second in which Maxim can learn the truth. I hope no one has forgotten that if he does there will be nowhere on this planet safe from his wrath. Maxim has not lost his fire, only forgotten it. But that fire has not forgotten he who once wielded it. That fire longs to ignite once more.'

Castellan felt the fear that crept into the room. It slipped under the door, unseen and unheard, and infected all who sat with him whether they showed it or not. Fear now meant doubt later. Doubt was worse than fear, which would pass in time.

Doubt only grew the longer it was left unchallenged.

'I know how to put out any fire,' Castellan said as he reached for a bottle of Finnish vodka.

He smiled and some of the bosses smiled too.

He went around the table, refilling glasses, leaving the Sector Five boss until last.

'Ah,' Castellan said, sloshing the remnants of the bottle around, 'let me get a fresh one.'

The bosses cradled their drinks, waiting until they all had one for what they presumed was a coming toast.

The Sector Two boss noticed Castellan had not unscrewed the top from the new bottle. The Sector Five boss did not see this as Castellan stepped up behind him. He did not see Castellan reverse the bottle in his hand so that he gripped the stem.

A single downward blow to the top of the skull was all it took to stun the Sector Five boss. Castellan did not even need to strike with full force. The bottle was dense glass containing a kilo of accelerating mass. It made a dull *thunk* upon impact and the Sector Five boss keeled forward in his seat.

No weapons were allowed at meetings of the Club, so when the loyal thief accompanying the Sector Five boss shoved a hand inside his jacket for his gun, he gripped only air.

Undeterred, he rushed to stand as his boss groaned, dazed and incoherent.

'*Do not leave your seat*,' Castellan screamed at him,

holding the bottle of vodka out with its bloody end pointed at the man's face.

The loyal thief froze, then looked around the table to the other bosses and their own loyal thieves, all sat still and unreactive. He lowered himself back down into his chair.

Castellan reversed his grip on the bottle and unscrewed the cap, tossing it away. Then, he grabbed the hair of the Sector Five boss and pulled him back upright, and levered his head back so he faced the ceiling.

There was no resistance aside from an incoherent rasping and a powerless waving of arms.

Releasing the Sector Five boss's hair, Castellan shoved the neck of the bottle into the man's mouth until it could go no further. With one hand holding the bottle in place, Castellan used his free hand to pinch shut the man's nostrils as the vodka drained down his throat.

'Know that once we commit to a course of action then it is the right course of action,' Castellan said to the other bosses, as the Sector Five boss choked and drowned. 'We can have no doubts because we cannot change what is done.'

Dazed from the blow to the head, it did not take long before the Sector Five boss became limp, and Castellan withdrew the bottle and released him to collapse forward on to the table in a disgusting spill of vodka, blood and vomit.

'Congratulations,' he said to the loyal thief sat next to the corpse. 'You are now in charge of Sector Five.'

'Thank you,' the man managed to say in a weak, strained voice.

Wiping his hands, Castellan said to the Club, 'Patience is all we need. Our friend who has already proved so useful informs me that this morning is only a minor setback. However hot, Maxim's fire will soon find nothing left to burn.'

The Sector Three boss said, 'Her trap has already failed, lest we forget.'

'No one has forgotten,' Castellan said, pouring himself a much-needed drink from a fresh bottle. 'Which is exactly why she has set not one trap, but many.'

FORTY-SEVEN

Killing was always thirsty work. Victor had several empty bottles of water in the footwell of the car he had stolen on the way out of Nice. He headed west along the coastal highway, the Mediterranean on his left, passing beaches and marinas with moored yachts and sailboats bristling on the brilliant turquoise water, almost all white and gleaming in the sun. In the distance, a haze of cotton-wool cloud clung to the hillside while the rest of the sky was clear.

The hillside was dotted with villages and lone villas along the coast. Phoenix's chateau overlooked the sea, and was only accessible by road after first detouring inland. A late-nineteenth-century building, it had fallen into disrepair by the time Phoenix acquired it. She had assured Victor it had been a steal given its condition but had not revealed the actual price tag. Her English sense of modesty at play, which seemed to be the only time she had any modesty in Victor's experiences of her. He could not envision the full refurbishment of the chateau within her lifetime, even if she died only of natural causes sometime in the distant future. Maybe that was the point: a project she could never complete because what would she do once the chateau was restored to its prior splendour? Victor saw the appeal of setting a goal that could never be achieved. Always striving meant always having purpose. Once, Victor had wanted to be the best, and that motivated him to train harder, practise longer and do his job to the highest standard. Then, when he had been a professional for too long and made too many enemies, simply staying alive had taken over as his singular purpose. And, like Phoenix's renovations of the chateau, his too was a goal impossible to realise. He was never going to live long. He had already survived for longer than he had once predicted. Each day since had felt like a victory, but one he had to earn again and again.

The grounds were designed for serenity and yet Victor would find no peace within them. There were no overlooking points of elevation for a sniper – Victor did not count the Alps on the horizon – and yet he felt far too exposed after climbing over the high wall on the north side. In the distance, islands rose from the sparkling waters of the Mediterranean. Immaculate lawns surrounded the infinity pool on three sides.

There was no garden, yet many gardens. Each had a different theme. Victor was no horticulturalist and the multitude of minutiae of seasonal flowering plants, shrubs and trees went over his head, although he appreciated fresh fruit, so the orangery was something he could imagine having himself if he ever had such wealth and such a reckless attitude to security. It was impossible to properly guard such a property. He figured a dozen competent security personnel would give the appearance of being well guarded and yet he would have no trouble slipping past twelve vigilant men. With so much space to utilise, so many needless blind spots created by the pavilion, the guest house, the servants' quarters, the endless decorative hedges, planters and statues, he could envision the alarm would only be raised when the person they were meant to protect failed to respond to the maid knocking on her bedroom door in the morning. Phoenix said the gardens were like a jungle before she had taken ownership and it had required every landscaper, tree surgeon and florist in the Riviera to tame it.

There were no guards patrolling. Only a few lights and cameras provided anything close to security.

It made no sense to Victor that someone like Phoenix would choose to live in such a place. Not only unprotected, but so brazenly inviting to enemies. And yet he had only tracked her down here thanks to the assistance and resources of an intelligence agency. He didn't imagine many who might want to do her harm had access to such advantages. Still, she had lived in a way he found needlessly reckless.

Inside, he found himself drawn to a particular reception room. It had been there the first time they had met and conversed. She had found him playing the grand piano, albeit with a clunking lack of practice. All such rooms had ceilings that rose over three times his height. The floors were polished parquet. The fireplace was so huge he would have no trouble incinerating a body within it.

She had portraits on the walls of old movie stars from the era when they would have attended the film festival in nearby Cannes and enjoyed after-parties of wild decadence at the chateau held by the previous owner – before he fell into spiralling debt and eventual bankruptcy. Phoenix said she had been born three generations too late and bemoaned the fact that she never had the chance to enjoy the roaring twenties, beyond the old movies she played most nights in the chateau's cinema room. She longed to wear low-waisted dresses, cloche hats and '*all* the pearls'. When Victor once suggested there was nothing stopping her, she had shrugged the comment away.

This area of the coast was known as the English quarter, for the original aristocrats that had once summered here. Then, for the influx of expatriates after the Second World War. She told him that the war had changed Europe so much it had altered its very soul. After so much bloodshed, there was no way back. The consciousness of the continent would be forever marred. No such conflict would ever be repeated and yet Europe would never escape its legacy. No one had really won that war because generations later, people were still affected. A Royal Navy serviceman who had seen unspeakable things would return home never to speak of them, instead drinking whatever it took to drown out the voices of those who had drowned and, in that inebriation, inflicting pain on his children who he would otherwise cherish. In turn, those children would grow up scarred by such experiences and, like their father, they would hurt their own sons and daughters, although in different ways. And those children would grow up with different scars, perhaps scars so raw they had no sons and daughters of their own. So the war that ended long ago was still stealing away lives decades later.

Of course, he knew Phoenix was talking about herself. She didn't need to admit it. He never asked her why she lived alone in a chateau that could house dozens. He wasn't sure of the exact measurements but there had to be a kilometre squared of space in just the chateau itself. It had eight bed-rooms, two of which were suites the size of family condos. Both of the latter had been renovated back to their origi-nal glory. Phoenix alternated between them, spending the summer in the south-facing master bedroom overlooking the coast, and the winter on the opposite side of the chateau, where she could retract the drapes in the morning to see the snow-capped Alps dominating the horizon.

In their interludes, she had been content enough to tell him about herself. At first, he had found this perplexing and assumed any insight she provided was merely manipulation or distraction. Victor generally only told anyone any specif-ics about himself if he was about to kill them and it wouldn't matter what they heard. Eventually, he had come to under-stand that Phoenix was honest with him in a way he could never be with her. He found this reckless. He felt honour bound at times to remind her of the inevitable conclusion to their business relationship and so she was putting herself at an eventual disadvantage by being so candid with him. He had not, of course. While it felt unfair in the purest sense – like cheating at a game with strict rules – Victor welcomed the additions to his mental dossier on her. When the time came, there would be no rules, he had always known. That particular game was one in which Victor would gladly cheat in order to win.

Now, he wondered if she understood this too and simply didn't care. He had found her once before, after all. He knew where she lived and she wasn't prepared to move. *I only run on a treadmill*, she had once told him, *and only then if the gym has a bottle of champagne on ice next to the machine.* So, when he already knew all he needed to know about her from a professionally minded perspective, what did it matter what else he knew? Knowing where she went to school made no difference in that context. Such insight did not make her any easier to kill.

He found no sign of her anywhere in the building. There was almost nothing to say it was her home. He had hoped to get here before she learned of the massacre in Nice's Old Town. Not unexpected to arrive too late, however. She was a smart woman. She may have had misplaced faith in the kill team's abilities – nine gunmen sounded a lot on paper – but she knew the risk of going after him. While not quite at his own level of prudence, she was a careful woman. No one became such a prolific broker of contract killings by forgoing caution. He imagined her far away by now. Perhaps she'd been far away long before he saw the open shutter in a building that should have none.

He couldn't blame her. He had always considered theirs to be a temporary arrangement. Betrayal was inevitable given enough time. His mistake was not killing her in that hotel suite when he had had the chance. When he had merely been pondering the merits of such an action, she must have already decided on his fate.

Victor knew that in most fights whoever threw the first punch tended to emerge victorious.

Hers, however, had missed.

She would try again, he knew.

Whether she had that second punch ready or whether she was now hastily preparing it, he couldn't know. But it made no difference. He should already be out of the country.

Protocol instructed him to get out of Europe altogether. Maybe never come back.

You'll like Relou, she had told him during their previous time together. *He's quite the mystery man too.*

If Phoenix thought he would run, she didn't know him at all.

Victor was going nowhere.

FORTY-EIGHT

In the early years after he lured her away from politics, Maxim had shielded Zakharova from much of the violence committed by the organisation, keeping her at his side as an assistant, then adviser, until, one by one, he had her running the Brotherhood's various operations. By the time he could no longer draw a veil between her and the reality of the business, there was no longer any need. Her will was as cast iron as her stomach. She was just as ruthless as he had once been.

And though Maxim was still technically the head of the Bratva, she was a far better boss than he had ever been. It was a source of genuine pain that he could never tell her that. Because, though he knew her well enough to know she had no desire to usurp him, he could not risk inadvertently lighting a new fire of ambition inside Zakharova. She respected him. She valued his opinion. If he told her she was a better boss than he then maybe she would start seeing herself as the true boss with Maxim on a throne that belonged to her.

The thought of Zakharova as an enemy terrified him.

He felt guilty withholding rightful praise, but was comforted by the knowledge she need only wait a few more years to receive what was hers in all but name.

When she entered the drawing room of his dacha, he was pouring her a coffee from a silver pot; it had been freshly brewed by his serving staff the moment security buzzed her through the main gate.

'How did the president take the news you were no longer coming to Belarus?'

'He was predictably displeased,' she answered in her careful tone. 'But he appreciates this is a personal matter that requires our undivided attention.'

Maxim lowered a sugar cube into the coffee he had poured, and stirred with a tiny silver spoon.

She nodded her gratitude as he presented the coffee to her. 'Oksana?'

'Is distraught.'

Zakharova sipped her beverage.

'I am to blame, she tells me,' Borisyuk continued with a resigned sigh. 'I should never have had Kirill go to America in the first place.'

'What do you want to do?'

Once, Maxim had considered proposing. Despite the lack of any affection between them, he had thought about it for his daughter's sake. Oksana would have been thrilled for him to have someone, he knew. It was a silly idea, of course. Zakharova would only decline the offer, however beneficial it might be to her in the short term, and she could never respect him again after that.

He told her, 'I want to hear your thoughts.'

'Kirill was facing many years in prison. Even with the

245

best lawyers we could get him, there was only so much that could be done.'

'For all his weaknesses, he was no coward. And he loved my daughter very much, whatever their marital problems.'

'He was always indulgent,' she said, ever tactful.

'I could believe an accidental overdose of heroin, but not painkillers prescribed by a doctor.'

'I feel as though you've already made up your mind.'

He thought about this for a moment, then shook his head. 'That mind you mention would like assurances, one way or the other.'

Zakharova said, 'Tell me what you need.'

'I'm going to be busy for the rest of the week,' he told her without looking her way. 'So, you will need to take care of the specifics.'

'Of course,' she said. 'I will reach out to our friends in Washington to make sure they know we expect expedient answers, with nothing left to assumptions. Naturally, I will arrange for Kirill's corpse to be returned just as soon as they have conducted the appropriate examinations and tests.'

'Yes, yes,' Maxim said, impatient. 'I know all of that. I want our people to look into it too.'

'I'm not sure that's a good idea,' she replied in a careful tone. Though they could talk with frankness, she had no wish to insult him. 'The Americans will be doing a thorough job, I'm certain, even without my call. I don't know what else our own investigators could achieve beyond drawing avoidable attention to Kirill's activities and –' she looked towards a framed photograph of his daughter '– his associations.'

'I didn't say I wanted a team of soldiers on US soil,

knocking heads together,' he explained, losing patience. 'I don't want a hammer. I want a scalpel.'

'I see,' she said after a moment's pause.

'You disagree with my strategy?'

'I think these things have a tendency to cascade in unpredictable directions,' was her tactful answer. 'Any one of those directions can be bad for business.'

'You're right,' Maxim agreed. 'Of course you're right.' He picked up the framed photograph of Oksana smiling. 'But I need the truth. I won't lie to my daughter, and I won't leave her with any questions unanswered. Maybe I am to blame. If so, I need to know. I need someone to get those answers, no matter what.'

'I understand the position you're in,' she said, setting her cup and saucer down. 'And you'd like me to reach out to him?'

Maxim nodded.

'There's really nothing I can say to dissuade you, is there?'

'If I can take away even a single tear of her pain, I will do so whatever the complications,' he said. 'Fetch me my scalpel.'

FORTY-NINE

It was afternoon by the time Victor reached Marseille. He had abandoned the stolen car in one of the small towns along the coast and taken the train the rest of the way. There was something unkempt about the city that set it apart from its neighbours on the Riviera. Many districts were centuries old and now crumbling. It was not as picturesque as Nice, nor as friendly. It was dirty around the harbour and the many open-air markets. Crowded. The crime rate was high. It had a long history of criminal activities, once being the primary route into Europe for the heroin trade. Organised-crime killings were frequent. The city housed many rival gangs in a constant struggle for territory and supremacy. The northern districts were most known for their gang-related crime. Many neighbourhoods were considered no-go areas.

Victor had always liked it regardless. He didn't trust a city that was too clean. As much crime happened in sparkling skyscrapers as it did in dark alleyways. At least the thieves in the latter operated under no false pretences and without laws not only protecting them but encouraging them too.

The immediate environs of the station were not pleasant. He saw prostitutes and drug dealers without needing to look. Thieves were everywhere, as were signs of homelessness and addiction. Two preachers, both with megaphones, competed to be heard, one offering salvation through Jesus and the other redemption via Mohammed. They were ignored equally by passers-by.

He knew what he wanted to find and yet had no idea how to find it.

Victor thought about what Phoenix had said the last time he had seen her. Relou, the tailor with whom she had offered to arrange a fitting. They were on excellent terms. She knew him some other way beyond his current trade. She called him a mystery man. She said Victor would like him; she seemed unreasonably confident of that fact. Which told him she knew Relou in the same way she knew Victor. Did that mean theirs had been a business relationship or that they too had strayed beyond those professional boundaries? He wasn't sure. At the time he had filed the information away in his mind for potential use at an interval far into the future. He expected to have followed up on Relou at some point, but way before he had the need.

Phoenix had told him Marseille was no Paris when it came to tailors, which both helped him and made looking for Relou more difficult. Had Marseille had its own Savile Row, or rue du Faubourg Saint-Honoré, as she had remarked, he would have known exactly where to begin his search. Neither the internet nor the phone directory was going to help him. Relou was a nickname, not a given name. It meant he was irritating, which Victor found odd as she seemed so fond of him. Perhaps, while she had appeared to be forthcoming about Relou, she had still kept her professional distance. Relou might have been a name she made up in the moment so as not to reveal too much to Victor. She might have made the initial offer with sincerity and honesty, and then realised she was saying too much and held back on giving away too many details.

With so many corpses in Nice and a threat still out there, wandering directionless around Marseille was no kind of plan. Victor could fit in almost anywhere and yet he was still an outsider here. If anyone had followed him, or was looking for him here, he was at a considerable disadvantage. He wouldn't know their faces until they gave themselves away. If they were locals, the difficulty in picking them out of a crowd would significantly increase.

He had no choice. He searched the city for tailor's shops, for Relou.

Any he found were shut on a Sunday, of course. He would need to come back in the morning. Still, finding them now meant time saved tomorrow. Marseille looked more welcoming in the morning sunshine. Like any city, it had extreme contrasts between its districts and neighbourhoods, rich and poor, but here in the centre the poverty was pushed to one side. Hidden away, almost, so as not to upset the tourists. And like any city, its retail centre was vast. Victor ignored the shopping malls, department stores and the large stores along the main thoroughfares. Instead, he looked along the side streets. In his experience, the best artisans were small outfits who lacked the means to pay the extortionate rents of the prime retail centres and had no need to do so as well.

Discerning customers willing to pay premium prices for excellent quality were also willing to walk a little further to make their purchases.

Globalism spared no one. Once there had been dozens of bespoke tailors of renown stretching across the Riviera. Now, such artisans were rare. International brands had swallowed up almost all of the fine independent establishments.

Relou would have his own store, bought with the proceeds from his previous career, and Victor could not imagine a tailor Phoenix spoke highly of belonging to a soulless corporate brand.

By the time the sun was setting, Victor stopped in front of a tailor's with no storefront, no well-presented mannequins on display. The simple signage showed the silhouette of a man in a suit above text reading *DEPUIS 1907*.

The lack of a storefront had obvious privacy and security advantages. The street itself was pedestrianised and narrow. Shadows had nowhere to wait and watch. No road meant no drive-by attacks and no vehicles parked up with a kill team waiting inside.

If this was Relou's shop, he had chosen well.

Victor intended to tell him so in the morning.

After performing countersurveillance, Victor slept in the worst hotel he could find. A rundown, filthy establishment in one of the most crime-infested areas of the city, where the centuries-old buildings had succumbed to so much subsidence and decay over the years that while there was maybe two metres distance between the buildings at ground level, the guttering of each rooftop almost touched. Drugs were sold openly on the street outside the hotel and escorts waited for the elevator while he took the stairs to his room. In other circumstances he would have stayed up until dawn and slept until noon. Instead, he slept while he could.

Another day, he decied, was all he could risk. Any longer and he might as well hand himself in to the authorities. One more day before leaving the city, then the country and finally the continent. He wouldn't plan his route so no one could intercept him on the way. He would let randomness decide the specifics later.

If he didn't find Phoenix soon, he never would.

FIFTY

Marseille looked more welcoming in the morning sunshine. Victor was performing countersurveillance before the stores had opened, continuing to watch out for other kill teams as well as the security services as he bought new clothes and disposed of his old ones. The tailor's he figured could be Relou's was along a narrow street shadowed by the tall buildings on either side. A café stood on the corner, followed by several fashion boutiques with large and elaborate signage that blocked any view of the tailor's sign until Victor was almost in front of it. Each storefront was narrow and yet the tailor's was narrower, consisting of no more than a door painted in glossy black and a brass intercom panel. He turned side-on to let pedestrians walk past him. The street was only wide enough for two people without having to squeeze or stand aside, or a single person and their shopping bags. He removed his sunglasses and hung them by the arm from his jacket's breast pocket. Shadowed from the sun, he was cool as waited a moment to ensure no threats appeared at either end of the street.

Time was not on his side otherwise he would take more extensive countersurveillance precautions. The longer he remained here, both in the country and in the region, the more dangerous it became. Leaving many corpses in the same place was never a good idea. There would be enormous pressure to find the perpetrator. Maybe a whole task force would be set up to find him. Even the best forensic experts would take days to fully understand the scene of the crime, which was the only upside. Initially, it would be hard to put the pieces together. By the point they knew for sure he was the only perpetrator, he needed to be far away. He intended to be on another continent in a place without extradition treaties with France. Then, months on the move. He had a reserve of identities and he would burn through them all by the time he deemed he was far enough away and enough time had gone by that he could go back to work.

He realised that without Phoenix to broker his contracts, he wasn't even sure how he would return to his profession. Years had gone by since he'd had contracted for multiple brokers. Though he still remembered the contact details for some of them, there were no guarantees such communication channels were still open. There was a good chance the brokers from his past were now dead or had moved on to other lines of work. Reaching out to one or more came with all sorts of risk. Before Phoenix, he had done some black-bag work for various intelligence agencies. Those handlers all thought he was dead now and he could not envision opening himself back up to the additional threats of working for them again – threats that had led to him needing to appear dead in the first place. Although, he could imagine the look on their faces should he turn up on their doorstep risen from the grave.

Problems for another time. Victor never looked too far into the future. He had to survive today before he could move his focus to tomorrow and the cycle began anew.

He used a knuckle to press the buzzer. He stood in a relaxed posture, head tilted down to hide his face from any watching cameras. While his new suit would no doubt fall way short of the quality provided here, it made him look respectable and smart. Like a customer.

'*Oui*?' asked the voice that came through the little speaker on the panel.

'I have an appointment,' he said. 'I'm here to pick up my new suit.'

A gamble. Whoever was peering at him would not recognise him as a customer, although it could be some weeks between the last fitting and the suit being finished. In his experience the best bespoke tailors worked to precise schedules. They did not admit walk-ins. They were simply too busy to be ready to measure and serve someone without an appointment. So he figured it was likely pick-ups would work in the same way. If no one was scheduled to pick up their outfit within the next half-hour, confusion would follow and then questions he could not hope to answer and within a few moments the ruse would be over. If a customer was due to collect their suit, then—

The buzzer sounded and the door unlocked.

Victor used a shoulder to push it open and stepped inside.

FIFTY-ONE

A small vestibule lay behind the door and narrowed into a short hallway, leading to the shop proper. The vestibule had enough space for a hat rack and coat stand, while the hallway was wide enough for a single person only. Victor took a few steps and felt boxed in and vulnerable. An enemy could appear in the opening ahead and Victor would have nowhere to go and nothing he could do about it.

No enemy did appear, although a man carrying a high-end garment bag entered the hallway as Victor was halfway along it.

He had neat white hair and a red face. Blue eyes peered over flabby cheeks at Victor. The man wore a navy three-piece, cream shirt and orange tie. The folds of his neck bulged over the collar. His mouth formed a thin smile of disapproval.

He stepped towards Victor, filling the hallway ahead of him. There was no way for them to pass one another unless the guy ducked and Victor vaulted over him.

'Well?' the man said, impatient.

Victor understood such people. Entitlement came in many forms and all were ugly in his experience. He knew exactly how it would play out if Victor failed to give way. The man would never backtrack himself. He was used to getting his own way and would be perplexed by the audacity of someone like Victor not immediately doing as they were told. The man would have no plan B, of course, because he had never needed one before. The entitlement would become obstinacy and should Victor still fail to step aside then that obstinacy would become outrage. At that point, the man would try moving Victor out of the way. He couldn't know all the many ways Victor could make sure that would be met with immediate remorse.

In Victor's experience, no one rethought their behaviour faster than someone in sudden and surprising agony.

He could dislocate the man's arm with almost no effort.

He could snap fingers one by one.

He could manipulate pressure points the man didn't even know existed.

There were all sorts of ways to inflict enough pain for the man to reconsider his entire worldview.

Victor stepped back into the vestibule.

The man released a sighing exhale. 'About time.'

He walked on by, the world turning to his designs exactly as it always had, and Victor let him.

The shop floor, albeit small, still had plenty of space for presentation. A scattering of round tables displayed shirts, ties, handkerchiefs and cufflinks. Further displays aligned the walls. Two high-backed leather armchairs sat in one corner with a small coffee table between them. A thick carpet the colour of caramel spread across the floor. Persian rugs lay across it in various places. The wood of the tables and chairs had the same dark hue, almost black except where the polished surfaces reflected the light in rich mahogany. The display tables had drawers with bright brass fittings.

In the silence, Victor heard a clock ticking. He saw none so it had to be a large clock in a back room or a small one beneath the counter. Either way, a device made of glass and polished brass and wood: no plastic, no electronics. The ticking of the clock had a solid, heavy resonance. There was something reassuring about the sound. As though he had stepped back in time to a simpler, more civilised age. The world advanced at a frightening rate outside of the tailor's shop. Here, though, time stood still and he was glad of it. Given the choice, he might never step back outside and return to his own time.

Then it occurred to him that maybe there was no clock at all and the sound was being emitted from a device of some kind. A tablet or a laptop. Like ambient music to set a mood. He didn't like not knowing the truth. It felt a cruel trick to make him guess and doubt reality.

In one corner of the shop floor stood a headless mannequin dressed in a Napoleonic-era soldier's jacket. He assumed it was authentic. An antique, centuries old.

'I'm in the process of restoring it,' a man said, stepping on to the shop floor. 'Musket balls through here –' he touched his left shoulder '– here –' he touched the sleeve of his right arm '– and here –' he touched his left breast.

'Ouch,' Victor said.

The tailor wore a stone-brown three-piece suit, a dark red tie and shirt of brilliant white. The jacket was buttoned and overlaid with a length of measuring tape that hung around his neck. He had a beard equal parts blond and grey. His hair was cut short to a fine stubble across the back and sides, and left a little longer on top, where it was thin and wispy. He wore round glasses with dark frames set low on his nose. Green eyes peered over the rims at Victor.

'If you look closely,' the tailor began, 'you can see how the threads differ. Assuming you know what you're looking for. Displayed behind glass and standing a metre away you won't see the difference.'

Victor responded with a polite nod. He glanced at the closest display table with its mix of conservative colours and ostentatious tones.

The tailor took a small step towards him. 'Monsieur Belouche to collect his navy blazer?'

'Not exactly.'

'I don't think you're Madame Monfleur here for her husband's repaired tuxedo.' He paused. 'So you must instead be that husband, although your tuxedo is going to look a little ... bulbous around your midriff. Congratulations on the diet. Perhaps you might have let me know to bring in the waist before today.'

'Bulbous is fine,' Victor said. 'I like a little extra room to manoeuvre.'

'In which case, maybe I can direct you to the nearest sportswear store for a tracksuit. You're not Monfleur's husband any more than you are Belouche.'

'I'm someone else,' Victor said.

The tailor pursed his lips in thought. He kept his palms together in front of his stomach. The two thumbs tapped against one another. It was a relaxed, unthreatening posture.

TOM WOOD

Victor often used the same one. Hands before the abdomen meant arms already bent at the elbow and muscles already activated. If those limbs had to move with sudden speed – whether to defend or to attack – they would be faster than ones dangling limp at the sides. Those hands were better placed to strike or grab or guard. Maybe a habit from the tailor's previous life or old instincts returning because he sensed Victor was a threat. Or just as likely a comfortable posture.

'I don't have an appointment,' Victor told him. 'I wish I did. I wish I were here to measure up for a suit, but sadly I don't have the need for a truly good one.'

'Everyone has the need for a good suit. I don't make *good* suits, however. When you wear one I have cut for you then you won't want to take it off again. When you lie in bed at night you will dream of wearing it.'

'Let me rephrase,' Victor said. 'I would dearly like one. But, for all my flaws, I will not knowingly waste such a garment.'

'What do you mean, waste?'

'Don't wear suede boots when there's a storm outside.'

The tailor did not cast his gaze downwards before he said, 'I'm afraid we cannot make exceptions for anyone under any circumstances. We are fully booked at all times. The only time we have a free spot is far into the future.' He looked past Victor to that distant time. 'If you would like to make an appointment to be measured then you will need to call us. In the morning, preferably. Please note, it will be many weeks before we can accommodate you for a fitting.'

'I was assured by a mutual acquaintance that an exception could be made for me.'

'Then they were incorrect or you have misunderstood,' the tailor said. 'Everything we do here has to be carefully scheduled. Every fitting, every thread of the needle. We never make exceptions, even for exceptional circumstances.'

'Not even for your old broker?' Victor asked.

FIFTY-TWO

There was almost no reaction and yet Victor detected it nonetheless. The tailor *was* Relou. His expression showed no change and his body language remained as it had been throughout the interaction: still and stilted. It was in the way he answered. They had been speaking at a certain rhythm, each responding to the other without hesitation.

This question, however, created the slightest of pauses before Relou answered, 'Not even for my mother.' At last, Relou moved. A polite step forward and a polite yet stern gesture towards the exit. 'If you please.'

'That's the unfortunate thing, Relou,' Victor said. 'I don't please.'

Relou paused for a moment and said, 'How do you know that name?'

'Do many people call you Relou?'

He shook his head. 'Only one.'

He held Victor's gaze. In another environment, he imagined Relou would take a quick glance to his left and to his right. Here, in his own tailor's shop, there was no need. Relou knew the layout blindfolded.

'You need to leave here now,' Relou said in a tone that was unthreatening, and yet Victor understood the threat because he was going nowhere.

In the same unthreatening tone, Victor said, 'I'm afraid I won't do that.'

'I'm not making a request.'

'You're squeezed between bigger stores on a thin strip of buildings so there's no workshop in the back. It's downstairs then, in the basement. The woman who answered the buzzer is there now.'

'So?' Relou said.

'Does she know what you did before you bought this business? How you had the money to buy it?'

Relou was silent.

'Then forget what you're thinking,' Victor said.

'You don't know what I'm thinking.'

'I know you let me through the door because someone's coming to collect their new suit within the next thirty minutes. If the rest of your customers are like the one I met in the hallway then the one due within the next half an hour is not going to like being told to come back tomorrow to give you time to clean up this room. Same goes for any fittings this afternoon that will need to be cancelled.' Victor glanced at the carpet. 'You'll never get the blood out. How long will it take to get a replacement put down? And that's without the very real chance you don't get away with it or the woman in the basement can't cope with the glimpse at the real you.' He paused a second. 'You need to think this through very carefully.'

Relou was thinking it through, Victor could see that.

He had no reason to believe Relou had been an impetuous professional and yet he had been out of the game for a long time. Evaluating actions and consequences might have been second nature once. Now, that skill might have been lost entirely. Relou might only think in immediacies, so Victor felt it pertinent to help him through that thought process.

'It's not like you carry a gun on you these days, is it?' Victor asked. 'It would ruin the cut of your suit, which would not be a particularly good advertisement for your talents in tailoring.' He rotated his head a little to look around the room. 'You keep one close, of course. Not in here. I'm guessing there's at least an antechamber out back before the stairs lead down to the basement. If so, that's where I'd keep it. If I were you, I mean. If, like you, I had retired I would not now be running a tailor's shop or anything else.'

Relou said, 'Then where would you be?'

'Once, I was naïve enough to think I might teach languages.'

'Naïve? How so?'

'I was reminded that none of us get to walk away without repercussions just because we would like to.' He touched his sternum with two fingers. Beneath his shirt lay a small scar. 'I was shot by an Accuracy International AW.'

At last, Relou's expression made an abrupt change. He was sceptical. 'Then you were born under a lucky star. A round from such a rifle should have cut you in half.'

'I don't believe in luck,' Victor told him. 'But I believed in windowpanes comprised of alternate layers of glass and polymer.'

'Believed?' Relou asked.

'The manufacturers of such windowpanes claimed they

were bulletproof,' Victor explained. 'Again, I had succumbed to a naïve fantasy. I should have tested the claim.'

'There's no such thing as bulletproof,' Relou said.

Victor nodded. 'I was young back then.' He paused. Thought about that statement, then clarified with, 'Younger.' He paused again. 'I'm not here because of what you were, I'm here because of who you know. I only want to talk about Phoenix and then leave. Five minutes of your day. How you want to spend those five minutes is entirely up to you.'

Relou was thinking about those five minutes, Victor could see. Only Relou's old way of thinking had returned. No longer a tailor, he was a professional once more. He was running through the various potential actions and consequences. Maybe a little slower than he might have done in his professional prime, but the same wheels were turning. No one forgot how to ride a bicycle.

'So,' Victor said after leaving an appropriate amount of time for Relou to think it all through, 'what's it going to be?'

Relou answered.

FIFTY-THREE

A little before six a.m. local time, a Gulfstream G650ER jet landed at a small private airfield in Minnesota. The thirty-metre-long plane had flown direct from St Petersburg, a journey of over seven thousand kilometres that took almost fourteen hours. The G650ER had a crew of four: pilot, co-pilot and two stewards. It cost almost $12,000 per hour to charter the plane, with a minimum $200,000 upfront fee. To buy new, the jet was just south of seventy million USD. The company who owned the plane had a modest fleet of three that were based in Eastern Europe and mainly operated on the continent and throughout the Middle East, flying wealthy individuals, corporate clients, oligarchs and oil barons, celebrities, and sometimes royalty. While transatlantic flights were not a cornerstone of the firm's business, they were not uncommon.

Most of their clients were regulars who wanted to bypass the inconvenience of commercial air terminals, have a bespoke travel experience to their own schedule, and make that whole experience far more enjoyable. Some wanted privacy more than anything else. Others had so much money they didn't know what else to spend it on. A few chartered jets just so they could keep their teacup Chihuahuas with them in their seats.

A profitable business that was bought outright in a sale finished only that morning, purchased by a shell corporation who paid well over market value to convince the owners to sell with extraordinary haste. It all happened so fast the four-person crew had not yet been told they had a new, anonymous owner. They would all keep their jobs. At least for the time being, because the new owner only needed the jets for a single purpose. Specifically, the new owner wanted the company's G650ER.

The plane could accommodate up to nineteen passengers in the height of modern luxury. There were leather seats and plush carpeting. The food available was restaurant quality and the wine list hand picked by an expert sommelier. On this trip, all ignored. The only thing that mattered was the Gulfstream's ultra-long range of 7,500 kilometres. It could fly direct from Russia to the US without the need to refuel at Heathrow, avoiding the inevitable delay, and the additional scrutiny that came with it.

The entire luxury plane had been used to take a single person across the Atlantic, who had brought his own food and declined all offers of wine or other refreshments, speaking maybe two dozen words in total during the long flight. Almost all of which were 'no, thank you' or 'I'm fine'. He didn't sleep. He didn't watch the recently released movies. He didn't flirt with the stewards who had come to expect ugly innuendos from those with too much wealth and too little decency. He only scrolled through documents on a tablet computer and made handwritten notes in a small notebook.

What work he was doing, the stewards had no clue. If he paused at all during the flight, they did not notice.

Cold air blew inside when one of the stewards opened the exit and stood waiting with a polite smile, trying not to shiver.

If the passenger noticed, he did not hurry to depart, engrossed as he was in his note making. When he had finished in his own time, he stood, collected his modest suit-case, and departed with a polite, 'Thank you.'

Calls had been made in advance of his arrival to ensure a specific custom agent handled the processing, which con-sisted of waving the man through with only the slimmest of checks.

With that out of the way, Maxim Borisyuk's scalpel was free to do his job.

FIFTY-FOUR

Victor was correct. A gun would ruin the cut of Relou's suit, which was why he carried a knife instead. He had been out of the profession for a long time, and if he had lost some speed, he was still fast. The palms held together in front of his abdomen broke apart as he adjusted his feet into a fighting stance, the left hand extending forward and the right darting into a pocket to withdraw the weapon: a small folding knife that extended out in a flash of reflecting light.

One of the round tables displaying a multitude of ties stood between them. Victor had been careful in his positioning. Relou could not simply attack with the table blocking him.

'You're going to ruin your suit,' Victor said.

He took a small step to his left in response to Relou doing the same, keeping the table between them and denying the tailor the opportunity to clear the obstacle. Relou was still feeling him out, unwilling to commit to the attack just yet. The table prevented a straight line to Victor and so any

269

attack would need to go around it, negating any chance of speed and catching Victor off guard.

'I can read your thoughts,' he said. 'Don't forget you're retired. You've spent the last few years using scissors and sewing needles, not fighting knives. However good you were, that's not you now.'

'Do you really think you're the first killer to show up at my door?' Relou asked, continuing to circle the table towards Victor and Victor continuing to circle away from him. 'My retirement has not been as quiet as you might think.'

'I'm not here to kill you,' Victor assured. 'I'm looking for Phoenix. She set me up. Not for the first time, granted. But this is the second and final time that will ever happen.'

'If you came here thinking that I would betray my former broker then not only are you wrong about me but you have no idea about her either.'

'You don't need to worry about repercussions from her; you need to worry about me.'

A mocking smile formed. 'You know even less about me than you did before if you think I will respond to threats.'

'I'm speaking in facts,' Victor said. 'But my preference is to keep this as civil as possible. You tell me what I need to know and I go on my way. You carry on life as a tailor as if none of this took place. Then who knows? Maybe one day I come back and get measured up.'

Relou's expression did not change. It was one of focus and intent. He circled the table with his gaze locked on Victor. There was no reaction to Victor's words. He was thinking, though, that was clear. Weighing up the proposal versus the alternative and trying to deduce the veracity of it. Could he trust Victor?

No, naturally was the answer. Because Relou understood Victor as much as Victor understood him.

Relou revealed nothing in his expression, but his movements gave him away. His slow side-steps to the left became a little less soft as he shifted more of his weight across to his left foot as it found the carpet.

'It doesn't have to be like this,' Victor said.

Relou wasn't listening. Then his side-steps became a little wider as he prepared to launch into the attack.

'Don't do it,' Victor said.

The intercom buzzed.

Relou stopped circling. Victor did the same.

Neither moved. Neither blinked.

The same voice that had answered Victor's own ring now spoke again. He heard it both faint and disembodied from the intercom outside and quiet and echoed from the workshop below.

'*Oui?*'

Victor could not discern the answer, then the door buzzed a moment later. Someone was here to collect their garment. Madame Monfleur or Monsieur Belouche, of course.

Relou gave Victor a look.

There was a question in that look and a suggestion, both expressed without the need for words.

Victor thought for a second, then answered the question and agreed to the suggestion with a nod.

In a fast, smooth motion Relou folded the knife away and slipped it back into his pocket. Victor stepped away to the nearest corner and took a seat in one of the high-backed armchairs.

He imagined himself as a customer waiting to collect a

perfectly fitted charcoal suit. He adopted a relaxed pose, elbows on the arms of the chairs and his legs crossed at the ankles. Relou returned to his original posture, palms together before his stomach.

Victor heard the entrance close and footsteps in the hallway before a woman stepped on to the shop floor. He kept her in his peripheral vision while he thought about the suit he was picking up. A bespoke suit, expensive. One he had been fitted for three times over a number of weeks after a number of weeks on the waiting list for that first fitting. How many weeks had he waited to collect it today, he wondered? Was he still excited by it or was he impatient to get his hands on what had taken so much time and cost so much money? This might be a gift to himself or a reward for getting that promotion, or was he so wealthy that all his suits were bespoke, each costing thousands of euros? Not the latter, he decided, because the suit he wore now was off the rack. He found a certain pleasure in creating such characters, imagining himself in different guises, living out a different life. Like the fantasy of reading his book on the beach, it was better than nothing.

The woman glanced his way as she entered before fixing her attention on Relou, who stood waiting to receive her. She wore dark jeans and a black blazer. Her shoes were flat and comfortable. Long auburn hair was bunched up into a bun. Brown leather gloves covered her hands. The garments were simple yet refined and expensive. No make-up that he could detect.

Madame Monfleur, Victor thought.

Then he thought again, considering the simple outfit she wore would be the perfect attire for a professional desiring to be smart yet not stand out. Her hair up prevented it getting in her way or being used against her. The gloves provided an obvious benefit.

Relou said, 'May I help you?'

She looked Victor's way for a moment before answering. 'I need to talk to you. Privately.'

'I'm afraid I'm very busy at the moment,' Relou said in a polite, regretful tone. 'I have a customer to attend to.' He gestured to Victor. 'Perhaps you could come back later? Tomorrow? I don't have the time to assist new customers without a proper appointment.'

'You need to make time for me.'

Little by little, Victor adjusted the way he sat, uncrossing his legs and planting the soles of his feet firm against the floor. He leaned forward, straightening his back so his head lay directly above his hips.

Relou gestured to the exit. 'If you please.'

She looked towards Victor, then back at Relou, and drew a gun from under her jacket.

It was a slick, snapping movement, her right hand darting to her waist where she had a belt pouch, and snapping back again clutching a compact SIG that she pointed at Relou.

He did not react.

She said, 'Now do you have time for me?' then to Victor, 'Stay in the chair if you want to live through this.'

Her gaze was on Relou, so she did not see the gun in Victor's own hand.

Only after he said, 'Oh, I'm going to live through this regardless,' did she look back his way. He had his FN aimed at her centre mass. 'You might too if you can hold your nerve.'

She released a heavy sigh of disappointment. Then smiled as she shook her head in disbelief. Victor could see she was annoyed at herself for being caught out.

She kept the SIG pointed at Relou and asked him, 'Who's your friend?'

'He's not my friend. He came here to kill me. Is that why you're here too?'

She said, 'I'm asking the questions here.'

'I think we all are,' Victor said. 'So perhaps we can prevent a bad situation getting worse and just answer the questions people put to us?'

Relou, staring down the barrel of the SIG, agreed with a nod. 'Sounds reasonable to me.'

The woman thought about this for a moment, then shrugged. 'Sure, why not? But I'll start.' She asked Victor, 'Who are you and why were you about to kill this tailor?'

'I had no intention of killing him. I only want information. It was he who was about to initiate violence. As for who I am: call me JT. Your turn.'

'I'm Salomé,' she said. 'I'm looking for Phoenix.'

'So is he,' Relou told her.

She turned Victor's way, her eyebrows pinched closer in surprise. 'Don't tell me,' she said, breaking into a smile, 'Phoenix set you up as well.'

FIFTY-FIVE

Beneath the shop floor lay a workshop where fabrics were cut and sewn. Victor had no idea how many different kinds of fabric he saw, but there had to be thousands. A huge variety of threads, colours and textures.

An old woman, small and hunched, looked surprised when Relou descended into the workshop along with Victor and Salomé. Relou took her to one side and told her to take the rest of the day off. Victor could not hear her exact words of protest. He saw her expressions of dismay, however.

She passed him, shaking her head and muttering to herself. They stood in silence for the two minutes it took her to leave. She slammed the door on her way out.

Relou explained, 'She's worked here since she was a child. For the very first tailor, his successors, and now me. One of the reasons we operate to such inflexible schedules is because she can't sew very well any more and I don't have the heart to let her go.'

Salomé's SIG was back in its holster. She kept her hand

275

near it as she paced around the workshop. 'Cute story but I really don't give a shit.'

Victor's own weapon was similarly put away. He felt no need to keep his hand near it. 'Watch your language, please.'

She cast him a look, expecting a punchline. When none came, she shrugged, then said to Relou, 'Where's Phoenix?'

He had a resigned expression. He was still loyal to his former broker and yet he understood his predicament only too well. When it had been just him and Victor then Relou had been willing to take a risk. Against Victor and Salomé, Relou knew when to back down.

'I don't know where she is,' he said.

Salomé released a heavy sigh and shook her head.

Victor was watching her actions more than he was watching Relou.

'I know where she lives,' the tailor explained.

Salomé said, 'We all know where she lives.'

Victor told him, 'She's not there. Which is why I'm here now. Anonymity has always been her best protection but it offers no defence against those who already know her. She doesn't strike me as the kind of person who would go on the run. She's not going to spend her life moving from one hotel to the next.'

'She'll have a safe house,' Salomé added.

'Exactly,' Victor agreed.

Relou's gaze alternated between the two of them. 'Why would she tell me where such a safe house is located?'

'Because she wasn't always this careful,' Victor said. 'No one begins this life knowing the extent of the precautions they need to take to survive it. I didn't. I had to learn on the job. I'm sure you were the same.' He glanced at Salomé. 'You, too.'

She shrugged with her eyebrows.

'She won't have said, *This is where my safe house is located,*' Victor continued. 'But she will have said something that can help us. Maybe she took a trip and let slip that she might want to live there or retire there or that she's seen a villa she's considering buying.'

'That would have been a very long time ago,' Relou said. 'Who knows if she still owns any such place?'

'That's for us to find out,' Victor answered.

Salomé growled in frustration. 'Just tell us what you know. Stop stalling.'

Relou was silent.

She said, 'Or do you want me to go and bring back your assistant? I'm sure she hasn't got far.'

'Leave her out of this,' he said.

Salomé paced around the workshop, coming to a stop at one of several sewing machines. 'Maybe I'll put her hand under this and we can see how many times she screams before you find your tongue.'

Relou, so calm up until now despite the situation, reddened with rage. He was thinking of the folding knife in his pocket and Salomé's throat, Victor was sure.

So he said, 'That's not going to happen.' Then to Salomé, 'I mean it.'

'We're on the same side here,' she said. 'We don't need to play nice.'

Relou's gaze was still on Salomé and her throat.

Victor told him, 'The old woman will be left alone but you need to give us something.'

'Why didn't you use the gun?' Relou asked him. 'Before, I mean. When it was just us upstairs.'

277

'Professional courtesy,' Victor said.

'And?'

'And I didn't want to coerce you until it was absolutely necessary. I prefer to be civil if possible. Which is why your assistant is perfectly safe whatever happens here.' He paused. 'But if you don't tell us what you know about Phoenix – and I know you know something – then it will be your hand under that needle.'

Salomé smiled.

Relou exhaled and nodded. 'Some years ago, long before I retired and in the early days of working with Phoenix, we weren't so careful. As you said, you have to learn these things on the job. We met in person to discuss contracts. We met in person for other things, too. She would tell me about the crumbling chateau she was restoring. I would tell her about the tailor's shop I wanted to buy. We trusted each other then. I still trust her now, which is why I find it hard to believe what you've told me. Anyway, she had a little getaway, as she called it, for when she needed peace and quiet.'

Salomé said, 'Where?'

'A cottage,' Relou answered. 'Inland, maybe one hundred kilometres. Near the village of Goult. I was only there one time.'

Relou bowed his head, ashamed.

Salomé looked to Victor, then gestured at Relou. A subtle gesture, asking a question with her hand, close to the gun at her side.

Victor shook his head, then asked Relou for more specifics on the cottage's location. Despite the single visit, the tailor remembered enough details for Victor to feel confident they would find it in a sparsely populated area.

Salomé shrugged, then said, 'Car share? I figure since we're in the same situation we may as well pool resources. Cover more ground, and so on.'

'Makes sense.'

Salomé headed up the stairs, calling back down to Relou: 'I'm sure we don't need to remind you that it would be a mistake to try and warn her.'

In a quiet voice he replied, 'I wouldn't even know how to warn her.'

'Remember you had no choice,' Victor told him. 'And if it helps, I'll make sure Phoenix understands that.'

The tailor nodded. His eyes remained downcast. 'Give her a chance to explain,' he said. 'You might feel differently if you understand why.'

Victor said, 'I don't care why,' and headed up the stairs.

FIFTY-SIX

He found Salomé waiting outside the tailor's shop. She had lit a cigarette. 'Do you think he's telling the truth?' she asked. 'About the cottage?'

'I think you convinced him of the need for veracity.'

'He would have been more convinced if you hadn't stopped me bringing back his assistant.'

'I didn't stop you,' Victor corrected. 'And it hardly matters now. What's done is done. And I need answers.'

'*Mais bien sûr*,' she said, blowing out smoke. 'I didn't recognise you at first. When I stepped into the shop just now you might as well have been a different person to the one I saw yesterday morning at that café.'

Victor pictured the woman seated outside the café. 'You wore a wide-brimmed hat.'

'A simple misdirection,' she continued. 'People see the hat, not me.' She wrinkled her nose. 'I preferred the beard. You looked more distinguished. Like a history professor. Now you look like a thug.'

'Thank you,' he said, in a tone she didn't understand.

He stroked his jaw, thinking of the beard he wore when working to do the exact same thing as Salomé's hat. Effective, but he should have noticed. He should have paid more attention. To his shame, his guard had been lowered by Phoenix's act. He had to give credit where it was due. Phoenix had to have been setting him up since the first time they met, knowing the day would come eventually for them to part ways and understanding such a betrayal could only be built from solid foundations.

'I was supposed to meet Phoenix too,' Salomé said. 'Which means she set us both up to die that day. You walked straight past me into the café and I thought nothing of it. Then, to my surprise, you walked straight back out and crossed the street and entered the office building. At first, it seemed unimportant. A stranger who changed his mind about coffee. The gunshots began a few moments later. Muted. Suppressed, naturally. I was slow to understand what I was witnessing.' She paused to rethink her words. 'Slow to understand *why*, I mean. I think it must have been the owner who realised next what those noises were, although he seemed unsure of himself. Civilians are so reluctant to believe it when civilisation is shown to be an illusion, are they not? When a man plunged headfirst into the road, there was no further denial.'

Victor listened.

'I thought you'd overstayed your welcome when you had not left and the police turned up. Which was when I decided to take my leave. Otherwise we might have had this conversation yesterday.' She paused. 'How did you know it was an ambush?'

'Open shutters,' he answered. 'That weren't open the day before.'

She thought about this for a second, then smiled wider. 'Thank you for saving both our lives.'

'How did you know about Relou?'

'Because I've worked for Phoenix for a very long time. She talks too much, no? That's what I thought then. Now, I realise it was all part of the act. The benevolent broker. No threat to anyone.'

He said, 'She fooled me too.'

She gestured. 'My car is this way.'

They headed down the narrow street, stepping around or stepping aside for the other pedestrians as the need arose. The breeze blew the smoke from Salomé's cigarette into Victor's face and the feeling was better than any sea breeze.

At the intersection ahead, a Peugeot was parked against the kerb. A man sat behind the wheel and a second man stood next to the car. He was south of thirty, tall and lean, in a baseball cap and hooded sweatshirt zipped halfway up. Cargo trousers. Practical walking shoes. Victor pictured a knife in one of the trouser pockets and a pistol hidden under the sweatshirt.

'You didn't tell me you're part of a crew.'

Salomé shrugged and tossed away the cigarette. 'You didn't ask. Is that a problem?'

'That depends,' he answered, 'whether you're in charge.'

She huffed and smiled as if there was no possible alternative. Maybe there wasn't one. Maybe she would never take orders from another person.

'JT's with us now,' she told the guy at the car. 'Same objective so be friendly. I need to make a call.'

She stepped away and fished out a phone. A clear sky and bright sun made the sandy paving stones shine a blinding white. The guy leaning against the car had on a pair of sunglasses.

He took them off when Victor drew nearer.

'I'm Miller.'

Victor nodded.

An American, Miller was about Victor's height, which was mostly in the torso. His legs were a little too short for his frame. He wouldn't be fast on his feet. His arms were a little too short too, so he would be more effective at extreme close range than his height might otherwise suggest. The hooded sweatshirt gave him a false appearance of bulk. He had narrow shoulders and thin legs.

Miller said, 'Pleased to meet you and all that. We're going to be close, I can tell already. Whatever you need, I'm your guy. Salomé says to be friendly then I'll treat you like you're one of us. Whatever you need, I'm your guy.'

Victor said, 'I don't need you to be friendly. Our intentions are aligned, that's all.'

'Everyone needs a friend,' Miller said.

'Not me. I work alone.'

'I can tell. You're giving off all kinds of leave-me-the-hell-alone vibes.'

'Don't blaspheme.'

Miller played with his sunglasses. 'Saying "hell" is blaspheming now?'

'It always has been,' Victor answered. 'So stop saying it.'

'Sure thing, padre. Like I told you: we're here to be your friends. You want us to mind our Ps and Qs? We'll do it. We'll even repent our sins and get baptised and join the Red

Cross if that's what you want us to do. Not just friends, but best friends. The kind of friends who do whatever you want.'

'Who's the guy behind the wheel?'

'Boulanger,' Miller said. 'He's French.'

Victor raised an eyebrow. 'Miller and *Baker*?'

'Not our real names, obviously.'

'Obviously,' Victor said. 'Why would friends use their real names?'

'So we can stay friends,' Miller said. 'What's your real name again?'

'Touché.'

Miller stood up straight. 'Look, this is far from your idea of a good time. I get that. We all would prefer to be somewhere else doing something else. That's not the way the cards folded, so why don't we just try and make the best of it, yeah? It's what Salomé wants, so it's what Salomé gets, okay? You refuse to play nice and Salomé comes down on me and Boulanger like a ton of bricks. Which means me and Boulanger have to come down on you like a ton of bricks. Which makes it two tons of bricks coming down. That's a shitload of bricks.'

'Don't curse,' Victor said.

Miller held up his red palms. 'Ps and Qs, gotcha. My bad.' He opened up the passenger door and motioned for Victor to climb inside.

'I'll ride in the back.'

Miller shrugged to say he didn't understand why but that it didn't matter, and moved to open up the back for Victor, who sat behind the passenger seat that Miller climbed into.

'I'm Boulanger,' Boulanger said.

He looked at Victor in the rear-view mirror. Boulanger

was a little older than Miller, although still young too. He had a far larger frame packed with mass. His shoulders were so wide and his limbs so thick that Victor wasn't sure how the man could even fit inside the car.

'Boulanger's our muscle,' Miller said with a smirk.

'No kidding.'

His face was red and shiny, and his eyes bloodshot. Victor pictured the heart beneath the massive chest beating at a ferocious rate just to keep so much size sitting still. Boulanger said nothing further, which made sense. If he talked as much as Miller then they would get nothing done.

A long time ago, Victor might have mistaken this to be an ambush in the making and pre-empted it with his own attack, but he understood more now than he had in those early days as a professional. He had learned how to read people, to spot the subtle signs of coming violence, and Miller and Boulanger showed no signs at all. They were both relaxed and a little bored. And most tellingly of all, they were tired. Boulanger was stifling a yawn and Miller let out a sigh of exertion as he lifted off his cap to scratch at his scalp. People about to murder someone were never tired, whatever their physical fatigue. Adrenal hormones saw to that. Had Miller and Boulanger planned to kill him, they would be mentally and physically alert, possibly restless and fidgeting with all the nervous energy.

Whatever this was, it wasn't a prelude to violence.

Victor was pleasantly surprised. He didn't trust these two men and he didn't trust Salomé either – because he trusted no one, least of all fellow assassins – and yet he was content to let it play out for now.

Finished on the phone, Salomé climbed into the back. 'How are you boys getting along?'

'Like a house on fire,' Miller said.

Salomé said, '*Allons-y*,' and gave Boulanger a little back-handed tap on the arm.

Boulanger responded with a nod and started up the Peugeot.

Miller seemed excited to be on the move. 'Let's go get this b—' He stopped himself, then turned to Victor. 'Ps and Qs, right?'

Victor nodded in answer.

Miller said to Boulanger, 'We got to watch our language around this guy. No taking the Lord's name in vain or anything like that either.'

'Are you serious?'

Miller said, 'As a heart attack. This guy's quite the character.'

Boulanger glanced at Victor's reflection in the rear-view. 'You kill people for money but you draw the line at swearing and blasphemy. How does that make any sense?'

Victor's tone was wistful. 'I never claimed to be consistent.'

FIFTY-SEVEN

They drove north from Marseille, following Relou's directions. One hundred kilometres. Near Goult. A long journey from the coast into the countryside of Provence. They passed through small towns and villages with the scenery changing many times from rolling hills covered in dry grass and palms to fields of shimmering wheat to seemingly endless vineyards.

The Peugeot was an old car. The interior was dirty. The upholstery was tattered and worn. It stank of old tobacco and body odour.

'Apologies for the ride,' Salomé said. 'Don't judge us.'

'It's disposable,' Victor said. 'I like that.'

She nodded. 'We'll torch it just as soon as we're done.'

Boulanger kept to the speed limit. Sometimes driving a little faster and other times just under it. Victor liked that. It showed some competence, although parking up a stone's throw from Relou's shop had not been a smart move. Given the intentions of those involved, they should have been more subtle. Miller should have insisted Victor sit in the passenger seat, too. Professionals, only they were still young. Still had a long way to go before they fully understood the nuances of their chosen trade.

The cottage Relou had described lay at the mouth of a narrow valley filled with farmland. It had almost certainly been part of one of the farms at some point when the whole valley had belonged to a single landowner.

Boulanger and Miller held back in the car while Victor and Salomé moved closer on foot. A simple stone building. Two floors. Maybe four or five rooms. In no way a defensible building or location from Victor's perspective. Although Phoenix was no tactician. Her idea of defence was not the same as his own. Her usefulness and her resourcefulness had kept her alive all these years.

That and eliminating threats before they ever got this close to her.

Salomé said, 'It doesn't look like much from here, especially compared to her chateau. I was expecting something more impressive.'

'A safe house that stands out is hardly safe,' Victor replied. 'Had we not known it belongs to Phoenix then we would never have given it a second look.'

Boulanger approached. 'There's no vehicle outside.'

Salomé shook her head. 'That means nothing. It could be out back or parked somewhere else so the cottage appears unoccupied from a distance.' She paused. 'A safe house that stands out isn't safe, is it?'

The Frenchman said, 'I guess.'

He seemed even bigger without the driver's seat confining him. Maybe double Victor's own weight and only a little fat. No human was built to carry so much mass, so Boulanger's build was due to supraphysiological amounts of androgens. Which meant he had a supply of drugs with him. Victor couldn't imagine an assassin carrying around needles and vials so it would be oral steroids then.

The temperature was mild and yet Boulanger was sweating.

Salomé spoke to him while gesturing to Victor. 'He and I will handle it. You guys stay here and keep an eye on the surrounding area. Give us a heads-up if you see anything or anyone out of place. I don't want a kill team sneaking up on us from behind while we are inside. Is that clear?'

Boulanger shrugged and nodded his answer, meaning he understood but also that he didn't see the point. Victor found that interesting. Even more so when she gave the Frenchman a stare of admonishment. She was not pleased with his attitude and yet Victor detected something else in the look she gave him. Maybe she thought he made her look bad in front of Victor.

Or maybe it was something else entirely.

Neither Victor nor Salomé needed to step inside the cottage to see it was unoccupied. The diesel-powered generator outside had not been activated for years based on its weather-beaten exterior. The grounds were overgrown. Paving stones were almost invisible underneath the rising weeds. Window frames had peeling paintwork. The glass itself was opaque with grime.

'Is there any point going in?' Salomé asked.

Victor circled the building looking for signs left by recent visitors, anything to indicate Phoenix or anyone else had been here. He found nothing.

'I suppose we might as well,' she said when he didn't answer.

She picked the lock while he continued his examination. She was fast. Faster than he would have done it.

The interior was as the outside suggested. Not a single sign anyone but they had set foot inside for years.

Salomé said, 'I'll check upstairs.'

Each step creaked and groaned as she ascended.

He walked the ground floor, which took less than a minute. The front door opened into a room that was empty apart from an old armchair and a painting easel in a corner. In the small kitchen, Victor found some non-perishable foodstuffs in cupboards whose hinges squeaked as he opened them one by one. Some canned fruit. Some Italian flour. Jarred Corsican olives in brine in the last cupboard he checked.

He almost closed the cupboard door but instead he took out one of the jars. The olives inside were fat and green. The label had been handwritten.

'Found anything?' Salomé asked. 'There's nothing upstairs except a bed without bedding. Not a single item of clothing. No telephone.'

'Olives from Montemaggiore,' Victor said, twisting the lid off the jar and plucking one out of the brine. 'Fancy one?'

'I'll pass, *merci*.'

'Your loss,' he said and dropped the olive into his mouth. He placed the jar back where he found it. Chewed and swallowed. 'What now?'

'Obviously, Phoenix isn't here and hasn't been for a very long time. Maybe Relou knew that and sent us here anyway.'

'I don't think so,' Victor said. 'He knew when he was beaten.'

'Then what do you suggest?'

He said, 'I'm not sure but it's almost time to call it quits and get out of France while I still can.'

'Don't be so hasty,' Salomé began. 'I have some contacts. They've been helping me so far. They might have had more luck with other leads.'

'Other leads?'

'Back in Marseille,' she said in answer. 'I have many friends in many places. Another benefit of not operating alone is you can do favours for people and have them do favours for you in return. You don't have to rely on yourself to do everything.'

'Sounds useful.'

'*Tout à fait*,' she agreed with a nod.

'How long have you worked for Phoenix?'

Salomé's gaze was on the scenery outside. 'For ever, I guess. At least, it seems that way.'

'You three always operate together?'

'Why does that matter?'

'I'm simply making conversation,' Victor explained. 'It's not often I get to meet fellow contractors who I'm not also trying to kill.'

Salomé smiled a little at that.

'You never wanted to ride solo?' he asked.

'Why would I?'

'More money. A fee split three ways is worth three times more split no ways.'

She said, 'It's not always about money. We're a team. After this is all over, you should stick with us. Try being part of a family for once.'

'I don't play well with others.'

'So you're a lone operator who can never be loyal to anyone?' Salomé asked him. 'That's a hollow exist-ence, *mon ami*.'

Victor did not argue.

'I can sleep easy in my bed because I know I'm part of a team,' she continued. 'Those boys have got my back and I've got theirs. Anything happens to me and they will go nuclear to avenge me. Do you have anyone out there who would do the same for you?'

'No,' Victor admitted.

Salomé let out a hissing sound as she lit a cigarette. 'That's what you get when you don't show loyalty. You receive none in return.'

FIFTY-EIGHT

It felt good to be out of jail. Not a surprise, sure, but Nikkitin had not anticipated just how good it would feel because every little aspect of life was now a thousand times more enjoyable. Even taking a piss was a pleasure now he was free to do so whenever he wished without a cellmate a few feet away.

'Trust me,' he told his little brothers, 'you should make sure you get pinched at least once. You can't appreciate what it's like to be free until you're first chained.'

'No need,' one of his little brothers said, shrugging. 'I appreciate my freedom several times a day.'

'We know,' another shouted in response, 'we can all hear you through the walls, tugging away on that worm of yours.'

Nikkitin laughed. It was good to be around these animals again. He sipped his beer slowly. After just two bottles he was already buzzed. Another benefit of a few months inside, although he wasn't about to admit his lowered tolerance to his little brothers.

A house party. In Nikkitin's honour, though he had none himself. His particular gang of little brothers were all young guys. No one had yet turned thirty. Most were not long into their twenties. Some were Russian nationals while the majority were US citizens, either expatriated or native born. Nikkitin was in charge even when he had been in jail, and he'd only been inside in the first place at Kirill's bidding. When Kirill died in the night, Nikkitin's lawyer made sure he was released soon afterwards. Nikkitin's lawyer was Kirill's lawyer, who was really a Bratva lawyer. Nikkitin had assaulted some guy in a bar owned by the Bratva. When the time came, the witnesses withdrew their statements and the charges had to be dropped. There had never been any danger of Nikkitin ending up with real time. Still, his little brothers never needed much excuse to throw a party.

The house itself belonged to the wider Bratva, although only Nikkitin and his crew made use of it. Somewhere to hang out and store product. Because they had taken to moving narcotics in medical supplies, there were boxes of vials, bottles and jars everywhere. A box of hypodermic needles was open at the top of one pile because the little brothers had taken to throwing them like darts to see if they could get them to stick into the door. Some had.

One of them approached Nikkitin. The guy was nineteen, with knees and elbows so bony and hard they all called him *konkretnyy*, concrete. He shuffled over with a furrowed brow and with the corners of his mouth downturned, as though he were confused or unsure of himself. He scratched at the back of his shaved head.

'Someone's here to see you,' Concrete said, glancing over

his shoulder and making a lazy gesture towards the hallway and the entrance beyond.

Seeing no one, Nikkitin chuckled. 'Is he a ghost?'

The guys nearby smiled or laughed.

Concrete did not join in. 'He said he's a servant of God.'

Figuring he had misheard because of the din of music, Nikkitin said, 'Say what?'

'He says he's a servant of—'

Nikkitin had not misheard. 'Then tell him to get lost,' he said, still smiling but running out of patience. 'This is no place for a priest. We have devils here.'

Concrete's unsure demeanour intensified into something like unease. 'He won't . . . I don't think he's going anywhere.'

'Get rid of him,' Nikkitin ordered, then reached for another drink from the nearby table. 'Can you believe this?' he said to one of the guys sitting with him.

'Boss,' the guy said back, although his gaze was not on Nikkitin.

Concrete hadn't moved. He stood scratching at the back of his head, still unsure of himself, still uneasy.

In a sudden rage at being ignored, Nikkitin hurled the bottle at the closest wall.

It smashed, sending shards of brown glass rebounding from the wall as foaming beer sluiced down the paintwork.

Concrete flinched, startled.

Everyone else in the room stopped what they were doing.

'Get rid of him,' Nikkitin said again.

Unease bubbling into fear, Concrete shook his head.

Nikkitin was lost for words. He was so taken aback that Concrete not only ignored his order but outright refused to obey that his rage melted away. He knew his crew were all looking at him. They were expecting him to stand up and beat Concrete where he stood for his disobedience. Instead, Nikkitin hesitated. He saw Concrete's fear of his boss was lesser than his fear of the visitor. Which made no sense. Unless . . .

'Bring him through,' Nikkitin said.

Concrete nodded and retreated. All eyes in the room were looking Nikkitin's way.

'Turn the music off,' Nikkitin told no one in particular.

The room fell into a near silence. The only sound was that of Nikkitin's breaths, in and out, in and out.

Then footsteps. Concrete's shuffling trainers on floorboards. A second set: hard heels on wood, yet somehow soft and echoing as though the laws of physics applied differently to them.

Concrete appeared with his head down. He stood at the doorway with his eyes averted and gestured back the way he'd come.

The man's shadow appeared first, dark on the floor. Then his silhouette in the doorway. Then he entered the room, unremarkable. Dark trousers and a dark blazer over a thin grey sweater. Maybe forty. The kind of guy Nikkitin could pass on the street and not look at twice, never think of again. A regular citizen living a normal, boring life.

But no such person would walk into a house full of Bratva asking for their boss without a single tell of anxiety. Such tells came in many forms, Nikkitin knew. Not only sweating or nervous tics. Some guys overcompensated and would put on displays of arrogance and bravado. They felt the need to state they were unafraid because they were afraid.

This man felt no need.

The way his gaze locked on to Nikkitin as though everyone else in the house had ceased to exist and Nikkitin was all by himself suggested this man might feel nothing at all.

The little brothers' prior expectation turned into confusion. None of them understood because they were all too young. They were too inexperienced, too soon into their Bratva careers to have heard of this man.

Nikkitin himself had almost forgotten about him. Out of necessity almost. It could be hard enough to sleep at night without that name haunting his dreams. Only the man before him was no mere nightmare.

'Do you know who I am?' the man asked.

At one time, he was called Nav, which was the name ancient Slavs gave to the Underworld. Some called him Chernobog, or devil. In recent years he was named Haros, though some might say Charos or Charon. Depending on where in the world he was found. They all meant the same thing, give or take, though pronunciations and translations muddled things. Which was why Nikkitin answered with a different name.

'The Boatman.'

It was the moniker the modern Bratva knew him by, for waiting on the banks of the River Styx to ferry the dead across was Maxim Borisyuk's chief enforcer and his most feared executioner.

FIFTY-NINE

The car was quiet on the way back to Marseille. Victor was thoughtful and he was sure Salomé and her two guys were the same. The sun was low in the sky by the time they reached the northern outskirts of the city.

'Where are we going?' Victor asked.

'To see my contact,' Salomé said. 'I am, at least. You boys can cool your heels until I'm done.'

Boulanger drove to an industrial neighbourhood and pulled up alongside a chain-link fence that rattled in the breeze. Behind it, shadowed in the dim light, were rusting train carriages.

Salomé told them, 'I'll see you soon,' and climbed out. 'Hopefully I'll have some good news when I do.'

Boulanger drove away. Through the rear window, Victor saw Salomé talking on her phone. She wasn't facing his way, however, so he could not read her lips.

'Where are we headed?' Victor asked.

Miller answered. 'Company property.'

'Details.'

'What do you want to know? It's an abandoned restaurant in a strip mall. Well, whatever the French call a strip mall, you know? Whole thing should have been condemned a long time ago, but no one has got round to knocking it down like they should have done with half of the buildings in this crumbling town. The other properties are empty. We might be a bit short on creature comforts. Can't beat it for privacy, though.' Miller exhaled as he stroked his beard. 'If those walls could talk.'

The sign for the strip mall had been disfigured by graffiti. The list of businesses below it was impossible to read. Pollution had stained it in a dense layer of dark grime almost the same colour as the lettering, which might have still been legible in the right light were it not for the many overlapping graffiti tags. A whole rainbow of sprayed colours competed for dominance. Victor could not make out a single word or complete symbol.

Spaces for maybe thirty cars in the lot out front and all but two were empty. A rusting BMW was parked in the furthest corner. It looked as though it had been there for years. A newer SUV was near it, with the interior light on and the engine running. Smoke drifted out of an open sunroof. When Boulanger parked up and the doors opened, the SUV left, and Victor saw a couple of teenagers inside, red-eyed and laughing as they drove away.

He noted a liquor store, a dry cleaner, a budget store, a café, a seafood restaurant and a convenience store. Some windows were boarded up, others backed with newspaper. Only the liquor store had roll-down security shutters.

Boulanger parked behind the strip mall. Aside from a

scattering of trash and urban detritus, the space was empty. Where the walls met the ground there were yellow urine stains and worse besides. Only ambient city light provided any illumination at all. A good place for an execution, Victor thought, although Miller and Boulanger still showed no signs of coming violence. No CCTV, no overlooking windows, no passing foot traffic.

Victor climbed out of the car and followed the two guys to the rear door of the seafood restaurant. Miller had the keys and unlocked the door. He held it open for Boulanger to enter first and then kept it open and gestured for Victor to follow. Victor never liked being flanked, even by those who posed no immediate threat. He obeyed regardless. He preferred to play along in this instance.

Inside the restaurant, Boulanger thumbed a light switch.

There wasn't much to learn about his environment, although Victor paid attention during the short walk. He saw doors leading to a storeroom, a cold storage, an office or break room, a staff toilet, public toilets, the kitchen and the restaurant floor. Boulanger used a flat palm to push open the door into the restaurant proper. A decent-sized establishment with space for maybe eighty or one hundred diners at any one time. Most of the furniture was gone, although some tables had been left behind, unsold and unwanted, one of which was evidently used by Miller and Boulanger, based on the accompanying chairs, the ashtray, newspaper, playing cards and many takeout coffee cups and containers for pastries, pizza and shawarma. But no seafood.

'You've been holed up here a long time,' Victor said.

Miller glanced his way. 'Say what?'

Victor gestured to the containers littering the table.

'Or big appetites,' Miller said with a grin.

Victor picked one of the used coffee cups from the table to get a closer look at it.

Miller watched him. 'We can go out for fresh in a little bit. No need to sip leftovers.'

Victor nodded and set the cup back down.

'A buck gets ten the lawyers are currently fighting over who should pay to knock all this down and start again. It's going to be years before anyone comes around here again. I'm betting we might just be done with this job by then.'

'What job?' Victor asked.

Miller hesitated for an instant, confused. 'Finding Phoenix. That's what we're doing, right? That's the job we're trying to get done.'

'I see,' Victor said.

A few other chairs were dotted around the space, either knocked over to their backs or side. One had been broken to pieces. Chunks of polystyrene from the ceiling tiles littered the floor, along with bits of wood from the furniture, flakes of plaster from the walls and shards of glass from smashed mirrors that reflected the derelict room back on itself in jagged fragments of loss and sorrow.

Four decorative pillars stretched from floor to ceiling in the centre of the room, with a low raised space between them. The pillars had been defaced with graffiti.

Miller shrugged off his hooded sweatshirt. 'We got a hot plate over on the bar. Some soup. Crackers. Stuff like that.'

The restaurant's bar occupied a corner of the space. As with the rest of the room, it had deteriorated and had been damaged by water leaks and vandals. Stools bolted to the floor remained in place, although the vinyl cushions had all been slashed and torn to frayed strips. Foam padding protruded from within or had been pulled free and tossed to the floor to form a yellow halo around the bar. Glass shards from many broken bottles mixed with the foam. A dirty hot plate sat on top of the bar. Groceries and enamel mugs stood next to it.

Victor was careful with his footfalls but Miller and Boulanger's steps crunched on the polystyrene and glass. Larger pieces of debris seemed to have congregated around the space's periphery, so Victor imagined the two men had kicked or thrown them clear as and when the mood took them. A red carpet covered the floor. Grime and water damage had darkened it to black in many areas. The polystyrene dust seemed almost as snow over it.

Miller picked at a frayed strip of wallpaper. 'You can call me crazy but I kind of like it here.'

'Hungry?' Boulanger asked as he emptied cans of soup into a pan that he set on the hot plate on the bar.

Victor nodded. 'Sure.'

Miller took a seat at a table and rubbed his palms together at the prospect of food, so Victor took it as his cue to take a look around.

The kitchen was in worse shape than the main restaurant floor, he found. It had tiled walls and a tiled floor, both so filthy that the blue tiles were a dull grey. The large cooking unit, made of stainless steel, was caked with old grease and grime. Pipes had been pulled away from the walls and bent at sharp angles. Some tiles were split into spiderwebs of cracks with neat holes in the middle. Victor imagined a hammer had done the damage. Takeout containers were everywhere, most ripped or flattened. The ceiling had almost entirely come away. Victor could see exposed wires and pipes and vents, all dark and decayed. The only colour that had not succumbed to the same rot came from two red fire extinguishers on one wall. This made Victor wonder about the quality of delinquents in this part of the city. Had this been a haunt of his wayward teenage crew those fire extinguishers would have been among the first items to be torn away. He could imagine having an epic duel with one of his crew, each trying to choke the other with carbon monoxide gas while the others watched on, laughing and shouting encouragement.

He saw no utensils, which was not surprising. They would have been sold or taken away by creditors long ago, and any missed would have been snatched away by the same people who pulled pipes from the walls or pulled away the ceiling for fun.

But such delinquents were not a thorough breed, Victor knew well.

He went down to one knee so he could peer beneath the long cooking apparatus. The space between the cookers and floor was even filthier than elsewhere. Victor peered into the darkness, searching through the debris until he saw the flattened box of a takeout container that lay on the floor at a slight incline because something was elevating it.

Victor stretched one arm to reach the box and move it to one side.

A kitchen knife lay beneath where the box had been. Smeared with dirt, although stainless steel from tip to grip. Edge dulled, of course. No chance of cutting skin, let alone clothing. The point, however, had lost no lethality.

Victor slid the knife to him and tucked it, grip first, up his left shirt sleeve. The handle was thick enough that his sleeve did a reasonable job of securing it halfway up his forearm. He adjusted the cuff, pushing the fabric against the point of the blade so it pierced through a few millimetres, further securing it. Any aggressive movement would shake the knife free so Victor would keep his arm as still as he could, and raised his fist to angle up his forearm from a vertical hang to about forty-five degrees. A natural enough position to avoid attention and his suit jacket would disguise the bulge in his sleeve.

He heard Boulanger's heavy footsteps nearing, and stood before Boulanger reached the doorway.

'Soup's ready.'

'Great.'

He stared at Victor for a moment then peered around the room with close interest to see if anything was different. 'Nothing to see in here.'

Victor agreed.

SIXTY

The Boatman did not look like much, Nikkitin thought. He had imagined a huge man with terrifying features. Seven feet tall with red eyes, perhaps. This man was maybe six feet. It was hard to tell in the dim light, but his eyes might have been a pale blue. He didn't look strong or powerful. He didn't look remotely scary.

Looks were deceiving, Nikkitin had learned. Though there could be no mistaking them physically, in a way the Boatman reminded him of the man who had last spoken with Kirill – not that anyone believed Nikkitin about that. Both men had a curious air of normalcy about them. There was no reason to look at them twice.

'I'm glad you know who I am,' the Boatman said without any sign he was indeed glad. 'Do you know why I'm here?'

'No,' Nikkitin answered in a quiet voice.

He felt the eyes of his little brothers on him. They saw what he saw and they had no prior knowledge. Nikkitin had not told them of the Boatman. To his knowledge, the

Boatman never came to the US. Nikkitin had slept better in that ignorance.

'I've searched him,' Concrete added, eager to please and show his worth.

The Boatman said, 'I carry no weapons.'

This revelation only added to the confusion of the little brothers in the room. The unremarkable man had no gun and no backup, so why Nikkitin's reaction?

The Boatman asked, 'What happened to Kirill?'

'He died of an overdose,' Nikkitin began. 'Painkillers for his headaches, they—'

'I do not require a summary of the facts,' the Boatman interrupted. 'I asked what happened to him.'

'I'm not sure.'

'He was your superior. His death means you will inherit his position.'

Nikkitin shook his head, desperate to dissuade his accuser. 'No, no, no. Never. It was not me, I swear it. I did not kill Kirill.'

'So, he was murdered, then? He didn't kill himself?'

'I'm not sure.'

'Who had access to his cell? A guard, perhaps? I would like a name.'

Nikkitin explained: 'Kirill always took meetings at midnight. He had an arrangement with the jail.'

'A routine, then,' the Boatman mused, 'that could be exploited. Who did he meet that night?'

Nikkitin was hesitant. 'Some hitman.'

'Explain.'

'Kirill hired him to shoot Grigori, but the cops arrested him and shoved him in the same jail as us. Kirill wanted to know why he had got himself caught. He paid a lot of money to make sure the murder could not be linked back to him.'

'Kirill spoke with an assassin the very same night he took a lethal overdose?'

Nikkitin couldn't bring himself to utter an actual reply, so he nodded instead.

'You didn't think there might a connection?'

'Sure, I did. But it was Kirill who asked to see him, not the other way around. He was angry the killer had got himself caught.'

'The assassin is still in jail, I presume.'

'They let him out the next day.'

The Boatman gave him a look of disbelief. 'He was not charged with the murder of Grigori Orlov?'

'No.'

The Boatman's head rotated right, looking for a moment to where Concrete stood.

'Do you not think this assassin was responsible for Kirill's death?'

'I don't know.'

'Who wanted Kirill dead? Which enemies did he have who might have hired a killer to get to him in jail?'

Nikkitin could only shrug. 'How would I know?'

'Hey,' one of the little brothers shouted at the Boatman, eager to defend his boss. 'What is this?'

The Boatman ignored the question, and asked, 'Why did Kirill have Orlov killed?'

'He heard Orlov was talking to the FBI. I guess he didn't want Orlov saying anything that might jeopardise his own deal.'

'What deal?'

'He was talking to the FBI himself,' Nikkitin explained. 'To reduce his sentence. I don't know the details; you'd have to ask his lawyer.'

'I will,' the Boatman said. His head rotated left, looking for a moment to where the rest of Nikkitin's little brothers were sat. 'Who knows about this place?'

'We do,' Nikkitin answered, gesturing to his crew. 'No one else is allowed inside.'

'That's good to hear,' the Boatman said.

He removed his suit jacket as he rotated his head back and forth, and slung the jacket over one shoulder, holding on to the collar between thumb and forefinger. A benign action, although almost nonsensical given the chill of the building.

Concrete, having stood still and awkward throughout the conversation, went to leave the room.

'No one leaves,' the Boatman said in a soft, matter-of-fact tone.

The little brother who had interrupted, shot to his feet. 'What is this? Who are you to tell us anything?'

'Sit down,' Nikkitin told him. 'Please.'

He did no such thing; instead, he drew a knife and held it up. 'Get out,' he yelled at the Boatman, stepping closer, 'before I peel your face off.'

The knife was a box cutter with a fresh blade.

Nikkitin's little brothers preferred such weapons. Small meant easier to conceal, and experienced knife fighters understood such short blades were often harder to disarm than their longer cousins. More blade length meant more to manipulate and greater leverage to exert. The small blade of the box cutter became a deadly point after only a few centimetres. There was almost no way of going for it without incurring serious wounds in the process.

Which was why the Boatman had taken off his jacket, Nikkitin saw.

Before the little brother could get close enough to threaten him, the Boatman snapped out his wrist, extending his arm and flicking the jacket through an overhand arc so that it whipped into the guy's face.

No damage, just distraction that initiated the flinch reaction that jerked the head back and made the guy retreat a step.

The Boatman used that moment to snap the jacket back, taking it into both hands to bunch up around both the knife and the fist holding it. The bunched-up jacket shielded the Boatman's hands from the blade. However sharp the edge, it was still a saw at a microscopic level and needed friction to be at its most effective.

The Boatman wrenched the hand down to drag the little brother off balance and dropped to a squat to pull him face-first into the floor.

He cried out as his nose broke and he lost teeth.

With a brutal twist, the Boatman hyperextended the wrist and torqued the knife from his hand. He made no effort to take it as his own and let it clatter away.

Still controlling the young guy's arm, which was now up in the air behind his back, the Boatman turned to face the next enemy who had been coming up from the rear. He had a knife of his own and was now halted in shock and fear.

Making sure everyone had a good look, the Boatman manipulated the arm in his hands so it stretched backwards across the shoulder blades of the little brother on the ground. The joint prevented the limb from stretching very far, until the Boatman set one hand at the elbow and pushed down hard, exploding the shoulder socket so the arm fell limp across the back.

For a second, the room was silent. No one could quite believe what they had witnessed. The little brother on the ground had a broken nose, had lost several teeth, and his right shoulder would never be the same again. He was pale with pain and shock where his face was bright red with blood.

'If we may continue now,' the Boatman said, rising back to full height.

Nikkitin's little brothers were brave and loyal to a fault. They could not let such a savage attack on one of their own go unpunished. Nikkitin saw it coming.

So did the Boatman.

His left hand shot out, grabbed a hypodermic syringe from the open box nearby, and drove the needle into the side of Concrete's neck.

Ripping it out again just as fast, the Boatman hurled the syringe, burying it into the left eyeball of the next closest little brother as he tried to pull a gun out from under his sweatshirt.

An arch of pulsing crimson spurted from Concrete's neck and he clutched both bony hands to the wound as he sank to his knees.

Before Nikkitin could beg for mercy, the Boatman was scooping up the dropped pistol from the guy with the needle in his eyeball, and pointing it at his face.

SIXTY-ONE

Victor ate the soup Boulanger had prepared. They all used the enamel mugs, sipping at first while the soup still steamed and then slurping as it cooled. It wasn't bad. Too much salt, of course, as always seemed to be the case with canned soup, although it helped with hydration. He left most of the soup: hydration or not, he didn't want a full stomach.

Water dripped from the ceiling, which had many gaps where the polystyrene tiles had fallen away, or where they remained in place but with holes in them from whatever had been thrown up against them by Miller and Boulanger in boredom, or from vagrants or delinquents seeking peace through destruction. Victor remembered times long ago when he had smashed and wrecked to gain some small respite from the drudgery of existence. When he had had nothing, destroying something was the closest thing to ownership. A flash of laughing faces in his mind almost made him smile.

He saw a distorted reflection in one of the broken

mirrors – of Miller regarding him with curiosity. Victor pushed his memories away, displeased with himself for lowering his guard. Only a moment of distraction, a few seconds of thought, could be fatal. He knew because he had exploited such moments to kill targets who might otherwise have seen him coming. Before he had perfected his talents of lethality, he had just waited. When he was young and inexperienced, he had used patience to overcome his immaturity and lack of competence. All targets were vulnerable at some point. Everyone let their guard down if you could just hold your nerve long enough. Victor, who had needed from an early age to be patient, had found success where others more skilled had failed.

Patience, he had found, could do that which talent alone could not.

'I know what you're thinking,' Miller said. 'You're thinking what foul deed did you do in a past life to end up right here, right now.'

'You read my mind,' Victor said.

'Not exactly the jet-set lifestyle you dream of, is it?' Miller said with a smile. 'Where are the tuxedos and cocktails, am I right?'

Boulanger finished his soup first, gulping down a second mug's worth before Miller was halfway through his own. The Frenchman then licked his fingers to get rid of some spilled excess, and wiped those fingers on the thighs of his slacks. He got up from his seat and left the room. To take his steroids, Victor guessed.

Now it was just the two of them, Miller asked, 'You like it? You like doing what we do?'

'Why do you want to know?'

Miller huffed. 'Why wouldn't I want to know? Curiosity is the default human position. Besides, we gotta pass the time while we wait. We gotta talk about something. I'm not shy. I don't mind you knowing a little about me so I'll go first. Yeah, I like doing this. See, no big deal? You can do it too—'

His phone rang. He made an apologetic gesture and took it from a pocket – a cheap burner phone, by the looks of it – and said, 'Yeah?' He listened to the voice on the line for a few seconds. 'Sure, everything's fine here. Take your time.'

He hung up without another word.

'Salomé?' Victor asked.

'Yeah,' came the answer, blunt and surly. He paced about.

'Any progress?'

Miller said, 'What?'

'Her contact,' Victor answered. 'Isn't she supposed to be finding out what they've learned about Phoenix?'

'Yeah, yeah. Sure. Making progress.'

'Which is?'

'You don't need to worry about the specifics, okay?' Miller said, voice rising. 'All that matters is staying calm and waiting for Salomé to get back.'

'I'm always calm,' Victor said. 'But do you think all this is going to work?'

'What does that mean?'

'*This.*' Victor gestured to the environs, to the soup. 'The act. I'm only here to find out what's going on, and now I know.' He gestured to the coffee cup he had examined earlier. 'There's lipstick on this and Salomé doesn't wear any. Who does?'

Miller drew his handgun, swift and smooth. 'No more questions.'

313

Victor raised his hands so they were about shoulder height.

Miller came almost within arm's reach, then said, 'You're going to be a good little boy and be patient and silent until Salomé's here.'

'With the rest of your crew? That's why we're waiting here, isn't it? The others are spread out in different locations.'

'What did I say about no more questions?' Miller growled.

'I saw a few yesterday at a hotel, only I convinced myself I'd been wrong. Well, they convinced me. I'm impressed. They're better than you. I gave you too much credit when we met earlier. You weren't relaxed because you meant me no harm, you were relaxed because nothing was going to happen until the whole crew was together. No one's taking any chances after what happened last time.'

'Shut up and lose your piece.'

Victor looked at his raised hands. 'Do you want me to keep my hands up or do you want me to lose my gun? I can't do both.'

Miller thought for a moment, then said, 'Don't you move an inch, okay? I'll take your gun.'

He edged forward.

Victor glanced down at his waistband. 'All yours.'

Miller reached for it, and Victor shook his left wrist to dislodge the knife's point from his cuff.

As Miller withdrew the gun, Victor dropped his left hand so the knife slipped straight out from his sleeve and into his waiting hand.

Miller didn't realise the danger until the blade plunged into his throat. The knife entered just to one side of his oesophagus. The point hadn't reached his spine, or else had been deflected by it, given Miller could still stand, although shock kept him rigid as a statue. There was only a little blood. The knife itself was plugging the wound it had created.

Miller's eyes were wide and his skin paled.

Victor said, 'The answer to your earlier question is yes.'

A croaking sound emanated from Miller's lips.

'I used to like it,' Victor admitted. 'Back when I started out. But I realised anything that involves you at an emotional level makes you a weaker professional. The more detached you are, the less you care either way, the better you'll become. But you have to work at it,' he continued. 'It won't come naturally. You have to force yourself not to care. You have to make a determined effort every second of every day until it becomes second nature. Now, it's like chopping onions,' Victor said as he prepared to withdraw the blade from Miller's throat to unleash the damned torrent of blood. 'Only without the tears.'

A shadow appeared in the doorway: Boulanger returning.

Victor left the knife buried in Miller's neck and went for the guns.

Only he could not prise either free. Shock had given Miller's grip hypertensive strength.

With no other option, Victor pulled free the knife and dashed to intercept Boulanger as he entered the room.

The Frenchman strolled in unawares, humming to himself, only realising what was happening as Victor rushed towards him. Boulanger had just enough time to draw his pistol, but nowhere near long enough to aim it before Victor reached him.

Given his size and musculature, a single wound might not stop him even if Victor pierced an artery or the heart itself, so he stabbed Boulanger in the head, aiming to drive the blade through the thinnest area of skull at the temple and into the brain beyond.

The sudden pain caused Boulanger to drop his gun, but that was the extent of the effect because—

The knife broke against his skull.

SIXTY-TWO

The tip pierced skin and punctured bone, then the blade snapped before Victor could drive it all the way through to the brain beneath. His angle of attack was not ideal, although it should have been good enough. While the knife seemed solid, the blade flexed more than it could handle.

Stress fractures acquired through many years of use, invisible to the naked eye, Victor reckoned, as the shard pinged away, reflecting the light in staccato flashes, leaving a little blood welling from the tiny wound in Boulanger's scalp and a broken kitchen knife in Victor's hand.

Now they were close, Boulanger grabbed him.

Without the point, the knife had a flattened tip, although the resulting new edge was fresh. Too wide to stab with, and too flat to use to slice, but it had two corners, both hard and sharp.

Victor swung the knife like a short club or axe, chopping those corners into Boulanger's arms and shoulders as the Frenchman hoisted him from the floor, ignoring the rapid, painful attacks that moved to the top of his head so he could hurl Victor back down with almost no effort.

He rolled to absorb the fall, yet could not jump to his feet fast enough to stop the huge Frenchman charging into him. There was far too much mass and acceleration to stop and as Boulanger collided into him, they tipped over a table.

While Victor was faster, he took the brunt of the impact, acting as a cushion for the Frenchman, who pinned him down.

Victor blocked and parried the first clumsy attacks as Boulanger pushed himself to his knees, before rocking his head from side to side so the more accurate follow-ups that got through his guard could not connect with full force.

Victor slipped one entirely, and Boulanger's tight fist punched the floor.

Which was why Victor mainly threw palm strikes and elbows. If he punched, it was usually to the body. A skull could be as hard as any floor if the punch connected just so.

If punching the floor had damaged Boulanger's hand, it made no real difference. His reaction was limited to a moment's pause.

That was all Victor needed to slide and roll out of range of the Frenchman's punches.

Victor scrambled to his feet, a little unsteady, his balance returning just as Boulanger was standing and rushing to intercept. When he swung another massive punch, Victor ducked beneath it and hacked with the broken knife, opening a gash across his enemy's thigh.

Boulanger roared and tried to grab hold of him again. Victor hacked at his hands, then his shoulder, then his neck. Quick, darting attacks. No real power needed to draw blood from soft flesh with the sharp edge of steel. The obvious drawback was a distinct lack of damage to his opponent. Victor's attacks caused pain, not injury. The wounds were too shallow. Even the blow to the neck that Victor had intended to puncture a carotid barely bled. Boulanger kept coming, undamaged and undeterred.

But he began to slow.

All that extra mass needed extra oxygen from a cardiovascular system built to do half the work required. His face shimmered and damp patches darkened his shirt under the armpits, and across the chest and shoulders too. His mouth hung open to gulp in air. Each time he hit Victor, Boulanger took as long to recover from the exertion of throwing the punch as it took Victor to shake off the pain and disorientation.

Then, inevitably, the punches that landed began to lose their snap. There was the same mass behind them, but increasingly little acceleration as Boulanger's fatigue rose. Hitting with less force meant Victor recovered faster than Boulanger. The more Boulanger attacked, the worse he made it for himself. The harder he tried to win, the quicker he would lose.

Victor elected not to explain the fatal error in Boulanger's tactics.

Instead, he grunted and grimaced with every patting punch, staggering with each impact until Boulanger was almost collapsing and had to slump against a wall in order to stay standing.

Which Victor judged was an appropriate time to drop the act.

Only the Frenchman was aware of his faltering

endurance. He still had his strength, and used it to hurl a chair at Victor.

No incoming missile of those dimensions was ever going to beat Victor's reflexes. It was a good throw, however, and would have struck square in the face had he not ducked low below its path.

Which had been the Frenchman's primary intent, Victor realised, as Boulanger exploited the moment by lifting an entire table and hurling it at Victor, who was fast enough to dodge most projectiles, and yet he had nowhere to go. The table was too large. There was no escaping it, and it knocked him to the floor.

The impact stunned Victor, who felt the knife leave his weakened grip.

Boulanger grimaced and let out a throaty growl as trickles of blood ran down his face from the many little rips Victor had made in his scalp. The Frenchman had more wounds across his limbs that he took a second to examine. All bleeding, all painful, though they were not going to stop him.

Victor struggled to breathe, his diaphragm paralysed. He rotated his head in a failed effort to locate the broken knife or any other possible weapon before Boulanger rushed him.

The Frenchman was unsteady on his feet, however, and his massive chest rose and fell with big, rapid breaths. He was so exhausted Victor thought his paralysed diaphragm might recover before Boulanger had his breath back. The other man pushed on, however. He could see he only needed one more big exertion and then he could rest.

With the wind knocked from him, Victor could do nothing to prevent Boulanger bending over to grab him by the lapels and pulling him back up to his feet, then tiptoes.

Victor tried to raise his leaden arms up in time to guard, but he was too weak and too slow.

Boulanger, face glistening both from sweat and from the vertical rivulets of blood, and bright red from high blood pressure, grinned despite his pain and fatigue, and head-butted Victor.

Who then saw only black.

SIXTY-THREE

It was a monumental effort not to weep like a child when faced with such overwhelming beauty. Every last reserve of his willpower had to be summoned in order to hold back the irresistible march of emotion. Should his very life be at stake – should the life of his only daughter be at stake – he could not pretend to be unmoved. He was not purely a monster, after all. And even the most hideous of monsters still *felt*. Whether a misshapen troll lurking under a bridge or a treacherous dragon hidden in the darkest cave, their monstrosity was not their all. He was more than the sum of the many evils he had orchestrated and the terrible agony he had inflicted upon the world. Because he could be brought to the verge of crying by art, Maxim Borisyuk knew he still had a soul.

'*Brava,*' he yelled. '*Brava.*'

He shouted his appreciation with such ferocity and clapped with such power that his throat was hoarse and his palms red and stinging.

He shouted louder. He clapped louder.

The prima ballerina smiled wide and joyful as she received Borisyuk's acclaim along with that of the entire auditorium. He could not see her eyes from this distance to know for sure that she was crying, but he knew those eyes had to be full of tears. He didn't need to see them because he could feel them threatening to slide down his own cheeks.

The rapturous applause went on for several minutes. By the time she and the other dancers had taken their last bow, only the old and infirm were not partaking in the standing ovation. Borisyuk had been first to his feet, of course. Bionic hip be damned.

He had done so with such speed and enthusiasm that he had shocked his bodyguard out of his slumber. The oaf had fallen asleep sometime after returning from the last interval, having slowly sunk lower and lower in the seat until his knees were far apart – his legs restricted from stretching out by the box's barrier – and his chin on his chest. Borisyuk had left the man to sleep, preferable as it was to witnessing his bored expression, although a single snore would have resulted in a kick to the nearest shin.

Good thing he had no enemies that would dare move against him in the centre of Moscow herself, or the bodyguard would still be wiping away drool while Borisyuk bled out in the private box. He gave the man a narrow-eyed look of disapproval in between shouts of acclaim.

Like many rich men who had been born into poverty, Borisyuk had not grown up loving the ballet. He had only ever gone to those early performances because his first wife had wanted to be seen as a patron of the arts among their peers in Russia's post-Soviet nouveau riche. At first, Borisyuk had been like his bodyguard. Only his stamina as a younger man had kept him awake through all those endless grands jetés and pirouettes. He had not understood what he was watching and so had become bored, then tired. The always warm Veliky theatre, the dim lighting and several generous measures of vodka never helped either.

But art was just like vodka. Those initial hesitant sips generated only aversion and revulsion until, almost without noticing, the taste for it was acquired. Borisyuk could never get enough of either vodka or ballet.

He had gone through two more wives since the days when he had been dragged, complaining like a spoiled infant, to his first shows. Now, he had no wife, and was too old and too content in bachelorhood to find another, so he came to the ballet, and sometimes to the opera, by himself. His bodyguard had no choice but to accompany him, so Borisyuk did not consider the man company in the purest sense. Oksana loved the ballet as much as her father, and yet was always too busy saving the world to come with him even before the unfortunate demise of her husband. He did not ask her to accompany him tonight.

On his way out of the theatre, he told one of the red-attired box keepers to send flowers to the entire cast. While the prima was the obvious star and superior talent, Borisyuk didn't like the idea of other dancers, less talented yet no lesser in work ethic, being left out. In the same way, he only sat at the head of all tables of the Bratva because of the combined efforts of all the uncountable *bratskaya* out there.

Luda Zakharova was waiting for him in his limousine, having spent the evening running his empire from her laptop and phone. In that simpler time never to be repeated,

Borisyuk hadn't even used a phone. Everything was done face-to-face. He needed to look his little brothers in the eye when he gave them orders to know they were loyal, and he wanted to see those enemies he condemned to death wail and beg.

'How was the show?' she asked him without looking up from her screen, her fingers tapping keys so fast they were a blur of motion to Borisyuk's old eyes.

'I will be seeing it again next week.'

'I'm so pleased you enjoyed it,' she said with no warmth in her voice, then tilted her head up from the screen to look him in the eye.

'I see that you've heard from the Boatman,' he said, reading her expression.

She nodded. 'While you were inside.'

'Go on,' he prompted.

'He is of the belief Kirill was murdered.' She explained what she knew: Kirill's midnight meetings, the killing of Grigori Orlov by a man who ended up in the same jail. But what she could not fully explain was:

'Why?' Maxim asked.

'That is currently unclear. However, I have been liaising with our associates in the Justice Department and have some intriguing information about the man who was arrested for Orlov's death and then sent to the same jail as your son-in-law.' She used the laptop's trackpad, closing and opening windows Borisyuk could not see, before swivelling the computer around to show him the screen and a photograph of a man. 'This is the face of William Pendleton. Arrested, but not charged. Released from jail once the twenty-four hours were up and sent on his way. That's the last anyone's seen of him.'

'Who is he?'

'No one,' she answered. 'At least on paper. While we're still digging, I have a feeling we're not going to find anything more on him if the Boatman is correct.'

'Casualties?' he asked.

She nodded. 'Your scalpel is more of a chainsaw.'

'If he cuts to the truth, I don't care how much mess he makes. Who hired this man to kill my son-in-law?'

Zakharova said, 'I'm sorry to say it appears Kirill was planning on making a deal with the authorities.'

Borisyuk considered this revelation for a long moment. 'A traitor then,' he said. 'But still Oksana's husband.'

'For a reduced sentence served at a minimum security prison,' Zakharova continued, 'Kirill would help investigators unravel Castellan's distribution network in North America. Given his involvement in that operation, I've no doubt Kirill could have damaged the supply of heroin from Marseille to such an extent Castellan might never have recovered. I would say that is plenty of reason to risk your wrath.'

Maxim thought about what he had been told. 'A motive alone is not proof.'

'My feelings exactly.'

'So have him find proof,' he told her. 'Tell the Boatman to pack up in the US and head to Marseille.'

'He was of the belief that time is of the essence.'

'Indeed,' Borisyuk agreed. 'But why are you telling me?'

'Because he called me from your new jet,' she explained. 'He'll be landing in France come the morning.'

SIXTY-FOUR

There was a moment after Victor regained consciousness that made no sense. He opened his eyes and found he could no longer see anything. Maybe blinded by the headbutt or an actual blindfold. It was only after a long moment that he managed to understand there was nothing impeding his vision. Face down on the floor, he was looking at the dark stained carpet of the derelict restaurant.

He blinked and refocused so the texture of the carpet sharpened into clarity. He could not smell the damp or the filth caked into the fibres, only his own blood. His nostrils were blocked where it had congealed. He tasted it too. It had remained liquid where it had seeped into his mouth. His nose wasn't broken, at least. The dull pain emanated from between his eyebrows, so he guessed he had been quick enough to angle his head downwards before Boulanger's own struck him. The force had rattled his brain inside his skull and ruptured the delicate tissues in his nasal cavities. Victor had no memory of the impact itself. Unconsciousness would have followed almost instantaneously. Tilting his head had saved his nose a direct hit and he had taken the blow about as well as could be expected. Maybe sparing his nose from being crushed had meant hairline fractures in one or both of his orbital bones. He couldn't be sure and wasn't about to prod them to see if excruciating pain followed. That experiment could wait.

He guessed he had been out no more than a minute or two. The blood in his nostrils had congealed, not crusted. He could still breathe okay.

He concentrated on his hearing, trying to build a mental image of his circumstances without having to move first. He didn't know if he was alone in the room. Maybe Boulanger had left him for some reason or was simply making no discernible noise. Victor had no desire to summon his return until it could not be avoided. And if Boulanger was still here, Victor wanted to maintain the façade of unconsciousness as long as possible and not draw the man's attention while he was still dazed and disorientated. It had taken enormous effort to make his eyes focus on the floor centimetres from his face. He guessed the rest of his body would be no easier to control. Every second he lay still gave him an extra second to recover.

Victor tried to keep his breaths shallow so his ribcage did not fully expand and draw attention. He flexed various muscles in his arms and legs to check for injury and function. Some took more effort than others, but most obeyed. He didn't expect he had the strength to stand just yet. He had a few minutes at least before he would be able to operate in a facsimile of normal function. The problem, however, was the longer he waited, the greater the intrinsic risk he was in.

If Boulanger came to kill him while Victor was still prostrate, it wasn't going to matter how much he had recovered. When Boulanger returned, Victor would rather be on his feet feeling awful than lying down feeling better.

For a second, he allowed himself the fantasy that Boulanger was not coming back. The Frenchman might have checked for a pulse after dropping Victor and not found one. A weak pulse felt a lot like no pulse to the untrained. Victor knew that not everyone who seemed dead was dead. In times past, morticians had looped a tiny brass bell around the big toe of newly arrived corpses in case that new arrival was not actually dead. When consciousness returned, the bell would chime and the person could avoid a premature embalming or burial. Victor couldn't help but wonder how often such a bell had been required, and hence how many unfortunates had needed to bang their fists bloody inside the casket, else wake up on the embalming table midway through the procedure, before the little bell had been implemented as a precautionary measure.

It was possible that Boulanger had mistaken Victor for dead.

He wasn't going to bet his life on it, however.

He felt a minuscule tremor from the floor. He figured Boulanger was moving elsewhere in the restaurant. Victor was thankful the Frenchman wasn't in the same room, waiting for Victor's senses to return so that he could be conscious and aware of his coming death. Some killers were sadists and would kill whether they were paid to do it or not. Victor had encountered many like that. The paycheque was little more than an excuse.

He heard no footsteps so Boulanger wasn't getting closer. His huge weight was sending those reverberations through the carpet, through the cement beneath it. Unnoticeable through soled shoes or even barefoot, yet Victor's whole body was stretched out on that same floor. With his eyes struggling to focus and his hearing muted, his brain paid closer attention to his other senses.

Get up, he told himself.

He pushed himself to his knees first. Bringing his head up over his shoulder made his vision blur and his ears whine. He felt a wave of nausea and took deep breaths with his eyes closed tight until it had passed.

No thunderous footfalls sounded in response so he knew Boulanger had not returned without needing to see him.

Free of the nausea, Victor tried to rise. Every small movement was a struggle, first raising one knee to plant a foot firm on the ground, then using a palm to push off from that knee. He was exhausted. He failed to find enough purchase on his own but reached out to a nearby table for support. He failed again. His senses were returning fast and he felt strong enough, and yet he couldn't quite coordinate his limbs. His balance was off, so that the solid concrete floor felt swayed by fierce waves.

He tipped over forward and jerked out his arms to brace against the floor to stop him falling. Then he dragged his knees up under him and used them to stabilise before he pushed up on to his hands. He had to pause there and rest for a moment, sucking in air until he was ready to try to get the rest of the way to his feet. He grimaced and grunted and every fibre of his body seemed to ache and resist his efforts. He shook under the strain, sweat dripping from his nose and chin, then pushed with his hands and jerked his legs forward and somehow managed to plant his feet. He balanced and brought his arms back beside his torso as he leaned upright.

Almost there. Although it felt like an eternity since he had first returned to consciousness.

He inhaled a deep breath and concentrated on trying to push the swaying floor away to extend his legs in more stable motion. He stood, faster than his balance could handle but he figured a sudden explosion of movement was needed to overcome his weakness. On his feet, the floor seemed at the mercy of a hurricane's swell. He took several steps in an effort to fight the waves and stay standing, trying to direct himself towards the closest wall so that when he staggered towards it the wall stopped his forward momentum.

He rested against it. Each second still standing was a precious victory. The wall felt damp and cold, and almost refreshing against his palms. He left handprints of condensation when he finally pushed himself away to stand without support.

As his strength improved, so did his awareness.

He could hear his own breathing again. The details of the room were in crisp focus once more. He could see graffiti on the walls. He could see the white of the polystyrene chunks on the floor.

He could see the broken glass of the mirror and the distorted reflection of Boulanger looking right back at him.

SIXTY-FIVE

Victor, his wits keen once more, knew he was still too weak to have any chance against the giant a second time. Even with his full strength, Boulanger had been too powerful for him with all that supraphysiological assistance.

Regardless, Victor pushed himself away from the wall and faced the Frenchman.

His gaze was already locked on Victor, who saw that Boulanger had not returned as first thought: he had, in fact, never left the room. He had been here with Victor while he was waking up and trying to stand. Boulanger had been here the entire time Victor had been unconscious.

Boulanger was sat on the floor, slumped against a tipped-over table. His legs were splayed out in front of him.

From across the room, he seemed exhausted and trying to get back his breath. He hadn't yet recovered from the exertion of the fight with Victor.

Who approached Boulanger to kill him while he was still

exhausted. After a few steps closer, it became obvious that there was no need.

'This is a first,' Victor said.

Boulanger's red face had become pale and shimmered with fresh sweat. He breathed with shallow wheezes.

Victor took advantage of the opportunity to straighten down his jacket and brush the dirt and polystyrene from his sleeves.

'Referred pain,' Victor explained.

Boulanger was clutching his left arm, high near the shoulder. His face was not merely pale with exhaustion, but with suffering too.

The Frenchman grimaced and his knuckles whitened as he gripped his arm harder.

Victor said, 'It's really your heart that hurts but the way the nervous system works means you experience that pain elsewhere.'

Boulanger was silent as Victor approached him.

'It's the steroids, of course. Obviously, you're carrying too much weight. Your cardiovascular system doesn't know if that weight is muscle or fat cells. Mass is mass. Every time your heart beats, it's trying to pump blood around a body twice as big as nature ever intended. You didn't think that would come with a cost? And then there's the blood itself. Too many red blood cells making it thicker than it should be because of too much anabolic signalling. That poor heart of yours that already has to contend with all that mass has to pump yogurt through blood vessels meant for milk. Now, it can't get enough blood for itself. You pushed it too hard.' He paused. 'This was always going to be the end result: whether now because of all the strain you just put on it beating me or in the future as an older man just getting up off your chair in the morning. Take comfort in the fact that it was all over the moment you stabbed yourself with that first needle.'

Boulanger looked up at Victor, eyes half closed. Still aware, yet weakening with every second.

He searched Boulanger's pockets; the Frenchman had no strength to stop him. Victor found keys to the car outside, a wallet with some cash, and Boulanger's phone. A burner, for sure, although a modern handset.

'I took things too when I was your age,' Victor admitted as he went through Boulanger's effects. 'Not anything as crude as anabolic steroids. I understood that an increase of size was not the same thing as an increase in proficiency. I'm not going to disappear into a crowd if I'm four feet wide, now, am I? The best fight is always the one you don't have to fight.' Victor gestured to himself and Boulanger. 'See?'

The dying Frenchman did not reply.

When the phone screen lit up, Victor held it in front of Boulanger's face and the screen unlocked.

'Tut, tut,' Victor said. 'I preferred stimulants. What we would call nootropics now ... compounds of that nature. I wanted to be faster. Not simply of action, but of thought. If I could process data faster then I would be better. That was my thought process in that time. I wanted to be the best, most competent professional I was capable of becoming. I realised eventually that such a goal was not only unrealistic but damaging. I had to first experience that of which I sought to conquer. Does that make sense?'

Victor waited for an answer. None came.

He opened up every app and found any messages had been deleted and the call history erased. No numbers had been stored either. While Boulanger had been lazy in using the facial recognition unlock, he had been careful enough to ensure the phone wasn't full of incriminating evidence.

'I'm overcomplicating it,' he said. 'I'll try to be more succinct. Simply put: I didn't actually know what it took to be the best. It was only a hypothesis. Ultimately, I learned that in order to be good in this line of work you need to be willing to do what the next guy won't. I don't mean from a moral point of view. We're all immoral by default. The exact shade of immorality is hardly relevant, is it?'

Boulanger wheezed harder. It might have been an attempt at an answer. Victor wasn't sure.

Although Boulanger had erased any communications he had had with Salomé or anyone else, the last webpage he had visited was still up in the internet browser.

Boulanger was following the news about yesterday's massacre in Nice's Old Town.

'Putting morality to one side,' Victor said as he scrolled through the news, 'I'll give you an example of what I mean. Let's say if you don't want to be killed in your sleep then you make sure you never sleep. At least, you never sleep when anyone expects it. You sit in a chair watching the door until dawn comes along to tell you that you survived the night. Then you sleep. If you're not willing to sit in that chair every single night for the rest of your life then it won't matter what stimulants or nootropics – or in your case steroids – you take. Because someone else out there will sit in that chair until dawn.'

The wheezing became a hiss, then the hiss fell quiet.

Boulanger made no further sounds.

Victor said, 'Thank you for making my point for me.'

So soon after the event, there was as much speculation and inference of the events as there was actual information in the news. Most of it was wildly inaccurate, of course, although a few specific details were known. Only one of those specifics made any difference to Victor because he knew exactly what had happened in that office building.

The detail was a genuine revelation.

'... *huit victimes confirmées* ...'

Victor scrolled through the reporting with renewed interest, waiting for elaboration or a correction. Neither came, so he opened up another tab to search for more up-to-date reporting. When he found the most recent information, it confirmed what he had already read.

Eight casualties confirmed.

Which meant one of Phoenix's original kill team was still alive.

SIXTY-SIX

Victor was taking a huge risk, he knew.

Returning to Nice broke so many protocols he doubted his sanity. He was a wanted man. He had killed an entire team – almost an entire team – and assaulted three police officers in his escape. What little the authorities knew about him would have grown exponentially since yesterday. Almost certainly, the café owner or other witnesses had helped sketch artists draw an approximate likeness, and maybe variations of that sketch had been composed to account for differences in appearance. Or, worse, investigators had mapped his movements with CCTV footage and knew about the haircut and shave. Beyond that, Phoenix was still out there, perhaps directing more contractors like Salomé and her people his way. Maybe the next team would not try to deceive him, and simply open fire.

Any one of them might have also heard the news about the survivor from Sunday's massacre, and anticipate Victor wanted answers.

Go, a voice inside his mind urged him.

But he wasn't listening. Not while Phoenix still breathed.

Salomé and the rest of her crew could wait for now. He had hurried away from the restaurant before she could return with reinforcements. There had been four people in the hotel after his arrival in Nice, so that was at least four more assassins. He wanted answers, but he wasn't going to get them from Salomé or her crew without a fight he wouldn't be able to win. Whatever they were doing, Victor needed his strength back before he found out.

With gunshot wounds, the paramedics would have taken the survivor to the Centre Hospitalier Universitaire de Nice. It was the closest hospital to the scene and had an emergency unit, unlike some of the other hospitals in the city. But it was getting late, so he found a rundown guesthouse near the airport where he could pay with cash and the host never asked to see any identification. He left Miller and Boulanger's car in one of the long-stay garages that served the airport, leaving it unlocked and with the keys in the ignition to encourage thieves to dispose of the evidence for him. He imagined Salomé would take care of the actual corpses. Anything that could lead back to Victor would also lead back to her.

After cleaning up, he sat in a chair for most of the night before sleeping for a few hours once dawn had come.

The host had prepared him breakfast, so he took the opportunity to refuel before boarding the tramway at the airport, buying a ticket with coins because the machine did not take banknotes. The tram was a smooth, comfortable ride into the city. He stood for the journey, paying attention to those who stepped on after him or at other stops along the way, and ignoring those who were already on board. He saw no one who pinged his threat radar and no one in a uniform looked at him twice.

He liked trams. Not as much as trains, but more than buses. The price for a ticket was very reasonable, with unlimited stops valid for over an hour. It made the city centre quieter and calmer. No gridlocked vehicles and honking horns. The whole city was more pleasant as a result. Cleaner, too, without exhaust pollution dirtying facades all day long.

When the tram reached the last stop, he disembarked with the other people, although only after most had already left. The walk to the hospital from the stop was short, about five minutes taking a direct route uphill. Victor's path, however, took almost an hour. When he arrived outside the main entrance, he was as sure as he could be that no one had followed him there.

He used a site map to locate the entrance for the emergency department. The survivor would have required surgery without delay, and then either close observation in intensive care or moved elsewhere to recover if the surgery went well.

In a large hospital that could be any ward or room.

Without a name, Victor could not just ask. Instead, he would have to enquire in a very specific way.

He walked the hallways of the hospital at a fast pace. Busy, but not hurried. He held himself in a way that said he had a purpose and required no assistance. He had no time for needless delays. A simple technique and an effective one in Victor's experience. Everyone understood what it was like to have a packed schedule and the frustration of someone interfering and eating up precious time and energy. Few people chose to be that someone if it wasn't absolutely necessary. Victor had walked into many places he was not allowed to enter by simply acting as though he *was* allowed. There was a domino effect to such things. Once one person had tacitly agreed to his presence, others followed. If he was already there then it must be okay. Even if he did not know where he was going or how to get there, he never seemed lost. The second benefit to a quick walk in such instances was that if someone did think twice about whether he should be somewhere then by the time they decided to act he had already left.

On a long, bright hallway, he turned a corner and saw three women heading towards him and two men. The men were together and wore casual clothing. There was no indication they worked here so Victor ignored them. His focus was on the three women. The closest was by herself, in a doctor's white coat. She looked exhausted, no doubt weary from a long, tiring shift. She cracked open a bottle of water and glugged it as she neared. If she noticed him, she didn't show it. Further along the hallway, the two other women walked together. Nurses by their scrubs. They chatted with one another. He read on their lips something about a new sitcom.

Timing was everything, so Victor waited until he was just about to pass the doctor before he stopped.

'*Excuse-moi*,' he said, turning sharply towards her and taking her by surprise.

She stammered a response and tried not to spill any water.

'*Je suis désolé*,' he continued. 'Do you know where I can find the cafeteria?'

The sign for the cafeteria was further along the hallway. Small, yet obvious for someone observant like Victor.

Although plausibly missed by a less-aware visitor unfamiliar with the hospital.

The doctor shook off her surprise and turned to point back along the hallway through which she had walked. 'Fifty metres. You can't miss it.'

'Thank you,' Victor said, noting the name on her little badge.

She continued on her way and he on his, walking with purposeful strides down the hallway, towards the two nurses. They had seen the interaction with the doctor, although from a distance. Which was close enough. Victor had made sure to make exaggerated movements and to catch the doctor off guard so she did the same. Even for two nurses engrossed in discussing the antics of a hilarious comedy show, they couldn't miss it.

He stopped in front of them.

'Pardon me,' he began. 'I'm Inspector Toussaint of the Nice police and I'm here to speak with the gunshot victim from Sunday's incident. Dr Lavigne told me you would know where I can find him.'

He had taken them by surprise in the same way he had surprised the doctor. He spoke in a fast, urgent intonation, as though every second counted.

The nurse to his left looked quickly to the nurse to her left. 'Isn't he on the B4 ward?'

The second nurse took a moment to find her words. 'No, not there. I believe he's up on the third floor, east wing.'

'*Merci beaucoup*,' Victor said, in the same fast, pressed-for-time tone.

He walked away, knowing they were both still a little surprised and a little confused, perhaps now realising they should have asked for more information on who he was, or some identification, but now it was too late and what did it even matter anyway?

SIXTY-SEVEN

Wearing a doctor's white coat he had lifted from a chair in the cafeteria, Victor entered a room with tall windows on the third floor of the hospital's east wing. Although risky impersonating a doctor, the coat spared him any further challenge while walking around the corridors between visiting hours. The coat had a pen clipped to the breast pocket and the hip pockets contained gum, change and a set of keys. The blinds were down about halfway, blocking much of the sun outside and still letting in plenty of light. He saw that it had started to rain. As well as a visitor's chair, a decent-sized sofa lay beneath the window.

The adjustable bed was the curative-care variety with wheels assisted by electric motors to help nurses and orderlies who would otherwise struggle pushing such a heavy piece of equipment. A little longer than a twin bed and about the same width. The metal gleamed and the cream-coloured plastic components looked bright and clean. Maybe a recent purchase or merely fastidiously maintained. As expensive as a family car.

The bed could be adjusted by the patient pushing buttons on a small panel near the head of the bed, or by hospital staff using their feet to operate paddles on the bottom support struts. The safety rails were set to the up position, both to ensure the patient did not roll out by mistake and also as a means of securing him. A set of handcuffs looped around his left wrist and around one of the thick plastic bars, the uppermost one, so as he lay almost flat the handcuff kept his arm straight out. Not a comfortable position. Victor imagined the doctors or nurses had argued with the police.

The height had been set so the guy was about level with Victor's abdomen.

Walker. The guy in charge of the first kill team.

Victor was surprised the Brit hadn't suffocated due to the hole in his lungs. A tough man, despite the smoking habit. The paramedics and surgeons must have done an exceptional job. No wonder French healthcare was consistently ranked the best in the world.

Walker's legs lay flat and his torso and head had been elevated to a small incline.

He wasn't sure if Walker was unconscious or merely sleeping. Both states were similar, naturally. The guy's eyes were closed and his chest rose and fell at regular intervals.

A clear bag of fluids hung from a steel support. A tube snaked from the bottom of the bag and attached to a cannula in his left forearm. Surgical tape kept the needle from slipping out of the vein. A patient monitor displayed his vitals. At rest, his pulse was slow. His blood pressure was a little on the low side too. Perhaps because he was sleeping or because of the medication they had given him.

Behind the bed, the headwall had many electrical outlets to

manage the patient-care accessories, including a call button that lay next to Walker on the pillow. Victor eased it away.

On the opposite wall, a TV showed the news. The volume had been muted but Victor could read the presenter's bright red lips with ease. Escalating gang violence was being blamed for the killings in Nice, which was a pleasant bonus if true. At a press conference, the mayor sought to assure citizens that such turf warfare would not be tolerated and the police were close to apprehending the suspects. Far too early to make such assertions, of course, but politicians had to be politicians. Still, if the police knew enough to outright contradict such claims then the mayor wouldn't have made them in the first place.

How long until they knew the truth?

Victor checked the medical record at the foot of the bed and saw Walker was on intravenous fentanyl to control his pain. And to keep him in a relaxed, semi-sedated state, Victor presumed. The drip was gravity fed so Victor unhooked the bag of fluids and set it on the bed's tray attachment, next to a plastic jug and cup. A small single-serving container of yogurt was untouched next to a white plastic spoon. Walker would still receive the medication, although the dose would now be much lower. Victor wanted him alert.

The effect of the decreased dose of fentanyl was almost instantaneous, else Walker had been in a light sleep. He heard, or else felt, Victor's presence. Eyelids fluttered open and took a moment to focus on more than the white doctor's coat Victor wore. When Walker's gaze met Victor's own there was confusion, then fear.

Victor slapped a palm over Walker's mouth before he could cry out in alarm.

'Shh.'

Walker's panicked breaths were hot on Victor's skin. The handcuff prevented any real movement and the weight and tuck of the bedclothes kept the guy's legs from moving more than a little. Only his one arm was free to move and yet he was too weak to move it in a way that troubled Victor.

In a quiet, reasonable voice, Victor said, 'If I was here to finish what I started I could just put a pillow over your face, could I not?'

Walker's eyes were wide and unblinking.

'That you woke up to see me standing over you instead of a blur of white should tell you that you're safe,' Victor continued. 'I just want to talk.'

The monitor displayed his rapidly elevating heart rate and increasing blood pressure.

'You really don't need to be afraid of me,' Victor said. 'Whatever happened before is in the past as far as I'm concerned. I don't bear you any ill will for trying to kill me and I hope you don't think worse of me for shooting you in the back and in the belly. I'm sure you can appreciate you didn't exactly leave me much choice in either instance.'

Walker's rising heart rate, which had more than doubled in a matter of seconds, was beginning to stabilise.

Victor said, 'You were doing your job. I don't judge you for that. I certainly don't condemn you for it. That would make me a hypocrite, wouldn't it? And when I'm already such a bad person why be even worse if it can be avoided?'

No answer.

'As far as I'm concerned we're only enemies when you're pointing a gun at me. The rest of the time there's no reason why we can't be polite. Does that make sense? Boxers often

346

hug after twelve rounds of hitting each other in the face, lest we forget.'

The British guy's heart rate began to slow.

'Please nod if you understand.'

Walker nodded.

'I'm glad you agree,' Victor said. 'I'm going to remove my hand now, so I do hope we can maintain this civility.'

He took his palm from Walker's mouth, who swallowed and sucked in some calming breaths. He made no attempt to cry out or call for help.

'Tremendous,' Victor said. 'There's rarely any need to be anything less than cordial. Just because we were enemies before doesn't mean we can't be gentlemen now.'

'You're kind of nuts,' Walker said in a weak voice. 'Do you know that?'

'I have my suspicions.'

The British guy almost smiled. Then he tried to adjust his position and clenched his teeth in sudden agony.

'Yeah, gut shots aren't pleasant,' Victor said. 'But think of it like this: you're only in pain because you're still alive. Someone told me that a long time ago and I think it helps. If we can truly realise that pain is only a message then we can decide how much we pay attention to it.' He shrugged. 'That's the theory, at least. No one can make pain go away with willpower alone, and yet I believe we can self-administer pain relief if we master that rationale.'

Walker's pain subsided enough for him to respond with a weak nod.

'Would you like to sit up?' Victor asked.

'Yeah. Cheers.'

Victor used his foot to work the paddles at the base of

the bed so the head of the bed tilted upwards and elevated Walker with it, who then quickly raised his free hand when he was content.

'Any more and it hurts,' Walker said, gesturing to his abdomen.

'How about some water?'

'That would be good.'

Victor poured some from the jug and then handed him the cup. He spilled a little as he sipped and passed the cup back to Victor, who set it down as he had found it.

Walker used the back of his hand to wipe water from his chin.

'Yogurt?' Victor asked.

He shook his head. He said, 'I'm good,' then, 'Why are you being so nice to me?'

'I told you,' Victor answered. 'You're only my enemy when you're pointing a gun at me.'

'You really mean that? Shouldn't we hate each other?'

'I don't hate anyone,' Victor said. 'Hate is not a very useful emotion when you think about it.'

'Then what do you want?'

'I merely want answers. I want to understand what happened. So let's start with who hired you.'

Walker hesitated, then said, 'I ... I can't tell you. You know how it works, right?'

Victor nodded. 'Have you spoken to the police?'

'Yeah, a bit. Doctors forced them out but they'll be back.'

'What did you tell them?'

'Nothing,' he insisted. 'No way.'

'I can get you out of here,' Victor said. 'If you help me, I can roll you out right now. I'll even set you up in a quiet villa on the coast so you can recover with a nice view. A private nurse to take care of you. Regular doctor's visits. Then, when you're fighting fit again, I'll ensure you can get out of the country without being bothered by the authorities. How does that sound?'

He said nothing.

Victor said, 'This is a genuine offer.'

Walker broke eye contact.

'Is that your final answer?'

On the monitor, Walker's heart rate began to climb again.

Victor let out a sigh. 'And there was me thinking we were getting along so well that we could do this without any unpleasantness.'

SIXTY-EIGHT

Walker looked back at him. Wide, questioning eyes as he analysed Victor's words. The inevitable cry for help was muffled with a palm that slapped down over his mouth before it could be released. The Brit struggled, but was frail and even a small amount of movement caused him debilitating pain.

'Gut shots aren't pleasant,' Victor said again.

With his free arm, Walker tried to pull away Victor's hand. The grip around Victor's wrist was so weak there was no need to actively resist. Within a few seconds, Walker had tired himself out. His chest heaved and his face had become red and sweaty.

Victor examined the patient monitor. Walker's heart rate was sky high.

'Probably best if we ignore this,' Victor said as he disabled the alarm feature. 'Don't want panicking nurses rushing in, do we?'

Walker made a muffled noise beneath Victor's palm. A quiet cry for help or a plea to stop.

'No one can hear you and you're not going to appeal to

my better nature,' Victor explained. 'Try and take some deep breaths and hold them in your lungs for a few seconds before exhaling. You'll feel calmer.' He paused. 'Now, let's take a look at that wound.'

With his free hand, Victor peeled back the tape that held the dressing in place. Walker grimaced as the adhesive tugged at his skin. He struggled as much as he could, which achieved nothing. Victor didn't need to push down with his palm as his bodyweight was enough to keep Walker's head in place, and with it, his whole body. He kept fighting with his free arm, however, which Victor had to swat away every so often because it was a nuisance.

Once the dressing had been removed, Victor could see the wound itself. A small hole just below Walker's ribcage on the right side. It had only needed two stainless-steel staples to close up.

'They've done a great job,' Victor said. 'You're going to have almost no scar. No exit wound either. You should thank whoever it was that decided to take subsonic ammunition. A regular round could have left you with a much nastier wound in the back. Hold still, please.'

It took a few attempts for Victor to hook his thumbnail under one edge of the first staple and the nail of his index finger under the opposite edge.

'Downside of keeping my nails short,' he told Walker. 'Won't be a moment.'

When he had a secure grip, he ripped the staple free.

Walker wailed beneath Victor's palm. It took a little application of force to keep the wounded man in place.

'One down,' Victor said, batting away the flailing arm. 'One to go.'

The second staple was trickier to remove than the first. Walker struggled a lot more than he had beforehand. Now he knew what was coming, his fear outweighed his pain. Yet his efforts achieved nothing except to tire himself out even more, which only made him weaker and easier to control.

'Would you look at that?' Victor said. 'All this flailing about has opened up the wound.'

A little bright blood seeped from where the scab had split.

With his thumb and index finger either side of the split scab, Victor stretched the skin in opposite directions.

More blood seeped out as the scab tore apart to reveal the small round hole in his skin. It was larger than the bullet had made because the surgeons had had to widen it with the extracting tool.

'This is going to hurt,' Victor said, and then inserted his index finger into the hole.

Whatever Walker's fatigue, he found new energy to buck and thrash. Victor angled his head so the attacks could not find his face. Weak fingers tried to claw at his eyes. The muffled cries beneath his palm were a little louder and yet nowhere near loud enough to be heard beyond the room.

'Slightly higher and it could have been very different,' Victor explained as he forced Walker's head down harder. 'Which is why I shot you here where there are no vital organs and staying clear of your abdominal aorta. Even so, the bullet must have missed your liver by millimetres. Guess I'm a little rusty with an MP5. Subsonic bullet or not, that would have been messy. You would have bled out before the paramedics could get to you or you might have died on the operating table.'

The insides of the human body were as warm as a hot tub. Victor rooted around with his finger.

'I can feel a lot of adipose tissue in here,' Victor said. Then, seeing the confusion amid the horror in Walker's eyes: 'That's visceral fat,' he explained. 'Which is really not good. It's why your abdomen sticks out but your belly doesn't jiggle. All the fat's inside of your abdominal wall. We need some of that, of course, for insulation. And as cushioning for all the vital organs in this area that don't get the benefit of a ribcage to protect them. Your kidneys, liver, pancreas and intestines would be pretty vulnerable without a layer of fat as a shield. Problem is, too much visceral fat is really bad for your health. I'm sure at this moment you're not especially concerned about your increased risk of cardiovascular disease or type-two diabetes, but you have a ticking time bomb inside you. If you could feel what I feel you'd be rethinking your entire diet model.'

He adjusted his arm for a better angle as he explored Walker's insides.

'You drink a lot, don't you?' Victor said. 'Our livers are huge anyway, yet yours is even larger than it should be. I can feel a rough texture here ... and here ... That's scarring. Cirrhosis. This is the moment when a doctor would implore you to stop drinking. Don't worry, I'm not the lecturing type. And the good news is the cirrhosis is currently limited to these two areas so if you cut down on the alcohol and adopt some more healthy habits then there's no reason you can't live a long and happy life.'

Walker screamed with his eyes.

Victor stared back at those screaming eyes. 'No reason health wise, I mean.' After a moment's pause, he said, 'So, shall I continue or would you like to have another go at answering my questions? Because with a little rooting around

I could easily check out your gallbladder next. Maybe the spleen afterwards if I really dig deep. Nod once to return to the Q and A or shake your head to continue the examination of your internal organs.'

Walker nodded and nodded and nodded.

SIXTY-NINE

Victor used sterilising wipes to clean his index finger and hand, and dumped the wipes into a yellow bin with a biohazard symbol printed onto it. He gave Walker more water. He gulped down an entire cup and gestured for more. He was pale and soaked in sweat, as were the bedclothes. He looked as though he had aged ten years in ten minutes.

'Talk to me,' Victor said. 'Because if I have to go back inside I'm not just going to examine your gallbladder, I'm going to take it between my fingers and I'm going to rip it out and hold it up over your face so you can take a good look at it while it rains bile down on to you.'

'I'm just a merc,' Walker said, fast and desperate.

'I worked that part out for myself.'

He continued after a swallow. 'Contractor. Private security. Firm in Gibraltar handles the paperwork. I do jobs for all sorts of different people.'

'How do you know Phoenix?'

'I don't know what that means.'

'It means you were subcontracted,' Victor said, disappointed but not surprised. 'Your crew on Sunday ... did you know them all before this job?'

'Some, not all. I don't know who actually hired us. You learn to stop asking questions, you know?'

'You need to give me something.'

'Castellan,' Walker said.

'Is that a person?'

He nodded. 'A man. In Marseille.'

'I need more than that,' Victor said. 'Who is he? What's his connection to your crew?'

'I don't know him, but I heard his name mentioned by the firm. He's a Russian. He's—'

'A Russian?' Victor asked. 'Bratva?'

Walker was confused.

'The Brotherhood,' Victor explained. 'Russian mafia.'

'I don't know anything about that. I think maybe the money or the guns came from him. That's it. That's all I know.'

Victor thought about this for a moment. 'Marseille is a big place, so where do I find this Castellan?'

'I don't know,' Walker told him. 'I really don't.'

'Okay,' Victor said, although he had no idea how Castellan connected to Phoenix or how he was going to use what little information he had been told. If Castellan was part of the Bratva, what did that mean? Was Phoenix using the Bratva to get rid of him or were they using her?

'Don't kill me,' Walker said. 'I won't mention this to anyone.'

'I believe you. Please know that none of this is personal either.'

'You're not going to kill me?'

'Why bother? You don't know who you're working for but they know who you are, and if I could find you, so will they. And they don't need to ask you any questions because they already know what you know and they won't want you telling any of it to the police.'

'I wouldn't,' he insisted, surprising Victor with the passion of his loyalty. 'The firm knows I'm reliable.'

'Well,' Victor began, 'you did tell me. And I didn't even need to tear out your gallbladder first.'

'They *know* me.'

Victor shrugged. 'Which is probably why they didn't rush straight here to use that pillow we talked about earlier. But as time ticks on they're going to start doubting that. They're going to start worrying, and then they're going to come to the conclusion that it's simply not worth the risk.'

'You're wrong.'

'Maybe, but I have no skin in this game. You'll know I'm right if they send someone you've worked with before. Someone you know and like. You'll open your eyes and you'll smile in surprise seeing one of your buddies. He'll tell you that he broke protocol to see how you are and bring you that pastry or sandwich you like. The snack isn't part of the act, you see. It's because he feels bad he's here to kill you.'

'You're wrong,' he said again, only quieter.

'If I had time,' Victor continued, 'I would wait for them. There's almost a guarantee they will know more about the job than you do since they have to understand what they're cleaning up to do it right.'

Victor took the clear bag supplying the fentanyl from the tray and set it to the highest point of the stand.

'It's an opioid,' he explained to Walker. 'I'm giving you a faster supply so you're going to feel woozy in a few moments. You're going to feel on top of the world and then you're going to pass out into a peaceful slumber. There's a good chance you won't even remember this conversation when you wake up again. All the rooting around in your insides might become nothing worse than a bad dream. Wouldn't that be nice?'

Walker said something incomprehensible.

'Oh, I forgot to mention that you're going to lose the power of speech too,' Victor added. 'Pretty quickly.'

He wasn't sure Walker understood him. He wasn't sure Walker even knew he was in the room. The increased dose of fentanyl had reached his brain and a blissful look came on to his face. His eyelids closed most of the way, as if both asleep and awake at the same time, and his lips widened into a contented smile.

The opioid was doing a magnificent job.

Victor missed them almost as much as he missed smoking.

He pushed the staples back into Walker's abdomen. Without the mechanical force of the staple gun, they didn't sink in as far as they had been. Close enough, he thought. Anyone examining the wound would think Walker had moved too strenuously and the staples had worked their way out before anyone considered the alternative. Maybe someone would receive admonishment for not doing a good enough job closing the wound in the first place. A fixable error, however. No one would lose their career over it.

He eased the door open and stepped outside into the corridor when he heard no indication of footsteps or people talking. As before, it was quiet. He could hear talking and a radio advertisement for an energy drink, although neither were near. He imagined a door was ajar around the corner and one of the patients had a visitor.

On his way to the stairwell, an elevator pinged open and two men in scrubs and doctor's white coats stepped out.

They passed one another, Victor ignoring them as they ignored him in return.

Then Victor stopped and looked back.

Unlike every other doctor he had seen in the hospital, these two were not wearing comfortable trainers to ease the discomfort of long shifts. One wore plain black leather slip-on shoes and the second had on hiking boots.

Victor waited until they had turned the corner, and followed.

He was not surprised to see them enter Walker's room.

One even carried a brown paper takeout bag.

SEVENTY

Four and a half minutes was all it took.

Victor lingered in sight of the door until it opened, then he walked to the elevator at a leisurely pace. Although he could not see them, the two men were behind him in the corridor, fresh from killing their colleague. They could have done it any number of ways in those four and a half minutes. Given the setting, Victor imagined a drug of some kind administered at a fatal dose. Or perhaps a pillow over the face as Victor had suggested. With the high dose of fentanyl Victor had supplied, Walker would never have known what was happening to him. He would not have been able to enjoy the food they brought him either.

By the time Victor reached the elevator, they were close behind him, their purposeful strides catching up as he had wanted. When he used a knuckle to push the call button, they were right next to him.

They said nothing and neither did Victor.

When they had emerged from the elevator a few

minutes beforehand they had not so much as glanced his way. He detected no shifts in posture or behaviour to indicate recognition.

The elevator doors pulled back and the three of them stepped inside the car.

Victor, having been closest and first inside, moved furthest until he was at the rear wall. He turned around and leaned his shoulder blades against it as though he were fatigued from a long shift. In a suit beneath the white coat, he could be a consultant. He jangled the set of keys to relieve some of the imaginary stress.

The two guys did similar, each moving to the perpendicular walls. The guy on Victor's right leaning against it while the guy to his left stood with arms folded in front of it after thumbing the button for the basement level, where the underground parking was located.

They both bore a look of satisfaction, almost triumphant, although restrained. A job well done.

Little smiles and expressions exchanged as each congratulated the other in silence.

Victor feigned ignorance.

Although a part of him could never understand that shared triumph. A job well done meant doing a job well, which should surely be the default position of any employable task. No one should strive for passable, so why would the minimum achievement be worth celebration?

In other circumstances, he might have asked for enlightenment.

He could not image this ending in any way conducive of polite discussion, however.

The doors closed.

They had left the brown paper bag, he noted. Maybe they hadn't wanted to carry it away. Maybe they figured a nurse could make use of it. Thinking about potential fillings made Victor feel disappointed they did not still have the sandwich with them. He could almost smell the fresh baguette. He was sure it was impossible to buy a bad meal in France. There might even be a law to that end.

The car descended.

'Fancy a cold one?' the guy to Victor's right asked, speaking English with a Scottish accent, perhaps assuming Victor was French and did not understand, or not caring if he did. Despite what they had just done, this was an innocent question.

The guy to the left gave a firm nod of agreement. 'I'd say we've earned it.'

He had a well-spoken, received-pronunciation accent.

The two guys continued their wordless backslapping until the elevator stopped on the next floor down. A doctor in a white coat stepped inside, went to hit a button, then said, 'Is this going up?'

'Down,' Victor answered.

She backtracked with a smile of self-deprecation. The Scot to Victor's right thumbed the button for the basement again.

As the door closed, the doctor said, 'I don't know how you do it.'

Her eyes were cast towards the floor.

Then she was gone and the elevator descended. The two guys were confused, glancing at one another and in the direction the doctor had been looking. They shuffled their feet in case they had missed something.

Then they realised.

To Victor, it seemed as if both men came to that same

realisation at the exact same time. The guy to his right looked at the Englishman's hiking boots while he looked at his partner's slip-ons.

Their previous smug triumph became ignominy. They exchanged expressions of blame.

How could you have missed this?

How could you?

Victor stood still, saying nothing and willing them to get over it. So they had overlooked one thing. No big deal. Only one person had noticed.

The trouble, of course, was that now they understood their mistake they couldn't stop thinking about it. Doctors and nurses on long shifts would wear comfortable footwear. That should have been obvious. These two wouldn't make that mistake again now they knew. Anyone pretending to be a doctor would give themselves away overlooking such a detail.

The guy on Victor's right worked it out first.

In the silent exchange of blame, it was the Scotsman who had been the first to concede the argument. He shrugged as if to say *it is what it is* and he broke eye contact with his partner. He looked elsewhere while shaking his head to himself. At the ceiling. At the floor.

Where his gaze lingered.

An amateur might have looked straight at Victor in that moment. Human instinct was to make eye contact when seeing someone for the first time and this guy might as well have been seeing Victor for the first time.

The gaze lingering on the floor did so because the Scot had noticed that Victor's shoes, like their own, were not the kind of footwear a doctor on a long shift would wear. Although the suit suggested he was more used to sitting behind a desk in a consulting room instead of pacing wards. Had they not interacted already, had they not recognised him from before, Victor was sure the guy would have dismissed his suspicion now.

Instead, he looked away from Victor's shoes, careful not to gaze at Victor directly, and regained eye contact with his partner.

Victor saw the gesture the Scot made. A subtle head movement that told his partner there was something of note about Victor. Nothing further was required because the second guy had noticed the Scot looking at the floor. He did the rest of the equation by himself.

They had worked together a long time, Victor saw. They knew one another well enough to have whole conversations without words. Given what they now knew about Victor, he did not relish the prospect of them as enemies.

Neither acted straightaway, which was to be expected. The hospital was a public place even if the three of them were alone. The elevator would have CCTV and they had murdered a man mere minutes earlier. They didn't want to cause a scene. They were here to clean up Walker's mess, not make their own.

Besides, they didn't realise Victor had watched them throughout their entire thought process and understood their conclusions. They thought he was ignorant of their revelation. They wanted to keep it that way.

There was a small likelihood it changed nothing, Victor figured. They were the clean-up crew. They were a separate entity to Walker's team so there would be no camaraderie between them that would encourage an emotional need for vengeance. The takeout said they had some past history, of course, but nostalgia hadn't trumped their orders. They could have been best friends once, godparents to each other's children, only none of that had stopped them killing him.

Might they have orders to find and kill Victor too? Possible, although he could not imagine them failing to recognise him if that were the case. Victor's haircut and shave made him look like a different person across a street or within a crowd. Not when they were all close enough for him to see every enlarged pore on the Scotsman's nose. A competent clean-up crew, of which they had already proven themselves, would know their target, even a secondary target, when they saw him. Only the shoes – only the doctor pointing out that single oversight in their approach – had caused them to look at Victor with new eyes.

He watched their conversation play out before him. No words. Just expressions. The Scot on the right was agitated, as though he was angry at the other guy for not noticing, while angrier at himself. The Englishman raised his eyebrows and sighed through his nose, more sanguine than his colleague. *What can you do?*

After this first exchange, they got down to business. How were they going to handle this? They had only two real choices as far as Victor could deduce. Either they continued on their way because their mission had been completed or they dealt with him.

A few subtle gestures was all it took. The Englishman tilted his head a little in Victor's direction, then performed a slight motion with his hands – a rotating of palms, an elevation of thumbs – that could have meant anything, and yet the guy on the right understood.

We deal with him.

SEVENTY-ONE

If the two cleaners were impetuous and decided to engage here in the elevator, then they would be at the disadvantage, not him. There was too little space inside the car for two guys to make a move and not get in each other's way. Even if they both had guns and drew them at the exact same moment, Victor was confident he would be triumphant. He was already in striking range without taking a single step. The instant they exploded into motion, so would he, striking the Englishman with a punch so Victor could whip his right elbow back into the second guy. Neither blow had to be perfect in placement to disrupt their actions, and with each man effectively one-handed as they were going for weapons, they would have no practical defence for his follow-up attacks.

It could all be over before the car stopped at the basement level and the doors pinged open.

They were competent cleaners, however. They were not going to initiate any violence when they were so exposed. Besides, they had no need to rush. As far as they knew, he was ignorant both of their original purpose and of the conclusion to which they had recently arrived.

The Scot raised his hands a little, showing the other guy a glimpse of his palms in a gesture for patience.

We take care of him, just not yet.

The Englishman responded with a nod, then patted his hip pocket so keys clinked.

Agreed, get him in the vehicle.

It would be a van, Victor knew. While the space and the privacy afforded by the back compartment were the obvious benefit, more than that it was the forgettability such a vehicle offered. Guys waiting around in a car drew the gaze. A van sitting idle was almost invisible.

That the Englishman had keys suggested they were the full extent of the clean-up crew, although there was a good chance there was a second pairing in a second vehicle or this guy had a set of keys as well as a driver currently waiting behind the wheel. That could also be the reason why these two wanted to get Victor to the van: because that's where they had backup. They might not fancy facing him alone given they were cleaners, not frontline operators, but he realised that wasn't the case.

The Scot on the right failed to hide his smirk of anticipation.

Victor added overconfidence to their list of disadvantages as the elevator reached the basement level.

His attention switched to pure observation analysis. He focused on the two guys: their hands, their eyes, their body language.

They stiffened in readiness for action, but it was to no greater degree than anyone else would make when expecting elevator doors to open so they could continue on their way. They were not going to draw their weapons and frogmarch him out of the elevator, not when he could refuse to move from the car that might be recalled to ascend at any moment, and not when they were in front of him. A bad idea he was sure they would never even contemplate. So they had to continue the pretence for a moment, at least. They had to get out of the car without alerting him or otherwise giving him a reason to stay inside and jab buttons. They couldn't know he was stepping out regardless of what they did because, like them, he wanted to take this away from cameras and witnesses. Besides, they still thought he was ignorant of their intent.

They would step out first and either hang back until he passed, using any number of pretences to explain their loitering – searching pockets for a receipt, checking the time, telling a joke – or walk at a slow, leisurely pace that encouraged him to pass them. He figured the former since they might not feel comfortable with a threat in their blind spot. Especially because he might take a different route altogether and throw off their plan.

He knew how they felt. He didn't want them behind him for the same reasons.

When the chime sounded and the doors pulled open, the three of them stood unmoving.

Then the Englishman to Victor's left looked his way and said, 'After you.'

Victor made no move. 'That's okay.'

He gestured at the open doorway as the guy did likewise, both smiling and seemingly friendly and polite. On appearances, a duel of good manners only.

The Scot said, 'Go ahead.'

Victor relented because he wanted to maintain the appearance of ignorance more than he wanted to be behind them. The longer they believed themselves in control of the situation, the greater the surprise when eventually he made them understand their delusion. He needed privacy to make the most of that moment.

So, when he stepped outside the elevator and into the garage, his gaze swept across the space to identify their van. An impossible task on the surface, yet the odds increased with every passing second. Maybe two hundred potential spaces, and only half occupied. He didn't know the exact percentage of vans on French roads, but ten to fifteen per cent seemed about right. In a hospital garage, as opposed to general usage, he figured the lower end of that scale. About ten in total. A few seconds of scanning and he counted twelve. Because the garage was nowhere near capacity, they would have been able to park pretty much wherever they wanted. Although the majority of visitors would choose to park close to the ticket machine and elevator, these two men wouldn't elect to park in the busiest area. They were here to clean up a mess. They would favour discretion.

Victor's gaze found two potentials parked in faraway corners with few vehicles nearby. They were at opposite ends of the space, however. One was closest to the exit ramp, which was a fine tactical choice. The other was in an area with poorer lighting and somewhat shielded from CCTV by free-hanging signage, which also made tactical sense to him. Both were reverse-parked, so that was of no help to him, and neither had bright paint or other eye-catching features that would rule them out. One had a local licence plate, the other was registered in Marseille. Both were cargo vans. Neither was brand new or old and rusting. At a distance, Victor could see no rental company stickers.

It was looking like a coin-flip until he saw the ceiling lights reflected in raindrops on the windscreen of the van from Marseille. The vehicle near the exit had no hint of rain, because it had been parked far longer – it had either fully dried or missed the start of the rain altogether.

He couldn't see, yet he imagined that the two cleaners behind him perhaps smiled or made some other sign they were pleased by his decision to walk in the direction of their vehicle. Victor saw no one on the other side of the windscreen glass. Any backup could be in the back compartment, of course.

Eighty metres of open ground lay between Victor and the cleaners' van. He walked at a casual pace to reinforce the delusions of the two guys behind him. Maybe 1.2 or 1.3 metres per second. About one hundred seconds of time. Given he was doing most of the work for them there was no need for them to act until he neared their destination. If he walked right up to the van, however, they were going to deduce for themselves that they had misjudged him. Therefore, he chose a car in that area of the garage. A shiny Audi that looked like it could be his own, or one he might pick out of a rental company's brochure. Once they realised he was heading towards it, they would use it as their strike point. Perhaps deciding to wait until his hands were on the wheel before they made their move; they couldn't know it would never get that far. Safer to act before that, however, when they could get their hands on him if it became necessary. So when he was right next to the Audi then, before he climbed inside, when the vehicle was in front of him and they were behind and he had nowhere to go. He could almost feel their thoughts and see the gestures they made between themselves as they worked out the details.

It helped that they were professionals, competent and careful, so he could think just like them. Had they been amateurs, their plans would have been far harder to predict. Options that he would never even consider probable because of the slim chances of success or the many avoidable after-effects might be their first, hasty course of action, as bad for him as for themselves.

With the echoing acoustics provided by the low ceiling and many cars, his footsteps seemed loud. He made no effort to tread with softer footfalls, which he did so often that it felt unnatural to now make so much avoidable noise.

The two guys behind him were louder. Double the foot-steps and they had to match his pace to stay at the same distance, so a greater propensity to scuff a heel or put down that heel with unnecessary force. They were second-guessing him the entire time, never quite knowing if he was going to stop or adjust his course. Those unknown factors would increase their stress levels. He didn't want them to worry.

Fear made people make mistakes.

Victor wanted them to do everything right.

SEVENTY-TWO

The air was cool and humid inside the parking garage. A breeze blew in from outside and swirled around the space. He felt it on his cheeks. He could smell the moisture when he inhaled. He smelled exhaust fumes too, faint and acrid. He had always liked the scent, somehow sweet to him. Maybe it triggered a memory he could not otherwise remember. Or perhaps the waste gases and particulates wafting in the air shared some similarities with tobacco smoke that his nostrils detected or his brain interpreted.

After all, as he had told Walker, he was not an ex-smoker, only a smoker who no longer smoked.

Victor slipped a hand into a pocket of the white coat and withdrew the doctor's keys, pointing the fob at the silver Audi. The two guys behind him could not see the fob was for a different vehicle and Victor wasn't pushing the button, but even from behind it would be obvious where he was pointing and they would hear the sigh of frustration he made before slipping the hand back inside the pocket.

Their steps quietened a little when they realised which car he was heading towards and they knew how much distance they had yet to cover.

A faulty key fob or radio receiver was a push of credulity, he knew, and yet they only had to believe it for a few seconds. Confirmation bias would help him out. They were improvising, which had no doubt put them on edge whatever their expertise, and now they were calmer, which made them more predictable, because they had been reassured they had it all figured out.

The malfunctioning key fob may as well have been a hug as he assured them, *You've got this*.

The Audi was about ten metres from their cargo van, with a scattering of other cars between the two. Then narrow lanes for moving vehicles provided a corridor of open space before the van itself. As he neared, and could see more through the windscreen, he detected movement in the back compartment. While just a shifting of shadows, it told him there was at least one more cleaner. Who could be unaware of what was happening. Victor had seen no earpieces or other signs of comms equipment on the two guys who killed Walker. No pressing need to stay connected, they would have decided, and better not to risk having anything on their persons that might give them away inside the hospital or lodge in the memory of a member of staff who might be a future witness for investigators. And if not in constant communication, they would have phones. One of the two could have sent a quick message while out of Victor's line of sight, although he decided they had not. They were cleaners, improvising. All of their focus was on following Victor and getting him to, and into, their van. They weren't going to take their eyes off him for a second, let alone tie up one or more hands using a phone. And if any such message had reached the one or more cleaners inside the van, they would have given it away by getting behind the wheel in preparation for a rapid exfiltration.

Which confirmed the two behind Victor had guns. If they were unarmed they wouldn't make any move without backup. Good, because Victor could use some untraceable weapons. No cleaner gun than a cleaner's own.

He just had to keep them confident a little longer, so they walked themselves into a trap.

When he reached the parked Audi, he walked alongside it to the driver's door, pretending he had failed to notice the two guys had picked up their pace as one broke off to come at him from the far side while the other rushed up behind.

Both already had their guns drawn as he looked up to acknowledge them.

Those pistols were pointed his way, but held low down to keep them from the CCTV cameras.

Both cleaners had flushed faces, although not from the momentary exertion. Their hearts were pounding and their blood was awash with adrenalin. The flanker, the Englishman, was sweating too, his red face shiny, and fluorescent light glinting from a drop at end of his nose. The Scot who had come up behind him said nothing, his mouth desert dry, fine motor skills made blunt and awkward by his autonomic nervous system going into overdrive. Simple deep breaths could have prevented all that.

Cleaners, not soldiers.

The Englishman managed to say, 'Don't move.'

Victor had his back to the car so he could see them both at

the same time. He raised his hands. Keys gripped in his right fist to use as a weapon should it become necessary.

He had no need to act scared. These two were so bubbling over with stress hormones they were incapable of recognising fear or its absence. Which suited Victor. When he lived under constant pretences, he appreciated not needing to add more if it could be avoided. He could act naturally and it wouldn't make any difference. He could explain to them every mistake they had made and exactly how he was going to use those mistakes against them and they wouldn't be able to process it. They would just say, *What?*

Still, guns were guns and bullets didn't care who fired them. Victor kept his movements slow and obvious as a result. He didn't want a round in the guts because he'd spooked one of these guys into a negligent discharge.

He had his palms showing and near his shoulders, portraying passivity while keeping his hands at a useful height at the end of arms locked and loaded in case they were going to do something foolish. While they weren't calm, they were competent and careful, so the Scotsman said:

'Drop your hands. Keep them at your side.'

'This way,' the Englishman added.

They shuffled to give him space to move away from the Audi and he did as he was told. He slipped the keys back into a pocket. He wanted his hands free for now.

His continued acquiescence further reassured them and helped calm them down. They had been hyped up for the initial move – when the stakes were highest and the unknowns many – and now it was all going according to plan, their heart rates began to slow. They thought the danger had passed. They failed to understand the danger was coming closer with every step they took ushering Victor to their destination.

'In the corner,' the Englishman said. 'Brown van.'

'I have a lot of money nearby,' he told them. 'I can take you to it.'

Neither responded for a moment, before he heard, 'You can't buy your way out of this.'

Interesting, he thought.

They had considered the idea, if only for a second, perhaps exchanging quick glances to see how the other felt about it. Given they had already murdered a fellow member of the their company he knew they had little loyalty to one another, but if even the idea of easy cash gave them pause for thought then this really was just a job to them. They had no more loyalty to their employers than to their colleagues.

Pure mercenaries, just like him.

Good to know.

He slowed as he neared the van.

'Round the back,' the Scot told him.

He stepped alongside the vehicle until he was next to the rear bumper. There was almost two metres of space between the back of the van and the wall. They had reverse-parked with plenty of space left for the doors to open.

Victor glanced back. The two cleaners had come closer now they were at the van. Almost near enough to touch. Both had their guns out, held low still, yet gripped a little looser. He could see their knuckles had more colour in them than when they first had their guns out next to the silver Audi.

The Englishman then moved around to the back of the van, and tapped a palm on the bodywork three quick times.

The door opened to reveal a single man inside the back compartment. His welcoming smile faded to confusion.

'Who's this clown?' the man asked, as British as the other cleaners, as Walker had been.

The Englishman answered. 'He's the reason we're in this mess in the first place.'

'Self-defence,' Victor added.

'Oh, our boy's not merely a clown, but a joker,' the man inside the van said, shaking his head. 'What's he even doing here?'

'Came to finish what he started,' the Scot answered. 'What else is there?'

'You guys killed Walker,' Victor pointed out, 'not me.'

They had nothing to say to that.

'Isn't our remit,' the new guy said after a moment.

'Same firm,' the Scot replied. 'Same problems to solve.'

'We're here to put out the fire, not chuck a load of petrol on it.'

The sound of a car entering the parking garage broke the stalemate and the new guy sighed again and nodded. He didn't agree with the decision, and yet he didn't want to stand around arguing about it. Whatever the outcome, it would be decided elsewhere.

'Come on then, up you get.'

He gestured for Victor to climb into the van. One of the others put a palm to his back to shove him up through the door, although Victor needed no encouragement.

This was exactly what he wanted.

SEVENTY-THREE

The Scot and the Englishman hung back while the guy in the rear of the van moved through the opening and into the front, where he climbed into the driver's seat. No one told him what to do, so Victor sat down on one of the two narrow boxed benches running parallel along both interior walls. He took the one on the same side as the driver's seat. If they told him to move to the other bench, he would upgrade his assessment of their competency.

The Englishman and the Scot climbed into the back of the van with him, the Englishman taking a seat on the bench opposite Victor, only closer to the front and the driver. The Scot pulled the rear door shut after him and sat down next to the back of the van on the same bench as the Englishman.

Neither said a word to Victor.

It wasn't ideal to have them so spread out.

The two guys in the back with him kept their guns in their hands. The first had his held by his side, resting on the boxed bench. The second kept his weapon cradled in his lap.

The engine started up and the driver pulled out of the parking space and headed for the exit. The garage was pay-and-display, so there was no barrier to slow them down. They were up the ramp and out of the hospital grounds within one minute.

The Scot and the Englishman seemed content with silence, both carefully watching Victor while having another silent conversation with expressions and gestures. There was no congratulatory backslapping this time. They were pensive. Maybe doubts were setting in.

'The firm won't like it if we go off script,' the driver said in a loud voice to make sure he was heard in the back. 'We did what we came here to do, so we should exfil. That's it. No side projects.'

'There'll be a bonus,' the Englishman said, sure of tone. 'What happened on Sunday is bad for the firm's reputation. Delivering up our new best friend here will go a long way with public relations. Trust me, we're going to be very popular at head office. Might even get promotions out of this.'

The driver was silent, thinking it through.

'Besides,' the Englishman continued, a half-smile sent Victor's way, 'this chap says he's got cash nearby.'

The driver shot a quick glance back, lips pursed. 'Is that right?'

Victor answered with a nod.

'How near is nearby?' the Scot asked.

'Edge of the city, about twenty kilometres.'

'No reason we can't take a detour,' the Englishman suggested.

The driver said, 'Stashed how?'

'I have it in a car,' Victor said.

'Why is it in a car?'

'Practical reasons. I don't have the pocket space.'

The two men in the back exchanged looks, each imagining how much cash would be considered too much to be carried around. A few thousand? Tens of thousands? More?

Victor said nothing further. He let their mercenary sensibilities do the work for him. The Scot and the Englishman were so excited by the prospect of easy money they didn't think to ask why this stash of money wasn't in the Audi Victor had pretended was his own.

'Where exactly?' the driver called back.

Victor, thinking about the Marseille plates on the cargo van, said, 'Parked near the airport in a private *longue durée*.'

The Scot and the Englishman exchanged more looks, then nods.

'It's on the way,' the Scot said to the driver, while giving the Englishman a smile.

He smiled back, then added, 'If he has a stash then we should check it out regardless. We can't ignore anything that might result in blowback for the firm. No point bringing matey boy in if we leave his mess behind.'

The driver shouted, 'Gimme a minute to think about it.'

'Take your time,' the Scotsman shouted back, then nodded in the Englishman's direction.

He whispered, 'It's on.'

They seemed pleased with themselves, certain the driver would come around. The Englishman was animated, high on a job well done, a potential promotion, and the prospect of some extra crash. The Scotsman had more control of himself. He kept his gaze on Victor.

The driver sighed and shook his head. 'If he tries anything, and I do mean *anything*, then we shoot him whether we've got the cash or not.'

'Of course,' the Scot replied.

'I want to hear you both say it.'

The Englishman, in his aristocratic voice, said, 'Cash or not, we shoot him if he tries anything.' Then to Victor, he added, 'No hard feelings, yeah?'

Victor, mentally rehearsing precisely how he would kill them all, answered, 'Not in the slightest.'

SEVENTY-FOUR

The van was quiet. Victor sat as passive as he knew how, listening to the traffic outside and paying attention to the number of times the vehicle slowed down or stopped. He paid attention to the duration of such stops, too, and how much the driver accelerated. He noticed how often the van took a corner and how severe the angle of the turn.

There were no windows in the back of the van, and he couldn't see through the windscreen without changing position, but he didn't need to see to know when they were out of the city centre and when they joined the coastal road that ran the length of the Riviera.

Just a little further, he thought.

The Englishman had grown bored, the thrill of going into action and capturing a valuable target had worn off, replaced by the adrenalin dump that was making him sluggish. The Scot was more alert, so Victor put him as the more experienced man. The more dangerous man.

There were three guys with him. Three pairs of eyes.

382

Three pairs of hands. Yet two of those hands were on the steering wheel of the van while two eyes watched the road, leaving four hands and four eyes. Of those four hands, two were holding pistols. One was simple enough to deal with; two was a problem.

'Nearly there,' the driver called, having followed Victor's directions to where he had left Miller and Boulanger's car.

The Englishman said to the Scot, 'How do you want to do this?'

Gaze still locked on Victor, the Scot answered, 'When we're close, you hop out and I'll keep our friend here company. Have a recce. Then we'll work out the specifics.'

Adrenalin rising once more, the Englishman swapped places with the Scot, so he was right next to the rear door. As the van began to slow to navigate the narrow streets, he reached out a hand to the door handle, ready and eager.

Victor had planned on waiting until the van had stopped moving to act, but this was so good an opportunity it was almost an invitation.

With the driver's hands and eyes already occupied, and the Englishman now voluntarily giving up his free hand, it left only the Scot now sat opposite.

'You'll need my keys,' Victor said.

'Take them out,' the Scot said. 'Nice and slow.'

Victor did just that, keeping his movements slow and deliberate, before tossing the doctor's keys to the Scot. A gentle throw, telegraphed so it didn't take him by surprise. Easy to catch.

While he snatched the keys out of the air without needing to take his gaze from Victor, he glanced down instinctively to put those keys in a pocket.

In that moment, there was only one pair of eyes looking his way, and no hands to stop Victor—

Kicking the Scot opposite him in the shin. A simple attack, quick and savage. No huge power was possible in the limited space for acceleration, but Victor required none. He kicked out with his left leg, rotating his foot clockwise so his heel struck the guy's shin dead on. The result was as good as instantaneous, the sudden excruciating pain causing the Scot to double over, his core involuntarily contracting and lowering his head in a rapid arch—

Straight into Victor's right knee, which was accelerating upwards at the same time.

The gun in the guy's right hand was useless because he was unconscious before he could even think about responding.

Victor's knee impacted against the Scot's teeth – clenched in response to the kick to the shin – and tore many from his gums, exploded more still, and the snapping jaw ruptured many blood vessels inside the mouth.

The doctor's white coat would never be the same again.

Several whole teeth, and dozens of fragments, rattled around on the floor as the van swerved and swayed, the driver panicking.

Instinct compelled Victor to stamp on the back of the exposed neck of the guy who crumpled down, yet speed was everything now. A mere second spent executing an already-disabled enemy meant a foot out of position and two seconds of killing time lost to regain effective balance. All the while the remaining threats adjusted to his attack.

They were failing to adjust.

The driver could do nothing with his hands on the wheel and his eyes on the road. At least, that's what he believed.

Countless hours of driving experience worked against him here because his instincts were to keep his focus on what he was doing when even a slight jerk of the steering wheel or a sudden tap on the brake pedal would have dramatically changed the battlefield for Victor and thrown off his momentum.

By the time the driver understood he could in fact intervene, this would be over.

The second cleaner in the back reacted fast, although that reaction was ineffectual.

The Englishman froze.

Maybe it had been years since he was last in any real danger. Maybe the only violence he had witnessed had been the kind acted out under his supervision or control.

A cleaner, not a soldier.

Victor was already springing from his seat before the man had shaken free of his shock.

He snapped up his pistol – too far – expecting Victor's rapid rise to bring him to full height. Instead, Victor only rose far enough to charge his shoulder into the guy's hips, slamming him backwards into the doors of the van while his gun was useless above Victor's back.

The doors flexed and warped, the air whooshing out from the cleaner's lungs, leaving him breathless and stunned while Victor wrapped his arms around the back of the Englishman's thighs and wrenched his legs out from under him.

There was too little room for Victor to maximise the power of the takedown, the warped and flexed doors slowing the cleaner's fall and preventing any devastating impact of skull on floor, although Victor only needed to overwhelm and disorientate the man to stop him making use of his weapon.

Which left his grip at some point during the takedown, so that when Victor went to disarm it, he found only empty fingers.

A downwards elbow strike stopped the Englishman's attempt to counter-attack. A second would have knocked him out, only the driver slammed on the brakes.

Victor lost his balance as a result, the prostrate Scotsman cushioning the impact as he fell forward to the floor, yet he found himself within reach of the Englishman's dropped gun that skidded his way.

The driver was already turning around in his seat by that point, pistol in hand, yet he had too much distance to cover to rotate his torso and head to see into the back and get his arm extended to find an aim.

Victor snatched the handgun from the floor and shot the driver three times through the seat. He jerked and spasmed with each impact, then slumped motionless.

With the driver dead and the Scot unconscious, that only left the Englishman.

Who had his hands up and his palms showing before Victor could even aim the gun.

SEVENTY-FIVE

'*Waitwaitwait*,' the Englishman urged, eyes wide and one already swelling up from Victor's elbow strike. 'You don't need to kill me.'

'Agreed,' Victor said, lowering the gun as he took a seat on one of the benches and gestured for the Englishman to do the same.

He did, although slower, palms still showing, looking relieved he was still alive despite grimacing.

'I don't take this kind of thing personally,' Victor said. 'But you need to tell me something to keep it that way.'

'Of course.'

'Where's Phoenix?'

'I'm sorry,' he said, 'I don't know who that is.'

'You know enough about Walker's job to know his target when you see him, so don't act ignorant now.'

The Englishman said, 'No, that's not correct. I told you: we don't know anything about his job.'

'In the elevator,' Victor began. 'You realised who I am.'

'Yeah,' he replied, a little sheepish with embarrassment. 'Although we were slow to put the pieces together.'

'How did you recognise me, then?'

'A couple of grainy CCTV shots the firm managed to get hold of,' he explained. 'You look different now, obviously. Once we clocked it about the shoes then I noticed yours and then everything clicked into place. You were the one wanted by the cops because you were the one who killed Walker's crew and put the man himself in the hospital. You're the reason why I'm here.'

'Why did your company provide you with my picture but not tell you the specifics of the contract Walker was working on?'

'Policy,' he answered. 'While the contract was obviously unfulfilled by Walker the job remains open, so there are privacy and security implications. We don't need to know Walker's job to clean up his mess, so we don't get told. Direct action is a whole other division. We don't overlap.'

Victor said, 'Then who do I speak to in the direct action division?'

'Good luck,' was the answer. 'It doesn't work like that. There's a whole internal AI system for divvying up the work so no one is ever exposed and criminally liable. You could talk to everyone in the company and no one would be able to give you any clear answers. Sorry, pal. You'll be chasing ones and zeroes to the moon and back. Private security has embraced AI technology in a big way.'

'You were given my picture. Why?'

'Why do you think?' He found the question humorous. 'In case you popped up again where you don't belong. I'm telling you the truth, I swear. I have no reason to lie. This is just a job. I don't want to die for it.'

'Who's Castellan?' Victor asked.

'The client.'

'Walker's client or yours?'

'Both,' the Englishman answered. 'Well, he's a client of the firm, I mean. Russian guy, one of those mafia Brotherhood psychopaths.'

'Why is he hiring a private security company to do his dirty work? He must have his own soldiers.'

'You'd have to ask him that.'

'I will,' Victor said. 'How do I find him?'

'Western port of Marseille,' the Englishman explained. 'I think he has a shipping company.'

'I thought he was a gangster.'

'I don't know his CV,' the Englishman said. 'Maybe he's both. Everyone's a criminal in this world, aren't they?'

Victor nodded. 'I appreciate your frankness. You've been very helpful.'

'Sure, sure,' he replied, almost smiling. 'Like I said: this is just the nine-to-five. There's nothing personal in all this. I know it's only business, you know it's only business.'

'Exactly,' Victor said, then gestured to the rear doors. 'On that note, could you kindly open them a crack for me?'

The Englishman nodded, happy to be of service. 'Of course,' he said, working the handle and pushing the door open a little. 'How come?'

'It's better for the ears,' Victor answered and executed the unconscious Scotsman with a single bullet in the back of his skull.

The Englishman cried out in horror, thrusting his palms higher as he looked at Victor with terrified, pleading eyes.

'No hard feelings,' Victor said as he squeezed the trigger.

SEVENTY-SIX

After closing the van's rear door and dragging the driver's corpse into the back, Victor removed the bloody doctor's coat and climbed behind the wheel. The driver had stopped the van in one of the quiet industrial streets near to the airport. For an emergency stop, the parking was commendable. Victor only spent a few seconds aligning the van to the kerb.

He was careful when he exited the vehicle. The suppressed gunshots would have been audible to any passers-by, although Victor saw no nearby pedestrians. It wasn't that kind of area, which was why he had wanted the cleaners to bring themselves here. Had anyone been close enough, the ambient noise of the airport would have dulled the muted reports so much no one thought twice about them. Especially with the nearby industrial units providing an excuse for loud noises.

Regardless, three corpses in the back of the van were going to cause a problem at some point. Nowhere close to enough time to bury or otherwise dispose of them, so Victor decided to leave the vehicle where it had stopped. It would be a while before the bodies began to stink enough that someone became suspicious, which would give him plenty of time to get out of Nice and give the private security firm in Gibraltar a call. He figured that once he had made them aware they had lost more personnel they would send a second team of cleaners to take care of the mess the previous three Brits had left behind. The firm cared about its reputation, as the Englishman had pointed out.

Victor made his way back to the airport, letting his route be guided by the other scattered pedestrians that expanded into crowds when he neared the larger hotels and cafés, bars and restaurants that served the business travellers and holidaymakers. Where they were found, so were the pickpockets.

Similar to the groups he had witnessed operating in the heart of the city, yet these were slicker and bolder, taking advantage of the density of new arrivals to take wallets and valuables. He noticed one spotter looking his way more than once. In his suit, Victor looked as if he would have an expensive phone or a good amount of cash in his wallet, and he was alone.

When the spotter glanced Victor's way again, Victor looked pointedly back and removed his sunglasses to ensure the spotter could not be mistaken he was the focus of his gaze.

Victor shook his head a single time.

The spotter froze for a second, shocked and uncomfortable, then shook his own head in the direction of his fellow criminals.

Message sent, Victor continued on his path, although now he saw he had a bigger problem to deal with than simple pickpockets.

He had a shadow.

A man in a blue cap was following him.

Victor wasn't sure when he had picked up the shadow, whether long before he realised, or within the last few seconds when the pickpocket crew had distracted his watchfulness. He detected no one else operating with the shadow, but there had to be more. Was this guy another of Salomé's crew, part of another team of contractors or someone else entirely?

He neared a church that was up-lit in green, blue, red and magenta. Unnecessary, Victor thought as he always did when he saw such modern illuminations on historical buildings that had been built without such intentions. He imagined the original architects would be appalled by the display, and yet it drew him nearer.

He heard a choir practising inside, and entered.

The church was both a place of worship and a tourist site. While it had a modern interior, there were signs advertising the crypt below that dated back to the Middle Ages. Victor lit a votive candle and made the sign of the cross. For all his strength, that simple movement taxed him as much as any physical conflict. He took a seat on an empty pew and bowed his head in reverence. He spoke no prayer and yet he heard many in his thoughts, recited by his own voice and those of the other boys. Much of their time had been spent reciting prayers, of course. Hail Mary, Glory Be, Our Father, Nicene Creed, and more competed to be heard inside his head. It was no surprise he struggled to control his memories when inside a place of worship, and he gave up after a moment's effort. Instead, he let himself remember. He tried to separate the voices and picture the faces of the other orphans. Only the most basic shapes and features came into focus. He found he could not recall a single name from that time. Not surprising, he supposed, given he had spent so many years trying to forget.

Footsteps.

He forced away the prayers and faces to concentrate on the present. He made no reaction as he pictured the man in the blue cap. No doubt he had trod with care in an attempt to be quiet. The hard tiled floors and echoing acoustics made such a thing impossible here, even with the choir singing.

The footsteps ceased after a few seconds.

Victor pictured the man had taken a seat somewhere behind him in order to blend in, so Victor took that moment to rise from his own pew and follow the signs to the crypt.

There were plenty of lights, and yet there were many dark corners and shadowed alcoves. The harmony of the choir reached down into the crypt, only here they were faint and disembodied, made eerier by the acoustics of the low ceilings and confined spaces below the earth. Aside from the curiosity value, there was little to do or see. Maybe the guy in the blue hat knew that and would wonder why Victor was taking so long, or maybe he had been instructed not to let Victor out of his sight.

Either way, it wasn't long before he came down to the crypt.

It was not a large space, only a few rooms, though it was confusing with its maze-like interconnections, so the man had no idea when Victor positioned himself in his blind spot.

Four quick steps brought him up behind the guy without him hearing. He saw Victor's shadow, although not soon enough to matter. Victor snapped on a chokehold, wrapping his right arm around the guy's neck so the carotids were pinched shut on one side by Victor's forearm and on the other side of the neck by his biceps. Victor clasped his hands together and squeezed the guy's head against his chest, increasing the pressure to agonising levels. The guy was significantly shorter so Victor had his knees bent to better apply the hold, so that when he straightened his legs again he stretched the guy up on to his tiptoes, further intensifying the pain and the panic as his own bodyweight worked against him.

The application of force was so sudden and violent that the guy did not have time to launch an effective counterattack. He instinctively grabbed at Victor's arm in an effort to pull it away. Whatever the guy's strength, leverage and body mechanics meant it was never going to work. It took a few seconds for him to process this inevitability and by then he was already weakening fast.

'I'm going to loosen my grip,' Victor told him. 'And then you're going to start talking. Ready?'

Victor relaxed the hold, although only a little.

The reaction was immediate, the guy throwing elbows back at Victor's ribs, whose own response was just as fast, reapplying the crushing force and walking the man backwards through the chamber, pulling him into an alcove as the elbows lost their power. Victor dumped him on to the floor.

He was still alive because Victor had already left enough corpses strewn around Nice, and for all his sins, he would not kill someone inside a house of God.

The guy's jeans limited the spread of the involuntary urination. Victor opted to ignore the hip pockets regardless. He collected the guy's gun and wallet from his jacket pockets. Maybe he had keys or something else of note inside the jeans pockets. They could stay there. Inside his jacket, he found a compact radio that linked to a wireless earpiece, which he removed.

Victor fitted the earpiece in place. He heard nothing but fizzing static as predicted. The guy hadn't had chance to call out a warning to his teammates. Down here, they wouldn't have heard if he had.

The wallet contained personal effects, which Victor found interesting. He had expected nothing more than cash. Instead, there were cards, receipts and a Provence driver's licence with a local address. Nothing seemed staged either. So, not operating clean or more likely using expendable credentials.

Worse, maybe this was his real identity because he was no shadow or assassin but a cop. Or, worse still, an intelligence operative. A member of the DGSI, France's internal security service.

No, Victor told himself. Cops or spooks would have swarmed in huge numbers the moment they had identified him, not put him under surveillance. The only uncertainty therefore was whether he was connected to Castellan, the private security firm in Gibraltar or Salomé.

Ascending back into the nave of the church, Victor found the choir had taken a break. He saw them chatting amongst themselves and sipping soft drinks while a young chorister checked hymn sheets.

'*C'était magnifique*,' Victor told him as he passed. '*Merci beaucoup.*'

The chorister beamed. '*Mon plaisir.*'

Victor was halfway to the exit when a voice came through his earpiece. French. Female. Familiar.

'Come in, Weiss,' Salomé said in a harried tone, then after a moment, 'Are you there? Answer.'

He couldn't know their system, although he understood the universal dynamics of such communications and he thumbed the send button twice in rapid succession to transmit two quick bursts of deliberate white noise.

Salomé said, 'If you're on him but can't talk, do that again.'

He did.

Salomé made a sigh of relief. 'Good, stand fast. Ziani will enter the church shortly and take over.'

Victor slowed his pace, wondering if he should leave before Ziani arrived or wait and deal with them as he had Weiss. If Salomé had her whole crew here then it made sense to get away before they had him boxed in, although he was keen to have another conversation with her.

'The others are en route,' Salomé said. 'Let me know if you need me. Otherwise, I'm in position out back.'

Decision made, Victor turned around.

SEVENTY-SEVEN

She was sitting on a bench, leaning forward in an anxious pose. She was looking nowhere in particular because she was focused on listening. Victor didn't need to hide his approach as she was paying no attention to her surroundings. She thought she didn't need to watch her six. She was aware of his presence as he reached the bench, but not who approached until he had sat down next to her.

Salomé froze in a moment of panic and deliberation, then her right hand darted for the gun she had holstered beneath her jacket.

Victor grabbed her wrist before she could draw the weapon. 'You don't want to do that.'

Again, deliberation. She was asking herself whether she should fight back or back down. She chose the latter. Victor felt the tension lessen in her arm and she released the pistol's grip. She lay that palm on her thigh and Victor let go of her.

'You don't need to do this.'

'Want and need are two very different things.'

Nearby, an old man and an old woman, both short and stooped, walked along a path. They held hands, both to keep one another steady and because they were just as in love as they had ever been.

'Do you see that couple?' Victor asked.

She nodded. 'I do.'

'They're the egg timer,' he continued.

She watched the old couple walk. 'I don't understand.'

'How long do you think it will take them?'

They were heading towards the nearest exit. A slow pace. Awkward, shuffling steps. No doubt both beset by many ailments.

She said, 'I don't know ... Why?'

'Once they've gone,' he explained, 'it's just you and I.'

She watched the old man and the old woman continue on their way.

'Maybe a couple of minutes,' Victor said. 'Maybe less.'

Salomé was silent.

'Open space, and just the old couple,' Victor continued. 'No overlooking buildings. No cameras. I can snap your neck and be on my way without anyone noticing.'

'You don't have to kill me.'

'I don't have to do anything,' he agreed. 'But you have to start talking and you had better be succinct.'

'I'm not your enemy.'

'You'll appreciate it if I require a little more convincing than that. Maybe start with who you really are.'

'I've already told you. I'm Salomé Sorrel. Like you, I worked for Phoenix for a long time. In fact, we're both pretty similar from what little I know about you. I was in the military, then I went to work for the Ministry of Defence. Internal security. Counter terrorism. Then I—'

Looking at the old couple inching closer to the exit, Victor said, 'I'd skip the biographical fluff if I were you and get straight to the point.'

'I know what you're thinking, but you're wrong. You need to listen to what I have to say.'

Glancing at the old couple creeping ever closer to the exit, Victor said, 'You don't know what I think and I'd really try and explain it in a way that isn't complicated. You don't have time for that.'

'We should speak elsewhere. We have a lot to discuss.'

'Oh, I bet we do,' Victor said. 'Less than a minute, I'd say.'

'Okay, okay,' she responded, talking fast, composing herself. 'The men you killed in that building, do you know who they were?'

'British mercenaries,' he answered. 'On the books of a private security firm based out of Gibraltar. The leader was called Walker. He didn't know who hired him, naturally.'

'Did you ask him about his contract?'

'I told you: he didn't know the identity of his client.'

She said, 'Do you know who sent them?'

'Phoenix,' he answered. 'She was the only person who knew I would be at that particular place at that particular time. I don't know why you're asking these questions when you're running out of time.'

'Phoenix sent the team?'

'You already know she did,' Victor said. 'Otherwise we wouldn't be having this conversation now, would we?'

'Phoenix didn't hire Walker.'

He gave her a look of scepticism. 'As you pointed out, there were a lot of corpses in that building that say otherwise.'

'Phoenix didn't send them,' Salomé explained. 'But I did.'

'Then you've made the worst and last mistake you're ever going to make.'

She didn't seem concerned in the slightest. 'I've made plenty of mistakes in my life but that wasn't one of them. A miscalculation, for sure. Because I failed to account for you.'

'If it makes you feel better, you're not the first to underestimate me. But compliments won't keep you alive. Why not shoot me in the back outside the café on Sunday when you had the chance? You said yourself I walked straight past you and you watched me cross the street. It would have been easy. Didn't want to get your hands dirty when you had others to dirty their own on your behalf?'

'The same reason I didn't wait to shoot you in the back when you left the tailor's shop, which is the same reason Miller and Boulanger made no effort to kill you before you turned on them.'

She looked at him as though he already knew the reason.

Victor felt cold. 'Walker and his team weren't there to kill me. They were there to kill Phoenix.'

SEVENTY-EIGHT

For a moment, he thought about the events of that day in Nice. Seeing the open shutter. Walking across the street. Entering the building. Gunfire. Death.

A kill team sent by his broker to ambush him.

A set-up.

Or so Victor had thought.

'I don't understand,' he said.

'Why would you? I don't imagine Phoenix ever discussed contracts that didn't come to you. Obviously, you're not the only professional on her books. She would be a pretty poor broker if she didn't know how to keep secrets. And we both know there was nothing poor with that one. If not the most prolific middleman in the business, she was right up at the very top in joint first place.'

Victor looked with new eyes at Salomé.

Who smiled.

'There you go,' she said. 'You're getting there all on your own without me.'

'You want to be the new Phoenix.'

'Not exactly,' she said. 'I want to be me, only sitting on her vacated throne.'

'Then why am I involved at all?'

'That's where things get messy,' she admitted. 'We didn't know you were back until my people spotted you at the airport. Naturally, we wanted to keep an eye on you.'

He thought of the man and woman who had entered the hotel after him. He had figured them for threats at first, until they had convinced him otherwise with the arrival of their colleagues. Of course, now he understood they had been shadowing without the intention of attacking him.

'When they felt they had pushed it too far, they withdrew. Then we didn't see you again until Sunday morning at the café. You weren't meant to be involved at all at this point. You stepped into this of your own accord the moment you left the café and walked across the street.'

Victor remained silent.

He was so used to dealing with threats when he saw them he hadn't stopped to consider there was no threat at all. At least, no threat to him. He hadn't even asked Walker about the kill team's target.

'After you attacked Walker's team, everything changed. Once there were gunshots and sirens, it was over. Phoenix wasn't going to show up with all that going on, and there was no team in place to execute her even if she had. I knew she would run, but I didn't know where. We've been looking for her as much as you have yourself. I told you the truth about that. Maybe we could have found her already had you trusted us in the first place.'

'I don't trust assassins, Ms Sorrel. Neither should you.

Why didn't you tell me this earlier? Miller and Boulanger might still be with us.'

'Because I didn't know where your loyalties lay at that point. You thought Phoenix set you up. Maybe once you realised she hadn't then you would cease to be friendly. Besides, I still needed to find her and maybe you knew more than you were saying.'

'But why the kill team in the first place? Phoenix isn't a professional. Like us, I mean. You didn't need multiple guys with SMGs.'

'Precaution,' Salomé began. 'Maybe she turned up with bodyguards, maybe a kill team of her own. I wasn't going to lose my chance by not bringing enough firepower. Besides, I don't micromanage. The mercenaries were given a job and they decided how to get it done. If they wanted to be armed to the teeth then who was I to stop them?'

He thought about this, imagining an alternate reality in which he had not noticed the open shutter or had not checked out the location the day before. Would Phoenix have showed up? Or had she anticipated the coming attack?

'You told me your crew was tight and yet you don't seem cut up about Miller and Boulanger.'

'We were close, but this is the business we're in. Besides, everyone's replaceable.'

'You're offering me a new job?'

'I'm saying I want you to keep your old one.'

'What's your leverage?'

She pretended to be confused.

'Drop the act,' he said. 'You couldn't have known how I would react to you killing my broker. You needed something on me, some kind of insurance, before you made your pitch.'

'I don't need to sell myself to you,' she said. 'That I'm even sitting here talking to you is all the pitch I need to make. Phoenix should have quit while she was ahead years ago. You of all people know that you stay around too long in this business and someone is going to come along to explain that to you sooner instead of later. For Phoenix, it was later. But it was inevitable.'

'Except she's in the wind,' Victor said. 'I thought she ran when the kill team failed. Now I think she saw you coming even before I did.'

Salomé's expression was tight. She tried to hide her annoyance but it didn't work. She saw Victor saw right through her.

He said, 'You didn't answer my question.'

'Which one?'

'I asked what insurance you had,' he answered. 'On me. You don't know who I am beside the name on my current passport. And it's not the team of dead mercs. You can't give me up to the authorities without exposing your own involvement. But it has to be something. You had to come into this with a card to play if I point-blank refused your offer. You'd prefer not to play it at all, naturally. You don't want me to feel coerced into working for you.'

She was silent.

'Trouble is,' Victor continued, 'if you don't tell me what insurance you have then my answer is no by default.'

She looked away for a moment, the sun on her face and the breeze in her hair.

'Kirill Lebedev,' she said. 'You killed him in jail about ten days ago. I know you did because it was me who hired you to do it. I have ... let's call it ... a good working relationship with a certain syndicate of Russians. The Bratva. I subcontracted the hit on Kirill and Grigori Orlov through Phoenix. Making a loss in the process, I might add. Several other jobs, too, although not with you as the contractor involved.'

'So you could build up intel on Phoenix.'

'To better understand her and her methods, yes. I wanted to step into her shoes, not build my own from scratch.'

'Who's Castellan?' he asked.

'The Bratva's top man in Marseille.' She paused to correct herself. 'Their top man in France full stop. He's been here for years. I'm sure every criminal in that town bows before him by this point. He's the one who put the contract out on Kirill in the first place. It's Castellan's shipping empire that brings heroin from the Black Sea all the way to France, and then on to the United States, where Kirill was part of the distribution network before he got himself on the FBI's radar.'

'The bosses back home couldn't take the risk of Kirill talking,' Victor said. 'I guessed that part. I told him as much before I killed him.'

'Not the bosses back home,' Salomé began. 'Just Castellan looking to protect his supply chain. They would never approve it in Moscow because Kirill Lebedev was the son-in-law of Maxim Borisyuk.'

'That name means nothing to me.'

'The head of the Bratva keeps a low profile these days. So, you're absolutely correct: you killing Kirill isn't a card I want to play.'

'Because it would not only put me in the crosshairs of the entire Brotherhood, but you too.'

She nodded. 'Mutually assured destruction. Which would be an assured waste of mutual talent. I want us to work together, freely and profitably. I don't see any reason why anything really has to change for you.'

Victor didn't respond.

'Unless,' she said, 'I've completely misjudged you and you have a connection to Phoenix beyond simple business.'

He was careful in his tone as he said, 'You haven't misjudged me.'

'Good,' she said. 'Because I need your help just as much as you need mine.'

He looked away to the church where pigeons jostled on its roof. 'Let me guess: Castellan.'

'While he's alive he's a threat to both of us. If he reveals to Maxim Borisyuk that you and I were involved in the assassination of his son-in-law then he's just as likely to receive Borisyuk's wrath. Which is why he's going to wait and find a way to give us up that protects himself at the same time. It's not a matter of if, but when. Castellan hasn't ruled Marseille for all these years because he can be trusted. And he can't live with this hanging over him for long. Castellan will turn on me – and now you – just as soon as he realises that this is the only way out of the hole he's in. He needs a narrative to feed to Borisyuk and if he can't tell a good story then he's a dead man walking. Phoenix's death allowed him to control that narrative, but now she's gone he has to look elsewhere. When we planned this, we never considered going after Kirill's assassin because Phoenix was the simpler, safer option. But that was then. And even if Castellan doesn't get to you, he's going to be – *compelled*, shall we say? – to reveal the truth to Borisyuk. Then, it's not only Castellan's branch of the Bratva after you, it's the whole tree. Do I really need to spell out why that's something you want to avoid?'

Victor thought about his time in Russia, his work as a professional just starting out. 'You don't need to explain anything to me about the Bratva.'

'Then help me kill Castellan before he surrounds himself with legions of his soldiers,' she said. 'That ring of protection will only grow as his fear of Maxim Borisyuk's response grows so we need to act fast. Help me kill Castellan and not only will we never need to look over our shoulders for vengeful members of the world's most widespread and vicious organised-crime network, we also get to be the ones they dial whenever they have a problem they can't solve themselves. Where I'm from we call that a win-win.'

He nodded. 'You make a compelling case, only you're taking a big risk coming to me like this. You're gambling everything on me saying yes.'

'There is no gamble,' she replied. 'I'm not just a better deal than Phoenix, I'm your only deal if you don't want Castellan after you, and beyond Castellan, the entire Russian mafia.'

The elderly couple had already left the churchyard, although Victor hadn't noticed until now.

Salomé saw this. 'Well,' she began, 'what's it going to be?'

SEVENTY-NINE

She looked peaceful. The sun gleamed on her hair and made her pale skin so bright it seemed to glow. They approached at a measured pace, cautious and unsure of the situation. No sign of the killer, yet that did not mean they were taking his absence for granted. The man in the blue cap knew from painful experience that just because you couldn't see the killer, it didn't mean he couldn't see you. His throat ached with pulsing waves of dull pain that intensified to agony with just swallowing the saliva in his mouth. He was embarrassed because of the ambush and because of the wet patch at the front of his jeans.

Weiss's colleagues didn't comment upon it. He had been through enough without adding mockery into the mix. Besides, they had more pressing issues that required their attention.

'What are we going to do now?'

'Bury the mess,' was Ziani's answer. 'Then back to work.'

Salomé sat on the bench before them. She seemed peaceful,

as though she were dozing, upright on the bench with her head lolling forward. Only the lack of movement revealed anything was wrong from a distance. Now up close, they could see the dark area of skin on the back of her neck where a radial fracture to her spine had ruptured surrounding blood vessels.

'The killer declined her offer,' the man in the blue cap said, needlessly.

'No shit.'

Responding to the urgent calls, the others arrived, hurrying into the churchyard and converging at the bench.

'I knew this would happen,' one thought it appropriate to say.

'What do we do?' another new arrival asked.

'We can't leave her here.' Weiss sighed. 'Fetch a vehicle and we get her out of the city. Dig a hole somewhere no one will ever look. What else is there?'

'I meant about the killer. He's taken out Miller, Boulanger, and now Salomé.'

Touching his tender throat, he said, 'I'm done.'

'What?'

Gesturing to Salomé, he said, 'No paycheque is worth this. Once she's in the ground, I'm in the wind and I'm never looking back. We backed the wrong horse.'

'While he's still out there he's a threat to us all.'

'Then you go get him,' he said with a mocking smile. 'See how you do.'

'I'm out too,' another said. 'Maybe not for ever, but this is FUBAR. He spotted us at the hotel, he killed Miller and Boulanger, and he was on us here too. Salomé's just found out how well he plays with others and I don't want to lose anyone else, let alone myself. We need to scatter and hunker down until it's safe to raise our heads back above the parapet. We don't really have any other choice.'

'We all have a choice,' Weiss said. 'So, let's let the Russians deal with him, or he deals with the Russians. Meanwhile, we lick our wounds, and think about making a comeback further down the line ... or not. Either way: I say scatter.'

Shrugging in defeat, Ziani said, 'I'm not going after him alone, so I guess we're scattering.' Motioning to Salomé's corpse, she added, 'Now grab her legs.'

EIGHTY

The Club wanted to meet again and the Club never met again in such rapid succession. At least, before now they had never needed to meet so soon after the previous meeting. The Security Council were looking to Castellan for answers. Not only that, they wanted a new resolution.

He knew exactly what they would say.

This is not what you promised.

We should never have trusted you.

This is all your fault.

Castellan brought a shot glass to his lips, spilling a little with his shaking fingers. He downed the vodka. It did not seem as smooth as it had once. He stared out into the night. The port was still awake, of course. It never slept. The port was never quiet. The whine of machinery and rumble of engines was incessant. Forklift trucks with tines the length of a man were in constant motion, lifting and moving shipping containers on to trucks or trains.

A chain-link fence surrounded Castellan's industrial unit.

On the other side of it were stacks of old, rusting shipping containers. He saw hundreds if not thousands of them in neat piles of varying heights, colours and stages of decay. Some were so dirty, so rusty, that their original paintwork was indiscernible. He found them strangely beautiful as they decayed. They acquired an individuality they had lacked in life.

Castellan nodded at one of the guards he had patrolling the grounds, who nodded back. Good men, ex-military, called in for added security now Castellan's scheme had fallen apart and the outsiders he had trusted to sever the connection to Kirill's death had failed.

'Are you sure you don't want a drink?' he asked his visitor.

'I am already hydrated,' the Boatman answered.

Whether he knew Castellan was stalling or not, he gave no indication. He seemed polite and reasonable in his questions. He didn't smile and yet he projected no hostility.

'Maxim's daughter is very upset about the death of her husband,' the Boatman began. 'So any assistance you can provide will be gratefully received.'

'I told you already: I don't know anything about any deal Kirill was making.'

'Would you have had him killed if you had known?'

'Don't be ridiculous,' Castellan said. 'That would be considered an act of war by Maxim.'

'Only if you were caught.'

'I think I've had enough of your questions for one night.'

'You seem tense,' the Boatman said. 'You have men with rifles everywhere.'

'I take security seriously. What of it? Now, I've humoured you long enough. If Maxim wants to talk to me he can pick up the phone and I will gladly answer. I will not, however, entertain the deluded fantasies of his lapdog sniffing around for conspiracies.'

The Boatman responded with a polite nod. 'If it makes things simpler, you may consider what I say to be the words of Maxim himself so we might finish this discussion.'

Castellan scoffed. 'If it makes things simpler? You're funny. I didn't expect you to be such a comedian.' He used the shot glass to gesture towards the door. 'Get out. Go back to Russia. Tell your master to beat some manners into you.'

The Boatman stood without moving and fixed Castellan with an unblinking gaze. 'I'm going nowhere.'

'You don't scare me. I know the stories and I know they're fairy tales spread to scare little brothers into subservience. In my town, you're no one. I'm bulletproof here. If I decide it, you'll never make it out of the port, let alone the city.'

When the Boatman still failed to move, Castellan prodded him in the chest. 'Get out before I decide to do Maxim a favour and have those manners beaten into you myself.'

Lightning fast, the Boatman grabbed Castellan's extended hand, running his index fingers over the knuckles as a thumb slipped beneath in a pincer. The Boatman wrenched the hand clockwise, rotating the arm with it until Castellan's elbow was pointed to the ceiling and the whole limb was locked and immobile.

With just one finger and thumb, the Boatman controlled Castellan.

'Go ahead,' he hissed. 'Break it. Snap my arm into a thousand shards if that's what you want to do. See what happens when I cry out in pain. Let's find out how dangerous you are when a dozen former Spetsnaz rush in here and barrel you to the floor. Let's see how your slick moves fare then.'

The Boatman held him immobile.

'What are you waiting for?' Castellan asked with a smile. 'I'm at your mercy. You can break my arm and you can kill me and no one is going to stop you.'

The Boatman seemed distracted, as though he was no longer listening, as though he no longer cared about Castellan.

'Did you hear that noise?' the Boatman asked as he released him.

Rubbing his sore wrist, Castellan was about to ask what he meant, only then he heard something from outside. Faint. Like a muffled cry.

The Boatman approached the window and Castellan followed, peering out into the night to where the guard had nodded to him. Except the guard was no longer where he had been stationed. In his place, a smear of blood glistened on the side of a shipping container.

The Boatman said, 'You have visitors.'

'Friends of yours?'

The Boatman seemed bemused. 'I expect they're former friends of yours.'

Castellan thought of the Club. Would they be so foolish as to move against him? Or was this related to the broker? Either way, he wasn't going to hide in his office while his little brothers defended him. For all his duplicities, he was as loyal to his men as they were to him.

He punched in the code to unlock his secure metal cabinet, and took out his personal weapon. He checked it over and loaded in a fresh magazine.

The Boatman watched him. 'We have yet to finish our conversation.'

'I'm busy,' Castellan said, feeling more secure with a rifle in his grip.

'Don't take too long.'

'Wait here,' Castellan said, thinking that after he was done with the intruders he would make good use of his little brothers and have them shred Maxim's dog to pieces. Maybe keep those pieces in freezer bags until the time was right to send them to Borisyuk.

Or, better yet, he thought as he watched the Boatman position himself to get a better view out of the window, eat them.

'Unless you want to join me?' he asked.

The Boatman smiled in return. 'I prefer to let nature take its course.'

EIGHTY-ONE

That dead bodies appeared so lifelike was an irony not lost on Victor. He had seen so many – had been the cause of so many – that after a while they ceased to differentiate themselves. One corpse was, give or take, much the same as any other. His victims had a certain uniformity. Maybe an inevitability.

The Russian at his feet was no exception.

Victor had counted eleven silhouettes guarding and patrolling the unit. All carried the familiar shapes of Kalashnikov assault rifles. Modern AK-74s, the same designation used by the Russian military. Castellan was taking no chances with his security. Aside from the guards, Castellan was the only one on the property that Victor had observed.

At least, until the visitor arrived while Victor was still conducting his surveillance. To the guards at the entrance, the visitor had given his name only as *Lodochnik*. The Boatman.

The Russian at Victor's feet had been alert and competent.

He hadn't died as easily as the previous two. It had been messy. He had cried out before the end.

Now, any further chance for stealth had gone. Eight left. Among the shipping containers, the numerous blind spots would cut down their numerical advantage.

They were already convening on the area because he heard someone yell, '*Syuda*.'

Over here.

No gunshots came his way. Not yet. They were aware there was an intruder, but they hadn't seen him. He retreated from the area before anyone could catch him in their line of sight, the stacks of shipping containers saw to that. Even those that were not stacked were taller than him, which gave him plenty of places to hide and yet formed a maze in which it was difficult to keep his bearings.

The same would be true for the Russians, of course, although they could spread out to hunt him down. They were more familiar with the layout, after all. For a few seconds he heard them calling out to one another behind him, encouraging speed and also recommending caution. Then they fell silent and he pictured them whispering to one another.

Some would skirt around the shipping container graveyard altogether to cut off any exits, he was sure, expecting him to flee now he had been discovered. Inside the maze and unable to move in a straight line, he would reach any such exit too late.

He had no intention of trying to escape.

Victor took a breath as he waited – a deep breath to override his sympathetic nervous system and its attempt to flood him with stress hormones. Once, it had been the only way to keep his heart from racing so fast it made his hands shake. Human beings were built to adapt. As a boy he had been terrified of pain. As an adolescent he had thrown up during his first firefight. Early in his career he had needed to control his breathing to stay calm.

Now, he did it to control his excitement.

He was never scared, even if his body responded as if that were the case. Many times he had shot people and been shot at in return. Many times he had killed those trying to kill him in return. With enough experience, humans could get used to anything. The memories he tried to forget but could not scared him more than any gunman. The humanity he fought a constant battle to suppress was his greatest enemy. Losing that battle was his only fear. Every time he let it creep back he made mistakes. He made bad calls. He acted in ways he knew he shouldn't. Each one of those actions brought him a little closer to death.

Victor eased back the slide to check a round was in the chamber of the Scot's gun. He released the magazine to check his count was accurate. It was not impossible for him to make a mistake, and even if such mistakes were rare, he always acted as though they were commonplace.

He kept his arms tucked against his flanks, elbows in line with the base of his sternum, hands before his chest, pistol at the height of his collarbones. He peered over the top of it. While not as accurate as using the iron sights, perfect aim wasn't necessary at short range and he wanted the weapon close to him where it could not be grabbed by an enemy making a sudden appearance around one of the many corners and blind spots.

Against men with assault rifles, he could not afford to miss. The moment he fired one of the cleaners' pistols he would give away his position. The rest would come running.

He needed to keep things quiet as long as he could manage.

Victor paused where the corridor of space between containers formed a corner.

He could hear quiet footsteps nearing. Careful, deliberate movements cushioned by the ground, hard and dry yet still soft enough to dampen the sound a little. Victor concentrated. It was hard to tell just how close his enemy remained. Maybe two or three metres. Or he could be close enough to reach around and touch. If Victor picked the wrong moment to attack, he might be attacking nothing except empty air. If he delayed too long then he gave his enemy the chance to change his approach.

Victor, while patient, never wanted to let an enemy dictate the battle. He slipped the pistol away.

He waited until the exact moment the footsteps stopped – when he deemed the man was as close to the corner as he wanted to get – then charged out.

Victor caught the man mid-inhale, drawing in a deep breath in preparedness to turn the corner himself, and went for the assault rifle.

The Russian had it in both hands, a strong grip hard to manipulate, so Victor thrust a hand up from below, using the V between his thumb and index finger to drive the rifle upwards and angle the muzzle clear.

Victor looped his free elbow over his enemy's arms, aiming for the temple but catching him on the side of the skull as he turned his head away from the strike.

Undeterred, the Russian wrenched his rifle free and retreated a step to create space to angle it back on target. Victor didn't let that happen, instead barrelling into him before he had a chance to shoot.

He grabbed the outstretched wrist from above in an overhand grip, wrapping his fingers and thumb around the joint to use his better leverage and manipulate the hand holding the gun before the Russian could resist. He kept hold of the weapon, but now the hand was hyperextended and the muzzle pointing away from Victor. The Russian was strong, however, and heavier. He used his greater mass to good effect, twisting Victor around on the spot as they wrestled for control of the weapon. Victor was on the outside of the guy's right arm, throwing short hooking punches with his free left hand into the Russian's lower back and ribs. He threw punches of his own, also left hooks, sending his fist over his own right arm and aiming for Victor's face. Victor turned into the punches, angling his head down and tucking his chin under his shoulder so the gunman's blows landed against his skull. Each one was a clubbing shot that sent shockwaves of disorientation through Victor's brain, yet the guy was punching bone. Adrenalin was masking the pain in his hand but he was wrecking his knuckles against Victor's head. The Russian just couldn't feel the damage yet.

Then he made a terrible error, electing to take hold of Victor's jacket when there was no need. He extended his left arm to push and control Victor's movements so Victor exaggerated them in a sharp, jolting motion, pulling the guy off balance and closer.

The AK went off an instant after Victor batted it to one side. The bullet blew a hole in the ground, then another as the gunman tried to force it back in line to shoot Victor, who was close enough to drop a headbutt into his enemy's face before sweeping his load-bearing leg out from under him. The rifle fired yet again, this time sending a burst into the sky as the gunman went over backwards with his arms flailing. He hit the ground hard, the back of his head thumping against it, and he went limp.

Victor stamped on his neck three times until he heard the spine break beneath his heel.

EIGHTY-TWO

Victor heard more of Castellan's men nearing, drawn to the gunfire he had tried to avoid – seemingly from every direction – before he had a chance to retrieve the dead guy's assault rifle. He left it on the ground and dashed through a hollow shipping container, trusting his speed to take him out of the danger zone. Maybe some saw him. Maybe none did. He couldn't afford to hang around to check.

He took a zig-zagging path through the maze, passing between containers or through hollow ones, until he could hear nothing but his own breathing, and stopped to listen.

He heard the heavy footfalls of multiple men running his way and he crouched low in the shadows until the noise had passed. They were close, perhaps only a single shipping container between them.

'*Which way did he go?*' someone called out.

The noise of the footfalls faded into the distance.

But not all.

Two Russians were more cautious, he heard. Close, too. Somewhere behind him.

He backtracked towards the sound and waited at the corner of the container. A couple of steps back so his shadow would not extend out past the corner and give away his position. The sun had dipped below the horizon but ambient artificial light tinted the containers orange and created deep shadows where the light failed to reach.

Victor knew they were coming, although he heard no footsteps. Based on the competence of the others he did not imagine they were experts at stealth, so he pictured trainers or tennis shoes: footwear chosen for comfort that just so happened to offer considerable advantages when trying to stay quiet.

Because he could not hear their approach, he watched the ground. In front of him, at the opening, it was a little brighter because of the ambient light. Where Victor waited, the ground was darker in the shadow of the containers.

Seconds passed. Still no sound of footsteps. Even with the soft soles of tennis shoes or trainers they had to be creeping forward at a slow pace. Maybe not so focused on their own noise but trying to identify Victor's. He pictured them checking every open container and every junction, unsure where their target lay hidden. No point listening hard for Victor if they didn't also look for him. With no cover besides the containers themselves, such checks required no more than a moment's glance.

The ground gave Victor a split-second's warning when it darkened, a shadow cast before the approaching gunman passed the container's edge.

Victor attacked with a downwards chopping strike,

connecting the edge of his wrist on the lead Russian's fore-arms, knocking them towards the ground, along with the rifle he was holding out in front of him. The guy's entire centre of gravity shifted forwards and he doubled over, off balance and stumbling into the knee strike Victor sent upwards at the same time.

The knee hit him in the face, cracking his eye socket and sending the Russian's head whipping up in response. Victor caught the man's skull in both hands as it flew back upright, then twisted the head in a violent circle that forced the Russian to turn his whole body until he was facing back the way he came, creating a human shield between Victor and the second aggressor.

Victor released the head, used the heel of his palm to strike the guy at the base of the skull where it met the neck, and shoved him so he collided with the second Russian before either of them understood what was happening.

The knee to the face and the blow to the brainstem put the first Russian out of action for the time being. He fell to the ground just as soon as the second guy shrugged him away, but the time that took gave Victor the opportunity to close the distance himself, so when the second Russian was no longer impeded and bringing his gun back to bear, Victor used both palms to simultaneously hit the back of the guy's right hand and the inside of his wrist, shocking the rifle from his grip.

It tumbled into an open shipping container, clattering somewhere out of sight.

The disarmed man launched an immediate counter-attack, using his left arm to catch Victor in the face with a snapping fist before he could pull back his own hands to form a guard.

While the Russian had no leverage to make the punch inflict maximum damage, the sudden shock of pain snapped Victor's head back and he felt his knees momentarily buckle.

He had his arms raised to catch the follow-up strikes, feeling the stinging impact of fists and elbows to his shoulders and triceps. He remained covered up and defensive while he shook off the effects of the punches. His enemy took this as a sign of imminent victory and continued the assault, throwing punch after punch. Each one caused pain, although nothing more. Victor felt the stings of impact lessen, the gaps between them extending. And in those gaps, gasps.

The Russian had exhausted himself with just a few seconds of relentless attack.

Not uncommon. Most people had enough physical fitness for a single all-out effort and would need a rest before they were ready for a second.

Then the guy threw a looping punch. It was the kind of strike people did when they were desperate and when they were running out of steam. He pulled back his elbow to launch the punch with maximum stored energy, twisting his hips to get all his weight behind it, gambling on one big blow to land and change the inevitable conclusion to proceedings. Victor saw it coming almost in slow motion – the punch took three times as long to reach its target because of the initial dropping of the elbow, which led to the inevitable looping arc that only increased the distance the fist had to travel. The Russian could have flicked out a distracting jab then followed with a straight cross before finishing with a left hook in the same amount of time, but rapidly rising fatigue and pain and fear had a habit of encouraging otherwise smart people to make poor decisions.

Victor darted closer so the Russian's punch hit only air somewhere behind Victor's head, which he then whipped into the guy's face. Victor did not feel the nose crush beneath his forehead, though he did feel the spatter of warm blood on his skin that told him the headbutt had ended things even before the Russian crumpled to the ground.

Leading with his knee, Victor threw his bodyweight down on top of the prone man, breaking multiple ribs as his knee landed on the Russian's sternum, compressing his entire ribcage until it could compress no further.

He wasn't sure how many ribs fractured because they all did so at the same time and the sounds overlapped into one sharp *crunch*.

The first Russian was beginning to recover and had pulled himself up to his knees, so was at a perfect height for Victor to snap his neck.

A ding of corrugated steel gave Victor enough warning to intercept another, who had been drawn towards the telltale sounds of breaking ribs and vertebrae.

Victor used his left hand to push the gun away as it appeared round the corner, opening up the Russian to an elbow strike as he stepped inside the reach, turning his torso into the guy's outstretched right arm and sending a second elbow after the first. Both struck the Russian in the cheekbone and sent his head snapping back, but he took them well, only stumbling back while his balance remained strong. Victor threw a third elbow, this time throwing it in a downwards arc to strike the guy's arm in an attempt to shock the AK from his grip. It didn't work; this Russian was so resilient Victor wasn't sure if he was high on painkillers or carved out of rock.

The latter seemed more likely as the guy threw a headbutt at Victor, who already had his own head angled downward to prevent any such attack hitting his nose. The gunman didn't care. He headbutted Victor, forehead to forehead.

A piercing whine drowned out all sound and his vision blackened.

The whine faded and his vision cleared an instant later, but only after Victor had staggered backwards, releasing his hold on the Russian's arm and giving him the opportunity to snap the gun back in line.

Victor jerked to the side as the rifle fired, the bullet ripping through the trailing fabric of his jacket.

The Russian swivelled to follow Victor's path, yet Victor was too fast. He darted forward, outside of the guy's reach, the long gun now behind him and no threat for an instant – in which Victor snaked his arms around the Russian's outstretched limb, locking it at the elbow and controlling it. While both his hands were occupied, Victor was defence-less and the Russian went to throw a punch with his free fist, only for Victor to sweep his load-bearing leg out from under him.

He went straight down, Victor maintaining control of the arm and stamping his heel again and again into the Russian's face until there was so much blood no feature was distinguishable and the only movement the man made was a jerking spasm.

EIGHTY-THREE

The Russians who had run past would be coming back now. Castellan's guys had been just too strong and too tough to kill without making a lot of noise in the process. Victor took one of the AK-74s and some spare magazines and waited for them.

As expected, they came, drawn by the noise and taking a few moments to identify the correct corridor between shipping containers where the commotion had originated.

They approached in two pairs, convening from different directions.

Victor, hiding five metres up at the top of a stack of containers, shot the assault rifle down into the four men, firing in controlled bursts until all four had dropped to the ground with multiple bullet holes.

He released the empty mag, inserted a second curved thirty-round magazine into the receiver and gave the bottom of the mag a quick thump with his palm to ensure a good fit. Unnecessary on one level because he knew how much force was needed through endless training and operational experience, but necessary to Victor who knew that the most lethal of mistakes came from the most avoidable of hubris.

An AK roared and a nearby muzzle flash brightened the evening sky.

Castellan himself.

Victor jumped from the top of the shipping container, moving out of the line of fire, landing on another, before dropping to the ground.

Castellan had anticipated this and had already rushed to intercept him.

They exchanged shots from extreme close range, firing blind from around the corner of containers or popping out for minuscule moments in case they found a line of sight. Fully automatic rifle fire – the noise was deafening: the gunshots themselves, the loud thuds of impact in the ground or shrill pings as they hit steel. Victor kept mobile, moving to different points of cover and concealment. Staying still was always the wrong thing to do in his experience. Any direction was better than no direction at all, even if that meant approaching the danger. Every change of distance and angle was more work for the attacker to overcome. It was hard enough to shoot straight when bullets were coming back in return, let alone if that target was never in the same place twice.

Castellan stayed in position. He had great cover behind a rusting forklift. Victor's bullets could not penetrate the vehicle and the Russian only had to expose a little of himself to danger.

That rigid adherence to one tactic was going to work against him, because each of Victor's snapshots hit a little closer.

Until Victor ran out of ammunition. He had been counting rounds, only the magazine had not been full in the first place. He hadn't known by weight alone. He switched to the Scot's pistol, although it could not compete with the AK at this range.

Castellan went to reload early, before the magazine was empty. A tactic Victor often employed himself in a prolonged firefight. Few things were worse than running out of bullets at the exact wrong moment when there were still plenty spare in unused magazines.

Castellan's mistake was what he did with the magazine he pulled free. He wanted to reload as fast as possible to leave the shortest amount of time with only a single bullet in the gun's chamber; with his right hand clutching the grip of the rifle and the released magazine in his left, Castellan had no hand to fish out a full mag. So he dropped the magazine from his left hand. The kind of thing that seemed insignificant in the moment.

Until it clattered on the hard ground, telling Victor in no uncertain terms that his enemy in that moment had only a single usable bullet.

Victor appeared out of cover, seeing Castellan's face screwed up in a scowl of self-admonishment as he rushed to fish a spare mag from a pocket.

As Victor dashed to close the distance, the scowl became surprise, then anger. Castellan shot the last bullet at him, firing the AK from one hand, making a hard shot against a fast-moving target even harder. The bullet missed, zipping clear over Victor's head.

Castellan backed away while he tried to reload in the couple of seconds he had before Victor reached him. When he saw he wasn't going to get the rifle reloaded in time, he ran.

Instead of shooting him in the back, Victor discarded his pistol to tackle him from behind. Castellan was strong, yet he was too slow, his attempts to fight back limited to stalling the inevitable. Still on the ground, Victor snaked his arms around the Russian's neck, snapping on a chokehold as Castellan heaved himself – and Victor with him – to his feet.

'Who are you?' Castellan asked, knowing he was beaten as Victor applied pressure to his carotid arteries.

'I'm the man you hired to kill Kirill Lebedev.'

'Whatever Salomé's paying you . . .' Castellan said, voice straining and croaking. 'I'll double it.'

'Had things played out differently,' Victor began, 'I'd accept. Sadly for the both of us, this is all one huge misunderstanding I'm trying to correct.'

'Then we can work it out.'

Victor relaxed a little of the pressure on Castellan's throat. 'I'm listening.'

'Phoenix,' the Russian coughed. 'There's still time. If you know where she is then give her up to me and you'll . . . get a powerful friend in return.'

'I don't know where she is,' he admitted. 'But I have an idea.'

'Salomé told you about Borisyuk,' Castellan said, able to breathe and speak unobstructed once more. 'I can make sure he never learns about you. I can—'

Three muted gunshots sounded from the darkness. Not automatic fire, they were three rapid single shots that formed a triangle of bloody holes over Castellan's heart.

Victor felt the impacts reverberate through the Russian as he jerked and shuddered, before a final hissing exhale escaped his lips.

He sank to the ground as the darkness moved, rippling into the silhouette of a man that stepped into the light.

The Boatman.

'Thank you for expediting my inquiry.'

Confused, Victor remained silent. The Boatman had a pistol, held down at his side in an unthreatening posture, and yet Victor could almost feel the danger radiating from him. No way Victor could reach any weapon before the Boatman snapped up that pistol, so Victor stood still and kept his hands easy to see.

'I work for Maxim Borisyuk,' the Boatman explained. 'But I am not your enemy. At least, not yet.'

Victor listened.

'I am here expressly to determine if Castellan was behind Kirill's death, which I have now done,' the Russian continued. 'So you may leave without interruption. But please know we may see one another again before too long.'

The Boatman backed away into the shadows.

Victor watched as he became one with the darkness. 'Of that, I have no doubt.'

PART FIVE

EIGHTY-FOUR

Tonight's ballet, *The Golden Age*, told the story of a young fisherman in the 1920s who falls in love with a cabaret dancer, Mademoiselle Margot, who also has the heart of a local gangster. A classic love triangle. Borisyuk thought the gangster pretty weak as far as criminals went, yet he loved every minute of it nonetheless. Combining ballet and tango to a score full of jazz was a refreshing treat, even if his preference was for more classical productions. As he understood ballet more and more, he recognised the merit in holding true to technique refined over centuries. He found much modern ballet went too far trying to reinvent that which had already been perfected. Change for its own sake was the height of arrogance.

After the curtain had closed for the last time, he gestured to his bodyguard and the two men left Borisyuk's box. Not technically his own, since the box was a part of the Veliky theatre, funded – at least on paper – by the federal government, and yet he had donated a little over one hundred million dollars to fund the restoration, finally finished only a few years ago. As the entire project had cost between seven hundred million and one billion dollars, depending on who was to be believed, Borisyuk felt it reasonable to think the box, and the entire floor with it, were as good as his own property. Only one other individual had given more towards the restoration, which was still a sore spot for Borisyuk. If not for the unavoidable disruption to the programming, he would have the theatre burnt to the ground just so he could pay for the entire rebuilding himself next time.

Most attendees were on their way to the cloakrooms to pick up their coats, bags and outdoor shoes. Borisyuk, however, was not quite done with the evening. He headed to the café on the third floor, which was his preferred watering hole at the Veliky. This particular bar was smaller than both the main one on the seventh floor and the champagne bar on the ground floor, and its secluded, out-of-the-way location meant only those in the know ever used it. His bodyguard preferred it for that reason too, although he was concerned about security while Borisyuk didn't like to wait for service. Too long without a vodka and his mask of good manners tended to slip to reveal the street thug beneath.

A few other people were already in the bar when Borisyuk entered. Still thankfully quiet, he was pleased to see. His gaze was drawn to a certain couple drinking champagne.

She was tall, her long neck glittering with diamonds. Borisyuk remembered a time when she had possessed a sadness so profound that he had found it almost impossible to look at her despite her beauty. She had been like an icicle, flawless yet frozen. Now she gleamed as bright as sunshine on snow.

'Izolda,' he said, taking her hand to kiss the back of it. 'Wonderful as always to see you.'

'And you, Maxim. Did you enjoy the show?'

He smiled and made a play at dabbing at his eyes.

She laughed at this. 'You old softie.'

He laughed too, then said in curt greeting to her husband, who was looking a little bored and irritated to be left out, 'Vlad.'

Vladimir Kasakov acted as though he had not noticed him and then responded in kind. 'Maxim.'

The Ukrainian was a man of impressive size and intensity, who had, unlike Borisyuk, never acquired the same love for the arts. He attended for his wife's benefit. Which had been why, naturally, he had donated almost two hundred million dollars towards the theatre's restoration. Borisyuk was sick to death of this fact being hinted at in the newspapers every time Kasakov's name was mentioned.

Izolda said, miming a little of the show's choreography, 'I think I want to take tango classes.'

'Tremendous idea,' Borisyuk said.

'What do you think, Vlad?' she asked her husband. 'Will you learn to tango with your loving wife?'

The big Ukrainian grunted his answer and they all laughed.

She gave him a gentle slap on the arm, then asked Borisyuk, 'Wasn't the gangster terrifying?'

'Oh yes,' he replied. 'I wouldn't want to come across him in real life.'

Kasakov, who unlike his wife knew exactly how Borisyuk had acquired his wealth, gave him a wry smile.

Izolda didn't notice. 'Don't you think in some ways the production was like *Dreams of Japan*?'

'Japan is like twenties' America?' Kasakov asked, confused.

The brute knew nothing, so Borisyuk said, 'Yes, I think you might be right,' and they talked a little until Kasakov looked as though he might fall asleep standing up.

'Business is good?' Borisyuk asked to spare him.

'Yes,' the Ukrainian replied. 'Considering. And you?'

Borisyuk held out a downward facing palm and tilted his hand to the left and to the right a few times. 'Not bad.'

Kasakov had been a guest of Russia – and un-extraditable as a result – since the latter days of the twentieth century after brokering countless arms deals that not only poured billions into the economy but millions into the pockets of politicians and civil servants. In recent years, he had some-how become exponentially more prolific, to the point some said there wasn't a gun sold anywhere on the planet without his prior approval. Borisyuk was always intrigued to hear more specifics from the man himself, and the Ukrainian was just as interested in the workings of Borisyuk's business – there was much crossover, naturally – yet ugly conversations were simply not for such beautiful settings. Even the unso-phisticated Kasakov understood such civility.

Which was why Borisyuk said, 'How is young Illarion doing?'

Kasakov went to answer but Izolda was far quicker, beaming as she told Borisyuk all about their young child's latest adventures and showing him many photographs and videos on her phone.

'A little short for his age?' Borisyuk asked, noting the boy didn't seem to have inherited his father's stature.

'I think he'll be a late bloomer,' Izolda said, before adding, 'I'm going to go and give the nanny a call. Excuse me, please.'

Borisyuk made small talk with Kasakov, moving to a nearby standing table to rest their drinks upon. Kasakov was keen to keep the conversation away from ballet and to current events, although he became increasingly distracted.

The source of that distraction was a man at the bar who sipped from a glass of iced water. He seemed to be on his own, and unremarkable, and yet Kasakov was clearly interested in him. Eventually Kasakov gestured for Borisyuk's leave, who nodded.

'Pardon the interruption,' Kasakov said to the man at the bar. 'But I know you from somewhere, do I not?'

'I was just thinking the same thing,' the man replied, speaking perfect Russian but with an accent Borisyuk couldn't quite place. Like a Russian who had lived overseas for many years or a foreign national who had lived in Russia equally as long. 'I believe it was in Bucharest a few years ago now.'

'Bucharest?' Kasakov said, frowning. 'I'm not sure I even recall the last time I was there. I don't travel often these days.'

'A hotel lobby,' the man continued. 'An associate of yours acted a little clumsily and ended up damaging my suit jacket.'

Kasakov's eyes widened and he nodded along. 'Yes, yes. I remember that. Although I don't remember you ... if that makes sense. Am I correct in thinking I offered to buy you a new one and yet you refused?'

The man nodded too. 'That's right. A very generous offer, but unnecessary. No one should be penalised for a simple accident.'

'That depends on the accident,' Kasakov replied. 'But at the very least you must let me buy you a drink. You don't mind if he joins us, Maxim?'

'Not at all,' Borisyuk said. There was something familiar

about the man to him too, almost as though they had known one another in another life.

They introduced themselves, the man calling himself, 'Vasili.'

Kasakov went to fetch the promised drink, leaving Borisyuk alone with Vasili.

'What brings you to Russia?' Borisyuk asked.

'I'm here to see you,' Vasili answered. 'I hope you don't mind me being direct but this is in relation to your business and my own.'

Borisyuk had not been expecting that and yet somehow was unsurprised. 'So I do know you. But how?'

'We've never met before,' he said. 'Although I did work for you, at least indirectly, when I was younger. Not that I ever knew your name or you mine. But that's a story for another time. Tonight, I'm here to talk to you specifically about Kirill Lebedev.'

Borisyuk stiffened a little. 'What about him?'

'I killed him,' Vasili admitted, with a bluntness that felt like a slap to Borisyuk, who glanced to where his bodyguard waited, nearby and always ready to react. The man before him did not look the same as the photograph Zakharova had shown him – shorter hair, no beard – but Borisyuk now saw the eyes were the same. Black and pitiless.

'What is this?'

Borisyuk's question came out as a quiet hiss.

'By now you'll know I was hired by Castellan in Marseille, who did so through my broker and went to extensive lengths to hide the order so it never got back to you.'

He chose his words carefully. 'And yet here you are rubbing my son-in-law's murder in my face.'

'Not at all,' Vasili assured. 'I'm here to admit my part as the triggerman. Needless to say, I would not have accepted the contract had I known Kirill's relation to you.'

'You expect my forgiveness for own your ignorance?'

'Not at all,' he said again. 'I'm willing to pay off the blood debt, of course. But if you will not accept that, if we are to be enemies, then at least we can both leave here understanding one another.'

Borisyuk thought about this and almost smiled to himself. 'Castellan always had more ambition than was good for him. Why do you think I sent Kirill to work for him in the first place? Kirill was always doomed to make a mess of whatever he was involved in. Better he screwed up Castellan's operations than my own. But just because my son-in-law was a fool that doesn't mean I can let his murder go unanswered. I have his wife, my daughter, to answer to.'

Vasili waited, unafraid of his judgement.

Borisyuk said, 'You work for me now. At least, you will until I've decided on the debt you owe.'

'I understand.'

'Understand what?' Kasakov said, returning to the table. He carried a tray on which sat a bottle of champagne in an ice bucket. He had the stems of three flutes between his fingers.

'No more shop talk,' Borisyuk said, taking the tray from Kasakov, who then set down the glasses on the table. 'Let's discuss the performance with our new friend.' Kasakov groaned and Borisyuk asked, 'Are you a fellow enthusiast of the ballet, Vasili?'

EIGHTY-FIVE

From Russia, Victor first flew to Istanbul before a second flight brought him to Bologna. In Italy, he had a choice of trains. The non-stop service to Milan took a little over an hour, and then a second train would get him to Genoa in under two more. Instead, he chose the slower route, going first to Florence, then changing at Pisa Centrale, before heading to Genoa. With over twenty stops between the trains, he had plenty of opportunity to disembark several times and catch the following service so he could flush out any shadows. There were none. No one could feasibly have tracked him or be waiting for him. Still, it was protocol to operate as though enemies were one step behind him and one step ahead at all times.

He took the ferry from Genoa to L'Île-Rousse. While flying to Corsica was faster, naturally, like many things in life travelling the most efficient way did not mean it was the better way. The last time Victor had been to the island he had flown into Calvi, a small provincial airport, only to be diverted to Bastia at the last moment due to strong winds. Corsica, he had found, was not only an island: it was almost its own continent. Entire biospheres could change and change again within an afternoon's hike in the mountains. No wonder every Corsican he had encountered in his professional life had been so formidable.

It lay about one hundred miles from the Riviera, and this particular ferry from Genoa took well over five hours, which wasn't bad. He had long ago learned the schedule was a lottery that depended on the urgency or lackadaisicalness of the captain far more than it did the printed timetable. Should it be a sunny afternoon after said captain had a well-lubricated lunch, all aboard might be glad the trip only took six hours without any scares near the rocks.

Victor enjoyed every minute of his journey. A ferry was not quite a train, although it was close enough. Both were slower than most alternatives, and both allowed a passenger a certain degree of freedom to move about. A long journey confined to a seat was torture regardless of the scenery's beauty, and the most uninspiring landmarks seemed all the more glorious when viewed at will instead of at a window's grace.

In fact, in many ways a ferry was almost superior to a train, Victor thought. The degree of movement possible on a ferry was incomparable. And few things in life were as satisfying as the feel and scent of a sea breeze while on the water. He remained in the sun a little longer than would be considered wise, and did not care. When his entire existence was based around managing risk, to throw caution to the wind was liberating to a degree he could not quantify. Sunburn was a small price to pay for such rare exhilaration.

He chose a larger ferry for both the anonymity of the

many passengers and the additional facilities. He didn't use the restaurant but he drank coffee in one of the bars. At this particular time of the year, the ferry was busy with tourists seeking to attend the Fiera di l'Alivu. Victor was happy enough to act as one of them, eager to experience the olive festival. It gave him easy cover. Sometimes it was hard to justify himself as a lone traveller with no obvious purpose. A pilgrimage of sorts solved that. He had no need of pretence on this trip. He enjoyed olives, especially of the green Sicilian variety, and liked the oil drizzled on to his salads. No lies were necessary to disguise his reality and yet he could not quite understand the fervour of those travelling with him. Some people *really* loved olives, he found, and were delighted to talk to other aficionados. He chatted with a Bulgarian woman married to a Finnish man, both intelligent and witty, whose chubby toddler could say no word coherently except 'Oli' as she thrust a little hand out for another.

Victor smiled along with the couple, although he wondered about the severity of the choking risk when such a small creature shoved whole olives into her mouth. Surely such an undeveloped oesophagus could not cope with an olive if swallowed without first chewing?

He reassured himself that such intricacies would always be beyond his comprehension. The parents seemed happy enough and the little girl endlessly ravenous for olives and equally capable of eating them without harm. He was content to defer to the superior expertise.

They made plans – which he had no intention of keeping – to meet up at the festival. They were indeed lovely, so he almost felt bad when assuring them he could not wait until their next encounter.

The sun was still warm and the wind fierce as the ferry neared the port. Foaming waves broke against the granite coastline. Clouds drew a veil around the mountains, except where the snowy peaks jutted out into the sky. Soon after disembarking, he ate figatellu from an energetic street vendor to sate his hunger while reassuring himself that no one could have tampered with his meal. The pork liver sausage was a little overly smoked for his tastes, sadly. Still, calories were calories and protein was protein. He had enough of both in his system for anything that would follow. The vendor also sold red wine, produced locally, but Victor declined the offer of a half-bottle to accompany his meal. He was certain the wine would be exceptional and assured the vendor he would be back to try it on his way out. Of course, he would not.

He spent an hour performing counter-surveillance around the town, only interrupting protocol to linger near two old men sitting on a bench, sharing homemade fig cakes smeared with soft goat's cheese. Both had pure white hair and faces tanned red-brown by endless afternoons in the sun. They spoke with the same Corsican accent, and yet from the way they argued over the ancestry of Napoleon Bonaparte, Victor deduced one man was of French descent and the other Italian. Their debate was equal parts heated and expletive-ridden and yet interrupted by bursts of infectious laughter and the good-natured sharing of food. He expected the two men had been arguing over who had more right to Napoleon's glories for decades and if not for protocol and pressing matters, Victor would have liked to participate. When they asked for his opinion, he feigned ignorance of the language.

When he deemed he had no shadows, he took a bus

inland to Montemaggiore. No one boarded after him, so he was able to take a window seat and relax for most of the ninety-minute journey along the narrow road that wound through the hillsides, passing medieval villages as it gradually climbed higher and higher.

He stepped off the bus late in the afternoon. Four hundred metres above sea level the air was still warm, although the mountain breeze was cooling. Olive groves surrounded the village on all sides, which rose with the hillside, the eighteenth-century church of St Augustin forming its highest point. Looking south, the backdrop was mountains shrouded in cloud and snow, to the north the Mediterranean spread dazzling to the horizon from the Gulf of Calvi. Victor smelled olive oil wherever he walked.

The streets were narrow between old stone buildings, some whitewashed, others painted in pastel colours. Many with climbing plants snaking from balconies. He passed a small monument of stone to the young men who perished during the Great War. There was one in nearly every town and village. In the square, skinny boys and girls played football, using a wall of bare bricks as a goal. The low afternoon sun gave them long shadows that darted back and forth with boundless energy. A miskick sent the ball speeding his way as he crossed the space and he elected to volley it back, to their surprise as much as his own. While he didn't see who called out to him, more than one voice begged him to join them as they had uneven teams.

With only three hundred inhabitants, almost all natives to the area, and only a few dozen buildings in the village proper, Phoenix was easy to find.

Hers was a villa at the southern edge of the village where

the hillside flattened and the mountain views were unin-terrupted. A simple dwelling, as plain and ordinary as her chateau was ostentatious.

He vaulted over the wall that surrounded a modest yard where potted olive and fig trees stood on ochre paving. The back door was open and he could hear quiet music drifting out. In French, a woman sang of the cruel hand of inevitability.

Phoenix was painting with oils when he stepped inside. She heard Victor's footsteps on the floor tiles and turned from her easel.

Unsurprised to see him, she said, 'What kept you?'

EIGHTY-SIX

She wore an oversized white shirt patterned by paints over many years. He saw stains of acrylics and smears of oils where she had wiped her hands and brushes. The easel held a tall canvas on which she had sketched the village and laid down the underpainting. Only a small portion had colours. He saw undisturbed blobs of dense oil paints on her palette. She placed it down on a table, pushing aside curled tubes of paint to make room.

'I was expecting you forever ago,' she said with an easy smile. 'What have you been doing all this time?'

'I had to go to Russia,' he said. 'To clean up the mess.'

'Bold play.'

He shrugged. He hadn't considered it bold in the moment. Then, it had been the most tactically sound manoeuvre to avoid the wrath of powerful enemies.

She said, 'I hear Castellan met with an unfortunate end. I hope that means you're squared with the Bratva now.'

'Not exactly,' he replied. 'There's still a long way to go in that area.'

'Quick to anger and slow to forgive, as always.' She paused. 'I would have warned you had I been able to.'

'Of course,' he said.

'Did you think it was me?'

He nodded. 'The thought crossed my mind.'

'It all happened so fast,' Phoenix said. 'Which I guess was the point. I've had this little place for years and years. Perfect when one needs to keep one's head below the parapet.' She changed tone. 'I have to admit, I did wonder if you would take their offer.'

'I was tempted,' he admitted. 'But that's not the way I do business.'

'No?' she said, somewhat sceptical of tone. 'Correct me if I'm wrong, but isn't that pretty much how you and I came to work together?'

'That was then,' Victor answered. 'We entered our arrangement from a position of parity. As individuals. Salomé didn't operate alone.'

'So you're saying it's fine when it's only you and me trying to kill one another. Not when it's you and several of them.'

'Something like that.'

Phoenix stepped to where a small radio sat near her paints. She turned a dial to increase the volume of the French singer's voice.

'She's singing about snowflakes,' Phoenix said with a smile as she swayed with the melody. 'About how beautiful they are, and yet it's an incredibly sad song if you really listen to it. She's singing about snowflakes but the lyrics are about life. Snowflakes are beautiful yet they are only so in the most perfect of conditions for their very existence. A minute change in temperature or humidity and that snowflake never forms. And should conditions be exactly right for that water to crystallise, then the snowflake it becomes has an inevitable expiry date. It cannot endure. Either it shall melt or it will be crushed into ice. Only for a short period between those extremes will it be beautiful. We should weep because of that beauty. We should weep every single day for that most cruel of fates.'

'We make our own fate.'

'Then we make our own cruelty too?'

'Someone told me,' Victor began after a moment, 'that once we are cruel, we are forever cruel. I'm not sure I fully agreed at the time, but only because I did not fully understand. He meant I could be a saint from this point henceforth and whatever my goodly deeds achieved they would not change my past. No penance can wash away so great a stain.'

The wound in his thigh ached, although he could not be sure the pain was real. 'The man who said this to me was a monster by his own admission. He did not try and pretend otherwise. He accepted what had been done cannot be undone.' He paused, thinking about what he was saying, in a way that was unusual for him. 'I told someone once that I was doomed to hell for the things I had done. So, in the case of inevitable damnation, there was nothing left to lose. Nothing I can do can ever change who I am or who I've been. Who I'll always be.' He shrugged. 'I'm okay with that.'

She examined his face, reading the expression. 'You want to know why I asked you to come back to see me after you'd finished with your procedure?'

'It's a question currently unanswered.'

'I was thinking of retiring,' she said. 'I had an inkling I may have been comfortable for too long, but when we last saw one another I wasn't sure. I thought by the time you had finished up with your procedure then I would have decided either way and could tell you in person if I was bowing out. To avoid any ... misunderstandings.'

Victor said, 'Considerate.'

'Practical,' she countered. 'I didn't want any such misunderstandings causing you to show up at my door.'

Phoenix looked at him.

Victor looked at her.

'What did you decide?' he asked.

'Those disloyal contractors made the decision for me.' She glanced around at the humble villa. 'Hence a hasty trip to this little hideaway of mine.'

'But what would you have decided had the choice been a free one?'

She thought, then shrugged with her hands. 'I don't think we'll ever know.'

He nodded. 'Similarly, I'm never going to know for sure at what point you realised Salomé was working against you.'

She listened.

'Because maybe that inkling of yours about being comfortable for too long was a little more than a hunch.'

She waited.

'And the best and safest way to see if you were correct was to have me play it out for you.'

'I said before that we're way beyond all of that,' she said in a careful tone. 'We have a good working relationship and there's no need to jeopardise it. Besides, here you are with

451

barely a scratch. I don't know your name but I know this is who you are. Let's not be coy about it. No one operates in this business unless they're addicted to risk. We tell ourselves we will walk away just as soon as we have acquired a certain amount of money. Or we pretend that walking away isn't so simple. We put up all the barriers ourselves. No one needs to do it for us.' She paused. 'The truth is we can get out just as soon as we choose. We just don't choose to.'

Victor remained silent.

'Now the status quo has been reinstated there's no reason we can't pick up where we left off. Don't let your paranoia get the better of you and ruin a good thing.'

'Paranoia is part of the job description,' Victor said. 'The end result is the same – we've both been exposed – so it doesn't matter what the truth is. We can't go back to normal now, so there's really only a single option.' He paused. 'No one believes me when I tell them that I don't take these kinds of things personally. It's only ever business.'

She took a deep breath. 'And that's what this is? Business?'

Victor nodded. 'I'm afraid so.'

'Clean slate?'

'Nothing clean about it. But we both knew this was always going to end with one of us looking down the barrel of a gun. It was only ever a question of which way around we would be standing.'

'That's not true,' she told him. 'That's just the way you think. When I said our prior aggressions were behind us, I meant it. You don't want to believe it because it makes this easier for you. But one day you'll realise you let your feelings get the better of you. Ironic, of course, because that's exactly what you think you're trying to avoid right now.'

He withdrew a small pistol, a suppressed .22 Ruger, and placed it on the table next to her palette.

'All you have to do is squeeze the trigger,' he said. 'But not here.' He pressed a finger under his jaw. 'Here.' He then pressed the same finger to his temple. 'You won't feel a thing.'

She looked down at the gun and swallowed. When she looked back at him there was no fear in her eyes, only acceptance. 'Do you mind if I finish listening to this song first?'

'Not at all.'

Later, the setting sun painted the medieval buildings blazing red in the village square. The skinny children were still playing football, their long shadows stretching into dancing marionettes.

Victor kicked the ball with them.

ACKNOWLEDGEMENTS

Writing never seems to get any easier and every book requires more than just my efforts to be its best. Thankfully, there are several people both old and new that have been worth their weight in gold. My longtime editor, Ed Wood, deserves a ton of praise for putting up with me at my most difficult moments and for continued support and consistently excellent editorial input. I'm very grateful for everything he's done for the series over the years. Similarly, my agent, James Wills, has been invaluable in many ways beyond his astute knowledge of the industry and contracts. Thank you to every friend and family member who has listened (without showing too much boredom) as this author rabbited on about Victor and his latest predicament. One of my oldest friends, Mark Smith, provided much insight into the life of a corrections officer with stories of his time guarding some of society's worst offenders. Johana Gustawsson receives both my thanks for helping me with French translation in my previous novel and has my sincere apologies for failing to include her in the acknowledgements of that book. Bodo Pfündl assisted immensely with comments and corrections from the roughest early draft all the way to final result, so thank you Bodo. Thank you also to Jon Appleton for his eagle-eyed diligence behind the scenes. Lastly, my heartfelt appreciation goes out to every reader who took the time to send me an email or a DM over the last year. Writing can be a lonely profession for much of the time and the many warm messages of encouragement and appreciation have really helped me through some of the darkest moments of self-doubt.

DISCOVER THE MAN BEHIND THE ACTION
TOM WOOD

© Charlie Hopkinson